# Determined To Be A Villain

## Tonya Adolfson

*Published by Fantastic Journeys Publishing,*
*Boise, Idaho*
*PUBLISHING HISTORY*
*E-Book released through Kindle*
*Soft Cover trial edition June 2016*
*Mass market edition/ XXXXXX*

*Cover art: Photo of fabric by John Farmer*
*Created in Gimp 2.6 by John Farmer*
*Cover Art copyright by Fantastic Journeys Publishing*
*Interior Art by Lorraine Barraras and Suzette Urbano*
*Edited by John Farmer, Gwen Bradley, and Stephanie Reese*
*Content copyright ©March 2016 Tonya Adolfson.*

*Published in the United States of America.*

*ISBN: 978-1-941276-98-3*

*The characters and events portrayed in this book are fictitious. Any similarity to real*
*persons, living or dead, common or deific, is coincidental and not intended by the*
*author, unless, of course, I know them.*
*No Augustinians were harmed in the making of this book, though a few folks were*
*roughed up a bit.*

## *Also by Tonya Adolfson*

**The Souls of the Saintlands Series**
Thine Enemy's Eyes
An Unpolished Gem
An Open Enemy
To Thine Own Self
Full of Sound and Fury
Determined to Be a Villain
All's Fair*

**Other Books**
Surviving Your Own Creativity
Filling Up on 500 (With Todd Adolfson)

*Coming 2017

# Reviews for the Souls of the Saintlands Series

## Thine Enemy's Eyes

"I loved it I stayed up late several nights because I had to know what happened! It's a great read with excellent pacing and such entertaining and rich characters. I loved the rich world she created and the details used to make it stand out. I cannot wait to read the second book to learn more about the characters and places mentioned! I highly suggest this book."
Maryanne Durant, Amazon Review

"I cannot wait for the next book, and hopefully, subsequent books to follow."
Steve Nunez, Dragonfleet Studios

"Tonya Adolfson's debut novel is incredible! Full of intrigue, wildly imaginative characters and set in a medieval fantasy world of such authenticity it blew me away. I would heartily recommend this to anyone, and can't wait until the second novel comes out!"
I. J. Smethurst, author of the *E.D.F Chronicles*

"The plot has interesting twists and turns to keep you going straight through the book. When it ends, it leaves you wanting more."
Shelley Wolf, Amazon Review

"…good political intrigue… good action scenes… Not to mention one of the heaviest cliff hangers I've seen in a while."
*The William Jones Review*

"This is a very well written book, and has more plot twists and turns then I could count, but each one made me all the more eager to keep reading and see where the story would end up."
Durin Boge, Amazon Review

"I've read and reread this book 5 times now, it's easily one of my favorites! The characters are well developed, the twists and turns of the story kept me guessing, and the story line easily kept me wanting more."
Chalyse Padigimus, Amazon Review

"I'm a busy professional without a lot of time to read and this book absorbed my free time quite enjoyably for the past week. It has a touch of the almost magical within an imagined realm akin to midevil Europe. It has romance without focusing overly on the taudry details as she has better things to do with the plotline. She develops several charachters including their background in succinct but inviting story telling and she juggles all of these charachters' knowledge gaps about the current situation of court intrigue quite well. I'm really curious to see what book 2 has in store for me."

Shiela Harmon, Amazon Review

"Some trouble trying to make sense of the geography at first; however, not sticking to a real world atlas got me over that hurtle. The story itself is very interesting with a nice twist at the end."

Rold DeDog, Amazon Review

"Tonya Adolfson has a way of drawing you in to make you feel like you are right there with the characters. I could not put this book down because I was so in love with the characters, I had to see what was coming next. She keeps you guessing until the very end. At times I found myself a little sad for a particular character and then later rejoicing with them. I strongly recommend this book and cannot wait to see what happens next in book two."

Kayla, Amazon Review

"This is the first book from Tonya Adolfson I have read and believe me, it won't be the last. She caught my attention for the first page and held it through all the plots and conspiracies. The setting is wonderfully imagined and the characters fully realized, and believable. A brilliantly written fantasy tale filled with exciting intrigue. I'm glad I bought this and the second book together!"

Samuel Sturkie, Amazon Review

"Tonya has definitely found her place on my bookshelf. Now have the first 4 books! Can't wait for the next one!"

Spencer Maschek, Amazon Review

"This is a fantastic beginning to a fantastic series. I could not put it down. An amazing world full of detail."

Adam Wells-Grube, Amazon Review

"Ms. Adolfson has woven a web that will catch you while you're not looking. The characters are dynamic, with relationships we can relate to and an intrigue so deep that I could not put the book down until it was over; and I was begging for more. There are few books that I have found that suck me in the way this one does."
Hannah Therrien, Amazon Review


**An Unpolished Gem**

"In a perfect follow through to Thine Enemy's Eyes, Ms. Adolfson continues to illustrate just how sticky the politics and personalities of her world really can be. She never lets go of you, even after the book is done. Just when I think I have a character figured out, they surprise me; I can't even tell how many sides to this story there are. I can't wait for book three!"
Julien McBain, author *Ghosts of the Past*

"It is difficult for second books in a series to have the same weight as the first. This is the rarer case of the second book surpassing the first."
Christopher Garcia, editor of *the Drink Tank*

"This book is just as captivating as the first book in the series. Again I was so enthralled with the characters, plot twists, and story line that I literally couldn't put it down and finished reading it in one day..."
Chalyse Padigimus, Amazon Review

"I love her writing style. She creates this world that becomes real to its readers. Oh and then there are these great characters with such richness and depth you cannot help but to love and in some cases hate them! She has written it in such a way you have no idea where or who, if anyone, the main character will end up with. There is such a depth in the story you just cannot put it down. I read it in a matter of hours. I know these are books I am going to read again and again throughout the years. It has to be a great book for it to have that kind of status on my bookshelf."
Maryanne Durant, Amazon Review

"Love the way the characters grow and mature. Can't wait for the next book!"
Shelley Wolf, Amazon Review

**An Open Enemy**

"I have flown through these books. I totally love the tangled story with so many twists ans turns. These are written by someone who knows how to keep their audience captive and I cannot wait for the 4th book!!! I have been dying to know what happens! This is definitely and awesome read every true fantasy buff should have on their shelf."
Maryanne Durant, Amazon Review

"By the time I reached this novel I knew I was going to be a life long fan. These characters hold pieces of the human experience that filled me with a sense of hope, left me speechless and at times exhausted me. An emotional journey filled with adventure that I will treasure and live over and again every time I read it for the rest of my life."
Anonymous, Amazon Review

**To Thine Own Self**

The whole series of these books are very cleverly written and very in depth with rich detailing and character development. I absolutely have read these books over and over again. There is a lot of action within the pages along with laughter and pain. The books tend to suck you in and show a world unlike any other.
Maryanne Durant, Amazon Review

Tonya Adolfson will take you further down the rabbit hole with this latest installment. There's only one problem. Nothing can prepare you for hitting the bottom. Riveting and jaw dropping twists that only add to the story are in store for all. Be grateful Book 5 is already out, for the wait would have been unbearable.
Steve "Warky" Nunez, Dragonfleet Studios

This series is 11 stars out of 10!
With some books, it's hard to read them again once you know the plot twists. But with Tonya, she weaves her stories with such sublime brilliance that you want to read them again and again. Whether you're caught up in the beautiful dream like dialogue between two star struck characters or breathlessly page turning during the heart pounding action

scenes, you will love this must-have series! Spoiler Alert: The books just keep getting better and better!

Ethan Shaw

"To Thine own Self" is a wonderful book full of love, sorrow, adventures, plot twists and turns, and everything you can imagine. Oh how it ended! After finishing the first thing I said (with a smile) was "I need to go send 'hate mail' to Tonya." In the note I told her "You're not my favorite Tonya right now." Now I wait patiently… well somewhat patiently, for book 5 to come out.

Stephanie Reese

"To Thine own Self" is book 4 in the Saintlands series that Tonya Adolfson wrote. This is a wonderful series full of intrigue, adventure, love and magic of the medieval times. This book transports you into the lives of the people and the lands to the point where you don't want to put the book down to go to sleep. I can't wait for the next book to find out what happens next. Tonya has become one of my favorite authors and deserves to have all her books read and reread over and over again. Each book is really that good. Thank you so much Tonya for giving us the Saintlands series

Tish Firmiss

"To Thine Own Self" is a dynamic continuation in the "Souls of the Saintlands" series. A delicate balance of action that moves the story forward without feeling overwhelmed or bogged down. This book in particular adds great detail to both the land and characters that have been introDûced. While this is the fourth book, she has not stopped adding new mysteries and plot changes that must only be resolved in the next book. I anxiously await the next release date so I might again join the world that has created and learn how everything is resolved. A truly wonderful book and series.

Krista Wells

I started this series wanting a good story, I'm now fully committed to this universe.

If you're this far along, you already know what a great story you've gotten yourself into. You know these characters are driven as only people can be, not just archetypes. What will stand out in this book is the attention to detail. It isn't just a dance, it's a dance you can visualize. It isn't just clothes, you can feel what the draping of the silk must feel like. Think of what your favorite characters and stories have come to mean to you over time. Now tell them to make room. By the end of this book, you will be hooked. There is no turning back.

Andrea Cortright, Animeland Convention Owner


**Full of Sound and Fury**

I have never felt such strong emotions from reading a book. I was immersed in this book so much so, that when a certain spoiler happens, I threw my book across the room and cried into my pillow.

After book shaming this title for awhile, I had to know how this book was going to end.

Warning! The ending leaves you craving the next book, and sobbing into your pillow. People who buy this book should invest in some tissues as well.

All in all, I'm excited to see where all of the relationships are heading, especially Myrgen and Catriona. I want them to be together, but after seeing that the author doesn't rule out ANYTHING from happening, I'm on edge hoping and wondering what fate will allow.

Steve "Warky" Nunez, Dragonfleet Studios


I am already reading it for the 2nd time. I love this book. Tonya Adolfson has done it again, another great book in the series. It starts with where the last book left off so that you are right back into the suspense of it all. She will hold you spell bound by what happens next and, by the end of this book, you will be wanting the next to keep the suspense going. Just when you think you know what will happen next, she throws you a curve and you keep reading to see what will happen. I love her books and can't wait for the next one to come out. I don't care how long it takes her to write it, I want to continue living in this series. What a great place to immerse yourself in. Thank you Tonya. Please keep writing this series.

Tish Firmiss, Amazon Review


The game Is Afoot!

We know what to expect from just about everyone, so nothing new on the characters. We've finally settled in to a few less surprises from our friends and focus more on moving the story along. And move it does!

The curtain is pulled back on the pantheons. We're getting A LOT more of the spiritual story than some might be comfortable with, but if people didn't see that writing on the wall by now, they haven't been paying attention. I like that it's ALL of them addressed pretty fairly, not just one or the other. And we're starting to see that no one belief is necessarily right or wrong (they're all right AND wrong), they all have their nuances. They have been part of the story the entire time. I'm happy to finally see them more prominent.

There wasn't the rip roaring page turner that the previous books have been. I was able to sleep at night reading this one, but make no mistake: the blazing fire has only transformed into an intense smolder. The honeymoon is over, but the relationship is only just getting started!

Bring on book 6!!

Andrea Cortright, Animeland Convention Owner

Words can't even begin to justifiably escribe the sheer awesometicity of this book series. Tonya builds a lore-filled world in a way that few others can achieve with masterful control of her characters. And just when you think you have a handle on things, she throws so many swerves, even Vince Russo would end up with whiplash. But everything that happens keeps you wanting to come back for more. Can't wait to see what she conjours up next.

Richard Englebert

To Dartanian Richards, who so embodied the character of Alexander, I can only hear his voice.

### Acknowledgments:

First and foremost, I'd like to thank all the people who were inspirations for this book:

Gwen for Gwen, John for Raven, Dartanian for Alexander, Jeff for James, Misha for Emmy, Morgan for Alan and Johannes, Rod for Xeno, Shanna for Fierah, Stephanie for Belladonna, Erik for Dom, Jared for Draethen, Dave for Octavius, Morgan Wolf for Morgan Wolf, Aaron for Duncan, Adam P for Ambroise, John for Myrgen, David for Henri, Jennifer for Ce'Nedra, Daddy for Thessius, Kim for Ysabel, Joe for Nicaise, Jenn for Flora, Aggie for Aggie, Allan Hobbs for Allen Hobbs, Andrea for Aislyn, and all the hundreds of friends and family that have been contributors to this book. Your work has been amazing and your lives inspiring.

A big shout out to the most amazing editors a gal could have: Gwen Bradley has helped with this project for over 15 years and still comments on the itintial drafts to this day. Also thanks to John Farmer for always helping with the read throughs. And Stephanie Reese, you are beyond priceless.

Thanks to Shannon Galarneau for being my agent and helping me fulfill the dream of Fantastic Journeys Publishing. I'd also like to thank Steve "Warky" Nunez for all his enthusiastic support.

And finally, to my wonderful family: Morgan and Misha, for being so tolerant of Mommy's work; to my Daddy, Ray Lamar Manley, for inspiring me to tell stories for the sheer pleasure of my audience; to my Mom, Rosemary Virginia Manley, for reading historical romances; and to the Great and Powerful Todd, for being everything a Prince needs to be.

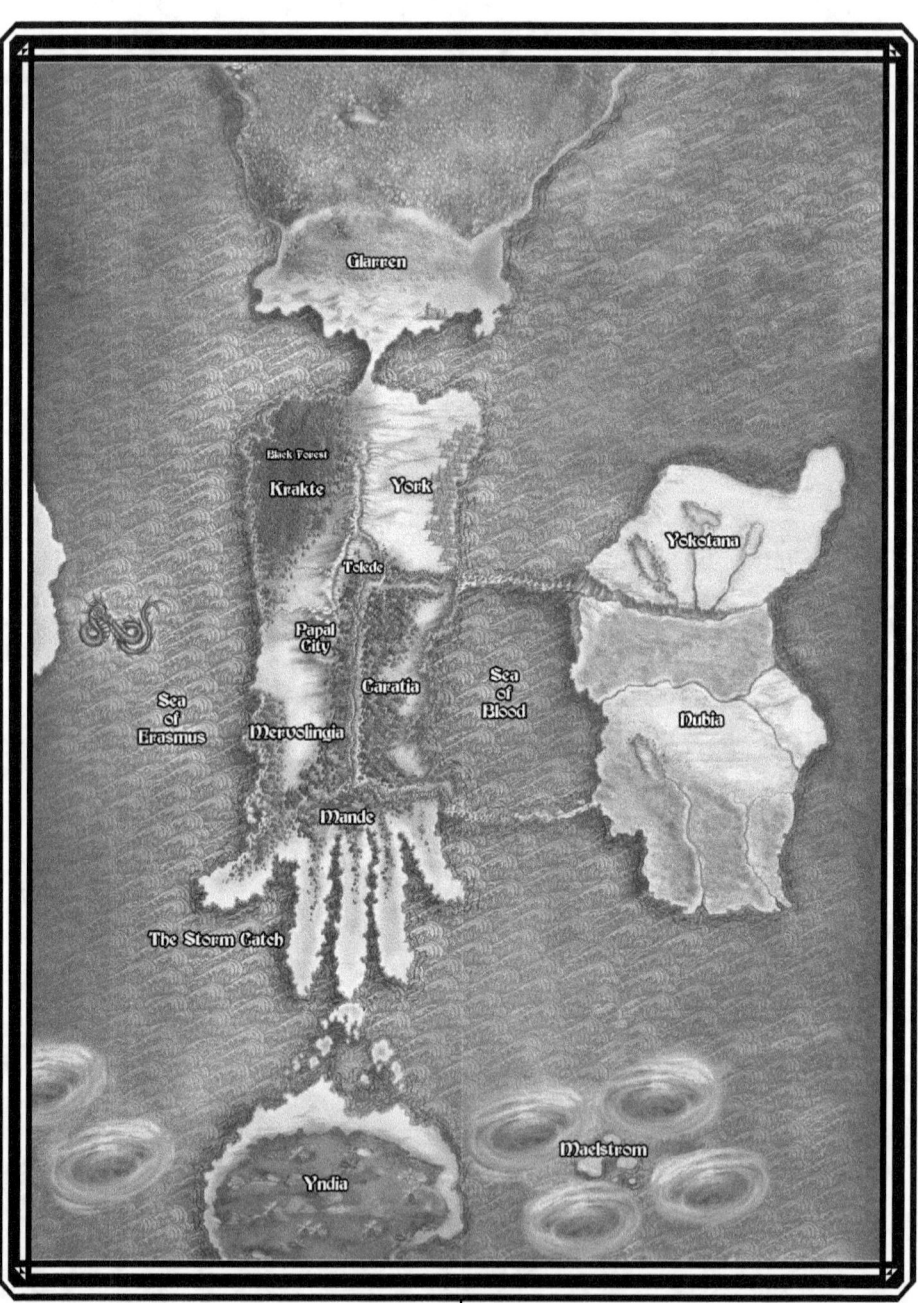

Glarren

Black Forest

Krakte          York

Yokotana

Tolede

Papal
City

Garatia          Sea
                 of
Mervolingia      Blood         Nubia

Sea
of
Erasmus

Mande

The Storm Catch

Maelstrom

Yndia

*The Karmic Hand* is a popular play among the incense houses and palaces of Yndia. Telling the tale of Kali and Shiva, it teaches the virtue of seeking balance in all things.

# Book One

"There are many paths in life. The most important choice you have is to make the first step."
The Karmic Hand

"Sometimes, not getting what you want is a wonderful stroke of luck."
The Dalai Lama

# One

## "I was determined to be a villain."
## Kali, The Karmic Hand

"You're bleeding, Saint Raymond."

The former Patron Saint of Barren Women saw the blood dripping onto his hand and knew the person speaking to him was likely to be an angel. Ever since Raymond non Nonnatus was thrown bodily from Heaven, the place where Gabriel had grabbed him bled near holy sites and people. Usually not a lot of blood, just a seeping wound, but enough to speak the truth of their grace and favor.

He had long ago gotten used to the pain so he didn't even notice that, but the wounds had driven him from cities on more than one occasion. Blood drew attention and when it could not be explained, people reacted out of fear more often than not. He wore scarves and stayed away from churches, which minimized the trouble, but he now shunned human contact in favor of not being hung on a city wall as a monster.

This was different. His neck was wet and now, there was blood on the backs of his hands where it had drenched his sleeves. Also, the pain was back. Had he not already been on his knees, he would surely have been driven there out of surprise.

He stood from tending the weeds near one of the great stones and looked behind him. He saw a young man, about twenty-five years old looking at one of the stones. The man's hair was long and dark brown, cascading in curls down his back in a ponytail. His eyes were gold like a lion's, and stood out against skin that seemed native to whatever region he traveled.

Raymond bowed. "You are mistaken, Uriel. I am no longer a saint. Your brother Gabriel saw to that."

"You caused the deaths of thousands and threatened the population of the world by creating the Soulless. It was warranted."

"If you believed that, then you would not address me as a saint." Raymond turned back to nurturing the rare scraggly grass that passed for foliage in the Yorkshire Wastes.

The Archangel Uriel touched the stone at the uppermost northern position. "You still tend this area, after all this time, Raymond?"

"It's the closest thing to Heaven I can be."

Uriel looked at the fallen saint. "Why would you want to be, after being cast out?"

Raymond laughed. "I have asked myself that pretty often these last three hundred years. Mostly, I think it's habit." He folded his hands in front of him. "What can I do for the Patron Saint of Spring?"

"Nothing really. I was just checking on something I left here." Uriel glanced behind him. "It's possible you may get visitors soon."

Raymond didn't like the sound of that. "Holy visitors?"

"Almost the opposite. Two men, one Nubian, one Glarren, travelling together."

"What should I do if they show up?"

Uriel smiled. "Don't interfere."

The archangel patted the monolith, then turned and walked away from the ring of stones into the Yorkish wilderness.

Gomez de Santander looked up from his plate of eggs as several people with parcels entered. Monique, the proprietress of the Wise Wench Tavern, came out from behind the bar, wiping her hands on a towel. Her dark brown hair was tucked under a muffin cap to keep it out of her dark brown eyes, and her slight frame disguised the wiry strength that Gomez had witnessed at least twice a day. She walked with the authority of not just an owner of this establishment, but a well-known and well-respected member of the community.

"Helen? Matt? What's going on?"

The woman in front had extremely long dark blond hair shot with silver-grey. She moved like a woman who knew she was not going to be able to work at this rate for many more years, so she was determined to do as much as she could right now. She progressed in the door to allow a few others to come in after her. All of them had parcels that looked like hastily thrown together bundles of clothes and items. A stout bald man behind the woman stepped into the conversation.

"The monsters surrounded the vineyard." He set his bundle down upon a nearby table. "First, they set up their encampments everywhere, surrounding the estate, then they came to us today in person. They told us to get our belongings and leave."

Helen shook her head. "I didn't leave when their leader, some giant-like thing, told us to a few days ago. They started drumming and bellowing all day and night to scare us out but I refused to move. I wasn't going to have our mistress hear that we ran from our home at the first threat."

"Then what changed?" Monique guided the couple from the doorway to the table with Matt's things.

"The Queen came down. She was…" Helen shuddered.

"Intimidating." Matt leaned on the table. "She didn't even gesture and they parted and bowed before her. She was half their size in the slightest case, but they deferred to her. Helen stood up to her and I was afraid the woman would order my wife's execution for her defiance."

"I wasn't about to let her destroy our *home*. Not without a fight, Matt."

"I'm right there with you, honey. I was then and I am now."

Monique sat down, waiting for them to explain and the couple followed suit. The other refugees lingered nearby, listening and waiting to add their own experiences. Helen sat, her back rigid and her demeanor simultaneously fighting pain and anguish.

One of the bystanders, a plump, pretty woman holding scribal supplies and documents, also rested her brimming satchel on the table. "The Queen said she didn't want to take any lives, for those were not replacable, but that she intended to destroy every building and crop held by Tangl. As 'repayment' for the insult of ignoring her letters."

Monique frowned. "What letters, Osondrea?"

"We aren't sure about any others, but she handed me this one." She reached into the satchel and pulled out a sealed letter. It was addressed to Lady Tanglwyst de Holloway.

Gomez stood, his plate of food forgotten. "May I see that letter?"

The group looked at the newcomer as he came over to the discussion.

Osondrea held the letter close to her. "I don't know you, sir."

"I'm Gomez de Santander. I run the King's personal guard at the palace. I'm here on Royal Business."

"Forgive me sir, but this is not royal business. This is personal business."

"The Queen of Krakte has chosen to attack the lands and property of a known fugitive from the Crown. This completely falls into my purview."

"Known fugitive?"

"She was part of the plot to kill King Charles. She escaped house arrest pending investigation."

The entire inn began yelling at once, and Gomez found himself surrounded by hostile, threatened people. Osondrea along with two others shoved him out the door and shut it behind him. He stood on the street, looking around. The half-goblin patrol guard looked at him as it passed but didn't stop its rounds.

Gomez thought about getting the local guardsmen but realized most of them were gravely wounded from encounters with the occupying army. So far, past the initial raid, there had been no additional fatalities but a few skirmishes had broke out against the half-Fae monsters both nights, and the humans had suffered the wounds. Gomez decided not to add to the destruction by pitting human against human over a legal jurisdiction. He had a few other ways to get the information.

He walked to the City Guard office at the end of the main town road. The blood from Asher's death left a mark on the floor, the final remaining testimony of the day the invasion happened. The Fae general Bartolemaus Johner, second in command to the Midsummer King Corrigan Starshadow, sat in the room, looking out at the town port to the west. The General was assigned to the human forces to aid with negotiations with the Krakten army as part of the rules of engagement.

"Captain de Santander."

"General." Gomez sat at the desk, folding his hands in front of him. His mind went to the people in the tavern. The Queen had not wanted to kill people on Tanglwyst's lands but she certainly had no problem murdering a dozen people in the streets when she came to town. Her stasis spell had frozen the whole town for a full day, suspending people where they were without stopping their awareness nor the environment. When she finally released the populace, the ones that could scattered to their homes. The ones that were damaged or dead, or too traumatized to move, were gathered up within the next day and taken to the local church.

The Queen of Krakte had told the General that she had sent letters to the capital for a month regarding the return of her daughter's body but Gomez knew Alexander's search for his bride had interfered with him getting them. They were no doubt piled on a desk with other unopened missives. The only thing worse than the idea of them unopened is the thought that Dominic DeMedici had opened them and ignored or discarded them.

He sighed.

The General turned. "Problems?"

"Beyond the obvious?"

"I suppose that's the question."

Gomez looked at the man-shaped creature. He had golden hair that flowed and shimmered like it was perpetually in a light wind in the summer sun. His beardless face showed a few lines to accent the bearing of a career military man. He wore shiny silver armor with golden accents and he never seemed to remove it. Gomez assumed he was a Fae but the Krakten Queen had been fully human so he wasn't sure. Apparently, humans could have high rank among the Fae.

Gomez weighed telling him. He might have insight into the situation and it could reveal if Bartolemaus Johner was human or Fae.

"The folks from Tanglwyst de Holloway's vineyards just arrived in town. The army is burning the estate. Apparently, the Queen gave the inhabitants a letter to deliver to the lady. She mentioned the letters that were sent before. I have no idea what to do about that. They refused to give me the letter."

"That is wise. If someone unauthorized opens a sealed letter given by the Queen, they will die."

"Well, they were unlikely to open it. They viciously protected it from me."

"This woman has loyal people, much like your King." Johner nodded to Gomez.

Gomez bowed at the compliment. "Still, I should let them know nonetheless. I don't want to find out later that my omission let someone get hurt."

Gomez got back up and went to the door, then turned back to Johner. "Death, you say?"

Johner nodded.

"Painful?"

Johner nodded again.

"Messy?"

"No. But they will undoubtedly be quite loud as they suffer."

Gomez looked at the inn. It was silent, but he didn't want to dawdle.

Johner tilted his head. "You worried about someone?"

Gomez shook his head. "I wouldn't say I'm worried, Bart. My lieutenant Nina would protect anyone *else* from opening one. But the man who opened the first one would have no mourners at his funeral."

Gomez felt a little smile cross his face, and he swallowed it before it put a spring in his step.

Catherine deMedici, the Queen Mother, looked up from her desk at the growing smoke from the fires towards St. Giles. A knock sounded on the open door and she turned to look at Charles the Messenger. The young man had ridden all the way from Patras with her and had been running her missives since she settled down to wait out the siege. She nodded entry to the man.

"Any word?"

"The *initial* reports of the fields of St. Giles burning were false. They aren't burning, but they're surrounded. A huge army has set up camp and the cook fires are large enough to make the countryside appear to be ablaze."

"Someone saw this?"

Charles nodded. "Yes. He's downstairs, if you want to speak with him. He also said that the fires were burning all the time but weren't consuming the wood. They produce smoke and heat and light, but they do not destroy."

*Faerie fire.*

But faerie fire didn't produce smoke, and there was an awful lot of that right now.

*They must have started burning something.* "Are they approaching here?"

Charles shook his head. "They appear to be camping to surround the county, covering all sides."

"What about the harbor?"

"He didn't go that far."

This eased her fears that the countryside would be destroyed and she was glad this place was safe. She had an investment in this Inn. The proprietor of the Benevolent Friar was a burly, heavy man named Svein and his wife was a slight, curly-haired woman Ealusaid. The stable boy was a young man named Zack, who had hooded eyes that looked like he was allergic to the hay he fed the animals.

"What about the missive?"

"Dropped off with the funds at the cartographer's. I don't have word yet about when they head up the mountain but I do have several runners prepared to tell us the news."

She nodded. "Good. Any other news yet?"

"The Patrols state that the spell holding people in place has broken but no one wants to risk entry so they are encamped outside of St. Giles, away from the army."

"Can the town send or receive messages yet?"

"Unknown. I can try to send a bird though. I brought some from Cliffbase in case you needed them. Granted, the replies will return there and not here but that can't be helped or changed."

She frowned, nodding. "No, I don't suppose it can be. But you have messengers set to run the replies here, correct?"

"Yes, Your Grace."

"I've been trying to decide if I want to remain here or go back to Cliffbase where I can get messages immediately."

Charles nodded his understanding. "I will make preparations if you choose that course."

They both knew that the inns were practically hovels in that town, with the only real trade being the messenger service on the top of the cliff. The service guaranteed delivery to whomever the missive needed to reach, even if the person's whereabouts were unknown, and Charles had reassured her that the service was legitimate. She had sent a missive to Alexander and now she awaited a response. She had told him where to find her and that was the only thing that stayed her hand in moving sites. In truth, she had commandeered the home of a city official in the town when they stayed there before, so she did not fear her privacy nor quality of housing.

"No. I said I would be here. There's no point in paying twice to let him know my whereabouts. Besides, this way I can keep an eye on the army." Though she did not say it, she also knew he had other ways to find her if he needed to, but best not give him a moving target. "Send a message to the Captain of the Guard in St. Giles. See if we can get a report. And send one to the Guard Office at the Palace. They should also have reports if any are available. I need to let them know where I am as well."

Charles the Messenger nodded. "They are making lunch downstairs, Your Grace. Do you want to come down or stay here?"

Her frequent stays had given her a small rapport with the couple who ran the Inn but the events of the past few days had made her more worried than social. Word had reached her of some sort of barrier stopping travel to the Papal City but she had paid it no mind. She had no more intention to go there than Cliffbase.

"I'm still not of a mind to make conversation, Charles. Please give Svein and Ealusaid my apologies."

"Of course, Your Grace." He bowed and left as she returned her gaze to the fires.

# Two

## "We fought as friends and played at being enemies." Shiva, The Karmic Hand

Uriel walked away from the standing stones where Raymond landed when he was cast out. The site didn't qualify as holy which explained why Raymond could be there. Uriel didn't much care for the division of the humans by the Church but this was what Heaven's keepers had allowed. In truth, Gabriel and Rafael didn't care about the manner of which they were being worshiped. The thing that mattered was the filling of the Well of Souls and that only happened if humans died while professing to serve Heaven. When they worshiped anything else, the souls went elsewhere.

Uriel knew that there were a lot more souls attributed to Heaven than currently were in the Well. He had spent millennia investigating this. He was the first to notice that the Well was diminishing, which had prompted the others to capture the Giver of Life.

Uriel unfurled translucent wings of light and took his musings to the cloudy sky.

*"This is wrong."* Uriel had looked at the cage where the Giver of Life was contained. *"You cannot hold this creature captive here."*

*Michael had nodded. "I agree. Taking her from her duties on the world will end poorly, resulting in many more harvests for the Bringer of Death."*

*"The Bringer has not been seen in a hundred years and the world still functions as if she walked among them." Gabriel gestured to the saints dispensing souls from the Well and placing them in babies. "The Well is diminishing. The souls are not returning to it. Having the source of Life here will turn more people to our cause."*

*Uriel shook his head. "If the Well runs out, then we will return it to the place we found it and let her fill it of her own volition."*

*Raphael ruffled his wings. "What makes you think she would do that again after we took it?"*

*The other angels stopped arguing at the reminder of their transgressions. Their villages had rejected and attacked the Bringer of Death when she came, so after a while, she simply didn't any more. The results were that people lived longer but they suffered for years in sickness and pain until the elders would simply execute them. Even then, the ground rejected the bodies of the slain unless they were hidden in wooden boxes. They originally wrapped them in linen or wool but after the cauls decomposed, the bodies were flung violently from the earth. Many had gone to burning them or storing them in caves.*

*Michael held up his hand to stop the bickering. "We will do this for a decade. If she does not refill the Well by then, then we must release both her and the Well back to the world. And we tell our people to seek the Bringer and let her do her work."*

*Gabriel and Raphael had frowned at the idea of admitting they were wrong. They argued against giving her back but in the end, Michael was stronger and the two agreed to the terms.*

*Lucifer had shaken his head, disgusted but saying nothing. Instead, he chose to head to the Purifying site to check on the souls of their worshippers who were less than kind while alive. The Giver did not add to the Well while still imprisoned and seemed catatonic most of the time. Gabriel and Raphael had grown more and more sullen as the tenth year approached.*

*Then the Soulless had been created and Michael had personally joined in the battle against them. His permanent removal from Heaven had stopped the plan to return the Giver to the world. Instead, they cut her hair and threw her in* the cage again. When the Saints threatened to free her, Gabriel cast down Raymond to demonstrate the precarious nature of the Saints' positions. The Giver was sealed away and when they added her hair to refill the Well, it had failed. Only her water would add to it and she rarely shed that, despite the torture and lonliness. The Soulless were defeated at great cost and Uriel no longer had allies to stand against Gabriel and Raphael. A war in Heaven would destroy it.

He had confirmed that the sword of Sir Richard of Kent was still in the stone monolith where he and Embertwist had hidden it years before. The alliance had been tentative, but the two had banded together to save the artifact from the hands of a corrupt church. As the only artifact of power left from the Soulless Wars, the rivals of Spring determined it was best hidden than lost or destroyed. Neither could say that the need would never arise again. Moreover, Uriel had not wanted to risk Gabriel or Raphael destroying it.

Afterwards, Uriel and Embertwist had met annually during the final day of their season, before Summer took over and their purviews were gone for another year. That day was tomorrow and their pub of choice was a day's ride away, but much closer by air. The small inn was on the main road in Mervolingia, skirting a Fae forest that separated the village of Cliffbase from the Papal City. It had good food and good ale and was both close enough to and far enough from each other's respective power centers to be literally neutral ground.

Uriel flew south for a while and was surprised when the cloud cover went from misty rain to grey smoke. He ducked down below the surface and saw the field near the border was in a controlled burn. There was a lot of devastation, but it seemed to be on purpose. The edges of the burn were precise, but he was suspicious. This was the season of growth, not the burning season. This was trouble. He flew on a while longer and was reassured to find the inn was not in danger.

That's when he saw the dome of thorns.

The Papal City had always glistened in the sunlight and could be seen for miles, but this glow was cut off from the sun by gigantic barbs and thick branches. He circled the area and saw that the monstrosity was all encompassing. He spied a small disturbance of red near the western edge and set down near it.

Flowers had erupted in a violent spray that looked from above like blood spatter. A large pool of them dominated the area where a sizable ballista bolt was pegged into the ground. Several more bolts were lying around but this one had the red flowers all over it and a trail of them leading away. The dome of thorns sprung from the earth within a stone's throw of the bolt and blotted out the sun.

He stood and approached the brambles, but felt the strong Fae aura permeating the growth. The thorns glistened with a sticky substance and even Uriel's power did not budge the barrier. The people within were undoubtedly scrambling to deal with the loss of the outside world but for now, even this resident of Heaven could not help them.

This is Embertwist's work. There is no doubt. He is the only Fae being with this kind of power at this time. I have not seen this level of energy since the War.

He looked around for a sign of where he went from here. The flowers went towards the north, surprisingly away from the woods. He followed them to a copse of trees on the border of Toledo where they suddenly stopped. He felt around to see if there was an illusionary building but found nothing. He could sense he was deep within the aura of the Fae here and felt an unnatural prickling all across his wings and skin. The feeling was enough to repel him and he took to the sky again to get away.

He flew to the inn and came down behind it. The holy aura of the Papal City was diminished and the aura of the Fae had elevated. Now, it felt like neutral ground might be at the edge of the thorny barrier. He didn't know for sure what could have caused Embertwist to expend his power, but he definitely wanted to wait and see if his friend kept their appointment.

Alexander Angloume, Heir Apparent to the throne of Mervolingia, looked around the area, scratching his head. Dawn had come while he and the Lady Tanglwyst walked to this place, so there was plenty of light to find the bandit camp. Yet there was no trace a horse or tent had ever been here. There was even a full grown tree where the fire pit had been. He turned to the lady, eyes searching beneath a brow scrunched in confusion.

"They *were* right here, weren't they?"

She looked around. "I would have bet my holdings on it." She walked to the edge of where the camp's horse corral had been and then went past that. Alexander followed her. She looked at a tree that had a rope tied in it.

Alexander pointed to it. "I *definitely* remember that. It was a snare they set that rendered me helpless."

"This is how they captured you?" Her hazel eyes were not subtle in their judgement nor their mockery. "A rabbit snare?"

"They were clearly hunting sizable rabbits. It lifted me off the ground. Frankly, if there are rodents of my size and weight in this forest, I'm heading back to Caratia, where it's safe."

She smiled at that, then looked more closely at the sprung trap. She let her gaze scan the forest before crouching near the ground. "I'm no ranger, but that print there looks like your boot."

She pointed to a mark on the disturbed ground. There were several others with it and he saw a print firmly in some softer soil near a tree root. He went over to each of the clearer ones and nodded, his foot beside them.

"They are." He looked around. "They all are. There are no other prints here but mine." He looked at her. "So either I imagined the whole thing and fought a phantom here."

"Drawing me into your hallucination."

"Exactly. Or these were…"

Tanglwyst sighed. "Fae."

He came over to her. "Tulio underwent a lot of changes when we entered the city. He became a woman, a very slight creature that was agile and had magical abilities. He was probably always this woman."

Tanglwyst nodded. She looked around again, then back to Alexander. "So, Cliffbase or St. Giles?"

He thought about having them return to Cliffbase. The road to the border town was not far from this spot. Then he remembered the accomodations available and looked to the west. Gomez was in St. Giles and he needed to get to him. He was still "looking for a bride" for Alexander and needed to be informed that Catriona was no longer a viable option. Gomez had covered for him while he pursued his heart but the guardsman needed to know that quest had ended. He looked at his companion.

Or had taken on a different face.

"What do you know about the road to St. Giles from here?"

Tanglwyst pointed to the west through the trees. "The main road from Patras to the Papal City skirts this forest and there's a nice inn where it forks around the woods. I almost stayed there but I saw your Mother arrive."

"Mother. That's right. I felt her fealty there when I was looking for you."

Tanglwyst nodded. She knew the sense of which he spoke because he had given her the Power of Sovereignty to save her life. It enabled the weilder to find every person whose heart held fealty to Mervolingia. The weilder was the *de facto* ruler of the country and she had returned it to him as he slept before disappearing. Throughout their entire ordeal, her fealty had not exactly flagged, but he knew her loyalty was not to *him,* but to the country. Wielding the Power left a mark upon the soul, and there was only one other person alive in the world who had that mark: his brother Charles, whom Tanglwyst was accused of murdering.

The reminder that she was a fugitive made him reconsider going anywhere in civilization. He could not pardon her from here. That required a writ to undo the one he had Gomez witness. In fact, for all Alexander knew, Gomez had to witness the undoing as well. That was something his mother would know. Having aided three kings while never holding the Power herself, she would know all the abilities of the thing. He nodded to the west.

"Let's head towards the inn then. My mother will know how to pardon you for the record."

"Okay." She nodded and headed towards the edge of the forest to the south. The road from Cliffbase to the main road lay that way.

He grabbed her hand, staying her progress. "Wait."

She turned to him. Her eyes went to their hands and then flicked up to his in judgement.

He released her, albeit reluctantly. "We should stay away from the road for now. Patrols."

"With me in custody, you'd be safe."

"And alone in this. I'd rather not be alone again. If you please, my lady."

She looked to the west and nodded. "Alright then." She went with purpose towards the inn, peering through the trees. "It's about a day's walk through the trees to here. The road would be faster but I will give you this. Understand, your mother will not be as forgiving as you. She might try to execute me on sight."

"I'll order her not to."

She closed her eyes, shaking her head. "No, you won't." She looked at him again, the scolding still there. "That's what caused problems before. You'll make no declarations nor write any laws or writs until your Coronation. You need to be sure you don't put the Power in anyone's hands but your own."

"You know, my *last* decision was so far the best one I made. You cleaned the Power of the taint I gave it."

"All the more reason why I don't want you marring it again with impulsive choices. Come on. We have some acreage to cover before we can rest."

# Three

## "Will I dream when I die?"
## Shiva, The Karmic Hand

"Good morning, Myrgen."

Myrgen turned from tending the small garden and looked up at the lovely Glarren woman with the long blond hair. He stood, smiling.

"Gwen! It's so good to see you!"

The friends embraced and he patted her shoulders. "Come inside. I'll make some tea."

"Thank you. How is everyone here?"

He dusted the dirt off his knees and picked up a basket of greens and carrots. "Fine. Tib is playing with some other kids down at Drake and Anika's. They'll be by for lunch if you aren't busy."

"Why don't we walk instead of having tea then?"

He nodded. "Sounds fine with me. I was going to wash these off for Anika but she can do that too."

They walked towards the sound of children playing in water and dogs barking as they joined in. Rose, the young woman who prepared Myrgen's room at Ashstone, waved to them. A young man Myrgen had not met came up and kissed her cheek. He smiled at the couple and Rose hugged the man around the middle as Myrgen and Gwen waved back.

"Myrgen!" Tib ran up to him and hugged him. "I'm so glad you're here."

"Where else would I be, big guy? Where are Drake and Anika?"

Tib pointed behind him, a slight scar running along his neck. "Over there." He turned back to Gwen and hugged her as well. "Hi Gwen!"

"Hi Tib." She held him close, then released him. "Go play."

"Ok." He ran off, stopping by Anika to get an apple before scampering off towards the water again. She and Drake waved to Gwen and Myrgen, who returned the gesture. Rainbows filled the air as the mists from the water splashing caught the sun. Birds sang in the trees and a cat ran by with a mouse in its mouth.

"So, what brings you by, Gwen?"

She took a deep breath. "There's a problem, you might say. It turns out that Heaven has taken a hostage. The Land needs you to rescue it."

"Me? I'm hardly the kind of person for the Land to send after a hostage. How would I even *do* that?"

"Well, I can't say yet because there is a weapon that you have to acquire first. It will be key to this mission. Without it, you can't hope to get into position to make the rescue."

"A weapon?"

Gwen nodded.

"And where do I find this weapon?"

"It's currently underground. In fact," she turned and pointed to the north, "it's that thing there."

Myrgen looked and saw a white line piercing the sky beyond the Caratian Mountains. It looked dangerous and frightening, like a giant granite sword stabbing the offending clouds. He felt his hip out of instinct and looked down when he found it bare.

*The White Granite Sword is missing. Where did I leave it?*

He looked around for Gwen but she was gone. The basket of vegetables slipped unnoticed from his fingers and started walking towards the Sword.

Smoke filled his nostrils and ash coated his tongue. He reached out, clawing at the ground around him and hauling himself from the black, hot soil. His body hurt but he could move and he could think. He felt his legs come free of their sheath. He was nude, covered in ground, cooled lava. Around him, he saw darkness lit by molten rock. He summoned the White Granite Sword to him and it responded before the thought was formed. He stood, again using it as a crutch, but only until he got to his feet. It slipped back into the black sand like it was dropped in a pool.

He stumbled forward, seeing a light that was not volcanic coming from the left about thirty yards away. He turned the corner and saw about forty people huddled by the mostly closed doors of the Meditation Chamber at Ashstone. A few people heard his approach and turned, frightened. He moved towards them and they parted, gasps of fear and awe punctuating the air. He pushed the doors open without stopping and flowed into the hallway.

He padded down the dark hallway, no light coming through the windows. A door to the ramparts led outside but no light came from there either. The only glow was from the stones of Ashstone itself. The grey rock was shot through with dark red veins and Myrgen now knew they were more than just lava. They were the Land's blood. Movement caught his eye down the hall, something the size of a man, but it made no effort to come at Myrgen.

He walked to the pile of shadows on the ground. In the middle of the hallway was a black scorch mark, nothing to say what made it, but Myrgen knew. This man was the dual-sword-wielder that he lost track of during the battle. A blackened wooden haft stuck in the oily mark, lightly charred but intact enough to be identifiable. A bloody trail stained the stones and showed a path to the nearby wall. There were three forms in a pile together.

One of them was Mathias, the man who took care of the stables. He had been slashed with a sword that had cut him fatally, and he sat in a sizable pool of blood. The man had handled Caratia's rather impressive horses as well as the smithing of the horseshoes and nails. He was not a small man and his heart had not given out easily. His cheeks were stained with streaks from his tears, partially washing away the blood splattered on his face.

Cradled within the arms of the stable master was a smaller body in two pieces. Drake, the wolfhound that Myrgen had given Tib as a puppy earlier this year, was with it, soaked in blood but resting his head upon the body. The boy's head was in Mathias' hand, held to his chest but Myrgen could tell it was not attached to the boy's body. Myrgen's heart seized in his chest.

*Not again... not again...*

His ears became full of the sounds of swords clanging on stone and steel, and the screams of Emilianites dying at the hands of Marcel and his guards. His voice abandoned him as he mouthed "I'm sorry" over and over.

Drake lifted his head at Myrgen and whimpered as he knelt beside them.

A moan escaped the stable hand's throat and he opened his eyes. "Stâpân…"

Myrgen touched the man's shoulder. "Help! I need some help here. There are people here who can help you, Mathias. Hang on."

Feet pounded down the hall as the folks hiding in the Meditation room heeded his call.

"I… failed… him… I tried…"

"Don't talk." Myrgen tried to press his hands upon the wound but Tib's body was in the way.

"Take him…"

Myrgen stopped his frantic effort and drew in a breath. He had seen where Mathias was going. He knew he would find Tib there. He swallowed, nodding. He took Tib's body from the man, being careful with the head to keep it with the neck. The dog looked at the boy and Myrgen fought the tears. Drake went to the small hand dangling, trying to get the boy to pet him. Myrgen had seen this before, with his son's dog.

"I need a cloth, a blanket please. Something."

One of the other people ran into a room and came back with a couple of blankets off a bed. He nodded to the floor and the man who got them spread one out. Myrgen lay Tib in it, and the boy's head shifted, resting to the side. Myrgen closed the boy's eyes as the dog lay beside him on the blanket. Myrgen let the dog stay for a moment, then he stroked the dog's head.

"Come on, boy. We need to let him go."

Drake sighed and Myrgen gestured for someone nearby to take him. A large man with a grey beard and long hair took the dog by the collar and tugged him gently off the blanket. The dog looked at the man, confused, and continued to watch as Myrgen wrapped the blanket around the boy. Someone handed him their belt to secure it. Another belt secured the feet. Myrgen stood and lifted the bundle. The dog was pulling at the collar and Myrgen nodded to the man.

"Let him come."

He walked down the hall to the Meditation Chamber, Drake beside him, looking up at the bundle. The doors stayed open but no one followed him in. He turned the corner and placed the body on the smoking ground. "Land, take this child, or preserve him until your Servant returns to send them on their way."

A stack of rock formed around the body, entombing it, leaving a large lump. Drake pawed at the stack for a moment, then sighed and lay down beside the mound. Myrgen petted he dog.

"I have to go and see what's happened. You okay here for a while?"

The dog's eyes shifted to Myrgen but he didn't raise his head.

Myrgen nodded. He stood and walked out of the chamber.

Outside, a woman handed him a pair of pants and a shirt. "They're from your room, Stâpân."

"Thank you. I didn't even realize I…"

"We could tell."

He dressed, looking at the dark hallways. After he tucked the shirt into the breeches waistband, he put his hands upon the wall of the castle, willing the shape to return to its former self. Light galloped into the hallways and the people looked around in relief. They walked beside him back down the hallway, where Mathias was being tied with rope in the other blanket. Nearby was a woman from the kitchen, a heavy, practical lady with a cheerful giggle named Rae. Myrgen remembered, for some strange reason, that she raised goats and used the yarn she spun from their wool to make hats. She was being hugged by her husband Jess, the man who had held Tib's dog, and she nodded, tears drying on her face, to something he said.

Myrgen put his hand on Jess's. "Thank you for your help"

"Where is he now?"

"He's with the body. The Land didn't take it so…"

Jess and Rae exhaled. She looked at her husband. "What does that mean?"

Myrgen looked at the people assembled who were looking to him for an answer. He didn't know how to explain what he had seen before the attack, back in the meditation chamber. He was shown an entity that helped people go to the place he had been, where Gwen was. The Death Bringer. He felt he knew her but that memory was elusive. He was not so arrogant as to think he could explain it to people who had always been at peace with death and the afterlife. Having seen it personally, and he was quite sure he had seen it, it was a good place to go. He had no idea what the afterlife was like for terrible people who worshiped the Land, but he hoped the Death Bringer did. He would ask her when she arrived.

Jess kissed his wife's forehead. "I think it means the Land is waiting for the child's mother to return before taking him away. So she can say goodbye."

Rae turned to Myrgen. "Are you going to go find her?"

Jess sniffed. "It might be smarter to wait here. She'll come back eventually. You'd be trying to beat a tenday head start."

Myrgen nodded. "Through inhospitable area. I want to see what needs to be done here. With Drake and Anika dead, I…"

"What?"

Everyone in the hallway gasped and several turned away, while others stepped forward in interest. A man from the back raised his voice. "How do you know they're dead?"

Myrgen swallowed the lump in his throat. "The Rite of Succession stones appeared after the battle. He was gravely injured and the Dûcesa had been killed by the Mandian King. Drake…" He fought the lump but it won, and he let the tears fall to get past it enough to continue. The people in the hallway began to cry again, their loss of Tib still raw.

"Was he taken?"

Myrgen nodded.

"Who else stood?"

"I did. I stood on the stone. There were only two."

"Then you are the new Dûce."

Myrgen shook his head. "No, I'm not. I died as well. I was in Summerland. I saw Tib there, and Gwen, and Anika and Drake. I saw R.." His throat seized again. "Rose…" He cleared it with a cough. "And many others have fallen. I don't think I was accepted as worthy."

"Then why were you returned?" Rae's eyes were red and wet.

He looked at her. "I honestly have no idea. Gwen told me there was a person held captive by Heaven, and that to get them out, I needed a weapon that was buried underground. It's to the north."

"Then you need to go north." Jess's voice was firm and the others in the hallway nodded agreement.

"Maybe, but I'm not going to leave here on some quest when there are people hurt."

"The Land returned you. You need to go." The rest of the people around him nodded and voiced their agreement.

"Yes, but I am Stâpân. Catr… *The Land* entrusted me with the protection of the people. I didn't protect them…"

Jess put his hand upon Myrgen's shoulder. "Yes, you did. We are all alive because of you."

*"But Tib is dead!"* Myrgen put his face in his hands and the people gathered around him. He felt their presence, their support, their love.

"Stâpân, he is in Summerland. He is safe. He will grow up, have a family. Drake and Anika are there too, to guide him. He will live and grow there. No one can hurt him there. He is surrounded by the Land. Even if his body does not go into the ground, it is not because he is not accepted by the Land. He is already there. This is now just meat left behind."

Myrgen felt this image was true. What he had seen in the afterlife was exactly what they were saying. He had a garden. He had always wanted one. That simple tilling of the earth to ease one's troubles had appealed for years now, almost a decade. And he had one in Summerland.

But not everyone was in Summerland right now.

"I believe the Land does want me to go. But it also wants me not to shirk my duties here. I'll tend to them first. Then I'll go."

This answer seemed to satisfy the people assembled.

Myrgen looked to Matthias. "What do we do for him?"

"We take him to his family. They will inter him."

He looked at the people. "Does anyone here know his family?"

Rae nodded and people came forward to pick up the body. The blood had soaked into the stones around him, leaving no trace that a man had died there. Myrgen looked at the surrounding stones, wondering how many of them had absorbed the blood of the people over the centuries.

The scorch mark where the blood of the invader had been still lingered and Rae noticed his gaze. She patted him on the shoulder. "Why don't you take this outside? I'll get that cleaned up."

"You don't need to." He looked at her husband. "You've done quite enough."

She flopped her hand towards him. "Pshaw. Drake is a good dog and it seems you need him more than Tib does. Don't worry. When the animal dies, he will see Tib again. It would be an entirely different story if Tib wasn't part of the Land, but he was." She leaned in, about to share a secret. "They say animals aren't let in to Heaven, so the Land claims them all."

Myrgen remembered the sights and sounds of Summerland. There was horse and cow, birds, insects, dogs, cats, chickens. It was no different from Caratia. It wasn't until he saw Gwen that it occurred to him that he might be dead. Even then, it hadn't mattered. He was home. "That just might be true. There were a lot of animals."

She sighed, as if the likelihood of her *not* being right was just silly, and Jess smiled.

The next several hours dealt with death in a way that Myrgen had never seen. The blood of anyone injured or killed was gone from the streets and grounds or were scorch marks that littered the area. People gathered their dead in heirloom bed coverings and blankets, mourning their losses while being strangely at peace. The crew of the Enigma joined in and Myrgen found out that Octavius had left town days before with some green-haired stranger. He smiled, knowing Octavius would be safe but in Raven's company, his sanity would be in peril.

People brought their dead to their homes and Myrgen was asked to accompany a few. Inside, they pulled back a rug or mat that revealed dirt floor and lay the body, still covered, upon it. They murmured prayers to the Land and then, in a soft *huh-hwaw*, the body entered the ground and was gone. The blanket or covering was lifted and the rug or mat replaced. On several occasions, Myrgen was asked to touch the body as it was brought back into the Land, and he felt it drop into the ground like the key at his neck had in St. Marguerite.

A couple people were without family, so the castle folk took them to the courtyard at Ashstone. They pulled out some stones near the trees and gardens and placed the bodies on the bare earth. The bodies were taken and in their place, flowers grew and bloomed. He looked around as about eight bodies were interred this way.

"Is this were all these flowers and trees come from?"

A woman from the bath area nodded. "This is our home for the dead."

Once the dead were committed to the ground and the scorch marks banished from the flagstones around town, everyone filed up to Ashstone for dinner. Flagons were raised and the Enigma crew was put to work filling in for the fallen. Everyone was saddened to hear about the loss of the Dûce, Dûcesa, and Tib, and many commented that it was good that Catriona was not around to witness it. Some argued Tib would not have fallen had she been there, but Myrgen assured them she would have been on the street or on the ramparts or in the Town Square fighting Cipriano, and he still would have died.

"The Land needed him more," was the regular toast, and many seemed to pass away the knowledge as easily as they said farewell to a ship that would be back next year. Myrgen knew their peace, and he knew Catriona would feel it too.

Thomas the Diminutive, a former Stâpân of Caratia, came up to him in the later hours, a few pints of ale in him. "Myrgen, what is your plan now?" He gestured to the empty thrones. "Do you know the procedure?"

"The final Trial? You stand upon the stones in the Square when they appear. You stand and be judged. But I was judged unworthy. I was taken and kept."

"Well," Thomas gestured up and down, "obviously not kept, but I see your point." He shrugged and took another drink. "The Land will choose someone. Sooner or later."

"Actually, I was going to talk to you about that. I need to leave Caratia."

Thomas frowned, an exaggerated expression under the influence of the ale. "Why? Catriona will come back on her own. She's just going to Glarren."

"The Land told me I needed to go north and get something. I don't know what it is but the Land said it was a very powerful weapon."

"Oh."

"I need someone to become Stâpân or Stâpâna until one of us returns."

Thomas nodded. "Okay. I got this."

Myrgen sighed. "Thank you." He was grateful to be able to turn the reins of the protection over to someone with experience.

Thomas stepped up on a bench between two diners and then to the table. "Everyone! Everyone!" He waited a moment for the talking to die down. "Our Stâpân needs to go get something for the Land. He will be doing the Ritual of Succession tomorrow morning at dawn. Be in the square. Thank you." He bowed and the commentary swelled again as Thomas descended his platform. "There. All taken care of." He patted

Myrgen's motionless shoulders and smiled at his stunned expression. "You're welcome."

Then Thomas wandered off to find his wife.

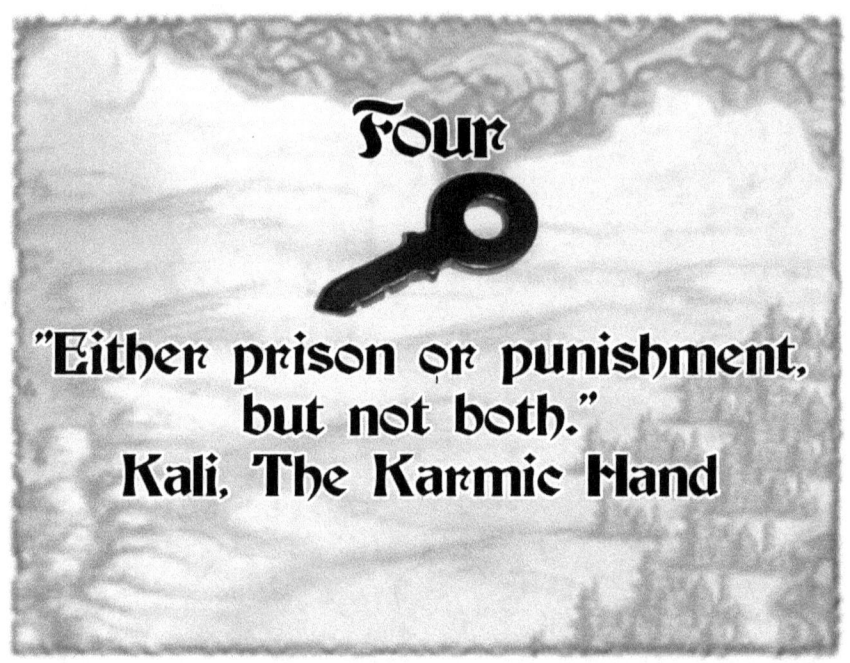

# Four

## "Either prison or punishment, but not both."
## Kali, The Karmic Hand

The lights of the Benevolent Friar flickered through the trees and both Alexander and Tanglwyst groaned in relief. Tanglwyst knew it had taken less than a night to get to the inn before, when she had discovered Catherine and her guards were housed there. This trip had taken well over a full day longer. She decided that Tulio had changed the travel times in "his" woods. With him (her?) gone now, that wayward magic was likewise missing. The resulting knots in her calves from the extra day of walking were her testimony to that.

*Well, that makes sense, she thought. After all, this wood spans half the country's width. Outside it, it takes a tenday to go by road. Inside, it seemed to move at whatever pace Tulio wanted. I mean,* she smiled, *he did decide brunch was after sunset on our first meeting.*

She stopped, leaning against a tree. "That's it up there."

Alexander looked at the lights. "You sure?"

She nodded.

"Then why are we stopped?"

She looked at the inn. "Your mother is in there. I'm a fugitive. That's a death sentence."

"Over my dead body."

She smiled at his naiveté. "Alexander…"

"My Lady, give me a chance to be your King. Please."

She was about to explain that this wasn't how any of this worked when a small breeze ruffled her hair. There was a scent of fire that was too strong to be just from the inn. Worse, it wasn't a wood fire. It was a grass fire and it was coming from the valley. She looked at Alexander who also caught the scent. They looked to the inn and ran to it. They stepped onto the porch of the Benevolent Friar and Tanglwyst stopped, staring at the smoke rising from her lands.

She gripped the railing, horror in her eyes as she scanned the valley. Alexander stood beside her, looking from north to south to see the expanse of grey darkening the sky. A patrolman came out of the inn and excused himself as he passed the pair. Tanglwyst reached out and grabbed the man's arm.

"What is that?"

The patrolman looked at her, then where she was looking. "St. Giles, milady. There's a Fae army encamped around it."

"Around the entire county?"

"Yes, milady."

Alexander looked at the man. "How big is this army?"

"Big enough to be a problem. Excuse me." The man left towards the stables.

Tanglwyst covered her mouth with both hands, trying to stem the tears. "I have to go. I can't stay here, Alex. My family is there."

"I'm not going to let you go alone. You might not make it there at all."

"And what are you going to do?" She gestured to the smoke encircling the lush farm area. "Mobilize your army? Even the Caratians couldn't stop a force this size."

"The Caratian army would not oppose these people."

Tanglwyst and Alexander turned to look at Catherine, her stiff frame rivaled only by the doorway.

"What do you mean, Mother?"

Catherine stepped between them, nodding to the encampments. "The Kraktens are Fae Worshippers. They are children of the Land, just like Caratia."

Tanglwyst bowed. "Your Majesty."

Catherine looked at the fugitive. "That is your home, is it not?"

"Yes."

Catherine put a hand upon Tanglwyst's. "I am truly sorry for your loss." She turned to Alexander. "I wish you had arrived two days ago. You would have saved me fifty ducats."

"I was busy." He glanced at Tanglwyst.

"Yes. You apprehended her. May I know how?"

Alexander looked at the fires and Tanglwyst could tell he wasn't sure how to explain what had happened. She decided to help him.

"Summoning."

Catherine looked at Tanglwyst, frowning. Her face was confused instead of indignant like Tanglwyst assumed she would be for a person answering for the Crown. "And it worked?"

Tanglwyst nodded, bowing in a gesture of I'm here, aren't I?

Catherine looked at Alexander again. "It's intact?"

"Believe it or not, Mother, is always has been. Elizabeth… did something to her."

"Oh."

Tanglwyst averted her eyes. "I am sorry for your loss, Your Majesty. I am ready to pay whatever punishment necessary for my crime."

"Indeed." Catherine looked into the inn. "Guards! Come here."

Alexander grabbed her arm. "Mother, no."

The guards came out of the door, surrounding the trio. Tanglwyst looked at the men, but did not try to run. Catherine looked at Tanglwyst. "Take this woman and give her thirty lashes with a whip for her crime."

"No." Alexander stepped between Catherine and Tanglwyst. "Mother, this is not your decision to make. You are not sovereign here."

"I am the wronged party however. This woman schemed to kill the King, my son."

"Against her will. She was compelled by a spell."

"So she is blameless?"

"Mother, she…" He looked around at the crowd now assembling. "I need to speak to you in private about this."

Catherine set her jaw. "Fine. Let's take this upstairs." She turned and entered the Inn.

Alexander took Tanglwyst's hand and started to follow but Tanglwyst balked.

"You said 'private'. That includes leaving me out of this."

"It affects you."

"And I'll find out about it when it's time."

"It's time."

She frowned.

"I will have these men pick you up and carry you in there if I must."

She rolled her eyes. "Fine."

"Thank you." He led her upstairs to his mother's room.

"Now, what is it you wish to say that will change my mind about what to do with this traitor?"

Alexander closed the door. "Sit down, Mother. This is going to take a while."

Alistair Hapsburg, the embodiment of Karma, pushed away from the pillar that showed him his son, James. He thought he had heard his daughter's voice and that was what drew him from his fugue. Ever since he had killed the previous incarnation, he had been very aware of a strange tilting feeling around him. It wasn't vertigo-inducing or anything, just a little like being drunk. He had taken to lying motionless on a white bed he conjured to give him a sense of normality and had not really done much else since he visited Hell. When he heard Gwen's voice, it drew him out, and when he couldn't find her, he found James.

James was traveling north with Myrgen's friend Michael. He was curious about the reason for the travel, then realized it was doubtless to tell the family about Gwen's death. That made him sad again but he was cried out at this point. Being a spiritual entity in charge of keeping the whole world balanced didn't prevent one from grieving the loss of a child, apparently. He sprawled back on the bed.

*Gloriana.*

Alistair sat up.

*If James is going to tell his mother about Gwen's death, then...*

He got off the bed and ran to the Pillar. He summoned forth his son's image and listened. They were talking to a man but Alistair could tell he wasn't just a man. That was a fallen Saint.

"Carrots?" James was surprised, apparently. "How do you have carrots out here?"

"I go and get good soil from the area around York, then I don't let that touch the ground. If it never comes in contact with the ground here, it doesn't lose its life."

They walked into the small house and James and Michael marveled at the setup, as did Alistair. All along the walls were large troughs built to house a hundred plants. In fact, the entire house seemed to be made of these troughs. They were about three feet deep and the entire ceiling was glass to let the sunlight in. There was a bedroom but even it was lined entirely in dirt and plants. There was enough food to feed thirty people.

Michael recovered first. "Raymond, there is more soil in this room than I have seen in this whole country. Where did you get it from?"

Raymond cleaned off some carrots in a basin and handed three to each man. "Mostly from Caratia. It has the best soil. I bring it over from the mountain."

"That's a hundred miles from here." James pointed behind them with a carrot. "How did you haul this much soil a hundred miles?"

"I made more than one trip." Raymond gestured to two chairs. "Please, sit. Tell me of your adventure."

The two young men sat, glancing warily at Raymond but eventually, after the carrots hit their taste buds, they relaxed.

Michael started. "We are traveling to Glarren to deliver bad news. My friend's sister died recently and we are going to their mother to tell her."

"Glarren is a long way from here. Why go overland?"

James answered this time. "My father is from here. We wanted to see the place where he lived."

Alistair put his knuckles to his lips. *Oh no.*

Raymond frowned, leaning back away from the two men. "Where did your father live?"

James and Michael seemed to notice the problem at the same time, judging from the look they gave one another. James continued munching. He pointed east, to the sea. "At the part of York that touches Caratia. We sailed past it a dozen times but he never stopped. He recently died too so I have a lot of bad news to convey. Since he never went there, I decided to go there on the way home. It turns out he used to travel to Persephone, looking for artifacts. One time, he just didn't come back and the people of the village assumed he died out there. He didn't, he went on to Mervolingia, but I wanted to see what was so important."

Raymond relaxed. "And did you find what that was?"

Alistair exhaled. *Smart lad.*

"Not really. There's a barrier around the thing. Can't get in. He drew pictures of what it must have looked like based upon the fallen towers and dilapidated buildings. But it doesn't look like he could have gone in. He would have had to bring his own food and water, though there are troughs all around the countryside that catch the rainwater."

Michael glanced at the troughs around the room and then back at their host. "You built those."

"Um, yes."

"How?"

"I gathered wood and built them, then placed them along my route to get the soil."

James stopped eating. "Then why were there ones on the way to Persephone?"

"It gets boring traveling the same road all the time." Raymond sighed and leaned forward. "Are there any changes to the landscape at all?"

James and Michael hesitated but then shook their heads. James picked up his last carrot. "But I don't know what it is supposed to look like. All I know is this trip. Is the entire country like this?"

Raymond nodded. "Top to bottom, side to side."

"Why do you stay here then?"

"It is where I am needed most." Raymond looked up. "You have much daylight and you have animals. You can make it quite far without stopping. Do you have food for them?"

"Chick pea cakes."

Raymond scowled. "Pah! I will give them real food. It is the least I can do for company." He stood up and left the building.

Michael leaned over to James. "Do you think Catriona is in danger?"

"From this guy? Hardly. She's trapped in that place. He can't get to her."

Alistair frowned. *Catriona? What place? Oh, please tell me she didn't...* He turned his viewing Pillar to look for his former fiancée.

There, underground, under Persephone, was Catriona. She was bound in some sort of mystical trap, suspended beneath the covenant. She was unconscious and she looked like she was being drained. Her body sagged from the loss of muscle and her black hair was starting to thin and fall out. Her clothes, very well made and fitted to her, hung on her like rags. Her boots were already loose on her legs and had she not been bound there, she would have lost them to gravity by now.

He caught a movement out of the corner of the room and looked. There was Raven Grasshair, leaning against the wall, watching her. He was awake and lucid but he seemed likewise to be wearing out. Lauriel was nowhere to be found.

*Raven...*

Raven looked around at the mention of his name. Alistair leaned in, excited.

"Raven? Can you hear me?"

"Alistair?"

Alistair swung around in excitement. "Yes! Raven, yes it's me. I'm in Karma."

"Uh... okay. How did you get there?"

"Long story. What's going on there?"

"Oh, well the Gold Wife decided she wanted to see me again. So she lured this woman in here. Apparently, she is the First Dûcesa."

"Catriona?"

"Hmm... why do I know that name?"

"It's the name of the woman we were talking about in the tavern in St. Andrew, when you were a cat? Catriona Morstadora."

"That name is really familiar."

"Morstadora was the name of the First Dûcesa. That was the dead giveaway for me that Catriona was her resurrection."

Raven tapped his head. "Oh! I know this one. Because the trap in this room will only spring for something more powerful than what it currently holds. And it let go of Magic to claim her."

"It let go... of... Magic?"

"Yep. Apparently, Magic has been in this room, being drained, for millennia. And it let go of that to take this woman."

"That doesn't make any sense."

Raven shook his head. "Nope."

"Why haven't you gotten her out of there? You're a mage."

"Yeah, about that. I tried. Trouble is you can't get out from inside. It's designed that way. You can get taken out, but it's a one-way thing."

"Who built this thing?"

"I have no idea, but I'll keep asking."

"Asking who?"

"Well, mostly myself, but I'm not very helpful."

"I'll see what I can do to get you out."

"Thanks. And you might want to hurry if you don't want her to change. She's only got a little while left. I keep doing what I can, but that is only keeping her unconscious and nourished. I'm using magic powered by her to feed and water her. She's effectively eating herself. It isn't helping her survive. If she dies…"

Alistair nodded. "I know." He swallowed. "Raven, is this part of the war you have been talking about for two hundred and fifty years?"

Raven frowned. "Probably not. I mean, for all I know, that dream all those years ago was about the battles we fought against the Inquisition."

"Haven't you had it since then though?"

Raven thought about it for a second. "Yeah, but that might just be me. Wilge talked through dreams and I think I just… you know… I miss her sometimes." He waved his hand. "That's probably all it is."

Catriona spasmed and Alistair let Raven work. He stepped back from the pillar and looked around. A trap like that, something that powerful, was not random. It was placed there. But what kind of entity would be able to make a trap that diabolical?

He closed his eyes and nodded.

Lucifer.

Catherine looked at her son. "So, he's alive?"

"And happy."

"And on a ship?"

"Making tea, last I saw."

Catherine turned to Tanglwyst. "But you knew none of this?"

"Embarrassingly little, Your Majesty."

"But you know about these amulets?"

Tanglwyst nodded. "That I am a bit more familiar with, Your Majesty. I saw where the vaults were in the Papal City."

"Which is now covered in thorns."

Alexander and Tanglwyst nodded.

"And you destroyed the amulet my son had."

Tanglwyst nodded.

"And you gave her the Power of Sovereignty to heal her?"

Alexander nodded.

"And you gave it back?"

Tanglwyst glanced at Alexander, then nodded.

"And now you two have some sort of bond."

Tanglwyst raised her hand. "I don't know about…"

"Yes." Alexander looked at Tanglwyst, then back to his mother. "Yes."

The sun had gone far in its trek across the sky in the telling of the tale. At first Alexander had been hesitant to give details but it became clear that leaving anything out would simply cause more problems. Tanglwyst had taken over the tale and she had filled in Alexander and Catherine of the things she knew, supplemented by Alexander's point of view where applicable. Catherine had watched their exchange and saw that Alexander had grown fond of this lady, despite the circumstances. Or perhaps because of them. She remembered the gossip from the palace brought to her by Charles and his colleagues while she was in the Papal City. Alexander had become interested in a new lady over the winter, but something had occurred to drive a wedge between them. She wondered if this was the lady but realized she didn't need to know those details. At least not at this time and place.

"So, what do we do now?"

"We proceed with giving me thirty lashes."

Alexander and Catherine looked at Tanglwyst.

"I don't think I will let that happen, my lady." Alexander folded his arms across his chest.

"You have to." As he started to protest, Tanglwyst held up her hand. "No, I mean it. I was a traitor in the eyes of the law and the Crown. I was involved with a plot to kill the king."

"You were compelled…"

"The people won't care. And your mother deserves justice."

"That's not justice. That's torture. Besides, Charles isn't dead. He's fine and happy with the love of his life."

"But the people don't know that."

"Then I'll tell them."

"You can't." Catherine's voice was calm and firm. "He faked his own death. If he is alive, you must either rescind the throne to him or

make him your heir. Either way, he would have to return to Patras."
Catherine looked at Tanglwyst. "I'm afraid the Lady is right."

"No. She isn't. I can't... I won't..."

Tanglwyst took Alexander's hand. "Listen to me. Yes, I was
compelled to do what I did, but I was not compelled to do all of it. Some
of those sins are fully mine. I deserve to be punished for those. This will
show that you are a just King, and not someone for whom the laws only
apply to people you don't like. You cannot show favoritism in this. It
will set a bad precedent."

Those last words held weight, more than Catherine understood, yet
they did the trick. Alexander walked away from the women, running his
hands through his hair. He turned back.

"We'll get you drunk. Passing out drunk. Then you won't..."

"No." Tanglwyst looked at Catherine. "You should probably
oversee it, at least the initial blows." She looked at Alexander. "You both
should."

Alexander set his teeth and scowled at the ceiling. Catherine could
see he was trying to figure out a way around it.

"Tanglwyst, will you give us a moment?"

"Of course." Tanglwyst opened the door and left.

Catherine waited until she heard the lady go down the squeaky
stairs, then turned to her son. "The woman is right."

"The woman is mad!"

"Also true. Alex..."

"Mother, don't. I got my gift of words from you and I know their
power. You convinced me and Charles to murder thousands just to get
rid of one man who you despised. Don't think for a moment I don't know
your tricks." He pointed to the door. "That woman is showing integrity
and remorse over her crime, something I've never seen you do over
yours. Now you want her blood to satisfy another vendetta. You won't
get it." He drew himself to full height and Catherine felt the push of the
Power of Sovereignty against her fealty. "I will let her take the
punishment for her crimes, let her pay her debt. You will stay up here.
You will not get to witness this. I'll not feed your bloodlust, nor let it
overrun me again."

Catherine nodded. "As you command, My King."

He stormed to the door and opened it. "I need a medical kit, and a
belt."

# Five

## "Art is the ability to paint with your soul."
## Shiva, The Karmic Hand

Myrgen opened the door to his room but the emptiness of it was too much to endure. He thought of going to Catriona's room but felt it would be even more overwhelming there. It was right next to Tib's. He remembered a note he had gotten under his door the morning of the attack. He walked over to it and picked it up. Inside was a key. The note explained it.

*To our friend,*
*To help you in the absence of our daughter. Go to the eastern tower, very top. We hope it helps.*
*D and A*

His tears wet the paper, threatening to smudge the writing, so he wiped it away and set it out to dry. He took the key and went to the stairwell at the end of the hall in his wing. The stairs were comfortably wide, spiraling around a narrow support core probably ten feet thick, with thin windows on the outside edge to let in the night sky. Sconces marked the inside wall, lighting the area, which was handy since he had not thought to bring a light himself. The door at the top was the only one. He used the key and opened to a wondrous sight.

The room had been set up to be an artist's workshop. Pigment powders of various colors sat in glass jars and bottles, waiting to be mixed with oil or water. Mixing trays, wooden pallets, and brushes sized from house painting to cat's whisker were likewise assembled. Canvasses already mounted were around the room on easels and there was even a single person bed for when he painted himself to exhaustion. A window looked out upon the harbor and he could see the *Enigma* in dry dock from there. He realized the angle from the other turret would not have that sight and the tears flowed again.

"Thank you."

He picked a canvas and turned to the paints. It took very little time to assemble the pigments he wanted to use for his concept, and by dawn, he had already sketched his idea. He stepped back, admiring the lines. It was a huge canvas, but he preferred that. He wanted it life sized. He had drawn the perspective lines and the moon for the lighting. True, the original situation had been twilight, but by the time this moment happened, it had been moonrise. He stepped back, and looked at it.

"Excuse me, sir."

Had he not been so focused, he would have started and possibly dropped his carefully made pigments. Instead, he looked behind him as if he has always known there was someone watching. It was the woman from the bath.

"I'm sorry to bother you. It's dawn."

"How did you find me?"

She blushed. "You left a trail of open doors. And there was a note."

"Ah." He looked at the painting. "What does dawn have to do with it?"

"The Ritual of Succession?"

"Oh!" He glanced out the window and saw the whole village assembling in the town square. "Damn! How bad do I look?"

"Um…"

He saw her apron had several pockets. Out of one was a comb. "You're the bath lady?"

"Yes. Livia. Livia Becskei."

"Well, we're gonna need to do this on the run, Livia. Start handing me things and I'll use them as we go."

By the time he had entered the town square, Livia had him combed, tucked, lotioned, soaped (which he accidentally used on his teeth first), and a couple cloves to cover the wine and ale breath from the night before. She confirmed he had no black flecks in his teeth, judging him fit to be seen. He thanked her and called for the White Granite sword without thinking. He checked his neck for the Onyx key and saw it wrapped around the handle of the sword. He nodded, swallowed, and stepped into the street to walk to the square. There were a lot of people in the park. He nodded to Thomas as the sun shone on the dewy grass.

He bowed to the people and spoke clearly in the early morning stillness. "My family. Thank you for coming to see me this morning. I've never done this before so I'm just going to get right to it." He took a deep breath and looked into the eyes of the people.

"In the attack, I was among the dead of that day, as many of you can attest."

Gasps filled the air and several people nodded. He recognized them as those fighting in the square against Cipriano's men.

"When I was in Summerland, I was visited by Gwen. She told me the Land was not quite finished with me. She showed me a place I needed to go. There is someone held prisoner in Heaven and I need to fetch a weapon that will aid in the rescue of that person. So I will be leaving here as soon as my duties are finished to retrieve this weapon. Since I can't protect the people if I'm not here, I want to turn these symbols of my office back to the Land to pick a proper Stâpân."

The crowd stood still, watching him. No one moved to step forward to be considered.

*Well, this country is used to the Land being wiser than them. I should go along with that.*

He looked around for a Ritual stone but none rose to meet him. He got confused and glanced at Thomas. Thomas shrugged.

*Okay then.*

Myrgen set the point of the sword before him and let it go, expecting it to soak into the ground and rise before the person that was worthy.

It fell over and lay at his feet. The Onyx Key didn't even soak into the ground, but lay upon the damp grass.

"Sorry. I guess I did that wrong." He bent over, picked it up, and willed it into the ground, which it did. He sighed, and nodded.

"Please, bring the office of Stâpân to my successor."

The sword and pendant rose from the ground. He looked at the people, frowning, and didn't reach for the sword. It stayed upright, then toppled over, hitting him in the shins. He barked in pain and the populace laughed. Thomas strode over to him and put his hand on Myrgen's shoulder.

"There's your answer, I think."

The people bobbed their heads in agreement and several turned to resume their morning duties. A couple yawned, looking like they might return to bed. At least four exchange money, loser of the bet to winner.

Myrgen sat on the wet ground, rubbing his shin. "I don't understand."

Thomas knelt beside him. "It's pretty obvious to all of us. Apparently, the Land isn't ready to release you yet."

"But what if something happens here?"

"Then we and the Land will deal with it."

Alistair thought about the last time he had gone to Hell. First off, he had been invited.

*He looked down at himself and found he was clothed in a white outfit with black embroidery. Elaborate scroll work dominated the cuffs and waistband of the outfit and cascaded down the front of the doublet and breeches. His boots and gloves were a contrast, black with white embroidery, as was his shirt. He wore no hat, but there was one beside him, white on top, black underside, complete with matching feathers that began white and faded black, and vice versa. He picked up the hat and saw a piece of paper beneath it, white on black paper.*

*Can we talk?*
*~Hell*

*He looked around, then picked up the note. It was real. He got to his feet and looked behind him. The Pillar was still there but Karma was gone. When he had been shown the true nature of the realm, it had been stark white and he had been nude. Now it was nondescript and he was resplendent. He couldn't understand. He looked down at the note.*

*Hell? How was he supposed to get to Hell?*

*A square opened up in the floor and a white spiral staircase descended into the space beneath it. It went to a room with a door of black ironwood set in a white wall. He walked over to it and twisted the handle. It opened, showing a corridor that ended in a large room about twenty feet away. Wide stairs led into the area that had books lining the walls and a large fireplace behind some elaborate carved chairs.*

*In one of the chairs was a man in beautiful black clothes with a long, fitted coat nearly touching the ground. He stood as Alistair entered, setting down a black glass mug of some beige liquid. There was a tray of similar liquid in a bowl next to an empty cup, and a tall tower of tiny, opulent cakes. The man was beyond handsome.*

*"Alistair, you got my message. Please come in."*

That had been entirely on the Archangel Lucifer's terms. He had requested the meeting, so he had set up the meeting place. He didn't know what kind of preparations had been done for Alistair's sake, but he has also seen the power of Karma when it came to making a place comfortable. He barely understood how to make the place livable for himself.

"I have a decorator, if you want to use him."

Alistair spun to see Lucifer in a beautiful set of blue and silver clothing. This time, he chose something from the Mandian fashion line. A long coat with brilliant filigree embroidery spun all around the cuffs, collar, and hem. The breeches and boots matched it entirely, like they were designed together. Where the coat opened, it showed of the continuation of the pattern upon the doublet. His hair was pulled back in a tail and he wore no hat, but he certainly didn't need one.

"Wow."

Lucifer spun, showing off the outfit. "Isn't it grand? It's a Fuccochio!"

"I don't know… wait, the Mandian designer?"

"Yeah. It's gonna be a real shame when he dies, though he may end up with you."

"Me?"

"Yeah, I've never met a fairer individual. He doesn't bump anyone to the front of the line, no matter who you are. I had to wait for a Mervol accountant to get finished. Luckily, the man didn't want anything too fancy."

Alistair walked up to inspect the work and Lucifer stood proud, showing it off. "That is impressive. All done by hand?"

Lucifer nodded. "He has a team of people who do the cutting and sewing once he does the designs so he has a fast turnaround. This is one of the very few benefits to not having the souls pure when they return to the Well. You can't get this level of creativity if you burn away all the sin. But that's not why you called me here. What's going on?"

"Oh. I... I want to know how to get to the surface."

"Surface of what?"

Alistair pointed to the viewing Pillar. "There. The world. Some friends of mine are in trouble and I need to help them."

Lucifer frowned. "Why should I help you?"

Alistair stopped for a moment, not expecting the question. Then he pictured Catriona in her wasted state and steeled his resolve. He reached into his bag of emotional tricks and looked Lucifer over for what would convince him.

"My job here is to keep the balance."

"Yeah, you're already not doing a very good job at that."

"Well, if I were gone, that would leave this place unmonitored. You could do a little unbalancing yourself, on the sly."

"Are you trying to appeal to my devious nature?" Lucifer folded his arms. "'Cus you're barking up the wrong brimstone."

"Oh."

Lucifer walked over to the Pillar, beckoning Alistair to join him. "C'mon. Tell me what's going on and let me see if I can help you out here."

"Why would the leader of Hell want to help me out?"

Lucifer held up a finger. "Oh, I'll extract a favor later, make no mistake, but the previous Karma wasn't exactly a great person and I'm interested is seeing some of the stuff they did undone. Now, what's going on?"

Alistair showed him the scene in the chamber beneath Persephone. Lucifer paused. He looked Catriona over very carefully. "What is that place?"

"It's a magical trap under a place in York."

Lucifer narrowed his eyes. "What does it do?"

"It grabs something and uses it as a *čaro* source, a magic well to drink from. It released its previous prisoner to capture her."

Lucifer didn't take his eyes off Catriona. "Dare I ask who the previous captive was?"

Alistair hesitated. This person was charming and informative, but Alistair knew he was in charge of all the Infernal realm. Evil. Still, Alistair was Karma. He was meant to deal with both sides equitably.

"Magic."

Lucifer looked at Alistair, a flash of awe crossing his face, then he looked back at Catriona, smiling. "Ya don't say." He stepped back, clapping his hands together. "Tell you what: I won't help you get to the surface because you don't need me for that. As a major arcana, you can go anywhere you like, and take anything you want with you. But I will help you help her. No charge."

Alistair frowned. "Why?"

Lucifer leaned on the table with the Pillar, staring with unbridled lust at the scene within it. "Because, my friend, I owe you now."

"What are you going to do?"

Lucifer looked at Alistair, a very sly grin spreading to his entire face. "I've got a guy."

Alexander opened the door to the room and carried Tanglwyst through to the bed. He had wrapped her in a blanket the instant he was finished with her punishment. Svein and Ealusaid came in behind him with the medical kit they had on hand. It was woefully understocked from what Alexander was used to, being an open basket with some bandages and a clotting herb. He lay her face down, careful to keep her covered. He turned to the innkeepers. "Will you get her some tea?"

"I can, but I doubt she'll be awake to drink it."

"Then get it for me."

Ealusaid nodded and left. Svein frowned. "Is there anything you need, Your Majesty?"

"Privacy more than anything. I need to tend to her wounds now." Alexander looked at the man. "Sir, I saw you holding a stein earlier. What kind of ale was that?"

"It's a strong brew. I was going to give it to her afterwards, if she survived it. Doesn't appear she's going to though."

"She's merely passed out from the pain. It was the best thing she could do. I made sure I didn't break any bones or cut her too deeply."

"Why would you do that for her?"

"Because she did it for me."

Svein grew silent a moment. "I'll get some of our stronger wine. And some well water. It will be cold and will help with that bruising. The stuff in the pitcher is still fresh."

"Thank you."

Svein nodded and started to close the door.

"Wait."

Svein stopped, looking at the king.

"This place is called the Benevolent Friar. Is it, by chance, holy ground?"

Svein shook his head. "No, nothing like that. We called it that because it was on the way to the Papal City."

Alexander sighed. "I guess it was too much to hope for."

Svein closed the door and Tanglwyst gripped Alexander's hand, surprising him.

"I wouldn't let... you do it... even if this... were holy... ground."

He smiled. "I wouldn't ask your permission."

"You had better... You aren't allowed... to do any...thing to me... that... I don't... permit."

He wanted her to keep talking, to make sure she wasn't going to die like the innkeeper had said. If she was talking, she could forgive him. If she was talking, she would tell him if he was damaging her more. He looked at the blanket, a few strips of blood seeping through the fabric. "I can't believe you permitted this."

"I can't believe... you did it... yourself..." She turned her head to look at him and the effort made her suck her breath through clenched teeth. "You must... really be angry with... me."

"I knew where your vital spots were. I didn't layer the hits on top of each other so the healing would take less time. I used a belt instead of a whip so it wouldn't cut the flesh as much. You can heal from bruises in far less time. And… if punishment is going to be dealt under my justice like this, it needs to be by my hand."

"Are you going to do… all the executions… in the city too?"

"I have so far."

Tanglwyst turned away, wincing.

"I am seeing some bleeding here. I want to look at the wounds. May I?"

"As long as you… don't need… anything strenuous… from me."

He smiled. "Just your permission."

She nodded and he tugged the blanket carefully out from under her. She tried to keep from whimpering, but he heard the wetness in her voice. He had wanted to forego the stripping of the prisoner, but by the time he had arrived downstairs, Tanglwyst had already gotten undressed. The inn's inhabitants had ringed the lady near the stables and Zack had tied her to the posts of the door. The medical basket was presented while a patrolman removed his belt. When the man stepped up to deliver the lashes, Alexander had put his hand upon the man's shoulder, holding out his hand for the belt. The King was unaccustomed to how to use a belt to do damage and it took the first ten lashes simply to really leave a mark. He almost stopped then, but the patrolman offered to finish for him. He realized these were going to be delivered regardless, so he did the rest himself.

The marks he left after that were more significant. He had lied to Tanglwyst when he said he was able to not layer the wounds too much. His ineptitude with dealing damage had the welts crisscrossing all over her back, rear, and legs. A couple lashes had flipped around to her stomach and the front of her thighs. The later lashes had ruptured the skin that was already swollen by that time and these were the source of the blood weals. One was especially nasty.

Ealusaid opened the door with a tea service obviously brought from the palace or the Papal City. It was silver and polished instead of crockery like the rest of the dishes that had housed lunch.

"Where do you want her clothes?"

"Were they befouled in any way? Did anyone spit on them, or worse?"

"Not particularly. She folded them on the porch and no one bothered them."

"I suppose it doesn't matter. She won't be wearing them for a couple days. Anywhere is fine."

Zack came in with the pile and set it down. He looked over the lady, then bowed to the King and left.

"Is it true, what you said there? That she was used by a Fae Follower to try and kill King Charles?"

"I'm afraid so. She still needed to be punished for her crime, but since anyone can fall prey to a spell at the hands of someone they trust, I can't really hold it against her."

"That's truly horrible. I know certain Fae are prone to mischief, but the person who did this to her is actually very much against what the Fae are about."

Alexander looked at her. "What do you mean?"

"Fae are kind of specific. If you change them, you change who and what they are and that destroys them. They may be able to change forms, but they are still the same Fae. To change someone's inner essence is very un-Fae-like. Changing someone to suit your desires, or someone changing themselves to suit their own desires, that's a human quality, not a Fae."

"Well, it appears the person who did this to her was half human then."

Ealusaid nodded. "That was my conclusion too."

"Did you find those herbs I asked for?"

Ealusaid scooted to the door. "Oh! Right. I'll get right on that."

"Thank you, milady."

The door closed and Alexander got a cloth wet in the basin on the other side of the room. He brought the cool towel over to the lady and placed it on her largest wound. It went across the small of her back and was the result of an accidental wrist flip that managed to hit only on the edge of the belt. The leather had managed to cut the already tender flesh when he drew it away. He really hoped Ealusaid could find the blood thinners and pain killer grasses he asked for. If he had one of his own kits, he could use a poultice.

Then he realized that the only poultices he had that would help here were the Cyprian herb ones. Great for him, deadly and mind-warping for her. The stuff Elizabeth had used on her had been unconditioned to a specific person, but his were attuned to him directly. It would make her his ever-loyal slave. He thought about what Ealusaid said, about the Fae

63

not changing people. It made what Elizabeth did even worse because she knew full well what she was doing. Since Elizabeth also had tried to make him her King, it was clear she had designs to do likewise to him. He shuddered at the thought of being forced to marry and love such a person. Then again, that was kind of what he was trying to do to Catriona.

He found he still missed the ship captain, and there was a part of his heart that felt it would never heal. Catriona had mattered more than life or breath to him for a decade. It was hard to shed that sensation. And he had loved her so completely. He wasn't going to feel like that again, he was sure.

He put the white and red clover flowers in a cup, stuffing it full and packing it in. There were other grasses that would have done a better job with surface wounds, since the clover was better ingested, but this would still help. When the hot water turned the liquid on top green, he dipped another cloth into it and started dabbing the cut with it.

A knock at the door preceded his mother's entrance.

"How is she?"

He sighed. "She'll be laid up for a few days but it will heal."

"What makes you think she'll stay put for a few days?"

"Because I'll make her stay put."

"How? By commanding her?"

He shook his head. "Mother, what are you here for? I'm working."

Catherine was silent for a minute. "I wanted to see how you were doing."

"Well, I'm fine, Mother, so you can be on your way."

"I know you don't think I care…"

"No," he turned to face her, "I don't. I think you care about you." He turned back to Tanglwyst. "And this woman is definitely not you. Now please leave. I don't want to be distracted. She doesn't deserve to be hurt any more than she already has been."

Catherine hesitated, then turned and left the room.

"You shouldn't be so… hard on her."

"Don't you start too."

Tanglwyst lifted her head. "Too?"

"Catriona said the same thing. She said Mother had always had the best interests of the kingdom at heart. I just very much disagree with her methods."

"Well, I hate to say it, but… if Catriona said so… that's probably true."

"I know."

She glanced down her back, flinching. "What… are you doing… back there?"

"I'm numbing an area. I fear it may need stitches."

She dropped her head back on the pillow. "Alexander, why don't… you go talk to your mother… and figure out… what you're going… to do about that army? I'm tired… and resting will… heal this faster than… stitches."

"I don't want to leave you."

"You're gonna have to get used to it… I won't be around… much longer."

Alexander sat back. He didn't like the sound of that. "What do you mean?"

"I have a shipping company… I'm gone all summer. And if I… get back on my feet here. …I'll probably be spending… time in Bordeaux, checking… on the estate… there. That's provided I still have one… after the army is done. I have a business… to run and I can't… be lounging around here. My only saving grace… is that Dominic has… enough money of his… own invested in my… corporation that he will… keep everything mobile and… flowing."

"Do you trust him?"

"No. But I know he'll work for… his own best interests… and right now, I'm still… an asset. Isabella takes… care of all the legal… paperwork and she doesn't… let her cousin ever get the… upper hand. It's a game with them." She looked at him without lifting her head. "Now shoo. Go eat or something… Let me rest."

"I'll be back in a little while."

Tanglwyst closed her eyes. "I have… no doubt."

Alexander left the room and looked at the door to his mother's. It was large enough to command the end of the inn, facing towards the fires surrounding St. Giles. The view of the valley was usually stunning, he imagined, but all he had seen in that room was worry and fear. His mother had gotten a few messages with lunch when he and Tanglwyst had told her the story, but she had not deemed them worthy of interrupting the story. In the end, it had changed nothing. Tanglwyst was still beaten for her crimes and they were no closer to having a solution about how to deal with the army in St. Giles.

He went down the stairs to the common room. Patrolmen were stationed at the door and the young man with the same name as his brother had set up shop as a messenger at one of the rear tables. He remembered seeing something once about Catherine having a stipend paid to an inn to maintain a room for her and he figured this must be the place. For all he knew, there were several of these around the country. Possibly even the world. He would have to make sure she wasn't using the kingdom's funds to pay for this. She had enough money of her own.

He went to the bar and Svein stepped from the kitchen, carrying a tray of wine and water. He looked at Alexander and then up the stairs. He set the tray on the bar.

"She alright?"

Alexander nodded. "She's sleeping. I don't know how long that will last. Her body is heavily battered."

"Yes. I believe that's the point."

The king looked away, not wanting to engage further and Svein swallowed.

"Sorry, Your Majesty. I… That was rude. Clearly you did not want to punish her."

"No, I didn't. And if I could find a way to make holy ground around here, I would. I would take care of that problem immediately. She didn't deserve that."

Svein started to take the tray back to the kitchen, then stopped. "Do you still want the wine?"

"Please. She'll need it when she awakens."

Svein nodded and went up the stairs.

A flash went through the room and Alexander looked up as the thunder rolled in. Rain started to patter upon the roof and the people in the inn quieted their discussions to look out the front window upon the valley. The rain bore down upon the fields and everyone watched to see which direction it was moving. There was an audible sigh when it started raining towards the valley.

Charles had gotten up and moved near the patrolmen at the door. He looked at one. "Will that put out those fires?"

The man shook his head. "Those fires weren't burning the wood, so I have no idea. If it were a regular fire, yes. Those weren't regular fires."

Charles sat down, frowning.

They heard a stomping on the porch outside and the door opened. Alexander heard the young stable hand's voice, and the two patrolmen stepped into the doorway, stopping the newcomer.

"The inn is full."

The person outside looked in. "Oh. Well, may I come in and get out of the rain?"

The men looked over at Alexander, who nodded. The guards parted and the man shook off his travel cloak before he entered. He unclasped his outer garment and put it on a hook by the door, then turned to face the room. His red cassock stood out against the lightning while his brown skin and hair blended into the wooden surroundings. He took off his red round hat with the insignia of the Papal City upon it and brushed the water from it. He looked up at Alexander.

"Hey, did you know the Papal City is covered in thorns?"

# Six

## "Listen to the world. It speaks on purpose."
## Kali, The Karmic Hand

Michael awoke in the predawn twilight with the urge to pee. There was just enough light to not trip over the unfamiliar terrain. He stepped outside Raymond's home, careful not to knock any of the wind chimes dangling from the eaves. The air was chilly and still, not having any vegetation to coax animals or insects to the area. No insects meant no birds either. He relieved himself and was about to head back in the house when he heard a snort over by one of the pillars.

He turned and saw a lion, sitting in front of one of the pillars.

His heart froze, then adrenaline pumped through his limbs, making him ready to fight or flee. When the animal didn't pounce, he stared at it, trying to figure out where to go and what to do. Then, he realized something: He recognized it. He *knew* this lion. It was the one he slew in his right of passage. It was the last thing he saw in Nubia.

The early morning light caused the light mist in its fur to glisten, giving it an ethereal nimbus. It blinked slowly at Michael, then sniffed at the pillar over its shoulder. It looked again at Michael.

"What are you doing *here, Leeu?*" He slipped easily back into his native tongue, despite not having used it for years.

The lion sniffed the pillar again, then stood.

Michael stepped back, prepared to run inside to get a weapon, but the lion simply walked away. He watched the fog swirl around its feet but the beast did not look back at him. He looked at the pillar and walked over to it. He saw a slightly damp spot where the lion's nose had touched the stone. He looked again for the animal, not entirely sure it was safe yet, then turned back to the pillar. He reached out to touch the spot when a noise behind him caused a shout.

James walked over to him. "Whoa. What's wrong?"

Michael rubbed his eyes. "I'm sorry, I must have been…" He looked around. "Do you see a lion?"

James looked around the area. "Nope. All these stones are smooth. I don't see any carvings at all."

"No, not carvings. An actual lion."

James frowned. "I wouldn't even know what an actual lion looked like."

"They are a large cat."

"What, large like," James held his hands apart about twenty-four inches.

"No, like," and Michael put his hand at chest height.

James whistled. "Uh, no. That would kind of stand out here."

"Yeah, I guess it would. What are you doing up?"

"You left. I heard you pee right practically by my head. That pretty much made *me* have to pee."

"Those walls are thick."

"Yeah, with a window."

"Ah." Michael looked again for the lion before giving up.

James put his hand on Michael's shoulder. "You okay?"

"Yeah, it just… it seemed so real."

James nodded. "You want to just head out? It's comfortable right now to travel."

"Yeah. I don't want to be rude to our host but since we're both awake, we can get a head start on the day."

"My sentiments exactly."

Lucifer entered his chambers and strode to the viewing Pillar in his own realm. The room Alistair had shown him was an absolute treasure. The man didn't even know what it was, but Lucifer figured it out immediately.

It was a Karma trap.

The previous incarnation must have made it. It was hidden, indiscriminate, and powerful enough to hold hostage whomever it got its claws in. And it had grabbed that woman in favor of the entity of all Magic. Lucifer knew exactly who she was. He now had the means to end Heaven's rule and take down his brothers, especially the one who orchestrated this whole deal in the first place. If he could get Gabriel in that trap, the real war would finally begin.

He looked at the woman, then at the man with her. He didn't know her at all really. She was the obsession of one of his recent playthings, but that had ended. The man though, he looked vaguely familiar… Someone from the Soulless War? Possibly. He studied the man, then saw the Fae connection. He followed that line to Corrigan, and that made Lucifer smile. War was what he wanted. Corrigan was gearing up for a conflict which meant there was a war involving Fae somewhere. He pulled back, looking for that. He found it in St. Giles. A lot of damage had just occurred there and he could hear some people cursing. Cursing and invoking harm on another person gave him a foothold and found someone that would be perfect for this. Righteous anger was one of the best gateways for him, especially in a Church official. He watched the priest for a minute until a monster went by and that got Lucifer's attention. He pulled back to view more of the area and saw the Fae army in Mervolingia. He pulled in to see who was running the thing and saw the flag of Krakte flying over a grand pavilion. He smiled. He checked and sure enough, it was the Queen.

Perfect.

He looked around until he found his linchpin. Any accountant who could afford a Fuccochio coat wasn't an honest man.

Dominic D'Medici filled the Pillar's surface, the amulet glinting in the morning light. He was sitting in the King's chambers in Patras, reading some letters. He still looked a little uncomfortable in the room and Lucifer decided that was just not acceptable. He put his finger on the image of the amulet and flicked it with a fingernail. It stirred the infernal creatures within it, amplifying the corruption inside.

Just a tiny bit. Nothing especially noticeable.

Suddenly, Dominic straightened and looked less apprehensive about his surroundings and more at home there. He set the papers on the desk and looked around the room with an assessing eye.

"They say some people just want to watch the world burn." Lucifer stepped back, admiring his handiwork. "I am that person."

Myrgen brought some meat into the meditation chamber after the Ritual of Succession. Tib's dog still lay before the bier Myrgen had built.

"Hey boy. I wanted to tell you I have to go. I have a task ahead of me that the Land gave me. But you can stay here. I'll have people bring you food and water to the door and I'll leave the doors open for you, okay?"

He set the meat on the ground beside the animal and Drake sniffed it, then went back to laying his head on his paws. Myrgen petted the dog and stood. He walked out of the chamber to Rae.

"Is he doing any better?" She wrung her hands.

Myrgen shook his head. "No. Part of me wonders if I shouldn't send him to Summerland to be with Tib."

"Is that something you think you could do?"

Myrgen sighed. "No. The idea of hurting an animal like Drake, whose only crime is loving the person he was given to," he shook his head, "I could never do that. If he's to die, it will not be at my hand."

Rae smiled and took Myrgen's hand, patting it with her other hand. "You're a good man, Myrgen. The Land chose well with you."

"Thank you. Can you make sure he has food and water out here?"

"Every day."

He smiled and left to pack for his trip. Once his saddlebags were ready, he went back up to the art studio. He covered the canvas to protect it from the light since he didn't know when he'd be back again. The candles had burnt down to nubs and gone out. He checked all the jars to make sure they were tightly closed and the brushes were cleaned. He lay them out to dry. After that, he closed the door and locked it.

He walked to the kitchen where the staff there had made several packages for his trip. One whole sack was just fodder for the horse. He was reluctant to take it but the amount or area he needed to cover coupled with the unknown factor of the weapon said the prudent choice was the horse. He hoped they could find water there. That was his biggest fear. He took the two sacks to the stables and tied them to the saddle bags on a powerful white stallion. The new stable hand, a young boy named Jon, handed him the reins.

"What direction are you going?"

Myrgen looked to the mountains he and Catriona, Michael, and James had taken not that long ago. "There. The quest is saying to go to York."

The boy frowned. "York? I hear that place is barren."

"It is. I looked upon it a tenday ago. I have no idea if I can make it to the place I need to go with the horse. But if it looks like the water situation is too dire, I'll send the horse home and go on foot."

"Diamond. His name is Diamond."

"Oh. Thank you." Myrgen looked at the horse and rubbed his cheek. "Thank you, Diamond, for letting me borrow your strength."

The horse whinnied and slammed his nose at Myrgen, who took it for the affection it was meant to be. He checked the straps, then mounted Diamond. Jon gave him a dozen carrots, tucked into the fodder bag.

"In case you need them."

Myrgen smiled. "I'm sure we will. Thank you, Jon."

He looked up at the face of Ashstone and clicked the horse to walk. He strode past the gardens that he now knew also housed the bodies of those Land folk who had no other families. People in the garden waved to him as he did and he waved back. He got to the edge of town when he heard a dog barking. He turned and saw Drake running like a demon after Myrgen. He stopped the horse and got down. The dog came running up, wagging his tail and panting. Myrgen rubbed the dog's face and ears.

"You want to come with me?"

The dog said nothing, being a dog. He did jump up and lick Myrgen's face though.

Myrgen laughed. "Well, if I'm to have a companion, I'd best be prepared." He led the horse and dog back to Ashstone to get more appropriate food for a dog than oat cakes and carrots.

Raymond awoke and found nothing unusual in the silence until he remembered he had guests. He sat up and looked around. The sun was up but it was not warm enough to burn off the fog, just to light it up. He could hear the very distant sound of horses and men talking, but only barely on the edge of his hearing. He sighed. He had hoped his guests would stay until at least breakfast.

He stood and found a note on the table, next to some bread. It had been a while since he had bread that was different from his own flat breads. A small note said "Thank you". He smiled. He knew they were safe out in the Yorkish wilds but it made him feel lonely. He wouldn't have wanted to leave the house here, but it would have been fine for a while on its own. There was a collection trough for water, which was a near daily occurrence in the early morning hours. It was the reason for the morning fog. Pretty much none of the plants needed him any longer. It would have been nice to possibly travel north and see the world.

*Well, there's nothing stopping you from that now.*

Raymond nodded to himself. That was true. That was very, very true. He could leave anytime he wanted and start over. Then he looked at the pillar where Uriel had gone and remembered.

No, no he could not. He had a duty to protect this place, and that duty was not yet finished.

Raymond gathered some water from the trough and went inside to make tea.

# Seven

## "We fear change, yet it is necessary to live."
## Kali, The Karmic Hand

As nightfall approached, Myrgen got to the inn at the top of the pass. He had taken his time with the ascent, being careful not to let Drake get stepped on by Diamond. This wasn't easy, since the puppy kept bouncing in and out of the horse's legs. They reached the top at late afternoon and although Myrgen figured he could get down the other side and camp at the base of the mountain, he tried to decide if that was better than staying in the Brew Ha House Inn at the top. The real deciding factor had been the arrival outside of the children running out to greet him. When he told Cecelia he had no money for a room, she waved him off.

"We don't worry about that. It's not like we aren't self-sustaining here. Come, tell us news of the city and that will be payment enough."

The kids were excited to play with Drake and he thought about leaving him here where he was safe. Then he looked at the hound and remembered it running out of Ashstone to come with him. Whatever convinced him to leave Tib's side was hardly going to be forgotten by a single evening's distraction. In the end, he supposed he would see how things worked in the morning.

He told Cecelia and Lawrence all about the attack on Zara. They were quite surprised that a Mandian had managed to pass all the protections of the Sea of Blood, and that was why Myrgen had been hesitant to leave. *If he can slip through, can't anyone?*

This went through his mind as he lay on the bed, courting sleep. His belly was full as was Drake's and the hound was on his back, snoring on the floor in that adorable way puppies do. He wouldn't have his baby face for much longer and when he turned gangly and adolescent in a year, he would be comical instead of cute, but for now, he was worth a smile just to look at.

Myrgen drifted off as he let his mind wander to the night prior to the attack. Dreams of hiking through a forest to hunt, a stone cottage erected by the Bringer, small stones with gold flecks, all wandered through him, staying long enough to leave an impression, letting him remember the story, but not the plot. And one other thing that made no sense:

A tall figure walking toward a winged figure, both well over ten feet tall. They turned to a relatively small figure of no discernable gender. The Tall figure handed something misty to the Genderless figure. The Winged Figure gave something misty as well, something moving. The two were combined and released into the night sky. Myrgen didn't know what they were but he knew they were equal parts right and wrong.

Drake flipped over and barked as the knock came at the door. Myrgen sat up. "Come in."

Cecelia opened the door to poke her head in. "Myrgen? Can you come out? I have something curious to show you."

"Yeah, I'll be right out."

Drake looked at Myrgen for praise at scaring off the intruder and Myrgen rubbed his ears as he yawned. He got dressed and he and Drake went outside for their morning constitutionals. When they returned, he greeted Cecelia.

"So, what did you want to show me?"

"Well, we have a long distance glass up here. We are pretty secure, but we are tasked by Ashstone to keep an eye out for things. It's part of our duty. We have birds here that we use and they are changed out regularly by the messenger in Zara. I was going to send out a bird today, but since you're going that way, I thought you might want to see it first hand."

He took the glass and Cecelia moved him over to the head of the path going to York. "Going that way? I'm not heading to Zara. I'm going to York."

"Yup."

He turned to where she pointed and put the glass to his eye. He saw huge expanses of wasteland going all the way towards Glarren. There was a small house by a far distant set of large stones. No water to be seen anywhere, though he saw what looked like a resting station. A covered area with a trough and a bench. That was encouraging. He looked west and was about to give the glass back to her when he saw what she meant.

When he had been here with the others, they had scanned the whole country as far as they could see with the spyglass from Catriona's ship. It had been desolate. Now, he saw something… confusing. There was a structure probably a couple day's ride northwest and it was *green*. He took the glass down, looked, and then put it back up. He couldn't see the green with the naked eye, but he could with the glass. He handed it back to her.

"Green."

She nodded, taking the glass. "If something is causing that area to be green again, and that rapidly, that means trouble." She went back to the inn, calling to Lawrence.

Myrgen looked at the area, they closed his eyes to see where the weapon was.

When he opened them, he was looking at the structure with the green.

"Okay then. Time to ride."

Ce'Nedra opened her eyes and knew something was wrong.

She felt *refreshed*.

It had been days since she, Henri, Felix, and Sylvaine had been trapped in the room by Dominic. There had been no sign of him returning, but that was to be expected. Dominic obviously knew what this room was and that it sustained the people contained within. Or he knew that the room would *not* sustain someone who wasn't a worshipper of Heaven. Either way, he put them in here to die, and as long as there was a chance someone still lived, none of them expected him to return. So, it wasn't that someone new was there.

She looked around. Henri was laying against the wall to her left, Felix to her right. Sylvaine was against the wall on the other side of the bed. They had pulled the bed away from that wall so she would have access. Ce'Nedra's understanding of Fae magics had allowed her to transfer the life-sustaining wards on the walls away from a divine source and to a Fae one. She noted that the Fae magics were stronger now than they had been when she carved the symbols. The Fae energy had been trace, and frankly, judging from the flavor, she had been drawing directly from the Land and not the Fae at all. That meant they were underground somewhere, but that was all she had figured out so far.

Henri and Felix were still asleep, but she could see in the ambient light provided by the other runes on the walls that their color was better as well. They were sleeping deep, and their breathing was healthy. She was far enough away from Sylvaine not to be able to hear her breathing but she didn't look as good as Ce'Nedra felt. That's when she noticed Sylvaine was out of position. The runes on the wall were symmetrical, and Sylvaine was not directly across from Ce'Nedra like Felix was from Henri.

*She's off the mark.*

"Sylvaine?" Her voice jumped through the room and startled both men awake. She jumped across the bed and knelt beside the young woman.

Felix got to his feet first. "What's wrong?"

"Sylvaine was not on the mark. She hasn't been fed." Ce'Nedra looked at Sylvaine's posture. She had bunched up her skirt and wedged it between herself and the wall, presumably to make the position more comfortable. Unfortunately, it had shifted her in her sleep so she was not in contact with the mark. Only by leaning right up against them could they get enough nutrition to survive. She leaned Sylvaine forward and untied the cord on her bodice, pulling it loose and opening it to expose her corset. More untying and the corset was loose, exposing her chemise.

"By the Fae, *why* are noble garments so elaborate?" She looked at the men. "Do you have a knife?"

Felix looked to his hip and pulled out a small utility dagger. "It might not be very sharp. I use it to open seals for the messenger's office."

Ce'Nedra took it and cut a slice in the back of the chemise, below the neckband. Felix was right, the knife was not sharp. However, it did expose her skin, which was the whole point. "Yeah, that never would have cut through the embroidered neckband, but it did the job."

Ce'Nedra put Sylvaine's bare skin against the symbol and it flared. Sylvaine started breathing better in less than a minute and color started returning to her cheeks. Everyone relaxed and Felix took over holding his beloved against the rune. Ce'Nedra stood and looked at Henri.

"How do you feel?"

"Me? I feel…" Henri did a little self-examination, "fine." He looked at his lady. "Really. I *feel fine.*"

"No hunger?"

"No."

She turned to Felix. "You?"

Felix nodded. "The same. I'm worried about Syl, but I myself feel better than I have since we got here."

She looked at Sylvaine. "I think she may have just saved our lives."

# Eight

## "Compassion is always the right choice."
## Shiva, The Karmic Hand

Catherine stepped out of her room when she heard her son's voice. He was talking excitedly to someone whose voice she did not recognize and that was unacceptable. With the King here, the inn should not be taking on visitors or patrons. When she saw the cardinal's robes, she stopped. "Your Majesty?"

Alexander looked at her and he was smiling, almost thrumming. "Mother, look! A priest!"

"I see that. Is… Has Tanglwyst…"

"No. But I know she won't have to suffer any longer."

Catherine followed the men into the room, and Tanglwyst awoke when the processional came in. Catherine saw the blood stripes on the sheet had turned brown and she worried the movement would undo any healing the lady might have managed.

"Alexander, please."

He didn't even acknowledge that she had spoken. "Sir, I need you to do it here." He waved his hands over the general bed area as Tanglwyst turned on her side, the bedding clutched to her naked body.

"Alexander, what are you doing?" Tanglwyst's face was pinched in pain as well as annoyance.

The priest shook his head. "Sire, I... I can't sanctify an inn room."

"Why not?"

Catherine and Tanglwyst spoke in unison. "Sanctify?"

"Sire, I'm sorry, but I can't."

Alexander frowned, as if hearing the man for the first time. "What do you mean, you can't?"

"Holy ground isn't my purview. I can bless food, drink, babies, but holy sanctification is well out of my skill range."

"A priest in St. Andrew did it all the way to the docks a month ago."

The priest shrugged. "He must have had a source. A baptismal font or holy soil from the church grounds."

"A font? You mean of holy water?"

"Yes."

"Which you just said you can make."

"Well," the priest glanced at the woman on the bed, then back at the King, "yes. Yes. I can do that. But I don't see how..."

But Alexander wasn't listening anymore. He grabbed the basin and threw the bloody water out the window. He grabbed the water off the nearby serving tray Svein had brought up and handed it to the priest. "Here. Well water. About as pure as we can get here."

The priest took the pitcher and Alexander backed towards Tanglwyst's bed. Everyone watched the pitcher as the priest shrugged and said a prayer. Alexander grew even more agitated as the prayer went on. When the priest finished, Alexander smiled.

"It worked. I can feel it."

"Alexander, no." Tanglwyst was sitting up on her bed, her look determined and her grip on the sheet tight against this stranger.

"I'll not have you suffer another moment, not when I can stop it."

Catherine put her hand on her son's shoulder. "What are you doing?"

"Stay out of this, Mother."

Catherine stepped between Alexander and Tanglwyst. "I will not. This woman has expressed she does not want this thing so you will not do it."

"You don't know what you're talking about, Mother. She needs this."

"No, I don't."

Catherine's eyes did not move from Alexander's. "It appears she does not."

The priest stepped back, holding the pitcher and staying out of the path of the royals.

Alexander set his jaw and Catherine felt her fealty pressed. He was exercising his Power of Sovereignty.

"Oh no you don't." Tanglwyst was on her feet between Catherine and Alexander. "Are you really trying to push the Power around me? Honestly? On me?"

Catherine felt the pressure ease up. Her voice was frozen in her throat.

"Tangl…" He tried to reach out but she batted his hand aside.

"If you do this, I promise I will take my newfound health and walk out that front door to St. Giles this instant, rain and all. You will not push my fealty or anyone else's just to get your way."

Alexander's will seemed to waver, then the pressure against her fealty fell away entirely. Catherine's breath let out. Tanglwyst was shaking and Catherine could see the woman was standing by virtue of her will alone. She looked at her son.

"Your Majesty, with all due respect, you should leave this woman's private chambers this instant." She looked at the priest. "Father, will you escort my son elsewhere?"

The priest looked between the royals and nodded. "Your Majesty, why don't we leave the women to get ready for bed?"

Alexander hesitated. "We will talk about this tomorrow." Then he left the room, his gait stiff and angry. The priest followed, setting the pitcher on the table on the way out.

Once the door was closed, Tanglwyst sagged and stepped over to the bed. She pulled back the covers and sat on the mattress. "Thank you, Your Majesty."

"I apologize for my son's behavior. He has grown up with a life of privilege and on occasion, it shows."

"That wasn't privilege. It was guilt."

"Guilt?"

"Yes. Catriona isn't the only one who can see things clearly. I have my moments as well."

"Catriona. That was the woman he went to sea to pursue?"

Tanglwyst nodded and pulled the sheet from beneath her bruised buttocks. She winced as it tugged at the tender flesh. Catherine took the sheet and helped the young woman get into bed. The welts on her backside were bad, not terribly bloody, but there were a few dark red marks across her stomach. From the shape of the marks, her son had ordered her beaten with a strap or belt. Not surprising. The likelihood of them having a scourge here was very low. There was a fleur shape starting to form and she realized the belt used had a metal tip, the kind worn by the patrolmen. The fleurs were on the two marks on her front side and she saw another on a thigh.

"He beat you with metal?"

Tanglwyst put her feet under the covers, nodding. "Yeah. Alex thought he was being gentle, but that was pretty much the same as a scourge."

"You mean he swung the belt himself?"

"Wasn't going to let someone else do his dirty work. I do admire him for that."

Catherine looked at the woman covering herself with the blankets. "He cares for you."

Tanglwyst shook her head. "No. He had his heart broken. I'm simply the nearest thing. I'm expendable. Trust me, I know this for a fact. I've already been discarded by him. I know my true worth."

Catherine sat on the edge of the bed. "I think you may be wrong about that. I know my son. He doesn't work this hard to help someone expendable. When a servant at the palace was killed by," she looked down at her hands, embarrassed, "by Charles, I understand Alexander brought the man to his own bedroom and had his wife brought to be with him when he died. That's the sort of man Alexander is. He helps people."

Tanglwyst lay her head back upon the pillow. "That's not a side I have seen recently. I know that when he is presented with an easy answer, he becomes someone I don't want to be around. The amulet, the Power, now this. I'm not going to be the reason he falls into the monster he was becoming." Tanglwyst closed her eyes, breathing deeply. "But I do know the side of which you speak. I saw it this winter, back when I was grieving too."

"You lost someone this winter?"

"To the same accident that claimed Alexander's beloved. We were… crutches… together."

Catherine had more to say but she could see the woman starting to fade. She patted Tanglwyst's hands. "You rest. I'll see you tomorrow."

"Thank you, Your Majesty."

"How is she?"

Alexander stood outside Tanglwyst's room, arms folded, head bowed but still training his eyes on his mother.

"She's injured, apparently at your hand."

"I didn't want to leave the task to someone else. If she was going to have to endure that punishment, I wanted to feel it too, not be apart from it."

"And how did it feel?" Catherine folded her hands in front of her, back rigid from decades of practice.

Alexander had not yet sensed any attempts to press upon his will like she could when spinning her stories, but he was also no longer susceptible to such things as monarch. The Power protected him against her now, just like it protected him against Tanglwyst's alleged "enchanted touch".

"Horrible." He pushed away from the railing and gestured to her room at the end of the walkway.

She complied. "That's good, Alex. That's very, very good."

He opened her door and they each lit a lantern within the room. The sky had grown dark with the storm and dusk had settled in. It had been an incredibly long day and he realized he had not slept at all during the night. He wasn't tired yet though. He knew it was coming, but it had not hit yet.

"Your companion said you two had spent time together this winter, after suffering a loss from the same accident that also claimed your beloved. That you were 'crutches' together. What did she mean?"

He smiled. "That's a very interesting way to put that."

"Which part?"

Catherine brought over a bottle of wine and two goblets but Alexander fetched the pitcher of water she had nearby, not wanting to get sleepy while things were still unresolved.

"All of that. Those were her words, I'll bet."

"Entirely."

"That man she loved and the woman I loved were once married to each other. Giovanni tore them apart, as I suspect you knew. Otherwise your ploy on St. Michael's Day wouldn't have worked."

She glanced away at the mention of the incident, then returned her gaze to his. "Not entirely. I knew you and Charles had gone from my estate in Cheryb on some wild adventure, escaping your guards who were there to protect you. That was because I knew Marco Giovanni controlled that area. It seemed only logical that mentioning that creature would spark some memory of atrocities at his hands. He perpetrated so many."

"You sent us to be around a man who could do those things, on purpose?"

"I needed you to see what power could do to a person. I had people there to protect you but you needed to see what could happen to you as rulers. Marco didn't even have the Power of Sovereignty and he was like that. Imagine what he could have done if he did. I married your father to avoid the fate of his previous wife, and he almost got me after your father died. I was only able to escape that fate by staying regent for Charles. Now he's dead, and I don't have to use the Crown to protect myself nor my country from a mad man." She looked at her hands. "When Plantyn started influencing your brother, I realized I might be sent home. And if I ever returned to Cheryb, I would have been obligated to marry that man and connect him to this throne. You saw what he was like. Do you honestly think any of you would have survived if that happened?"

"Obligated? How?"

"By the Church. They negotiated my marriage to Henry and Marco paid the previous pope to insure he got me next. The contract was set in Heaven, and I could not break it lest we all be excommunicated. If that happened, the throne would fall to the Papal City and they could put whomever they liked upon it."

Alexander pushed back from the table, his stomach churning. He had seen so much corruption in the church in the last week but he had no idea just how bad it was. "What about the new pope? When it changed hands, did you talk to him about it?"

"What do you think I was doing all that time in the Papal City? But he never saw me. Although Gregory is new, his advisors are the same.

They never let me near him. It doesn't matter anyway now. The beast is slain."

"Yes, you have Catriona to thank for that. She was the one who killed him."

Catherine's eyes showed her confusion. "Killed? But he committed suicide."

"Yes."

Catherine sat back as well, processing. Then she blinked several times as something seemed to come to her. "You tried to put an assassin on the throne of Mervolingia?"

"I tried to put a woman who could defend herself against assassins on the throne of Mervolingia."

"But it didn't work."

Alexander sighed and shook his head. "No, it did not."

"Would you like me to speak to her?"

Alexander snorted a laugh. "Oh, I would pay a ransom to watch that exchange." He shook his head, the smile fading but not disappearing. "No. But thank you for offering. She's… She's in better hands now."

He paused, thinking. Myrgen had changed. He wasn't shifty anymore, and Alexander was the cause of that, at least in part. Hunting Catriona, tricking Myrgen, chasing them, hurting them, lying, all that was behind him now. He had given in to a moment of grief and weakness and signed a Writ of Destruction the second Marie had left him alone with Charles again. The second he realized he was going to be King, Alexander had signed away his soul to rid Catriona of the one obstacle between them. He had taken the easy solution, and it had dictated his reign until he had given it up to save the woman in the other room.

"And so am I, Mother. Tanglwyst told you we were crutches together. Well, when one is healing from a devastating blow, having two crutches enables you to walk. We were helping each other walk this winter. But I was stupid. I had moved on but when I thought I might see Catriona again, I threw away the only thing helping me through it. I discarded my crutch before I was able to walk. Catriona wasn't coming back to me. She was avoiding me because she knew she could never live the life I was trying to force upon her. And in the end, it cost me everything to try and do it anyway."

They let a long silence spin between them, the processing complete as they exposed their vulnerabilities. It was Catherine who broke it.

"The lady in the other room, she deserves a bit better than you have been doing. I think I understand why her words mattered so much. Were you at your brother's desk when you signed the Writ?"

"Yes. Why?"

"And you used the quill and ink there."

"Yes."

"That is where the real power lies. The ink well is enchanted. It is the thing that houses the Power of Sovereignty."

"What? How?" He shook his head. "How can that be the source of this Power?"

"The Power is there through decree, which was written in that ink at the Papal City centuries ago. The Church imposed some sort of implement upon all the countries under its purview after the Soulless War. They wanted to ensure that the lineages in control of the countries were not being manipulated by evil creatures. You see, many of the monsters were contained somehow within the confines of York, but some got out before the bag was closed. They destroyed whole villages. The only place safe was holy ground. The Church took that as a sign that Heaven was the only protector against these creatures. When they sent their Inquisitors to destroy the monsters, the Church also sent out other tools to protect the people. Ours was the ink well."

"Do you know what the others were?"

"I only know one. Mande has their crown. A single jewel at the back houses the Power for them."

"How many countries were given these things?"

"All of them."

"The false ritual?"

"Written in the ink with the design flaw that it is fake. Within the palace is a single declaration. It says that the Heir is designated by the Throne. Only one of the two need be alive or aware in order for the Power to change hands, though the holder of the Power must be willing to give it up. It also says a false ritual will be written that will draw the attention of any usurpers and prepare them for their own destruction.

"And it says that the first act done in this ink will tell the Power what kind of monarch the Throne wants to be. Then the Power will ensure that action."

"So, Charles' first decree was…"

"To say I need never bow before him again." She took a deep breath, shaking her head. "He did it before I could stop him, before I could explain about the Power. You also left before I could talk to you, but when I saw your determination, I realized it was too late. You had already written with the ink."

"Did Charles know?"

She shook her head. "There was no point in telling him, no more than there was in telling you. I thought perhaps I could speak to your bride and let her know. She could have then decided how to proceed. I knew I would no longer be in a position to advise. But I would need to speak to her before you gave her the Cyprian herb or it wouldn't have mattered. In the end, if the knowledge died with me, then the inkwell might have been broken or discarded in time and the Church would have no more sway over Mervolingia or its Crown."

"I'll tell Tangl. She'll have a good idea what to do. She's the one who broke the spell in the first place. It turns out that the decree made by the last monarch doesn't carry to the next."

"No, it doesn't. And yes, she did in fact save you. But it also means you do not have to worry that this action on your part today is going to dictate what your reign will be like. Not until you use the ink for the first time."

He stood and walked over to the window. The dark had settled in and the fires were so numerous, they looked like a single line, but if he concentrated, he could make out the individual dots. He nodded to the encampment.

"I still have to figure that one out too." He turned back to his mother. "But not tonight. I want to talk things over with the Lady. She has a clearer head than I about this and can see things I can't. I need to give her time to heal. And before you ask, yes, I mean time, not tricks. I won't take any shortcuts."

"You will need to explain that to me."

Alexander nodded. "I will. Just, not right now. Good night, Mother."

She bowed and he left the room.

# Nine

"Sometimes, your best
audience doesn't know what
you're talking about."
Kali, The Karmic Hand

Myrgen crouched down after saddling Diamond and looked at
Drake. "Ya know, these kids here don't have a dog. And I'm not sure
what kind of trouble I'm riding into. You sure you still wanna come with
me?"

The dog jumped on him and licked his face. It knocked him
backwards off his feet and Myrgen fell, defeated. He rubbed the dog's
ears and let himself be accosted by the companion. The kids laughed
from the doorway of the inn, despite repeated attempts by Myrgen to get
them to rescue him. After a minute, he got to his feet and braced himself
so Drake couldn't take him down again. They rode down the pass road,
this side having a steep, straight path in addition to the winding one.
Drake sniffed the rocks, peeing on them occasionally so he could find
their way back, if it fell to him to get them home.

They rode at a trot for the most part. Myrgen let him run alongside
Diamond, stopping to rest when Drake started to fall behind. Once, when
Drake fell asleep while they were resting at a water stop, Myrgen made
a sling out of his blanket and tied it so Drake could sleep. It was bumpy

going because Myrgen let the horse run for a bit, but Drake slept nonetheless. Traveling, it appeared, was hard on a puppy.

When they stopped near dark, it was at another water station. The horse drank and there was a second basin for Myrgen and Drake, as well as a small partial shelter. The night looked like it might rain and a small fire pit was inside the three-and-a-half sided building.

"This is pretty convenient, isn't it, boy?" Myrgen looked around the shelter. "And it looks like our friends probably stayed here too. This fire pit has been used in the last tenday."

Drake wagged his tail.

Myrgen brought out his bedroll and laid it out, then went back and got the saddlebags. He unsaddled the horse for the night and fed him, tethering him to the building. He brushed him. "Sorry I don't have a shelter for you too, Diamond. Hopefully, if there's a storm, it will come from the north." He looked up at the shelter roof. "Although, whoever built this *did* extend this roof to be a partial shelter if I tie you here…"

He re-tethered the horse to a post on the other side of the trough, out of the open air. He nodded, happy with this, then looked at the slowly darkening sky.

"Better get to work on our supper, right, Drake?"

The puppy lay down on the bedroll and watched Myrgen unpack the saddlebag with the food. Tib had trained him well in the time they had, but there had been little else to do in the stone room. Drake knew not to take food from the bag, though it smelled good. Myrgen handed him a chunk of venison jerky and Drake took to chewing on it like a bone until it was gone.

"The kennel lady, what was her name? *Orsolya*. She was smart about that venison stuff for you. It only makes sense that the army would have provisions for their dogs too." He took the special bag from the saddle bag and pulled out the two rocks. They had veins of different rock through them. "And these? Brilliant." He put the two rocks in the fire pit with the flat sides up and pushed them together so they touched. The rocks changed and heat started coming from them as well as light. Myrgen gestured to them. "Look at that, Drake. And if I turn them over, they heat up without the light, in case I need to stay hidden. This whole kit is brilliantly done. No wonder the army is undefeated."

He set the flat metal plate with the lipped edge on the rocks, then rummaged around for a moment. He pulled out a metal cup and a stone fork that was a spoon on the other end. The edge of the spoon was serrated. "And this? Stone because of the Land and because it won't get too hot too fast, but you *can* warm it up and it helps your food stay hot when you eat it!" He smiled at Drake who stopped gnawing long enough to look at Myrgen. "Not that you need any of that."

They talked for a while, though the conversation was very one sided. Myrgen cooked up a carrot in some water with some powder thrown in from a pouch in the food bag. He gave one to Diamond as payment. He was certain to narrate the process and the childhood significance of each step, though Drake just nodded, not really paying attention. Once all that was done and eaten, he put the now cooled plate down for Drake to clean, then stepped outside to pee and clean the plate from water in the basin. He was careful to wash the plate without submerging it.

"Gotta drink this tomorrow. Though I'm not saying you didn't do a thorough job cleaning it."

There were hooks on the back wall and Myrgen hung the saddlebags there. It freed up floor space but put the food out of reach of the puppy. The bag that the venison was stored in was wax sealed to keep out water and dust while keeping the stuff inside clean and fresh. It also stopped Drake from being able to smell which one was the dog treat bag.

"Though I suspect you saw which one it was so it's not like you're fooled by that."

Myrgen took Drake outside so he could poop and pee, then kicked some dirt over the scat. "This helps hide the scent from predators, though, I don't know if that works. You could probably tell better than me."

They went inside and Myrgen got in the bed roll. Drake lay down beside him. "It's so quiet here. No birds. No insects. Nothing. It's like I'm back in the meditation Chamber. Just the sound of the fire rocks."

Drake snorted.

"But that's probably best right now…"

Myrgen drifted off to sleep in the middle of the sentence.

It was well after moonrise when Drake heard the sound. He got up, careful not to disturb Myrgen. He went outside and looked around for the sound. He got around to the northern side before he saw the lion. It was walking north, having just passed the shelter. It looked back at Drake, the full mane framing the cat's face. Drake sat down, and watched it go north. Then the rain started coming in from that direction and the great cat disappeared. Drake went back inside and lay down just as the rain started pelting the roof of the building. Myrgen stirred, but didn't wake, and Drake lay down and watched him until the rain lulled him back to sleep.

*Myrgen stood before a river of smoky black stone. Gold flecks glittered within the flow, sometimes thick, sometimes thin. On the other side of the river stood Catriona. She wasn't looking at the river. In fact, it was as if she couldn't even see it. She smiled at him and he knew she was about to step off the bank. If she did, she would be lost.*

*He tried to shout, but the roar of the river was too great. If only she knew the danger, she would know not to step in. He needed to get over to her, but the current was strong and swift.*

*What do I do?*

*He held up his hands, gesturing for her to stay where she was. She frowned, not understanding, He gestured for her to read him. She nodded, and focused upon him. He felt her look into his soul and he let her know the danger. She looked at the river, confused because apparently she couldn't see it. She looked at him again and nodded, trusting him.*

*He put his foot in the river, but for him, the river was solid. She saw him take the step and took a deep breath, waiting. He took another, but this time, the stone was spongy. Not completely, just like he was stepping on moss. The next step was thicker moss, but still stable. However, he did some calculations and realized that he would not get to her this way. He looked at her and let her know.*

*She swallowed, and nodded.*

*He took another step and this was like stepping on a bog. He made sure not to put his weight in either the front or back of his foot but it worried him what was going to happen with the next step. Quicksand? How did you deal with quicksand? There needed to be something beneath it to stand on, or something supporting you from the other side. He looked at her.*

*I love you.*

*She set her jaw and knelt down. She placed her hands on the ground. A spur of land progressed towards him and he took a deep breath. He moved his other foot so he was standing on the boggy earth, then carefully slid his foot forward. As expected, he felt the stone give way like it was thick liquid. He started to return to the previous footing, but with most of his weight on the boggy foot, he felt it giving way. He refused to go down that way and took the step into the quicksand. He flailed, and his hand grabbed the boggy stone behind him. It stabilized him so he could think without going under, but it wasn't stable.*

*Catriona extended the land again and now he felt like he might be able to reach it. He lifted himself on the bog and threw himself across the quicksand. Catriona sprawled out across the land, reaching out her hand. She touched the river and her eyes turned to jade. Her demeanor altered as well and she became more adamant. She push the land with her other hand and spikes grew out of the water, like teeth.*

*He swam through the quicksand until he felt a current start to pull him. His pushed his way towards a spike but the current became stronger a hand span away. He was lost.*

*He went under.*

*He felt a hand grab his and pull him from the river. As he grasped the spike of land, he looked up into kind, jade eyes. The Death Bringer smiled at him, and he felt himself go down again.*

"Not bad." Lucifer folded his arms. "I hope that gets the message across."

*It won't. Not on its own. But I can send more of a nudge, if you'll allow me access.*

Lucifer nodded. He stepped away from the viewing pillar and a delicate woman glowing white in the dark surroundings stepped forward to the Viewing Pillar in Hell. She was transparent, being only a shade of the creature being held in the cage in Heaven. Because of his proximity and connection to Heaven, this spirit could come here. After all, it was suspended over Hell in the first place, to intimidate her.

She smiled. Bringer would be so proud of her, actually using deceit. She hoped she would be able to tell her personally.

Giver touched the Pillar. Her captors had cut off her connection to Bringer by putting her in this cage, but they could not remove her access to dreams. These Pillars were her channel into that realm but this was her first chance to actually touch one. She reached into it and stroked the hair of the man on the horse in the wilderness. As she did so, she gently pushed a thought into his mind.

*Remember.*

She made it all encompassing. Romantic love, fraternal love, maternal love. It was one thought but it would be all he knew. Not obsession. Just a simple understanding of true love. He knew it. He had known it before, with his own child and his first love. Bringer had not touched those people, but she had touched this man. That connection was strong enough to bring a message to her, but it was like passing a note through an intermediary, one that can only be one word. A simple, one word message that would only truly matter to the reader and the one who wrote it.

Remember. That was all that needed to be done. Because once she remembered, there would be nothing to stop them.

She withdrew from the pillar and looked at Lucifer. *It is done.*

He nodded and glanced back up. "You heading back, or did you want to stay here a while?"

*How aware are they?*

Lucifer glanced at the ceiling. He could see Raphael watching from the window in front of the soul production floor. Saints took tiny drops from the Well of Souls and hovered over small vessels made from parts of the angels' wings. Gabriel was being harvested of his feathers as they spoke.

"They haven't noticed the body yet. They probably just think you're sleeping.

*In a way, I am.* She contemplated watching longer, but did not want to linger. It would only cause problems. *I should return. I don't want to be missed.*

Lucifer nodded. "As you wish."

She spied the plate of petit fours. *Although...*

He hid a laugh, glancing up the shaft to his brother, who did not hear him. He went to the plate, picked it up and knelt before her, head bowed and plate extended on both hands. "I always make them with you in mind. They are my favorite gift from you."

She touched one, consuming it. It disappeared from the plate and she was enveloped in its richness. They were made of the soul stuff he collected, the stuff that was part of her very essence. He always made them because it was a way to get some of the untainted souls into her, strengthening her. If he hadn't, she would have faded from existence long ago. That was how she could cry souls in the first place. When he had first given them to her, she was almost gone. It was only through this exchange that she continued to plot against her captors.

She bowed in thanks and took another one before turning to the hole. She nodded, indicating she was ready.

He glanced up and caused a problem with the naming of a vessel. Raphael threw open the door to the cage chamber and stepped out to chastise the saint trying to insert the soul. She nodded to Lucifer and rose back into her body.

# Ten

"Ignorance may be bliss, because knowledge requires either action or responsibility." Kali, The Karmic Hand

Michael looked behind him and saw the lion following him and James. It padded along after them, not running, not roaring, just keeping pace. Michael looked at James, but James was oblivious to the danger behind them. He shook the reins on his horse and picked up the pace a little, not running but moving a little quicker. The lion fell back and Michael started to relax.

Then he looked behind him and it was there again, but a little bigger. This scared him and he kicked the horse into a trot. James looked at him, worried and looked behind them. He didn't see the lion though, so he pushed his horse to a trot to catch up to Michael. The lion grew larger and large with each step. Soon, Michael had the horse running in a panic and the lion was larger than Tanglwyst's house, chasing them. It reached out with great claws and jumped for him.

Michael started awake and James looked over at him. "Fall asleep?"

Michael nodded. "Apparently. I guess I wasn't as ready to leave as I thought."

"Eh, there's just not a lot to keep you occupied. I'm lucky, I have these books."

"Well, stop being a monster and talk to me about the contents. What's the route we're taking?'

James pointed to the north. "Up there is a land bridge. We should be there in time to cross it but in the event that the snow run-off has filled the bay, we'll take a ferry across the Glarren Sea. I was thinking we might be able to cross before it filled, but the last several days have been pretty warm. I think we're gonna have to pay to get across."

"The bay gets full enough that it accommodates boats?"

"Yeah. In fact, the Yorkish navy patrols up there. It's a big trade port for Krakte and Glarren as well."

"A city? In this area?"

"Alistair tells me the destruction of the soil didn't extend up as much as down. It makes sense, there aren't a lot of bugs when you get to Glarren, at least not the flying kind. It's too cold year 'round."

"What does your family do up there?"

"Sheep. We graze them all over the landscape up there and then package and sell the wool in Kilmory. That's the landing point of the ferry."

"Do you miss it there?"

James shrugged. "Sometimes. But I've enjoyed travelling the world with my unc... my *father*. Geesh." James shook his head. "That's still weird to say."

"Hasn't he been like a father to you?"

"No. He's been like that skirt-chasing uncle that always seems to have things going his way. My *father* has been like a father to me and trust me, that really wasn't easy."

"Why?"

"You might say I had a lot of adjusting to do growing up." He tapped the book in his hand. "This is explaining why." James looked at Michael. "In that box on the horse is a locket with me and Gwen in it. There's an inscription that says, 'So you don't forget the faces of our children.' I kind of want to make sure that gets to my mother."

"Why would he write that? Why would your mother be in danger of forgetting you?"

"That's what I want to ask her."

Michael nodded, then glanced back over his shoulder. He didn't know how long the lion image would be with him, but he had the feeling it wouldn't be leaving anytime soon.

It took very little time for Sylvaine to look healthy again, and after she got her own deep slumber, she, too, woke up "amazingly refreshed."

"So, what happened?" Henri asked Ce'Nedra. They sat at the table while Felix and Sylvaine sat on the bed.

"Simple supply and demand. The runes have a constant flow to them. We were all using that flow at the same time, so it had to divide by four constantly. Once you weren't using the rune, it only had to feed three with the flow."

Sylvaine nodded. "So, if we don't all try to feed at once, we can rest and be healthy."

"It's a start."

Henri smiled. "It's strange how these little victories are so uplifting."

Ce'Nedra nodded. "Wait, there's more. The energies have changed. Before, there was a lot of energy flowing through the holy runes. Remember how bright they shone when Dominic dumped us in here? And when he returned with you two?"

Henri nodded.

"When I changed the energy they drew from, I'm pretty sure the only reason we had any sustenance at all was because we were drawing directly from the Land. I think we are underground."

Felix interrupted. "You can tell the difference between magics?"

"Not really. I can identify *Fae* magic. What was here before was divine, obviously. But the energy I drew upon for these runes wasn't Fae. The only other option was Land."

"Why?"

"Because the Fae are part of the Land."

Sylvaine frowned, leaning forward. "So, Heaven isn't really at war with all these other faiths. It's just at war with the Land."

Everyone nodded in understanding and revelation.

"So, what could have changed?" She looked at Ce'Nedra, then at the men. "Did the cell here relocate?"

Ce'Nedra shrugged. "It seems unlikely, but then again, this whole situation seems impossible."

"Well," Henri looked at his companions, "there must be an explanation."

"There has to be." Ce'Nedra looked at the Fae runes. "The trouble is how to find it."

Henri looked at the runes, then stood to go over to one. "Well, how are they fed the energy in the first place?"

Ce'Nedra sniffed. "I think there must be a similar rune on the outside. They don't exactly have to be right over each other to supply the energy. It could be as simple as a source rune that distributes to the smaller ones, like irrigation rows in a garden."

"Is the energy outside still divine?"

"Yes, I'm sure of it or I could create a doorway to get us out."

Felix frowned. "Then where is the Land energy coming from?"

Ce'Nedra smiled and patted the wall. "This is still carved from stone. Stone is, by its very nature, Land. You can't build anything out of natural resources that isn't connected to the Land."

She stepped back and looked at the wall and ceiling. "Unfortunately, crafted items can be *blessed* by the Church, diminishing its properties and connection to the Land. But if you know what you're looking for, you can still find the base nature of the item."

Felix nodded, also looking over the room. "So, like holy water is both divine and Land?"

"Yes. Water is ever changing, also by its very nature, and air is elusive so it is seen more as part of Heaven than the Land. Both are easily used by the divine to channel those energies. But things that come out of the Land, like wood, stone, and ore, maintain their solid connection to the Land."

Henri's fingers wandered to his stump. "What about fire?"

"Fire is a reaction, not an element. You actually need several components to make fire, including air. It is practically its own entity and therefore, it doesn't have to obey either side. That's why covering a fire with dirt or water can achieve the same end. On the other hand, it also can aid any side without compromise."

Sylvaine sighed. "Like Holy Fire."

Ce'Nedra nodded. "Or Hellfire. Or lava. Fire does not choose a side." She looked again at the walls. "Anyway, as long as the symbols on the outside stay active, they supply the base energy and I can convert it. But it is steady. We aren't getting more energy but we aren't diminishing it either. As long as we rest in cycles, no more than two of us at a time, we will be able to survive this until we figure out how to get out."

Henri looked at the symbols, crouching down beside the closest one. "What are the chances anyone can rescue us?"

Ce'Nedra glanced at her beloved, then at the others in the room. "Dominic is unlikely to return unless he has no choice. We can't *make* him come here unless…"

Everyone in the room focused upon Ce'Nedra.

"Something designates this as a connection to his amulet. That means the energy is already here to get him to this place. We just need to figure out how to call him here."

Felix stood. "What can we do to help?"

She turned to each of them. "Well, the first step is figuring out where our loyalties lie. So, tell me why you put your faith where it is."

Sylvaine shifted, her eyes worried. "Why?"

Felix answered. "Because if we don't all believe the same thing, we can't help. And right now, our captor is counting on that dissention to make us kill each other so he doesn't have to do it."

The revelation hung in the room like a smell and they looked at one another for a moment before they turned their focus inward. They were there because Dominic wanted to be rid of them. If they killed each other, he won. With these quarters being so small, conflict was inevitable.

Sylvaine's voice was small when she spoke. "I was raised in Mande. The Church is the only faith allowed. I've never known another. When the King came through and healed the villagers and the children that were hurt by my husband, I saw some of the people. They were so happy and whole and *clean.*" She looked at the others. "There's no other way to explain it. They smelled and felt and looked *clean.* I so wished he had touched me so I could be that clean as well. His gift came from Heaven. It worked at the Church and on the road after the priest blessed it. I don't think I could let go of the hope that Heaven will save me as well."

Henri sat at the table. "I saw that too. I was talking to him and getting instructions for how to handle things in the town, going from that moment. He talked and healed and talked and healed. They were both so natural to him, he didn't even realize he was doing miracles. He had good ideas but he also had another, pressing matter he needed to take care of.

He was distracted enough to not linger, but I knew his infusion of holiness was going to help everyone."

Henri looked at Ce'Nedra. "When that goblin attacked me, you saved my life. It was with fire though, and that coupled with the goblin attack in the first place has made me very solid in my worship of Heaven."

"Yet our lives are saved right now by Fae and Land magic." Felix leaned against the wall opposite Ce'Nedra. "As a traveler, I *know* the power of the Fae. Every inn worships them, every waysign is a tribute to them, carved symbols that I now recognize as protections." He gestured to the runes on the wall. "I have seen these things over and over and now I know for certain that the Church has never been the one I, or probably any of the people in the Messenger Office, worship. I've never felt comfortable in a church."

The four looked at the dynamic that was now present with these confessions. Felix and Ce'Nedra stood across from each other, Henri and Sylvaine sat opposite each other. There was a small tension in the air that these were now battle lines.

Ce'Nedra broke that.

"Good. That's equilibrium. This prison is half Heaven, half Land. Without *both* energies, we won't be able to solve this."

Everyone relaxed and she smiled.

Felix took a deep breath. "It sounds like you need to start teaching us all a little magic."

Ce'Nedra nodded. "There is magic of a divine nature at work here. It will take all of us working together to get it to function. Do you want to try?"

She looked at her companions.

Henri sat back, smiling. "Well, I'd love to but I have all these reports to write so I don't know if I have the time."

Sylvaine looked shocked, then figured it out. "I'd also like to help, but I have to get ready for the Ball at the palace."

"I have a few messages to deliver for His Majesty, I'm sure."

Ce'Nedra rolled her eyes. "I just remembered I have a stew to make."

The friends laughed at each other's "time commitments", then settled in to learn how to channel the energies in the room.

# Eleven

## "What one knows it is sometimes useful to forget." Shiva, The Karmic Hand

The rain from the night before had cleansed the valley air of the brown-grey smoke and Catherine sipped her tea and counted the encampments she could see. There were over a hundred. If each fire warmed only three soldiers, which seemed unlikely, that was still a considerable force. And they came from Krakte, with monsters instead of men. The army wouldn't mobilize without their King or at least knowing his whereabouts. This situation needed to be handled.

The door down the hall opened and Alexander stepped out, looking disheveled, but rested. He waved to his mother, then knocked on Tanglwyst's door. Catherine picked up the tray her tea came on and walked to stand beside her son. He looked up, nodding.

"That's very kind, Mother."

"Well, it would be inappropriate for you to go in to a young woman's chambers unchaperoned."

He frowned. "Do you truly think I would…"

She shook her head. "Of course not, Your Majesty. I want to see how she's doing too."

A weak moan from the other side of the door called their interest and the door opened. Tanglwyst stood, barely, wearing her shirt and nothing else. She gestured to the pair to enter, then hobbled over to the bed again.

"Alex, remember how I told you yesterday that I did not want your magical healing?"

"Yes, of course."

"I was a damned idiot."

He laughed. "Can I help you now then? I still have the water right here."

"Yes. Why are you still standing there?"

He smiled as he got the basin and used the pitcher to wet a towel. Catherine set the tray on the table and turned back to see Tanglwyst bent over the bed, her shirt exposing her bare legs and rear. She was glad she had set the tray down or she would have dropped it in shock.

"Alexander!"

The King and his friend looked at her, their faces concerned. He sat up a little straighter, concerned. "Mother? What is it?"

The marks across Tanglwyst's body were extensive. When Tanglwyst had protected her, she had been covered, and Catherine had only glimpses of the damage. There was no part of her exposed skin that was not black and blue. She could make out several fleurs across the woman's rear and lower back as well.

Her voice caught. It was so similar to the body of a young woman found on the Cheryb grounds that Catherine almost screamed. Her initial shock at the familiarity of her son was gone, replaced in its entirety by remembered nightmares she had long since outgrown. She stepped a little closer, her hand outstretched. Her shaking fingers touched the bruises on Tanglwyst's back as tears ran down Catherine's face. Her lip shook, threatening to let out the scream she had given upon her discovery of one of Giovanni's victims. She turned to look at Alexander.

"You… you did this?" Her voice was strange, even in her own ears and she felt her rage pulling back, like a wave from the shore before a tsunami.

Alexander swallowed, then nodded.

Catherine backhanded Alexander across the face, knocking him to the floor. The pitcher crashed, breaking into shards at Tanglwyst's feet. The cloth he held hit the ground as well and he knelt, waiting for any more assaults. Tanglwyst leapt onto the bed, turning to face them. Catherine backed away from Alexander, unable to speak. She felt faint, sick. Her vision wobbled and she sat in a nearby chair until she could steady herself.

Alexander stood and Tanglwyst nodded to Catherine. He walked to her, putting a hand upon his mother's shoulder. "Are you alright.?"

She looked at him through a haze. "Y..yes... Please, forgive me, Your... Your Majesty..."

He closed his eyes, bracing himself. "No need. It was no more than I deserved." He looked at Tanglwyst, who said something, but Catherine was only hearing the blood in her head now. She was fighting to stay conscious but felt herself losing. She felt arms around her and her feet, moving, then softness and warmth. She felt the world swimming, and then she saw blackness.

Alexander came back in Tanglwyst's room, closing the door behind him. "She's laying down now."

"Do you need to be with her?"

He shook his head. "Not right this second. She should be fine, at least until I can handle this." He reached down and picked up the cloth. It still felt holy, but the water was starting to dry out and he only had the cloth to use to get this done. The cardinal had likely left already, being as it was so late in the day. "Do you still want me to do this?"

Tanglwyst pursed her lips. "Yeah. As much as I hate to sacrifice my pride for my comfort, I started thinking that we might need to get going today. There's a lot to do that can't be done from here."

"Alright then. Let's see what I can do."

She turned around, keeping her feet on the bed, and lifted her shirt again. He placed the towel upon her bruises, the worst ones being across her rear and lower back. The towel barely covered the whole area, but he hoped it would be enough. He put his hands upon the cloth and called out to the healing power he had experienced several times in the past few weeks. Something he had used once and been denied for a decade, now was almost common knowledge to him. He felt the glow of Heaven fill him and move where he directed it, into the lady. He felt her welts and bruises fade into nothing, and even dealt with a small bout of nervous nausea as well. He heard her breathing normalize and she relaxed beneath his touch. He removed the towel and inspected the skin.

Her bruises all over her body were gone.

He smiled, tugging her shirt back down. "There. All better. How do you feel?"

She turned around and sat on the bed, her feet curling beside her. "Much better. I kept waking up all night when I moved. Now I feel like I could ride a horse clear to Patras." She moved and got off the bed on the other side. Alexander leaned down and started picking up the broken pieces of ceramic from the floor.

"I don't think there will be many small shards but I'll get a broom and make sure." He opened the door and carried the ruined pitcher downstairs. He threw them in the common hearth, then went to the kitchen to get another. Svein and Ealusaid were not in there but he heard their voices out back. He decided not to bother them when he saw a shelf with three similar pitchers on it, and he grabbed one. He found the broom beside the shelf and returned upstairs with them. Tanglwyst had changed back into the breeches, shirt, and doublet she wore traveling, and was pulling on her remaining boot when he returned.

"It's a good thing I hurried. You didn't even knock this time."

He looked at the door, then set the pitcher on the nearby table. "Oh. Yes, I'm sorry. I was not thinking."

"What were you doing instead?"

He shrugged. "Nothing. There was literally nothing going through my mind at all."

"How is it men can do that? I never get a moment's peace."

"It's a gift." He used the broom to find the stray chips of earthenware under the bed. It occurred to him then that the tiny shards would require a dustpan or something to get them up. His royal privilege seemed to be makng another appearance. It's not like he had never *swept* anything before either, but he had simply not been thinking.

*Time to stop that practice.* "We need to figure out what to do here. I'm not sure where to go now."

"We will, but first," she stepped over to him and hugged him, laying her head upon his shoulder, "thank you."

He held his arms out from them for a moment, then put his free arm around her waist. Although he knew better, he still felt worried he would hurt her. "For what?"

"For everything."

He let the broom go and encompassed her. He didn't even notice it hitting the floor.

"Gladly, my lady."

# Twelve

"Have a thief and a city guard on your payroll, but don't let them be the same person."
Kali, The Karmic Hand

Tanglwyst opened the door and tried to take the broom from Alexander, but he sidestepped her. "I'll be right back. I need to tell Svein and Ealusaid that we dropped the other pitcher."

"Alright. I'll be here."

He smiled, a genuine smile that lit up his face. He gave a little nod and bounded down the stairs, two at a time.

She closed the door and picked up the towels and bandages from the previous day. She really was grateful for the relief. Yes, she was ready to take the punishment she was due, but the more she lie awake last night, the more she smelled the wet smoke in the air. Her home was surrounded by an army and she was very afraid for her people. Twice she almost got up and took a horse but the one time she tried, the pain dropped her like she was a thousand pounds. Had Alexander been on hand, she would have had him heal her that second. As it was, it took her almost an hour to get back in bed. When she awoke later, she almost wet the bed instead of trying to move. But her pain had dulled a bit and she was careful in her movements. By the time she saw Alexander again, she would have had his children if he would have made the pain stop.

She heard him coming up the stairs and waited to see if he would knock this time. He did and she smiled. It was progress. She opened the door and stepped out.

"Where are we going?" He looked at her door then back at her.

"Your mother's room."

"Why?"

"Because she knows more about running the kingdom than either of us and she's inclined to help you."

He glanced down the hall and she saw the mark his mother had made upon his cheek. She reached up to touch it, then stayed her hand as he looked at her. "Does that hurt?"

"A bit. Is that towel I used still in there?"

"Yes."

"May I use it?"

Tanglwyst opened her door and they went to the pile of towels.

"Good. It's still damp." He placed it upon his cheek and she saw his hand glow a pale gold. When he took the towel away, the injury was gone. "That pretty much finishes that off. There was hardly any holy energy left." He tossed the towel back onto the pile.

"It did the trick."

He looked uncomfortable. "She wasn't wrong to do it."

Tanglwyst bit her lip. "I don't really know what to say here. Alexander, you were more than lenient. If Charles had actually died…"

"I would have put you to death myself like I did Elizabeth, but he didn't. And this wasn't your fault."

"It was my idea to take Alan. Catriona never would have risked her life to save me but she would have to save Alan. I put myself under lock and key to make Nicolai hate her. Elizabeth may have cast a spell but she didn't create that part. She just unleashed it."

He took her hand. "Did you feel anything for me this winter?"

She looked away and felt herself blushing. "Alex…"

"Because I felt something for you. Yes, it was probably just my broken heart using your broken heart to make myself feel whole again. But I cared for you. I just wasn't over her. No more than you were over Nicolai." He turned her face to his. "The evil magic in our lives took advantage of that. Yes, it brought out the worst in us, but at least we know what that looks like now." He let go of her chin. "I know I won't be going easily into that darkness again." He raised her hand to his lips and kissed it. "And I have you to thank for that."

Her eyes felt wet. "You hurt me."

"I'm sorry for that. Then and now."

"I don't trust you."

"I don't blame you."

"I probably hate you."

He smiled. "And I just may love you. But I don't want to risk saying so until I'm sure."

She laughed, her tears coming regardless of her wishes. He hugged her to him and she returned the hug. He broke the hug first, and brushed a tear away from her cheek with his thumb. "You sure you want to go to her like this? She may get ideas."

"She'll find out sooner or later that I cry when the wind blows. I'll just blame it on the smoke."

He nodded and they walked down the hallway and knocked on Catherine's door. There was a rustle of sound and a faint "Come in." Alexander poked his head in the door. "Are you feeling any better, Mother?"

"Yes, yes. Please, come in. Is Tanglwyst with you?"

"Yes."

"Good. I'm sorry for my behavior in there, young woman. I…" Catherine looked around, baffled. "I have no excuse."

Tanglwyst walked over and knelt before the Queen Mother. "I have seen that look you had in my own mirror. You don't need to reveal anything you don't wish to."

"Thank you, my dear. Alexander, are you hurt?"

"I had a small scratch but it wiped away. Obviously just a bit of dirt or something."

Catherine looked skeptical, but accepted his assessment of the situation. She got out of bed as Tanglwyst got out of the way and stood, her body much more steady than when she entered the room. "What do we need to do now?"

"That's why we're here, Mother. Tangl believes you might have some ideas about what to do next. I wanted to give you time to rest but we both fear there is not a lot of time left. We have no idea how long that army has been there…"

"Almost a tenday."

"What?" Alexander exchanged a look with Tanglwyst.

"Yes. The reports came in a few days ago. Here." Catherine walked over to the desk and pulled out the reports Charles had copied. She handed them to him.

Alexander and Tanglwyst read the reports, horror showing on their faces as the patrolman's account hit their minds. When they finished, Tanglwyst sank into a chair at the table and Alexander looked out the window. "Have there been any reports from Patras?"

"None here but there's no reason to expect them. No one knows we're here."

"By the Saints. Gomez."

Tanglwyst looked up and Alexander closed his eyes. "He's alive, and moving. That's more than he was doing before." He looked at Tanglwyst. "I thought he was just keeping up the pretense of finding my bride but he was likely trapped in that spell."

"What do we do?"

Catherine looked out the window. "We need to tell people where you are. It's the reason I sent the bird to you, at Cliffbase. I needed you to come to me. Luckily, the Saints put me in your path so we could solve this."

"If I wasn't here, what would you be doing today?"

"Probably sending word to Dominic about the army and telling him I was here, awaiting your arrival."

"Well, I certainly wouldn't trust Dominic in this situation." Tanglwyst looked at her companions. "I think he has the amulet from the Scarred Man. We both know what those things can do to a person."

Alexander nodded and closed his eyes. "Something is happening here. I don't know what. But Dominic *definitely* has one of those amulets. And he's going back and forth to Mande."

"I suspected he was doing something shifty. There were... signs." Catherine frowned, her look seeping anger.

Tanglwyst also frowned. "Signs?"

"He was wearing a Fuccochio coat. He had not been away from the palace long enough to get it legitimately, yet it was not a copy."

"What?" Tanglwyst shook her head and rolled her eyes. "Of all the vain, arrogant, foolish things..."

"What's a Fuccochio coat?" Alexander looked between the two women who seemed to be bonding over a secret of fashion. He wasn't sure how he felt about that.

Tanglwyst got the nod from Catherine to explain. "Fuccochio is a designer in Florentine and he is very exclusive. He will not ship his works because they need to be fitted on the person. They are so well made that a Fuccochio coat is an heirloom in wills in Mande. They have lasted for generations."

"He made your father's coronation clothing."

"The stuff he was buried in?"

Catherine nodded. "That was decades ago and, as you may remember, he wore it quite often."

"I do remember, even though he died when I was five. That clothing was beautiful. Dominic was wearing something that elaborate?"

"No. It was a subtle work. Not meant for royalty and probably cost him quite a lot of his salary, but with the embezzlement from your company my lady, I'm sure he could afford a single coat. But they take a tenday to fit and Fuccochio won't bump your project to the front of his order list, regardless of your station. Even the King of Mande waits his turn."

"And people tolerate this?"

"Yes. Heirloom."

Alexander shook his head. "Well, this is far more about fashion than I think I needed to know but I see what you mean. We need to handle him."

"Alex," Tanglwyst's face now showed concern, "we can't. The room? Anyone who investigates him could end up stranded. For all you know, that's already happened."

He frowned, then closed his eyes again. He felt for the fealty of his people and looked for anyone who was somewhere they shouldn't be. He found Dominic in Mande again and then seconds later in St. Andrew.

"He just jumped. To St. Andrew."

"What's he doing there?" Catherine leaned closer.

"He's in the... I think he's in the City Offices."

Tanglwyst exchanged a look with Catherine, then went back at Alexander. "Well, business would just be opening up so that wouldn't be suspicious. What could he be doing there?"

"Visiting Henri, I suppose. The City Official that helped me after..." He frowned, pushing away the memory of leaving hundreds of injured and ill to their fates while he pursued Catriona. "Wait..." He turned his head. "He's not visiting Henri. Henri is there." He pointed behind them. "In the Papal City. Below it."

Tanglwyst's eyes went wide. "The vaults. They are connected to the amulets."

"Why would he put them in one of these vaults?" Catherine's voice took on a sharpness borne of concern.

"To get them out of the way. There are at least four of them in there: Henri, Ce'Nedra, Sylvaine Rochefort? And Felix, from the messengers office at the palace. The Saints only know what could have brought them into Dominic's path. There may be more if there are people without fealty."

"So what do we do?"

He opened his eyes. "I don't know. We can't get to them, not with the thorn barrier around the city. It was Fae, I'm sure of it."

"Henri and Ce'Nedra must have found something out he didn't want them to know." Tanglwyst shook her head.

"Like that he had one of these amulets."

"How did he get them in there?" Catherine was puzzled by the references.

Tanglwyst cleared her throat. "Well, there were actually two amulets. One was a holy relic from the Inquisition. I researched it when I was in the Papal City. That amulet had a room that was attuned to it. It was a safe room, so to speak, with no access except to use the amulet to arrive and leave. When you are in the room, there's no way to tell where you are, what country, if you are underground or under water. And they are self-contained. The one Duncan took me to had a bed, a desk, and runes that glowed in blue light around the walls near the floor. Duncan said I would be safe there.

"When I was attacked by the Scarred Man, he took me to another one. It wasn't the one Duncan had used. I figured out that meant each amulet had a separate room attuned to it. While I was in a secret chamber below the Papal Palace, I saw a series of vaults with the Saints' symbols carved on the outside but no other opening. They were the same size as the ones I went to. I think those are the secret rooms."

Catherine leaned on her elbows. "You said something before about an amulet that you destroyed at the inn in Caratia."

"Yes. The one Alexander had was new, different. I don't know if it had a room or not."

Catherine looked at her son but he shook his head. "I never checked. But it was destroyed the same way the first one was: Fire."

"You had two, Alexander?"

"I borrowed his from Duncan, then another one presented itself to me after Duncan's was destroyed. She's right. That one was... very different. It was more corrupted. It almost killed Tangl."

"The one Alexander had was new gold. From central Mande near the capital. From the craftsmanship and the content, it had to be made in Vincenzia."

"How good are you at knowing your gold work?" Catherine's tone was half curiosity, half skepticism.

"I have a mine there."

Alexander looked shocked and Catherine leaned back. "You have a mine there?"

"It actually belongs to the company. I'm caretaker of a mine that is owned by the Church near the border of Mervolingia. It has two entrances: One Mervol, one Mandian. Anything that is harvested on the Mandian side goes to the Church there, but the same veins feed the Mervol side, which is all mine as payment."

"Alexander, I want to go on the record that I approve of this marriage."

Alexander sputtered. "I have not even..."

"When you do, I approve."

Tanglwyst leaned in. "If he does, I'll refuse. He has more appropriate people to marry to seal alliances. Like possibly the princess Gilian of Mande."

Alexander frowned. "She's a child. I met her. Besides, Cipriano wants Alan as her husband."

"Cipriano won't get that. Catriona would never allow it. You're a great second choice."

He looked about to protest, then gave a tight lipped frown. "This is not a discussion for this time."

Catherine looked back and forth between the two and hid a slight smile behind drinking some wine. She then started thinking, and frowned again, setting the goblet on the table. "What if that's why Dominic wanted the coat?"

Tanglwyst looked at the goblets, thinking. "You mean to make an impression upon Cipriano?"

"He tracks everyone who buys one. If you can afford a Fuccochio, he wants to know you."

"If Alexander won't marry Gilian and Alan won't marry Gilian..."

Alexander nodded. "Then being married to the man in control of all of Mervoliniga's holdings would do just fine." He looked at his mother. "And if he gets his hands on the Crown of Mande…"

Catherine looked away.

"Alexander," Tanglwyst rubbed her face. "We have to stop him."

"How?"

Catherine smiled. "I think I have an idea. And I don't need to go anywhere at all to do it."

# Thirteen

"There is no reason to discriminate based on what a person is born with."
Kali, The Karmic Hand

Catherine called Charles the Messenger into the room. "Charles, we need to get information to the Kingdom Chancellor about the situation in St. Giles, if he doesn't already know. We also need to let the Royal guard know where the King is."

Alexander raised his head from the missive he was writing. "And if St. Giles is receiving messages. How would we check that?"

"There's a patrolman, Sire, who has been to the village several times. I can bring him up."

"Please."

Charles the Messenger left and returned a few minutes later with an older man with brown eyes and greying blond hair. He bowed.

"Your Majesty, this is Patrolman Allen Hobbs. He also has a regular route that goes between here and St. Giles."

Allen bowed to the King and Queen Mother, then nodded to Tanglwyst. "My lady. It's good to see you are here and safe."

"Allen." She went to him and grasped his hand in both of hers. "I'm so glad you're safe. How is your family?"

"They are nervous about the fires but they are fine. I moved them to Cliffbase when I heard about the suspension spell."

She shuddered. "Did you see it? I just read the report and it shall haunt me for a year."

"Thankfully, no. I'm glad the missus had already done her shopping for the tenday. She just missed it."

Tanglwyst drew a breath. "Did you see anything at the estate?"

"Only that it was surrounded. I stayed to the Road Wood and they didn't notice me. If someone were to travel that way, they could bypass the army and get to Patras."

"Well," Tanglwyst shook her head, "I have no interest in going to Patras. I need to get to St. Giles."

Alexander stood and walked over to them. Tanglwyst released her friend's hand. "Mother, do we have a map of St. Giles?"

"Not really."

Charles the Messenger raised his hand to get their attention. "There's the cartographer in Cliffbase, Magdelena. She'll have one, and of the local countryside."

Tanglwyst looked to Alexander. "What are you thinking?"

"I want to figure out where everyone is. See where the gaps are. That will show us where we can go in St. Giles and not be discovered."

Catherine stood. "You will not."

"Mother…"

"You are the King of Mervolingia. You will not be sneaking into a town infested with a Fae army."

"Half-Fae, ma'am." Patrolman Hobbs looked at the ceiling just over her left shoulder.

"What?"

"I'm pretty sure they are only half-Fae."

Alexander gestured to Hobbs while looking at his mother. "See? Only half."

"We will conduct things from here, Alexander. There's nothing you can do there that can't be accomplished right from this room."

Tanglwyst nodded. "It's true. All the missives and meetings with the Krakten Queen can be conducted right here. That frees me up to…"

"The Hell you will." Alexander's tone mirrored his mother's from seconds before.

"How is Charles supposed to get the letters to the inhabitants of St. Giles?" Tanglwyst looked hard at Alexander.

He drew an exasperated breath. "You're not going anywhere without me."

"No, she's right. She should go and scout." Catherine looked at Charles. "The map idea sounds like a good start. I take it you plan to use the Power to locate featly holders?"

"I can find specific people if I look for them. It seems likely I can locate groups if I try. But she's not going to 'scout'. We have patrolmen to do that."

"I'll not send someone to do something dangerous when I wouldn't do it myself." Tanglwyst crossed her arms.

"That's a lie. You sent Dominic and Myrgen and Duncan and pretty much anyone else to do things you didn't want to do." Now Alexander was crossing his arms.

"Didn't want to do. Not that I wouldn't."

"I will command you to stay."

Tanglwyst bristled. She unfolded her arms with deliberate care, slowly, and her eyes went hot. "You will do no such thing. You have already used my loyalty to this kingdom against me twice. You compelled me to come to you, almost killing me. You sacrificed an innocent animal, the love of your life, and probably your best friend to that. You took a loyal servant who saved my life, and exposed him to a thing you knew he was recovering from, but you didn't give him what he knew. You gave him something he couldn't fight, couldn't beat. Have you even checked on Duncan since you took the amulet away? Do you know where he is? What has happened to him? I mean, don't you at least owe him that after he murdered your rival?"

Catherine's eyes flicked to the patrolman and the messenger, who were now looking decidedly uncomfortable about being witness to this. She started to motion to send them away but Tanglwyst went on.

"Then you gave that Power over people to me. I appreciate that you saved my life, but I'm even more appreciative that it has made me immune to your machinations. You have no Power over me, Alexander. You can't compel me to do a damned thing. That's why I stood between you and your mother earlier when you tried to push on our fealty. Because, contrary to your fantasies, you don't have my fealty. This kingdom does. The Crown does. But you? You. Are. Expendable."

She raised her finger and pointed at him. "So don't you ever threaten me again. If you died right now, that Power would die with you and cleanse this country of this ability. You need to remember that before you go wielding it against the people trying to support you. There are only two reasons why you are still holding it. One, the Papal City is covered in thorns so the Pope can't rescind your appointment, and two, because I gave it back. If either of those things weren't the case, I would rip that from you this instant."

She looked at Catherine. "Forgive me, Your Majesty, but I fear I have a headache. I'll be in my room, should you need me." She looked at Alexander. "You stay the Hell away from me."

She walked from the room without waiting for dismissal by either royal.

Alexander grabbed for her. "Tang…"

Catherine's hand was on his shoulder, shoving him back down into the seat. "What part of 'Stay the Hell away from me' confused you there?"

"She's…"

"Upset as hell and I agree with her. You have things to do for this kingdom. You will sit there and do them." She nodded to Charles the Messenger. "Please shut the door. If the lady decides to leave and go about her own business, I don't want my son to be able to do a damned thing about it. Patrolman Hobbs, you may return to your duties but I would appreciate it if you didn't repeat what was said here. The Lady is worried for her people and feeling helpless. Her words should not be held against her."

"Of course, Your Majesty." Hobbs bowed and left the room, as did Charles.

Catherine sighed. "That woman is dead."

Alexander nodded. "I know. She was just scourged for being a traitor and now she threatened me in front of two witnesses."

"Two? That door was open and there is no wall between the common room and this one. The entire inn heard that."

Alexander looked at the closed door. "I need to fix this. They'll kill her if she tries to sneak out."

"Yes, they will. But I don't know if that isn't the best thing for the Crown."

Alexander whipped around to stare at his Mother. "What?"

"She can't be compelled or controlled by the Crown, she's got money enough to get into or out of anything, and she has Papal ties. She's a very powerful ally, but also an equally powerful enemy. Right now, she seems inclined to be the latter."

Alexander put his elbows on his knees, running his hands through his hair. "What is wrong with me? I knew she had a problem with the compulsions. I just can't seem to control these days."

"You have spent your life not having to control yourself. You went off after that other woman for years, never having to answer to anyone. Not even me or your brother. You were never really prepared for the Power of Sovereignty to fall to you. I honestly never expected it to have to. When Elizabeth became pregnant, I thought the problem was solved. Then she had a girl and I realized it wasn't."

Alexander looked at his Mother, shaking his head in confusion. "What does that have to do with it?"

She cocked her head.

He stood, angry. "What does that have to do with anything? You have long since proven women are perfectly capable of ruling. Why should Emmy be shoved aside simply because of her sex?" He gestured to the closed door. "That woman held the Power and she managed quite well, far better than I have so far. Clearly the ones with the intelligence here have been the women. Charles gave away his authority, I became a murderous, obsessed monster. But so far, the only woman to have held this Power has not only managed to avoid its control, but has wielded it justly. And if she is now immune to it, I would be too. I could help Emmy, or Tanglwyst or you or whomever not to fall to its corruption. But I don't see how my gender has done a damned bit of good."

"What are you going to do?"

"What should have been done immediately." He went to the door and opened it before Catherine could stop him. He stormed down the two doors to Tanglwyst's and knocked.

The door opened and she closed her eyes, calming herself. "What?"

"I need to do something. And you need to witness it."

"Why?"

"Because it's important. And right now, you are the only other person who will understand."

He straightened his back, pulling himself up to his full height. He turned to face the common room, which was filled with patrolmen, messengers, and a couple of slightly anxious innkeepers. Catherine came from her room at the end, measured steps closing the distance between her and her son.

"I'm making a declaration that I intend to be my first official act when I return to Patras."

Tanglwyst stepped up to him and grabbed his arm. "Alexander, don't."

He turned to her and drew her up beside him. "No. This is a good one. It's the right thing to do." He looked back at his people. "There is an army camped half a day's ride from here, one that will take several tendays to gather a force large enough to battle it. I intend to be there with my men and women who will stand against this invader. And that means I might fall in the fight."

A murmur went through the hall and Alexander looked into every eye there. A few glanced at Tanglwyst and fingered their weapons.

She squeezed his arm and spoke without moving her lips. "This isn't helping."

He put his hand upon hers and looked at her. "This woman has seen the worst of me," he turned to his mother, "and this one has seen the best. Both of them have something in common that I have never seen a man I know accomplish: They have told me I was wrong and stood their ground when I protested. A Sovereign needs people like this, people with integrity. And that's why I am declaring my niece Marie Elizabeth Angloume to be my heir, until such time as my first born child, of either gender, comes of age." He turned to Tanglwyst. "For what makes a good ruler is integrity and intelligence, and I have not yet a woman who does not meet that criteria."

He released the Power he had been gathering and a flash rippled from him, hitting everyone in the inn. It flowed out of the building and he could feel it touch every soul. It connected with the people on the road, in Cliffbase. He felt it go to the people stranded in St Giles, in Patras. He felt it touch Henri and Ce'Nedra and that gave him hope. It went to Morgan Wolf, and the Baron and Baroness there in St.

Marguerite, to Aggie and Flora and Martin at the inn, to the people he saved and failed to help in every town. He felt it in Fallon, Emmy's nurse. He felt it all over Patras. He touched the souls of people he had never met and resolved to meet them. And he touched the soul of his Mother, and he felt pride from her.

But there was one person he did not feel, the one in front of him, and he smiled at that. He was never going to be able to control her, and that was probably best. "Do you approve?"

She shook her head, fighting her own smile. "You don't realize the precedent you just set."

"Yes, I do. And when I return to Patras, I'll use the Quill to write it into law."

"You did the right thing, even if it was just to ease my anger at you."

"I didn't do it to appease you. I did it because it needed to be done. Mother knows what to do here. We can head out as soon as the things I need to write and sign are done. We need to get you to your people."

"Alexander…"

"I would let you go on your own, but I'm not sure I should let you out of my sight. I'm not the smartest person when you aren't around."

She smiled. "You aren't the smartest person when I am either."

He nodded. "I'll accept that." He took her hand. "I apologize for my comment earlier. I was afraid I'd lose you. I shouldn't have said that. My fear for your life does not supersede your rights to your own decisions. Not yours, not anyone's."

"You seem to have a hard time remembering that."

"Thank the Saints I have you around to remind me regularly."

Her smile faded. "I won't always be."

He stroked her face. "I'd like to change that. Marry me."

# Fourteen

"I would rather have a friend who told me I was an idiot, than a friend who told me I was grand."
Shiva, The Karmic Hand

Tanglwyst blinked. "You're a mad man."

"I think we've established that."

"Alexander, you can't just make a grand gesture and expect my pain to go away. It's not that simple."

"I know. And I'm not expecting it to. But I can't correct things if I'm not with you. You have the ability to make me see my way clear. I can't think of a better choice, for me or the kingdom. So help me make the right decisions."

"I don't love you."

"I understand that isn't necessary." He turned to look behind him. "Isn't that right, Mother?"

Tanglwyst looked at Catherine, who had settled into a spot not far from him, not intruding, but witnessing. She nodded.

"I'm not royalty."

"Also not necessary. I decreed before I left Patras that I was going looking for a wife, regardless of her status. And Mother already gave her approval."

Tanglwyst laughed. "And I said I'd refuse."

He shrugged. "I'm hoping you were lying."

"I'll think about it."

He kissed her hand. "I'll accept that."

She looked down at the people in the common room, then went back to stand in her doorway. "You have work to do. Get going, king."

He bowed to her, then gestured to his mother and her room. As they walked back, he looked back at Tanglwyst. She watched him get to the door and open it. Catherine went in and he turned, lingering. She smiled then gave him the tiniest of nods. He smiled, then gave a small bow. She shook her head in exasperation and closed her door.

Catherine watched her son as he closed the door. She wasn't quite sure how she felt about the proposal, but the decree was a good one. There might be hope for him yet.

He saw her watching him. "What?"

She turned away, smiling. "Nothing. Not a damned thing."

"Uh-huh."

She pointed to a few partially drafted missives on her desk. "What's left to do on those?"

He walked over to them. "I have a few things I am directing people to do. This letter is to Dominic. He needs to explain at court where I've been so I have told him this:

'*To the citizens and clergy of Mervolingia,*

'*A month ago, this kingdom suffered a great loss. With the death of both the King and Queen of Mervolingia, I was left with a difficult decision. I had not yet married and had done no real courting, yet I was going to be assuming the throne. This was unfair to pursue a soulmate after I had been coronated so I took the opportunity to seek a Queen immediately.*

'*But I had also learned through my brother that the finest women in our kingdom aren't always the ones we are shown. My brother loved a common woman with all his heart and she had borne him a beautiful son. However, he was unable to legitimize him before passing away. I have placed his family in a safe country and provided them with the means to live as befitting a royal cousin. Moreover, I learned his lesson and have left no social class unavailable to be a candidate for Queen.*

'*Many people have been contacted and consulted with, and I have narrowed my options. I hope to return with a suitable fiancée within the month. Please prepare to meet her and to behold her as your queen after the last harvest.*'

"I plan to have this taken to the messenger service in Cliffbase and copied and distributed from there."

"Ah. So Dominic can't interfere with the word getting out, even though it goes to him." Catherine nodded approval.

Alexander smiled, arching an eyebrow. "Exactly. That man is doing something shifty and I don't want him interfering with the distribution of this missive." He signed that paper and set it aside to let the ink dry.

"What name are you thinking of for your Coronation?"

He frowned. "I haven't even thought of that. Thanks for reminding me. It would have been very embarrassing to get up there and not have that answer." He looked at the next missive. "This one goes to Gomez:

'*Gomez,*

'*I am at the Benevolent Friar Inn on the road between Cliffbase and the Papal City. My mother is here as well. I have heard and can see the Krakten army from here and have included a letter to the leader of the Krakten forces. I will leave it to you to determine how best to be our emissary, at least until I can be there to handle negotiations personally.*

'*The pursuit of Catriona has failed and we no longer have her nor Caratia as an ally. Though not hostile at present, I am not certain how to proceed to repair the damage I have caused. Hopefully, my future queen will be able to fix the problem but for now, I will not be communicating much with that dark and distant people out of respect for their losses. Likewise, the situation with Lady Tanglwyst has been resolved as well but with far better results.*

'*I don't know if you have heard any rumors, but the Papal City is cut off from the world at present by a giant magical dome of thorns. It is assumed to be Fae magic and it sprung up as I was escaping the City. I am not certain of the circumstances regarding it but I did witness the formation of the barrier. I believe the thorns are also poisoned so any attempts, from without or within, will result in sickness or possibly even death. We do not yet have a course of action on dealing with this problem but I hope to have it resolved by the time my Coronation arrives.*

*'I plan to leave here in a few days to try to get into St. Giles. With
any luck, you'll get this missive before I get there and it will give you
time to prepare. If you can send messages, send them to Cliffbase, with
a copy going to Patras. If it turns out I am unable to enter St. Giles, I'll
send to Patras for any missives and will set up a command encampment
outside of the influence of the town. I hope to be within sight of St. Giles
but if I cannot, I may return here or to Cliffbase where I can at least
oversee the army. They have a messenger service there that can get a
missive to anyone in the world. It might take more time but I will be able
to guarantee replies.*

*'If you can, find out why the army is there. If you can send messages,
send them to Cliffbase. We have a messenger who is getting deliveries
twice a day.*

*'Stay strong. We're watching you and the situation.'"*

"That's an awful lot of information for a guardsman."

"He's more than a guardsman, Mother. He's probably my best
friend."

"Really?" She looked to the occupied valley. "I truly have been out
of touch with you boys. I was hesitant for you to tell the populace about
Charles' infidelity with Marie, but in the end, both he and Elizabeth are
dead for all intents. And you explained they were in a safe country so
dissidents will have a hard time locating them."

"That was my thought too. I can't legitimize Francois but I can
acknowledge that he is my nephew."

"He named his son Francois?"

He stood up straight, his eyes squinting in concern. "Yes. He and
Marie almost didn't make it. I got there just in time to cut the child from
her belly. Had he been born normally, they both would have died."

Her shoulders sagged. "I am so sorry." She shook her head. "Damn
that ink and that Power. Had I my will, I would forbid all magic and
practice from our country."

He went to her and hugged her. "Blanket decrees are what caused
this mess in the first place, Mother. I mean to stay away from them unless
I'm certain they are for the good of the country."

"The one you made there, about Emmy, was a good one."

"I have seen far too many women be more capable and competent
than the men often charged with their care."

She looked at him. "Will you tell me about them?"

He stepped back and sat her at the table. He started at the beginning, with Charles and Marie's first meeting. It felt like there was no need to hide any of it anymore. The charm of Marie truly came through in Alexander's tale and more and more, she regretted her forbiddance of the relationship. But Catherine had been given the power to control the King for the best interests of Mervolingia and a bastard to claim the throne would have caused a civil war. Especially when the mother was a commoner that the king truly loved.

Alexander's description of what Marie did to and for Charles and what Elizabeth's interference caused angered Catherine. She felt it was inappropriate to put Alexander in that position. He had never been trained nor given much opportunity to learn how to govern, and she believed that was the source of all the recent madness, though she never said it. Alexander was speaking to her and this was the first time since the St. Michael's Day Massacre that he had done so. She wasn't about to remind him of her transgressions.

His tone changed significantly when he spoke of Catriona though. She could hear the pain in his voice, like he was speaking through a burnt out husk of what was once his heart. The woman seemed beyond belief and she figured he was making her supernatural now that she was no longer available. She hoped Tanglwyst would be able to handle it if she stayed with Alexander, and be smart enough to know if she couldn't before she committed to anything. Catherine hoped that was what Tanglwyst was doing at that moment.

When he had finished, she nodded. "That was quite the adventure."

"Yes. But there were a lot of lessons to be learned and I hope we all learned them." He pointed at her. "There were a few there for you too."

"That there were." She sighed and glanced at the door, then back to him. "What are your intentions with that young woman?"

He folded his hands and put them on the desk in front of him. "I hope to marry her, if she'll have me."

"Will she?"

He looked at the door. "Probably not. But hopefully, I can keep her nearby as an advisor. I will offer her a paid position should she be unwilling to be my wife. Perhaps Chancellor."

Catherine smiled. "No, my dear. She's a businesswoman, a rare creature in this day and age. She isn't going to abandon her own fortune to tend to yours."

"Then hopefully, I can have her as a friend."

"You have a lot of trust to recover. What *actually* happened this winter?"

He leaned back, casting his eyes at the ceiling. "Augh... Catriona and I acknowledged our feelings for each other in Aquin, right before the end of the month. I spent all of Benedine in ecstasy. I had been pursuing her for almost a decade. Then she went to a meeting and her husband was in the room. They had both thought the other dead, and even the records of the town had listed them both as deceased. It was quite a shock. She had denied herself any form of emotional intimacy out of her feelings of guilt. She blamed herself for his death.

"When they saw each other, they talked for a tenday. They decided, based upon how they felt for each other a decade before, that they would become a family again. It was doomed from the start. It turns out Nicolai, Catriona's husband, had captured Tanglwyst's heart."

"Ah." Catherine nodded. "That's what was behind the potion. That's what it fed off of."

"Yes. So she, as Elizabeth's best childhood friend, told the Queen about her heartbreak. Elizabeth had her take a room at the palace any time she needed. Tanglwyst visited often enough for Emmy to know her. She was the one who gave Emmy that blue and gold tea set."

Catherine looked puzzled, not really knowing every one of Emmy's toys since she had been gone, but she waved Alexander to continue.

"Well, Emmy used that tea set every day, anywhere from twice to eight times each day. Whenever someone visited her room, she made them tea. Once, Tangl and I ended up in the same tea party. We chatted and Emmy enjoyed it. We met like that every day for two tendays. Real affection seemed to grow from it." He shrugged. "At least it felt real at the time. Then, just as suddenly as they started, Emmy stopped having tea parties. So, I invited Tangl for tea in the anteroom. We had a few of those and I felt my heart healing. She did as well. There was a ball slated for the turning of the year and I asked her to save me a dance. In truth, my plan was to dance every dance with her.

"But as I was getting ready, I stopped by to see Emmy and talk to her about Tanglwyst. And in Emmy's room playing was a young man whose features were very familiar to me. Alan, Catriona's son, was playing with Emmy. All my plans left my head and I spent the rest of the night talking to him about his mother and him. I found out Nicolai had come to work at the palace. That meant, in my mind, that Catriona might show up here to fetch Alan that night and I stayed right by him just in case."

Catherine closed her eyes and shook her head. "Leaving the lady unattended at the Winter Ball. Oh Alexander. I taught you better than that."

He stared at his hands, his eyes getting wet. "It still stands as one of the things I'm most ashamed of. Not my greatest crime, not even against the lady. Merely the first. After that, she became susceptible to Elizabeth's machinations. Once Elizabeth was dead, Tanglwyst was put under house arrest. Duncan was sent to help her escape to the Papal City and when he lost her because of me, I had Gomez witness me placing a Summons upon her.

"Then I was an ass, and left Patras to follow after Catriona."

Catherine stood. "You what?"

"I know."

"That's horrible. That is sheer torture, madness-inducing torture. To have to find you and for you to keep moving away…"

"I know. I was under the spell of the Power by then, paying the price for my arrogance. She didn't matter, just the pursuit of the thing I felt entitled to. Tanglwyst finally broke it herself by removing her fealty. It saved her life but not before hurting a lot of people, including killing the horse she was riding to death to reach me."

Catherine turned away, her stomach churning. Alexander had never been told about the dangers of the Power, only about some of the uses. He had not even been given full access to the tome outlining the Power. Catherine had hidden the tome behind her wardrobe in a secret safe and part of the reason for her return was to talk to Alexander about it. It appeared he had learned all the lessons of the tome the hard way.

"And you somehow think this woman might allow you to marry her?"

He shook his head. "No. I don't. But she deserved to be asked. I was falling in love with her this winter. She helped me heal when I thought it impossible. One of the things Gomez and I determined was that he was going to have these sashes to give out to women of marrying age that were intelligent, honorable, strong willed, and self-sufficient. We figured that it would be a great way to elevate women in the kingdom. If a Stewart of the Sashes deemed a lady worthy of meeting the king, then she would have prestige amongst whatever village she was from. Even if she wasn't chosen to be queen, it was enough to be in the running for the title. She would be empowered to accomplish whatever she liked."

"Tanglwyst already seems to be like that without your consent nor prompting."

"She was the model, more or less. I had not completely lost all affection for the lady. I kept feeling tugs at my heart to go to her. Maybe to ask her to tea. But my obsession was too complete. I'm hoping she will see that she is very important to me and that she will at least allow me to be her friend again. With any luck, she'll be on hand to help me not make mistakes with the kingdom or the lady who becomes queen."

"Have you any candidates?"

"Supposedly. Gomez has the sashes. I imagine he's found a few he deems worthy." He sighed. "There are but three women I know that I can say I feel I would extend that offer. One refused, the other has died thanks to my obsession. Tanglwyst is the last one. After that, I will happily be alone until I die and let Emmy inherit."

Catherine sat back down. "Let's hope she stays around."

Alexander nodded. There seemed to be no more to say on the subject. She nodded to the stack of papers. "What else is in that stack?"

Alexander lifted the letter to Gomez. "The letter to the leader of the Krakten army. Tangl's pardon. An apology to St. Marguerite and acquisition of funds to rebuild."

"Rebuild?"

He glanced up at her. "Fire. Nasty one."

"Oh."

"Letter to Cipriano, thanking him for his offer of marriage to Gilian but telling him that I am not able to accept that offer at this time. Someone, I don't remember whom, thought I might be suitable to Cipriano's sister Laura, but he offered me his daughter."

"He offered marriage?"

"It was a power play."

"Well, naturally."

He picked up the last page. It had only one line on it, at the top. "And a letter of apology to the Stâpâna of Caratia."

"It looks… sparse."

He bobbed his head. "Yeah. I'm not really sure how to word it."

"You? At a loss for words?"

He stared at the page. "I'm afraid so, Mother."

She waited for him to say anything else, but he didn't and he eventually put the last paper back under the stack. He stood and looked out the window at the encamped army.

"You need to address that too."

"I know. Again, wording."

"Well, I have something to add to it when you send word to Patras, giving instructions." She went to her own stack and picked up the top one. She handed it to him.

He read it. "That's pretty open ended."

"I know."

He sniffed it. "Lemon?"

"It helps preserve the ink. I'm not sure where it will have to go."

"Oh." He looked at the letter again. "Alright. Any ideas what mine should say?"

"That the populace needs to know there is an invading force that is encamped around St. Giles. It does not seem to be penetrating farther than that, but that the Mervol army needs to assemble at the border of the county and await your arrival."

He nodded again.

"Make sure that letter is with yours and that should ensure we have an army that can withstand the assault."

"Thank you for your generosity, Mother."

She smiled. "Well, you didn't get the army you thought you'd have. That will help with recruiting."

"That it will. Thirty thousand ducats from your own accounts to whomever is bearing this letter should go a long way. I'll be sure it gets to the right hands."

Catherine smiled. "Oh, it will. I have no doubt."

# Fifteen

## "Dream without delusion."
## Shiva, The Karmic Hand

Tanglwyst walked down the stairs to Charles the Messenger's makeshift office. She kept an eye on everyone around her in case someone decided to discipline her for yelling at Alexander. After all, she had been flogged the day before for her crime and after chastising him, she fully expected to be accosted by the witnesses. She was actually relieved to find only Charles and Ealusaid in the common room.

The innkeeper went to the bar. "Did you need something?" Her tone was neutral and professionally friendly.

"Just heading to the privy."

"I see." Ealusaid glanced at Tanglwyst's shoes, then at her gloves. She gestured to the back door. "Come through the kitchen. The guardsmen had eggs earlier and the front stoop is a bit foul smelling."

Tanglwyst glanced at the front door, then at Charles who was copying a missive from Alexander. She followed Ealusaid into the kitchen. Svein wasn't around and Ealusaid glanced out back before letting her out. Ealusaid lowered her voice. "Where you headed?"

Tanglwyst frowned. She had hoped no one would notice. "My family is in St. Giles. I am in part responsible for Elizabeth's fate. I believe there's a strong chance the reason the Krakten army has gone that far and not further is because they are holding my estate hostage. I'm going to trade myself for them. I know Sovereigna. She's here to make a point, not an invasion. If I give her the guilty party, she'll take me and leave."

"You sure?"

"No. But I'll make that argument."

Ealusaid glanced towards the stairs and the kitchen doorway. "You're very much at risk right now. The guards have muttered about your fate. Several were quite offended at your treatment of the King, but others were not. After all, he proposed afterwards. Obviously, he forgave you, so the argument goes. Charles was under the impression His Majesty would prefer to keep you with him, so if you plan to slip away, you need to do so without him seeing you. And I would steer clear of Cliffbase since he has runners coming back and forth from there twice a day."

Tanglwyst looked to the east. She had indeed intended to go to Cliffbase to send a few letters. There was some business she needed to take care of, since it was looking like she might not be sailing this season. She was starting to worry that her company would be lost and she might need to release her claim on it and turn it over to her daughter. If she didn't and the company failed, the Church would take it away. One of her ancestors already sacrificed her own spiritual calling to keep that from happening. She wasn't going to risk the company when she could die from a "nasty fall" sponsored by a loyal guardsman.

"Charles believes I should be allowed to stay?"

Ealusaid furrowed her brow. "Yes. Why?"

"Do you think he'll let me send a few messages?"

A few minutes later, she was returning to her room with several sheets of parchment, ink, and three quills. A few hours later, she had three letters before her. The first one was to Alexander. It had taken several drafts, but in the end, she had decided to keep it simple. She could not marry him, not on the heels of being disciplined publicly. She was no longer a fugitive, it was true, but his entire reign would be questioned if he made her his Queen. She would not do that.

The second one was to Othon, her personal guardsman, and his wife Isabella, her lawyer. It told Isabella to draw up the transfer paperwork for turning the Tanglwyst Trading Company over to Kyri, and laid out the specifics for the information, including her Will. It also told Othon not to seek her killer if she ended up dead. Tanglwyst was willing to accept the fallout from her actions. She didn't need a vendetta in her name to sweep through her household. Too many lives would be lost that did not need to be.

The third one was the hardest one, and the one she dreaded the most. She picked it up and read it again.

*Myrgen,*

*I wanted to let you know what has happened to me, in case Mother and Father seek you to find out. I do not know at this time if I'll make it back to Patras to see them. Alexander has punished me for my crimes against Charles, based almost entirely upon the fact that Catriona spared me. He determined, as have I, that she saw what Elizabeth did to me. Please, if you see her again, thank her for me.*

*I have been proposed to by Alexander, but I have declined. It would be beyond inappropriate to accept. I suspect Catriona faced a similar decision and chose the same and likely for the same reason. I understand her more than I ever thought I would and I want to make sure she knows I regret my actions upon our last meeting in Patras. She was merciful and I am glad you are in her company. You cannot find a better companion. Please be a good friend to her.*

*I have seen Grandfather recently. He is safe in the Papal City, but a curse has sprung up around the place in the form of a dome of Fae thorns. I do not know what will happen and I do fear for his life. However, I have no solution. If the Papal City itself cannot break a Fae spell, then no one can. Caiaphas was there so I believe he will protect Grandfather. He's become a cardinal so he is privy to any plots. He was the best of us so I have faith.*

*I am turning the company over to Kyri. I can't be certain I will survive my next move so it is best to make sure the company is in someone else's hands before the Church gets it. With the Papal City cut off, the local branches will become desperate for power and I don't want my company to be a bargaining chip or goal. Isabella has the letter and will know what to do if I turn up dead. The Church will need my corpse to make a claim so do not let them bypass that part of the ancient decree. If there's no body, there's no death.*

*Take care, my brother. I love and miss you. Be happy.*

*Tanglwyst*

She took the letters down to Charles. "What else do you need to send these?"

He looked at them. "Any special instructions?"

"Like what?"

"Like needing the Guaranteed Delivery?"

She remembered the service Tomas and Symonne offered on the top of the mountain. She smiled. It might be nice for them to know that she was alright. "That's pretty expensive."

"Her Majesty has been funding the service."

"Personally?"

"Yes. Except for the royal missives from His Majesty. Cliffbase has an account for the Crown right now. Once Their Majesties decided to set up shop here, the service in Cliffbase was given a letter of credit. I understand a payment has already arrived to cover previous expenses plus a month of similar activity."

"So, I can set up an account and the money can arrive later?" Tanglwyst was impressed.

"Yes."

She amended the company letter to have Isabella pay her correspondence fees from the business coffers retroactively and thanked Charles for his time.

Upon returning to her room, she sat on the bed to think. *My next move* she had written. Now she just had to figure out what that was.

Charles set aside the letter he finished copying to let the ink dry and looked at the letters the lady had brought. He didn't even blink, but picked up the top one and opened it, his routine of copying all missives for Her Majesty now automatic. He barely acknowledged the contents of the letter to Myrgen, the words on the parchment not even seeming real anymore.

The one to Isabella DeMedici caught his interest because of the name, and he actually smiled. The king had proposed to the lady. If she was abdicating control of her company, she must be considering his offer.

Then he read the one to Alexander, undoubtedly put there by mistake because it was the bottom page of the stack of pages. He went back and re-read the letter to Myrgen. *My next move.* He looked up at the second floor.

This might require direct intervention.

He gathered the letters and walked upstairs to the Royal Suite. He knocked on the door and was admitted. He bowed.

"Your Majesties, I have received missives you might need to know about." He turned over all three letters to the royalty.

Catherine reached for them but Alexander took them first. He read the proposal refusal, sighed, and handed it to his mother. She too sighed and shrugged. The one to Isabella was next and he frowned at this one.

"This is a bit disconcerting." He handed the letter to Catherine.

After reading it, she looked at Alexander. "You can't let her send this one."

"Why not?"

She glanced at Charles. "Because if she lives through whatever happens, she'll be destitute. She's a woman. She needs to have her own money. Trust me."

Charles knew what the Queen Mother meant. Had it not been for her own ability to finance this endeavor, they would not be as solvent as they were in this inn. Having the Crown in debt to anyone was dangerous but at least this way, it was to family.

Alexander frowned. "I don't know that I feel comfortable telling her what she can and can't do with her own money."

He looked at the last letter, the one to Myrgen. He grew still, swallowing as his eyes flickered in pain. He set the letter down on the table and turned to the windows. His posture had altered, no longer showing the duty-tinged-with-merriment he had shown since his proposal. Now, Charles saw anguish. There was a long silence as Catherine read the letter. When she finished, she looked at her son.

"What do you want to do?"

With a strange and unexpected, yet controlled, authority, he raised his hand. "Please leave me."

Charles the Messenger bowed immediately and Catherine paused, then did likewise. They closed the door and looked at each other. She had left the letters on the table inside.

"Let's give him some time. Have you copied the missives?"

Charles nodded. "All but the one to His Majesty."

"Then return to your duties. I'll wait here."

He nodded and went back down the stairs.

# Sixteen

"I'll not deny my emotions for
the sake of a stranger."
Kali, The Karmic Hand

Alexander looked over the occupied county as he had done almost hourly since arriving at the Benevolent Friar. For the first time, he did not see them. He was seeing the words on the parchment behind him. Catriona's face on the ship, the wind in her hair. She wore it braided at sea, but there were always wisps that escaped her most measured attempts. He remembered her laugh, and her kiss when they finally surrendered to their own desires. He remembered how she looked on the bed beside him. He remembered his anger when he saw her crossing Ashstone's courtyard in Myrgen's blue long coat, the sense of betrayal and fear that she had been stolen from him.

Then he remembered the blood from Gwen. The Granite Arrow had sought his life and Gwen had taken that killing blow for him. The arrow fired by Myrgen to save the woman they both loved. His cheeks felt wet and he caught a tear about to drop from his jaw. He dropped to the floor, letting the loss and despair actually consume him. He thought about Catriona, thought about all he had destroyed and wasted, all the lives he had sacrificed. He cried for Gwen, for Alan, for Catriona. Gwen was her best friend and he had taken that from her. Alan had loved Gwen too.

His obsession was beyond reprehensible.

And he was losing another friend now. Tanglwyst was obviously looking for an escape plan, undoubtedly to go to her people. She didn't seem to think she'd live through it. The barest touch of the idea of her death grazed his mind and all of his angst and fear and despair broke free. Furious tears splashed on his pants and shirt but he let them flow unhindered.

The door opened a tiny bit and Tanglwyst's voice interrupted the room.

"Alex?"

He looked up as she stepped carefully inside, not opening the door enough to permit anyone or anything else. She saw him kneeling on the wooden floor and she went to him, kneeling beside him. He turned to face her as she put an arm across his shoulders. He turned into the gesture and rose up to fully embrace her. He cried until spent and she did not pull away.

"I'm so sorry, my lady. I should not have read your private letter."

She stroked his hair. "No, you probably shouldn't have. But thinking about it now, it was stupid for me to hand it over to the royal messenger. It only makes sense that he give you something that is correspondence between a former enemy of the state and a fugitive from the King's justice."

"You weren't thinking of him like that. You were thinking of him as a brother."

She nodded.

He pulled away. "Did you write Morgan yet?"

She blinked. "No. Not really. He doesn't know much about…"

"Yes, he does." He stood, helping her to her feet. "You should write him. Let him know what's going on. Tell him especially about what happened with Myrgen." His voice wavered for a moment. "And Catriona. He really needs to know."

He went to the table and picked up her letters. He handed her the one to Myrgen. "Make sure this gets sent. He's at Ashstone in Caratia. You may not need the service Tomas and Symonne offer but they will have someone who can go into Caratia, at least."

He looked at the refusal. "Did you mean to have Charles deliver this?"

She shook her head. "Not exactly. I penned it first and set it aside to dry. The letter to Isabella is long and I gathered it by mistake."

"You were so sure about your course by then?"

"Yes." She looked down and reached out for his hand. "Then I felt you fall just now, felt your despair. I don't know if everyone could feel it but Catherine was extremely worried. She didn't even hesitate to admit me."

"You felt my despair?"

"Like you were doing it right in front of me. I could feel your tears on my cheeks. I felt your deep sense of loss. I almost felt you reach out to me, but it was like you pulled away at the last second."

"You didn't need to be bothered with this. After all, you had already made up your mind."

"Yeah."

She looked at him, his red face and puffy eyes. His hair had fallen into his face and he ran his hand through his hair, then wiped his fingers across his cheeks to dry them. His nose was rubbed raw from his sleeve, which was also wet. She shook her head.

"Saint's Blood. This is ridiculous." She reached up and kissed him.

He was surprised for a moment, then drank in the kiss fully. He embraced her, his lips finding her cheek and neck as well. She nuzzled into his neck, returning the embrace. Their lips met again, and he rested his forehead upon hers.

"Please don't leave me."

She shook her head. "I don't think I can."

He looked at her, worried.

"I don't mean like that. You can't compel me anymore, Alex." She kissed his hand. "I want to be here."

He kissed her again and held her close.

"I'm still not marrying you."

He nodded. "Ok."

"I mean it."

"I know."

"And I don't love you."

He smiled. "Liar."

He felt her smile into his shoulder. He stepped back from her. "What do you need from me?"

She touched his cheek. "For now, this will do." She kissed him again. "Soon, I'll need to go to St. Giles. I don't quite know how you want to handle that."

"I don't either, but we'll figure it out together."

A knock interrupted them. Catherine called through the door. "Your Majesty, do you need anything?"

He looked at Tanglwyst. "Do we need anything?"

"I think she's worried about you being alone with a woman in her room."

He looked around. "Oh. Yes, I guess this is her room. Do you want to go elsewhere?"

"Depends upon what we're going to talk about."

She walked over to the door and opened it enough to poke her head out. "Is there any cold water? His Majesty needs to freshen up."

Catherine's voice sounded relieved. "Yes. Of course." Then whispered, "Are you alright?"

Tanglwyst smiled. "We're fine. The letter to my brother brought back old memories."

"Ah. I'll return in a moment."

Tanglwyst closed the door. "Your virtue is intact for another few minutes."

"Well, that's probably for the best. I really should go to my wedding a virgin and not shame my father." He curtsied, then looked back out the window. The sight sobered him as it always did. "I still need to deal with that, and I'm at a complete loss."

She slipped her arm into his and he kissed her hair. "What are your options?"

"Mother wants to send letters. Keep me here in safety."

"But you don't think that's the right course."

He shook his head. "I think it's the Kingly course, but I don't like having my people where I can't help them directly. I'm a little more action oriented."

She smiled. "I know."

"I'm very sorry about this last winter."

"You'll find a way to make it up to me."

He smiled, kissing her. "I will. I promise."

The door opened and Catherine came in with a pitcher and a couple towels. She glanced at the couple, then bustled over to the dresser where the basin and a second pitcher sat. "Do you still need the room to yourself?"

He glanced at Tanglwyst. Her hair shimmered in the candlelight, but he could tell she had not been able to care for herself like she was accustomed. She had only the one set of clothes and they were pants and a shirt instead of a gown like his mother wore. She looked perfectly comfortable though. "Do you need anything, my lady?"

"No. But we need to develop a strategy for that." Tanglwyst nodded to the army. "And we need to stop getting distracted."

Catherine started to leave the room again, but Tanglwyst walked to the door as well. "Your Majesty, take a few minutes. We'll get some food and ale and be back."

Tanglwyst held the door open for Catherine and they left.

# Seventeen

## "Make a companion of Nature, not a slave."
## Shiva, The Karmic Hand

Tanglwyst closed the door to Catherine's chambers and started to go towards the stairs, but Catherine stopped her.

"Do you mind if we have a few words in private?"

Tanglwyst paled a little and Catherine smiled. She went to her son's room and opened the door. "Neutral ground." As Tanglwyst entered, Catherine called down to Ealusaid. "Can you bring us up some food and ale to the Royal Room? Thank you." A nod from the innkeeper released Catherine from her appointed duty and she closed Alexander's door behind her.

"Is this going to be the obligatory death threat if I hurt your son?" Tanglwyst waited until Catherine chose a chair and sat.

"Let's just consider that spoken. I'm sure you've heard it before."

Tanglwyst winced like she had just been slapped, but she hid it from Catherine.

Catherine waved a hand, dismissing the subject. "I want to know what you had planned when you were going to leave."

"Oh." Tanglwyst explained the plan to go to Sovereigna.

Catherine sat back when she was done. "And you know her well enough to think she would agree to this?"

"I think she probably loved her daughter. I think she has heard of her daughter's fate. I also think she has heard of Alexander's treatment of Elizabeth's execution."

"I know her too. We used to correspond regularly. My greatest fear is that she will require the life of Alexander in exchange for Elizabeth's."

"Then tell her the revenge has already been extracted when she caused Charles' death. Her child for yours that she killed."

Catherine glanced down. "I'm not sure that will work. Charles isn't dead so if she has a way to tell that, she can still make that demand."

"Ah. And if she does?"

"Then we will have war."

Tanglwyst sat back in her chair. "What do you think we should do?"

Catherine shrugged. "Give her a suitable substitute."

"Will that work?"

"I don't know. If she will accept you as her hostage, then it should be you. My concern is that she will not accept you as a hostage and will want to kill you. I don't think that will sit well with Alexander right now."

"What alternatives do we have? Besides war?"

"Defeating her somehow." Catherine frowned. "How would you do it if this were business?"

"You mean a hostile attack?"

"Yes."

Tanglwyst smiled. "Well, I used to have this Vincenzian glassworks factory. Beautiful works of art came from there. I also had a rival named Urien Atreides. Every year, Urien would make a run at getting the glassworks factory. About every other year, he succeeded. Then, Isabella became my lawyer and managed to get a handle on the factory and defeated his machinations. We then married and combined our companies."

"You're married?"

She nodded. "At least I was about three years ago. I haven't seen him since. I think he has become a pirate or something by now. I've had controlling interest in the company all this time."

"Interesting."

Tanglwyst squinted at Catherine. "So I think that's the answer. Get a DeMedici on the task and let them find the way through. Then marriage." She smiled. "You wouldn't happen to know any, would you?"

"DeMedicis?" Catherine smiled, stroking her chin. "I've got a guy." She pointed at Tanglwyst. "But she's more than just a Queen. She's also a Fae Worshipper."

Tanglwyst put her elbows on her knees, steepling her fingers by her lips. "I don't know anything about Fae." She pointed her fingers at Catherine. "But that look says you do."

Catherine smiled, an idea forming. "I do. So tell me, what do you know about this holy power of Alexander's?"

Tanglwyst waited while Alexander actually hugged his mother goodbye. They had done as much as they could at the inn. It was time to leave and see what could be done in St. Giles. Although there were several horses stabled at the Benevolent Friar now, they decided against using them. Patrolman Allen Hobbs had told them the route he had used to get near the port town and horses would be an impairment to that kind of travel. They would be cutting in and out of the woods between Patras and Cliffbase and they were better off on foot where they could hide.

"Are you sure you won't take a few guards?" She kept her voice low so they were making as little sound as possible. There were still guards at the front of the Inn but they were stationed outside the doors, watching the fires.

"No, Mother. We need to maintain the impression I am still here. That's why we're leaving before dawn and going on foot. Make sure Charles is seen in the window every day."

"I shall. Please be careful. I have lost enough children."

"We will."

She turned to Tanglwyst. "You take care as well." Catherine hugged Tanglwyst, which caught her by surprise. While they embraced, Catherine whispered, "Remember what we planned."

Tanglwyst nodded. "I won't forget."

They parted and Tanglwyst and Alexander pulled up their hoods against the pre-dawn dew. They had both changed into dark green clothes that would give them cover in the shadows and help even if sunlight caught them. They nodded their readiness. Catherine went back inside and went to the front doors. They heard her asking the guards something, so they took their chance and slipped across the road to the south. They kept to the woods, taking advantage of the nearly new moon, which was why they chose this day instead of any previous ones. This would give them three nights to get past any patrols by the Fae army. Allen had given them a hand drawn map that marked shelters he had erected to hide him from the road so he could rest. There were several right up to the main road into St. Giles.

They each had packs with food they had secured the day before. Catherine, who had an uncanny knowledge of fairy tale creatures, had assured them that some of the monsters had excellent senses of smell so they were packaged with herbs to help the packs smell like the woods. It might affect the flavor but the food would still be good. They moved as quick as the lack of light would allow, which still managed to put a significant distance between them and the Inn when dawn finally arrived. They found one of the blinds Allen had mentioned and stopped to rest. They each had water but Allen had also left provisions in case they were needed. That was promising.

They didn't speak, both worried their voices might carry to a passing patrol. Here, this far from the actual army, they weren't really at risk, but getting into the habit of silence now would help maintain it when they were closer and under more stress. They shared a comfortable closeness though. Tanglwyst still could feel his emotions and that helped her understand what he was going through. He seemed likewise to be able to understand something about her, because he didn't push when she needed space and didn't leave when she needed closeness. She didn't know if he was just gifted, or if there was more to it. She also didn't care.

They got back on the move and covered even more ground. By the time dusk arrived, they were across from the army and able to smell their campfires. They found another blind and this one had a bedroll. They broke silence for the first time, keeping their voices low.

"How do you want to set up watches?" Tanglwyst glanced at the army through the trees.

"Are you tired?"

"Yes, but we both are." She looked around the blind. "Wait. What's this?"

She tugged on a couple ties inside and unfurled a blanket with leaves of fabric attached to it. They perfectly mirrored the larger bushes and shrubs in the area. The edge of it was attached to the blind and when it was unrolled, it hid the back opening. Inside the blind, with the flap down, there were peepholes on the sides and front. She could easily see someone or something approaching. She motioned to Alexander to join her and showed him.

"Allen is a genius."

"I know."

The bedroll covered an area of gathered moss and it was far more comfortable than she expected. Still not a bed, but she wasn't going to be sleeping deep in this occupied zone. There was barely room for both of them, this clearly being something Allen set up for himself alone, but if they stayed close it would be fine.

He gestured to the bed and sat beside her, watching the flames across the road. She held his hand and closed her eyes. She drifted in and out of sleep, starting awake at every crack of a stick real or imagined. Alexander would hold her hand or stroke her hair to calm her and eventually, she actually rested.

She awoke in the middle of the night to Alexander nodding off. She slipped him to the bed amidst minor protests, then got up and went outside to urinate. She could hear the army across the way, half earth-shaking snores, half grunting laughter and chatter. She finished peeing and was about to stand when she heard the grunting and sniffing of a large beast. Her hood was down but the lack of moon made the forest just shadows against shadows. Then she saw movement, a place where the fires across the way were blotted out, then came back into view. She slipped to her knees off the fallen log where she had done her business, fastening her pants as quickly as possible while still being quiet. She didn't look down at her hands, keeping her eyes on the fires, and she felt certain she had skipped a few buttons or put them in the wrong holes in her haste.

She stayed low to the ground and near the trees, stopping to listen every couple of feet. She got to the blind without incident when she heard the grunting and sniffing coming from the log where she had just been. She didn't know what had discovered her pee, but she wanted to make sure it didn't find her. She checked her knees to make sure she hadn't knelt in it, thereby leaving a trail right to the blind. Her pants were dry but when she checked her boots, she found them damp. She swore to herself and reached into the blind for the small stash of water Allen had left there.

She slipped from the blind and crawled away, edging towards the road and the fires and making a little noise to draw the unknown away from the blind. She drug her feet a little to get the urine off her boots. Once she was within sight of the road, she stopped and poured water on her boots to rinse the last of the urine from them. She put the waterskin in her doublet and climbed the tree she had leaned against. She only got about ten feet up when the thing making the noise came through the trees.

She saw in the starlight of the road a half-ogre, if the fairy tale drawings from her childhood could be believed. It had a huge head and bulbous nose but the body was almost human proportions. Granted, a sizable human, like Michael, but still just human. He sniffed the tree with his huge nose then around it, trying to pick up the trail. He wandered around for what seemed like most of the night but was probably only a couple minutes, then went back to the road. It pulled something from a tree branch and started moving back towards the fires. When it got to the road she saw it had killed a deer and was dragging it as easily as a toddler with a rag doll.

She waited until she couldn't hear or see it, and then waited a bit more to see if it had a hunting buddy. When she saw and heard nothing else, she got down and returned to the blind. Alexander had not stirred and she was so grateful, she curled up beside him and put an arm across him. He took her hand in his while not waking and she fell asleep.

# Eighteen

"Danger within and danger without."
Kali, The Karmic Hand

Alexander woke to Tanglwyst's exit. Her movements were cautious and he could feel her apprehension. He sat up and looked through the leaves in the blind. He could see the morning movements of dozens of monsters a mile away but the encampment stretched much farther than he could see. He poked his head out to see where Tanglwyst had gone. She was checking the ground near a fallen log and he slipped out, glancing behind them.

"What is it?" His voice was a whisper since she had obviously found something.

"Just checking something. I used this last night and a half ogre almost caught me. I hid in a tree to evade it."

*"What?"*

She cast a nervous look around at the hissing whisper and she gestured for him to keep his voice down.

"You didn't wake me?"

"There was no need. It's not like it chased me and I narrowly escaped. It was sniffing around here and followed a trail I accidentally left."

He looked around and saw part of a large foot print in some dried mud. He sighed, then looked at the lady.

She reached out and squeezed his hand.

He understood the gesture, but it didn't make him feel any better. Still, there wasn't time to dwell on it now. She gestured to the blind and he went back and gathered their things. She came along a few moments later, straightening her pants. It was his turn for privacy as she reset the blind to the status it was in before they arrived. He had to admit that the flap on the blind made it practically invisible, and if Allen planned to use it again, he would need to be able to find it.

They set off through the woods at a brisk walk, keeping low to stay in the shadows. The area had shrubs and spotty sunlight, but it was not impassable. They kept sight of the road to avoid going too far towards Patras, until Tanglwyst pulled up short, her eyes on the valley. She squinted at the army area and pointed. Alexander could see a husk of some building in the distance and he felt her heart beating stronger in fear. Had she felt like this in the night, he would have been startled out of a dead sleep.

She looked up at a tree, then at the building. She went to the tree and started climbing. He put a hand on her ankle, his eyes questioning. He flicked a glance up the tree, and pointed to his chest. She shook her head, then pointed to his eyes and to the army. He nodded. She climbed and got to a place that satisfied her. She pulled out a small spyglass he had forgotten they received from another patrolman, and looked across the field. She stayed up there for several minutes before climbing back down. The look on her face was not less troubling when she landed beside him. She handed him the spyglass and pointed to the tree. He climbed up to the same place and put the glass to his eye.

He saw a wide variety of sizable creatures that seemed to be bred for hideous ferocity. A few were playing with short swords that looked like mere daggers in their clawed hands. One of those dropped the sword on one of the others, cutting off a thumb. The thumb bled for a few seconds, before it started to grow back. The monsters laughed at the game and the process started again. Beyond them was a large, burnt husk of a building. The mansion was well into the valley with the signs of vast vineyards all around it. Some of the vines were still intact, despite the encampment around them, but whole acres of crops were lost on the other side. All that was left of the home was the hearth fireplaces, of which there were several, and a couple timbers that still gave off a little smoke.

He looked down at the lady, who pointed to the northwest. He put the glass again to his eye and looked where she indicated. There were people moving about in the village, but he could not tell if they were human or monster. He looked to the north more and saw a pavilion that was beyond the scope of beauty. It was gold and silver, and had several rooms and turrets. He could even see dragon heads on the top of the poles, and they seemed to be occasionally spewing harmless fire.

*That must be the Krakten Queen.*

He knew they had nothing so resplendent in the Castellan's Hold, but then again, they had no reason to. He hoped no one saw that and expected Mervolingia to match it. He wasn't even certain how to try and with them having to field an army now. If he couldn't solve this diplomatically, there wouldn't be enough money for extravagances, especially with the Papal City inaccessible. He climbed down and handed the glass back to Tanglwyst. He wanted to talk but he honestly had nothing to say. She seemed to understand and nodded. She squeezed his hand and he took her in his arms. He could sense her concern about her household and he tried to comfort her as best he could. He held her for a few minutes until they felt the need to move on.

They continued their trek, but they ended up stopping and hiding several times now that the Fae army was mobile and awake. Some of them had large eyes and those seemed to be especially good at spotting movement. Three of these shot some arrows at a smoky sky, then a few seconds later, three large geese hit the ground dead. They fell from such a height that their bones snapped upon impact, which seemed to delight the monsters. Alexander and Tanglwyst were sure to be hidden and still whenever they caught sight of those after that.

The exaggerated features seemed to dictate the skill. Tanglwyst recognized some with bulbous noses, and they both were extra quiet and still when a party of rabbit-eared beasts trotted past the perimeter. The monsters seemed to stay on the far side of the road but it was clearly by choice and nothing else. The couple barely managed to avoid a hunting party of tusked pig creatures that emerged from the trees in front of them. The pigs were hauling a dead boar between them on a pole in a strange display of cannibalism. Halfway through the day, the couple located a blind of Allen's that had been crushed and ransacked, and that made them mindful that the camouflage wasn't always a benefit.

When dusk approached, activity picked up. The hunting parties had submitted their prizes and the chefs of the defense force returned them ready to roast. Singing and dancing became the new mayhem, something the groups settled into as routine. Tanglwyst and Alexander spent nearly half their daylight stopped so the opportunity to cover some ground the second night made them almost reckless. They ended up resting when they couldn't travel unseen in the daylight and moving in the shadows during the night hours. The merriment let them slip by guard patrols and by midnight, they could see the lights of the city streets.

Tanglwyst started to head into town but Alexander put a hand on her shoulder. They were far enough from the army to be able to speak but he still kept his voice low.

"Remember the border?"

She stopped, the blood running from her face as she recalled the tale of the town held hostage. She swallowed and looked around. "There's no Mervol presence here yet. What are we going to do?"

He looked around, then nodded to the trees towards the cliffs overlooking the sea. "I have a place we can go. I think it's far enough away from the town to be safe. This way."

The lion was huge. Every time he looked behind him, Michael could see it. It was no longer chasing him because it no longer had to. It was large enough to more than dominate the horizon, it *was* the horizon. He could not look behind him and not see this beast. He ran forward, watching it and when it stood and raised its paw, he screamed out.

Hands grabbed his shoulders and spun him around. He looked into the eyes of a Nubian woman, her hair in thin dreadlocks. She was older, probably about sixty, but her hands were strong and muscular. She stopped him, shaking him to get his attention.

"Michael! Why are you running?"

Michael opened his eyes and looked at the small fire rocks in the shelter. Raymond had apparently built these a day's ride apart because he and James had encountered three of them now. Water, fire rocks that warmed with sparks from a flint and steel, even once a bag of jerky though neither of them could identify the animal. Every day felt and looked the same, every night was eerily quiet, every nightmare, the lion got bigger. This was the first time he encountered the woman though.

Nubian to be sure, but obviously from a different area than him. Her lips were thinner as was her hair, though those could have been from age. Her eyes had experience and knowledge. She was not a slave raised where she currently lived. She had been through a lot, probably more than he had. Her eyes, for being so experienced, were also very kind. He hoped he would get some guidance from her in the dream.

No, at more than twice his age, she had *definitely* been through more. Myrgen had taken his life from potentially being a nightmare to living and working in the Mervol palace. He had seen other Nubians in the world, but he had never been able to connect or talk with any of them. Charles had a problem with slaves and his distaste drove them from social climbing households all over Patras. Catherine's family had multiple slaves but she had none personally. She was where Charles got his dislike of them. Charles had insisted Myrgen employ Michael at the palace the instant he was brought there. Myrgen, of course, had no problem with that.

He hoped to see her again and this time, when he rolled over to go back to sleep, he didn't dread the darkness.

# Nineteen

## "Sleep brings peace, and waking brings joy."
## Shiva, The Karmic Hand

It took about half an hour to find it in the dark but Alexander came across the cabin overlooking the sea. A cove that could conceal a moderate-sized ship lay below and the way to it was hidden from the road by a half mile of woods.

"I haven't been here in some time. I hope it is not in too much disrepair." He entered the cabin and dared to breathe in, looking for Catriona's scent. It was blissfully absent, and he exhaled in relief. He wasn't certain he could have stayed if he smelled her.

"This is good," Tanglwyst looked around. "Very secluded, yet still close to town. Defensible."

"Yes. I'm not sure if being a fort was part of its design, but it will serve us for now."

"So, how are we going to do this? Shifts again?"

He shrugged. "We could. Though I'm not sure it would matter much. This place is defensible, but it's also a funnel. If they find us, we're caught. Unless you wanted to throw us both off a cliff."

She smiled. "Don't steal the covers or I might."

She sat on the edge of the bed, fighting with her coat. The buttons refused to come apart and she exhaled, frustrated.

He raised an eyebrow, "Do you need help?" He felt as if he should be dwelling more on the army that was situated not much more than an hour from them, but the woman before him seemed to dissolve his rational thought.

"Apparently." She closed her eyes. "I don't know. I guess I'm just…" She opened her eyes. "Do you think they got out?"

"Do you want me to check?"

Tanglwyst's eyes glittered with resisted tears. "That's right, you can do that, can't you?" She clenched her fists, trying to stop them from shaking. "Please."

It took a bit but she went through everyone she knew. Many were missing. He returned to undoing her buttons while she let her tears fall on his sleeves.

"Sorry to be so..."

"Hey." He lifted her chin. "Don't think the worst. The ones that are missing, like Helen and Matt, might not have given me their fealty. I only saw a large grouping of people, in town but if they were loyal to you, they would have withdrawn their fealty when you were accused. I have no doubt that information was already here. Gomez is trapped in that town as well. I'm more impressed that he's still alive. And I think I can only feel about half the folks in that city."

She sighed, then nodded. "You're right." She lay back, stretching and he caught himself admiring her form. She looked at him and he looked away, blushing.

"Forgive me, my Lady. I'm a bit distracted. I think the circumstances are making me act different than normal."

"You mean monster armies don't usually draw out your more romantic side?"

He smiled and stood. "I'll give you some privacy to get yourself settled."

"Thank you."

He stepped out of the room, dropping the curtain across the open doorway. He didn't know what was going on in his head. He was concerned that entering this place where he spent those magical nights with Catriona would bring back his longing for her full force, but his inappropriate thoughts were more on this Lady than that one. He hoped his assessment was accurate regarding her people. If she had suffered the number of losses that her tally indicated, then the threat of war was beyond just occupation. He wasn't sure a diplomatic option would be open if Sovereigna had murdered Tanglwyst's household.

His hands balled into fists as he felt anger at the possibility, and he calmed it lest she feel it. He didn't want her acting rashly because he was angry. He needed to keep his negative emotions in check. The Lady didn't need more emotions. He marveled at her ability to control her fear in the woods that first night. He was having a very difficult time. Then he realized that she was probably feeling that same worry and anger. That was why this was so hard. They were feeding each other's fear and sorrow.

He cleared his mind and unclenched his fists. He thought of better things, the water, the sounds of the soft wind through the trees outside. They filtered the sound from the village and the army, so much so that the place seemed peaceful. They could scream in pain or passion and be safe here. He knew the latter to be true for certain.

He shook his head. "Best keep that to myself."

Tanglwyst stepped out of the room. She had shed the coat, boots and socks. "Alex? Did you say something?"

"Just talking to myself. I'll keep it internal. Please. Get some rest."

She walked over to the cold hearth and draped her socks over the kettle hook. She set her boots beside the door. "Are you planning on staying out here?"

"Let me have a bit of time to myself to figure that out, if you don't mind."

"Just so you know, it's alright if you join me. I feel safe with you."

He kissed her hand. "Thank you, my Lady."

She bowed and he returned it, then she ducked back behind the curtain.

He stared out the window over the kitchen counter and watched the sea in the moonlight. He spent about an hour letting the sea hypnotize him, guide him, settle him. He could feel Tanglwyst's presence within him and it was comforting. She was hurting, and he needed to be there for her while not taking away her power in this situation. She had a calm within her, a plan, and he needed to trust that she knew what she was doing. He would find a peaceful solution if at all possible. Then they would go to her home and rebuild.

When he finally pushed away from the counter, he felt he could rest. When he came into the room, she was asleep, facing away from the door. He got out of his own coat and boots to make himself comfortable. He settled into the other side of the bed best he could, avoiding jostling her too much, and keeping space between them.

She rolled over, bumping into his arm. She opened her eyes. "Oh sorry..."

"You're fine. I'm sorry I woke you."

"Did you sort your thoughts properly?" The curtain on the window was open, letting in the starlight reflected on the sea. It provided modest sight once one's eyes had fully adjusted, enough to see a bit of color. She looked at him with eyes bright and kind, hair flowing behind her. She had removed the customary braid for the night, and the waves of red on the pillow complimented her eyes.

"Mostly."

She smiled. "Good." She closed her eyes, reaching over and taking his hand. She brought it to her lips, then set it back down.

He smiled in return. "Thank you for your concern"

"Mmhmm..." As she drifted off, she kept hold of his hand, her grip comfortable.

He watched her sleep, not nearly as tired as he should be. They had been in peril for days and the stress would cause anyone to break down once they had a chance to relax, yet he was still thrumming with energy. He wanted to talk, to kiss, to make love with this woman. He remembered his apprehension in St. Andrew, when he broke the spell the goblin put on her after attacking her. The memory brought with it everything he had done wrong and he was reminded of why she had refused his proposal, why she had been willing to leave him and go to her death travelling alone alongside Fae-held lands. He was as much a monster as those beasts beholden to the Krakten Queen. He just had a better disguise.

Tanglwyst stirred, opening her eyes to see him looking at her. He smiled and stroked her cheek. "Hi."

She smiled. "Hello. Have we met? You look... familiar..." She raised her hand, pointing at his face in a circular motion. "Something here... I can't quite place it... I think the smile is throwing me off."

"Really? I've found it quite common of late," he kissed her hand, "ever since I was thrown out a second story window."

"Sort of redefined you as a person?"

"There's a good chance it rattled my brain." He winked.

"That would explain a lot." She frowned. "Have you slept at all?"

"I think I dozed off momentarily once or twice."

"Is it because I'm here? Do you need a bit more privacy?"

"No, no it's not that. I enjoy having you so close."

"Then what?"

"I decided that watching you rest and taking in your splendor was far more important than sleep."

She closed her eyes. "Ah. That explains it." She rolled over onto her back. "I'm still asleep and this is a dream."

"You normally dream about me?" His fingers traced her shoulder.

"Mmm... I refuse to answer that on the grounds that you'll turn into a bear and chase me around while wearing an odd hat."

He put his hand to his chest in mock offense. "You think my hat is odd? I spent hours picking it out, trying it on in front of the other bears to see what they thought. And here you've gone and broken my confidence." He sighed, defeated.

Her laugh broke the night apart and she turned her head, looking at him. Once again, he was struck with the urge to kiss her.

"Now, if this is a dream," His hand found its way to the back of her neck, meshing with her hair, "you should have no qualms with this." He pulled her head to his and his lips found hers. Her response was tentative at first, nervous, but then she likewise brought her hand to his hair, prolonging the kiss. Her touch was powerful and she smelled of vanilla and desire.

"So, did I become a bear?"

She smiled, stroking his face. "No, but I haven't given up on that as a possible outcome. There *is* a Fae Queen nearby."

"Then let's give her another Queen to talk to."

"You don't have another Queen."

He looked at her hair and face, luminescent in the dim light. "I'd really like to change that."

She sighed. "Alex. I can't do that. I shouldn't even be doing this much. You have a duty to this kingdom and you being available might be necessary in this upcoming conflict."

"You think Sovereigna has another daughter?" His brow furrowed at the thought.

"No, but she might have a niece or something. Or she may make the request that you marry her."

"Marry a woman as old as my mother?"

Tanglwyst smiled. "You've never seen her."

He watched the pale light play across her features. "I don't need to. I already have the most beautiful woman in the world right here."

"Wow. You really *do* know just what to say." She touched his cheek. "Saint's blood, I want to just go with you, to indulge in your offer and think of you as mine."

"Then do it. Claim me, my Lady. Make me yours."

She rose up and put her hands on either side of him, lowering herself to kiss him. He gathered her hair in his hand, his lips reveling in hers. He felt his body responding to her and ran his fingers along her side, very tempted to brush her breast with his thumb. He was straining already and sat up to flip her onto her back. Her hair splayed out upon the pillows and for just a moment, he remembered another woman in that exact same position. In the dark, they could be the same person.

He sat back, breaking away. "This is not a good idea."

She raised up on her elbows. "What do you mean?"

He didn't want to tell her the truth, that he was afraid he would call her Catriona in his passion. Instead, he went a different way. "I have gone so far as to propose and you refused me. I need to be more mindful of your decision. This feels too much like coercion on my part."

"Alexander, I'm quite capable of having sex with a man and not falling in love."

He kissed her hand. "I'm not so strong. I kissed you once to break a spell and in so doing, I cast another. It would be beyond inappropriate to use this situation to satisfy my own needs without regards to your wishes. Once was enough and frankly, I'm not sure I've regained your trust yet."

"This seems like an awful lot of thinking for a man who couldn't even remember a dustpan with a broom a few days ago."

"I'm trying to change that." He touched her face. "You deserve better."

She sat up and looked at him. The dark was enough to hide his own guilt but he started to worry she could read him. She studied him and then nodded. "Alright. Let's see how this looks in the morning, ok?"

"I would appreciate that."

"Do you need to be in another room, or can you stay here?"

"I would love to wake up again by your side."

"That's the right choice." She let him put his arm around her and she lay on his chest. "But expect no mercy if you turn into a bear."

He smiled, nodding. "Duly noted."

She settled into a comfortable place and he settled into sleep.

# Twenty

## "There are only two types of politicians – those who give bribes and those who take them."
## Kali, The Karmic Hand

"Your Lordship! There's a missive from the King!" The messenger stood panting in the doorway. He looked like he had run from the messenger office on the first floor all the way up to the King's Chamber where Dominic had set up shop. He reached out for the missive and scowled at the broken seal.

"Why was this opened?"

"The missives came to the Grande Guarde's office. Lieutenant Richeleiu opened them."

*Well, I might have another to drop off in the sealed room.*

There were two letters within.

*"To His Lordship Dominic D'Medici, Chancellor of Mervolingia,*

*An army from Krakte is surrounding the port of St. Giles. If any missives have been delivered to the Palace, please get them immediately to the Benevolent Friar Inn on the road to the Papal City. The Messenger Office in Cliffbase is currently handling correspondence until such time as one can be set up for the military near St. Giles. Please use the enclosed letter to garner the army and send them to the occupied zone.*

*In addition, there is a considerable stipend with this missive for the transport of the body of Elizabeth of Krakte to the area as well. She needs to be reassembled as best she can and her bones treated and laid out. Please oversee this.*

*I can be reached for the next few tendays at the Benevolent Friar. After that time, I shall be on the road to St. Giles, awaiting the army. Please dispatch the reserves in Patras to that end now.*

*His Majesty ad Lidum Alexander Angloume"*

The second missive was in Catherine's own hand.

*"To whomever is the bearer of this letter,*

*Please grant a sum of Thirty Thousand Ducats from my Personal Accounts to aid this person in whatever endeavor they need.*

*My scent is my marker.*

*Catherine D'Medici, Queen Mother"*

He sniffed the page and it smelled of lemons and vanilla. He figured it was some sort of verification for the bank. He glanced at the messenger.

"Bring me everything that has come for His Majesty at once."

"Yes sir."

The young man left, closing the doors behind him.

*Thirty thousand ducats!* He could pay off his debt to his relatives and still have twenty thousand to do with as he wished.

*But you still have to rally the army first.* The voice that hissed in his mind was familiar and wise. He knew it wasn't real but it seemed to have very good advice. He went to the door and opened it. "Fetch Lieutenant Richelieu for me."

The guard on the left nodded and bowed, leaving just the guard on the right.

"Get my valet at once."

The other guard bowed and left and Dominic closed the door. Thirty thousand ducats. There had to be a way to get all that money for himself. He just needed to think. *Elizabeth's body to be delivered to St. Giles.* He could see to that personally, ensuring every dime of that went to him. The amulet made that easy. He could just grab her body in the night and go. He would do that tonight, once he got all the missives. He could be there by dawn, indispensable to His Majesty.

Except he'd never been to the Benevolent Friar.

He shrugged. "No matter. I'll go to the area outside of St. Giles. I've been there enough times."

A knock on the door admitted Lieutenant Nina Richelieu. She came in, all tall and willowy, her uniform crisp and clean. Her smugness irritated Dominic beyond control. She gave a stiff salute. "You called?"

"Do you know how to contact the General of the Mervol Army?"

She nodded, again crisp and professional. More than she had ever been. It made her even more loathsome. "Do so. Tell him to get the army to St. Giles. And hurry up. He needs to be there before I am or I'll have your badge."

"At once, sir." She gave another crisp salute and spun on her heel. She left with as much efficiency and she entered.

Dominic smiled. There was no way she could get the army there before him. He fingered the amulet. His little friend here could ruin her, and if she fought the dismissal, he would simply put her with Henri and his wench. Out of sight, out of mind.

His valet showed up in the door and bowed. "You sent for me, Sir?"

Dominic was glad the word had gotten around to call him "Sir". He had been sure to frighten his valet and a few other folks by taking them through the shadows. He demanded respect or he would show them the pits of Hell within themselves. It had worked well. Fear of him was affording him the respect he deserved and it had apparently gotten all the way to Nina. Good.

"I am going to meet His Majesty in St. Giles. Get my things ready and a carriage immediately. I will leave at dawn, with or without it."

The lad blinked in a stutter. "O... of course. Right away, Sir." He ran out of the room and towards the Chancellor's Quarters.

A messenger arrived with all of the letters to the Crown tied in a bundle. Dominic frowned. He was going to open them and see what was being said. With them bundled like this, that would be a problem. The top of the bundle had the royal wax seal on it too. His enemies were clearly trying to thwart him.

There was an inn at the crossroads on the way to St. Giles. Tanglwyst had invested in it to give it a boost about a decade ago and he knew she had a room set aside for her use about this time of year. The sailing season was already in full swing but they were usually accommodating regardless of the season. Or he could really show off his power and require a pavilion set up for His Majesty's Chancellor and have it ready immediately. He simply didn't know where the royal pavilions were stored.

"Boy."

The messenger looked at him.

"Where would one get a pavilion for His Majesty?"

"The Royal Castellan, sir. He's in charge of all of the regalia outside of the palace."

"Good. Send him to me."

The boy nodded and left.

Dominic almost danced with glee. Not only would he show up before the general, ensuring Nina's dismissal, but to be there with a full pavilion and everything set up would be even better. He would tell the Castellan to assemble all the parts out in front of the palace before sunset, then he would take his valet and the other two servants he had traumatized, and take Elizabeth's body and the whole lot to St Giles. The servants would set up the pavilion in the night and he would be nice and cozy, with the King's prize and missives a tenday before the army could assemble. The approval of the King would be assured and he would be able to rub it in everyone's face.

There was a part of him that fought the vindictive, petty egotism he was displaying, but he had long since stopped listening to it. Once Alexander knew he could rely upon Dominic, he would endorse the marriage to a prominent member of the Mandian royal house. Why, Dominic and Alexander could become immediate family. He would never again have to concern himself with being at risk. Maybe he should pay a visit upon Catriona and do away with her, getting the Giovanni fortune she stole as well. Just because she might look like the slave his father married to offend his family, she couldn't be any real kin. That priest had lied. Dominic just didn't know why.

In the end, he had been denied his fortune, but his current plan would wash all that away in a single night. And the best part is that it would be coming from Catherine's own coffers and not the kingdom's. He would get more in one night than he had embezzled from Tanglwyst in all the years he'd worked for her, and Othon could do nothing about it. As he reveled in the idea, he went to the desk. He wrote down all the money he would make and all the power he would have, the quill starting to shred by the time he finished, though he had hardly used any of the ink, apparently. He had thought repeatedly about locking the doors to keep out whomever kept refilling the ink, but in the end, that's all they ever did. His method of keeping his letters in the locked drawer had kept anyone from touching his missives, but it didn't stop them from refilling the ink.

By the time the Castellan arrived, he had a thorough list of his accolades in the pocket of his Fuccochio coat, and a list of everything he needed for the Royal encampment. He told the Castellan, whose name he didn't even care about, to get everything ready to go by dusk. The man frowned, and Dominic snarled the order, projecting his authority. The man's face contorted as if to complain about his treatment but Dominic held up the missive from the King.

"His Majesty has demanded I get his encampment ready immediately. You don't want to go against His Majesty's wishes, do you? After all, I will be seeing him soon. There is a war party encamped upon the county line of Bordeaux. Unless you want to be on the front lines of the battle, I suggest you do what you're told."

The man stiffened and bowed, leaving before Dominic could get any worse. That probably was for the best.

# Twenty-One

## "He who holds the ladder is as bad as the thief."
## Kali, The Karmic Hand

Tanglwyst awoke when the sunlight brought morning to the room. She opened her eyes and looked around. She was still in Alexander's arms but he was sound asleep. She realized that the arm she was laying upon was probably likewise. He didn't stir when she got up and she was glad for that. She noticed he slept quite deep when they had been together, yet she also remembered seeing him around the palace at all hours of the night over the winter after she started seeing Nicolai again.

*Well, he's in a far more stressful situation these days. It shouldn't surprise me that his body is giving out.*

She wanted to aid him in dealing with the invasion but seeing the soldiers up close had made her waver in her confidence. She closed her eyes and calmed her breathing so as not to wake him, then got up and slipped into the other room. She put on her socks and boots, expecting to step outside to do her morning business when she felt a light draft from a partially closed door.

A back room with a door and a large barrel tub revealed a privy with a pit apparently dumping into the sea below, and reveled in the convenience of not having to empty a chamberpot. Clearly there was fresh water nearby since sea water was not a useful cleansing agent. She would look for that when she finished.

The bath room had several tiny treasures that would be nice to use, a sea sponge and what looked like lavender soap. A couple small chests and one larger one revealed towels with ornate embroidery the likes of which she did not recognize. She would have to ask Alexander which friend gifted them to him. Whomever she was, her style was unique. The cottage was quaint and simple, with intelligent features. She wondered what it would be like to live here all the time.

She went back to the main room and looked out the window above the sink onto the sea. She was glad to be here. St. Giles was always her first stop of the year and the Sulocco should be in port within the ten-day, if it wasn't already here. She thought of his face as he toured the magnificent decks and passenger berths, saw the elegant woodwork and ate the delicious and exotic foods she enjoyed on her travels. It was her greatest inanimate joy. Well, one of them anyway. Not that he would be able to tell the difference at first. Her twins were designed that way.

In every port, there was something personal and unique that was the specialty of the village. In St. Giles, it was the famous Wise Wench Tavern. In Pardua, in the Storm Catch, there was a restaurant that specialized in exotic fish and fowl that the storms brought in. They were always harvested humanely, which was why she supported that business. She could afford to be selective in her patronage. She had worked tirelessly to do so.

She heard him stir and her heart raced, but the sounds returned to sleeping instead of to getting up and joining her. The feel of his lips last night returned to her mind and her body responded like it just happened again. He had wanted her as much as she wanted him, she was certain, but something had stayed his hand. She fought the self-doubt that beat at her consciousness. He said he was showing her respect, she was going to take him at his word. He had been feeling guilt when he spoke of putting the Summoning Spell on her. She knew he regretted all that had gone before and despite her better judgment, she forgave him. She took a deep breath and shook her head.

There was no doubt. She was in love.

She pushed back from the counter and opened the cupboards, looking for tea. Such staples were often kept in containers against the weather, especially in a seaside place like this. This cupboard held a few provisions, but that wasn't unexpected since he said it had been a while since he had been here. She figured there would be a few dried goods left behind and often around here, so close to the Yorkish-Krakten border, that meant tea.

She found a dark pouch which had a foreign scent. Again, she couldn't place the origins of the tea, and it confused her. She knew her imported items. She could identify glass from Veniche versus Florentine, gold from Mande versus gold from Mervolingia and the fact there were two things in this cabin she could not identify disturbed her. She opened the other cupboard on the opposite side and saw earthenware of the same ornate design as the embroidery. Whoever stocked this place apparently loved colorful flower motifs. She turned over the plate to find the maker's mark and found she did not know the symbol. She looked at all the pieces and they were all made by the same person. The quality of the work and the beauty of the design indicated this was a master craftsman.

She put the dishes back in the cupboard, leaving the mugs she had grabbed for the tea on the counter, and blinked, realization dawning. Simple but sturdy furnishings capable of making a long, overseas trip. Unfamiliar items with identical motifs. Unknown teas. There was only one place in the world she had been denied access in all her travels and all her business dealings.

Caratia.

He had brought her to *their* home. The home where they had expressed their love for each other. And he didn't tell her.

She leaned against the counter, suddenly ill. She wasn't even sure if this was his in any way. There were no signs of his touch at all. Nothing Mervolingian was here, save the ground upon which it sat and with Catriona being a Land Worshipper, Tanglwyst couldn't even be certain of that. She now wasn't even certain he was kissing her last night. He was probably pretending she was Catriona. In the dark, he couldn't have told the difference.

*That was why he stopped. Not out of respect for me, but out of respect for her.*

She fought the tears and took a breath. The air was stifling and she opened the door and stepped outside. She couldn't hear anything above the sea and she felt the need to run. She closed the door so as not to wake him and ran as long as she could through the woods. After a while, she stopped, her breathing labored through the sobs. She put her back against a tree and slid down it. How could she be so stupid? He wasn't over Catriona. He was barely able to deal with a letter to Myrgen about the woman. And he was now laying in the bed they shared. She knew from personal experience how hard it was to spend time in a bed where you held the one you loved more than anything. Her own first love had been ripped from her and she was left to cry into his pillow every night until his scent faded. She knew that pain.

She wasn't willing to be a substitute for anyone else.

A door banging caught her attention and she craned to see what made it. A small house door had opened and a young Nubian woman in her twenties came around the side to gather some wood that was in a stack nearby. She looked up and saw Tanglwyst, then dropped the wood she had managed to grab.

"My lady, are you hurt?"

She shook her head, standing. "No. I'm not. At least, not physically."

"Where did you come from?"

She glanced back at the woods but decided not to reveal Alexander's hiding place. "The coast. I was just clearing my head. Forgive me for bothering you."

She turned and looked around for where to go now. She couldn't go back to Catriona's home and she couldn't go elsewhere. She decided to keep walking and started to leave.

"My lady. Stop!"

She spun to look at the woman, her heart racing with fear. "What?"

The woman picked up a branch and tossed it behind Tanglwyst. Vicious energy grasped the branch and caused it to burst into flames. It hit the ground and went out, an instantly smoking husk of carbon.

"You've entered the Queen's control. You can't leave."

Alexander started awake, fear gripping him like ice. He looked around but he was alone. "Tangl?"

No answer.

He stood and rushed to the main room. The privy door was open but the front door was closed. The house was empty. His heart slowed in its pounding but he still felt the fear. He cast about for some sign of what was wrong and saw a bag of Catriona's tea on the counter beside a couple pieces of earthenware decorated with bright flowers. The blood ran from his face and he closed his eyes.

She had figured it out.

He leaned against the counter for a moment, then went and got his boots. He saw her coat on the end of the bed and remembered the fear. She might have left willingly, but she encountered something that frightened her. He shoved on his boots, grabbed her coat and ran out the door. He felt for her and found her to the north. He ran towards her, brushing past the branches and knocking them aside, occasionally getting slashed across the hand or cheek. As he got closer, he slowed. He reached out for her.

*Tangl*...

He felt her moving east and ran again. He never saw the barrier, but his Power did. It flared and bounced him back, spilling him to the ground. He raised his arm against the light and let the Power fade down again. He stood and looked around. There was a small house with a Nubian woman carrying an armload of wood.

"Milady!"

She turned. "Another one?

"Did a woman come past here?"

She nodded.

"Is she hurt?"

"No. I stopped that. She would have been had she tried to go through that barrier. Don't come any closer or you'll be trapped too."

"You stopped her from being hurt?"

The woman pointed to the ground near him. A burnt piece of wood sat on the forest floor. He looked back up at the woman. "My lady, I owe you a great debt. What is your name?"

"Aislyn. Aislyn Cortright."

"That lady you saved is the woman I love. Where did she go?"

She shifted her weight with the cut wood. "She said she had an office in town. She's going there."

"I won't forget this. Thank you for helping her."

"You aren't going to be foolish enough to cross that barrier are you?"

He stepped towards it, holding out his hand. The Power of Sovereignty glowed around him and pushed him back. He put his hand back down.

"There is no chance of that happening, I fear."

"By the Stones, what is that?"

"Something my brother gave me."

He looked through the trees, then picked up the coat of Tanglwyst's he had dropped. He walked away, releasing Aislyn from his questions. He shook his head and hugged the coat to his chest. He could still smell her on it. He swore at himself for not telling her before they went there. She would have understood. It was a safe house on purpose. She would have been fine with it. But he was too afraid, and now she was trapped in a town occupied by a vicious queen. He barely contained his fear for Tanglwyst's life.

He got to the cabin and went back into the bedroom. He grabbed his own things and put them on. He wasn't going down without a fight. He took her coat and tied the arms around his waist. He found the leather thong she used to tie back her hair and put it in his, getting his hair out of the way. He left the cabin without looking back and strode to the road. He looked up towards the town, then down towards Patras. There would be an army coming soon and the letter they dispatched would be to the palace by now. He figured he would have support here within a day.

And Tanglwyst was a very smart woman.

He sat in the middle of the road to wait.

# Twenty-Two

## "If one is to wage a war, one needs to have a strategy." Shiva, The Karmic Hand

Tanglwyst entered her office in St. Giles and Preston Cowley, her manager, looked up. He was a young man but had slightly older man's features: A balding head, greying beard, and gentle blue eyes. He stood, stammering and then ran to her. They hugged and he stepped back.

"What are you doing here?"

"Slipped in accidentally. Have you heard from anyone at the estate?"

Preston took a deep breath. "Boy, have I. Everyone is here."

Tanglwyst brightened. "Everyone?"

He nodded and she hugged him again. She looked behind her to tell Alexander, and realized he was not there nor would he be. She looked at the floor and sighed.

"What is it?"

She looked at her friend and shook her head. "That, my dear, is a very long story. Is my apartment available?"

"Yes. The Sulocco is in port so everyone is staying on her while this is going on."

"The Queen's control extends to the harbor?"

Preston nodded. "She made a special dispensation for your flagship."

She nodded. "That doesn't surprise me. I have a plan for how to take care of this situation."

Preston sat, waiting to hear what it was. She shook her head. "I can't tell just yet. I need to take care of some things first. Do you know where Gomez de Santander is?"

"The guardsman?"

She nodded.

"He's in the guard's office. He's made several enemies since the spell came down."

"How?"

Preston glanced at the door and stood again. "Come, I'll tell you on the way. There are a lot of people who'll want to see you."

"Let me get cleaned up first, if I can."

Preston gestured to the back of the office to a set of stairs going up the wall. She went up and looked at the large open area that was her office away from Patras. This was her home base, far more than Le Fleur Street. Her office covered about half the footprint of the building, completely open when you came up the stairs. There was a wall along the south side and a large desk before a series of paned windows that looked out onto the town and sea. She went in the door to the left and saw her bedroom was clean and waiting. She had a well in Patras because dealing with the river water was inviting sickness. She had done likewise in here and had a pump to draw the water to a half keg near the floor. A pipe connected it to a hole out the back of the building where she was able to pull a plug and have it drain. She went to the bathing area and took a half an hour to scrub and clean herself.

She reveled in the cleaning process, despite the water being cold. She had not bathed since the Papal City, not thoroughly. She had forgotten how much it mattered. She let her mind go to Alexander and check on his state of mind. He was angry, frightened, and determined but he was safe. She let him know she was safe as well, and he seemed to relax. She felt regret and guilt from him, and she turned away from it. She wasn't ready to deal with that yet. She closed her eyes and felt him touch her shoulder. She felt his arms around her and almost heard him say I'm sorry.

She shook it off and closed down her emotions. He should have told her. That he didn't, that he hid it, was the problem. He simply wasn't learning this lesson. She wasn't fragile or complicated. She wanted him to talk to her. That was all. She felt him nodding, felt him apologizing again and realized that she couldn't truly cut him off from her feelings. That annoyed her. She should be able to keep some things private. But if her emotions was what he wanted, then fine. Emotions were what he'd get.

She focused upon everything she was feeling. Betrayal. Rage. Fear. Worry. Determination. Angst. Intolerance. Rage again.

She felt him accept it, and that kind of infuriated her even more. Not that she wanted him to fight back but... She frowned, not even understanding her own mind. And she didn't love him after all. Not after this. This was a violation. Bringing her to the house he shared with his lover was...

She threw up her hands in frustration. She felt herself chewing him out in her mind and him just taking it. And then she wanted to punch him for making her feel like this. She felt some gratitude from him then, undoubtedly because he wasn't right there for her to rip apart. She stood there for another few moments, then her mouth curled a little and she started to laugh. She was standing, naked, in her wash tub, yelling at her paramour who was a mile away and he was grateful for the distance. For all she knew, it was all in her head. She grabbed a towel and dried off, shaking her head and dropping the whole incident.

The safe house had been just that: a very safe house. Catriona knew what she was doing. He would be ok there, but she didn't want him conducting a war from it. That was a sanctuary of Catriona's and he was not allowed to reveal its existence to anyone else. He seemed to agree and she got the feeling he was waiting elsewhere. South. She got dressed in some proper clothes of indigo, her red hair rich against the color. She put on town boots, which were of rich burgundy leather but softer than her traveling ones. She braided her tresses and smoothed cream upon her skin to repair some of the damage of the past two months. Soon, she was ready to face the world again.

The streets of the port city were better than Patras because it had gutters running to a sewer, which was actually a series of naturally-occurring warrens that ran to the bay. Grey water and black water filtered through tunnels of stones and sand so that it was less hazardous by the time it hit the sea. The frequent rains kept the sewers clear and working. Tanglwyst wondered if Catriona had anything to do with that too. The sewers were a natural feature of the cliffs but she wondered how natural it really was.

Never the less, the streets were clean and she could hear the market from her bedroom window when she opened it to let in some fresh air. She leaned out and looked up and down the street. She thought she saw something in the road in the distance to the south but could not make out what it was. There was a red line in the road where someone had marked the edge of the barrier. This was smart. If only there had been something like that in the woods. Ah, but even if there were, she would not have seen it. She had been running blind and now was trapped like all the others.

She went downstairs and Preston handed her a stack of papers. "These are all the letters that arrived. We can receive them but not send replies. The birds are destroyed when they pass the barrier."

She nodded. It was all business related and she felt certain Preston had more than enough skill and intelligence to handle the business until now. She didn't need to review.

"How is Steven?"

"In Patras, Ma'am. He left to visit his father before the occupation and he will be there for a while. I received a few letters already, but I haven't been able to return a reply."

"Has anyone thought to go to the edge of town and toss the letters through?"

"They burn up."

She snapped her fingers, remembering the log. "I knew that. Can you shout?"

He frowned. "No one has tried. There hadn't really been anyone to shout to."

She grabbed her skirts and went for the door. "There is now. What's the story with Gomez and our people?"

"He tried to pull rank here, demanding letters that were yours, and telling us you were a traitor and your lands and all your property was forfeit to the Crown."

"Gomez? That doesn't sound like him at all."

"That's what I was told."

"Hm. I'm going to see him."

"Oh no you're not."

"Preston…"

"No. Uh-uh. That man has it in for you."

She put her hand on his. "Preston…"

He patted her hand. He knew he was safe from her love touch, being as he was already in love with someone else. "He has orders to imprison you."

She smiled. Apparently Preston had withdrawn his fealty to the Crown. "I'll risk it. I actually have something for him from Alexander that will solve this. I need to take it to him personally though. His Majesty entrusted it to me. I'll be back soon, I promise."

Preston looked irritated, but nodded nonetheless.

She left the building and turned to the guard's office. As she passed the market stalls and taverns, she heard a murmur of recognition. Someone ran into the Wise Wench and shouted that she was here. She kept on her trek to the guard's office and startled Gomez when she walked in.

"Lady Tanglwyst?"

"Gomez. The King is waiting outside of town. Would you like to see him?"

Gomez looked at a man clad entirely in silver armor, then stood and went towards the door. "Hell yes."

The man in armor followed the pair out but kept a distance.

"How did you get here?"

"Accident. But it was a lucky break after all. Alexander has been needing to speak to you for a while. Did you get his letter recently?"

Gomez nodded. "I was surprised but grateful."

As they walked back through town, people streamed out of their homes and businesses. They followed the pair to the edge of town. The dot in the road saw them and stood, coming towards them. It took only a few minutes to confirm that it was Alexander. He strode up to the barrier and reached out his hand. Tanglwyst did likewise out of habit, and Gomez grabbed her before she touched the red line.

Alexander looked gratefully at Gomez, then turned his attention to Tanglwyst. "My Lady, I'm so sorry."

She held up her hand. "I know. I shouldn't have run off. It was childish. But I'm very glad to hear your voice."

People murmured behind them, hope in their voices.

Gomez stepped closer. He bowed. "Your Majesty."

"How goes the search for my bride, Gomez?" Alexander smiled.

"I've had my hands full here, you might say."

Alexander folded his arms across his chest. "So I see. If you had wanted a vacation…"

Gomez held up his hand. "I'm good, Sire." His face turned serious. "What is the situation there?"

Alexander turned to the east. "The valley is occupied, the Lady's manor house and crops are burned. But they are not advancing."

The man in armor cleared his throat. Gomez turned to him, then gestured. "This is General Bartolemaus Johner, Emissary of the Fae Army."

The General stepped forward and walked to the King. This caused a surge in the crowd behind them as people thought the barrier was down. Alexander ran to the red line but his Power raised up when it came in contact.

"Stop! The barrier is still up."

Someone near the edge of the road didn't hear him and ran for the edge of town. Gomez shoved Tanglwyst back and dove for the man, tackling him before he got to the barrier. He had an apple in his hand and it fell and bounced to the barrier, where it was instantly fried.

Johner did not even change his stride. He came to Alexander and bowed. "Your Majesty. I am General Bartolemaus Johner, the Voice of Command for Corrigan Starshadow."

Tanglwyst had heard that term before but could not remember where. Something she had seen on a page in the Papal City.

Alexander frowned at the General. "Why are my people trapped in there?"

"To keep them safe. Her Majesty has long been awaiting you."

"Where is she? I believe we should talk."

"She is in her pavilion, as I'm certain you have seen. I will take you to her, if you like."

Alexander looked at Tanglwyst. "Only if I may bring my advisers with me."

The General looked at Gomez and Tanglwyst. "I'm afraid not. The barrier stops anything from getting out."

"You got out."

"I'm not just anything, Sir. Do you have any advisers on this side of things?"

He sighed. "They are en route. I managed to get a head start."

"Noble. Well, I am here to advise so let me do that. Please, let us go to your own pavilion."

"I don't have a pavilion."

"Then borrow mine, Sir." The General gestured to the road behind him and a magnificent pavilion of blue and gold, with the arms of Mervolingia hanging as banners and flying as flags, appeared in the road behind them. It was as resplendent as the Queen of Krakte's and the fleurs on the pinnacles blew flower petals that seemed to be made of fine, razor-sharp silk. The townspeople uttered gasps of awe and Tanglwyst felt a shiver of envy as she gazed upon it. Alexander shot her a look of amazement and she pictured him as a great bear with a strange floral hat and almost bust out laughing. He glared good-naturedly at her and followed the General to the tent.

Gomez stepped back and bumped into the crowd. He turned and pushed through the group, excusing himself as the people looked on. Tanglwyst went with him.

"Once he gets set up, he'll be able to send messages to people."

Gomez nodded. "I hope that's soon. We're starting to run out of supplies here."

Tanglwyst stopped. "You are?"

"Yes. The only reason we are as flush as we have been is because everyone was gearing up for the sailing season. With crops burnt and no traffic out, we are having a hard time imagining this siege not leaving several of us dead. What does His Majesty have in mind to break it?"

"I'm not sure of all the details. He has sent for several things from Patras. I'm certain the letters have been delivered by now and the Mervol army is being assembled."

He glanced over to the east, catching glimpses between the buildings of the countryside. "I don't know what they can do against those monsters. When they first got here, a few patrols walked the streets. Then it became clear we couldn't leave so the army was sent back to the valley. What else does he have?"

She glanced back and saw that the townsfolk were still gathering at the barrier. She nodded her to the church up ahead. "Come, let's talk in here."

"Why there?"

She glanced back at the crowd. "Because they can't hear us in there."

"Is everyone ready?" Ce'Nedra looked at her companions.

Henri and Sylvaine were on Sylvaine's wall, all three hands resting above the symbol on the baseboard. They nodded. Felix was beside Ce'Nedra on Felix's wall, doing likewise. He also nodded.

"Now, remember the light you saw yesterday, the one that we use to feed? Look for that light now in your wall. It will feel like a faint heat under your fingers."

All did as instructed. Felix picked up on the heat sensation before the other two did. "I feel it."

"Are you sure?"

Felix nodded.

Ce'Nedra exhaled. "Then prove it."

Felix cut his ring finger on his left hand and placed the blood on the wall. He concentrated on the blood flowing where he had sensed the heat.

The blood shifted towards the heat, but then stopped.

"Keep trying. You've blooded the wall. Let that guide you." She looked to Henri and Sylvaine, staying out of contact with the walls and far enough away not to influence their magic. "What about you two?"

Sylvaine shook her head. "I don't understand. I don't feel heat, but I almost feel… cold?"

"Cold is also a reaction, but it might be that you feel air. That's probably good. What about you, Henri?"

"Nothing. Not even the cold." He looked at his stump. "Is it because I don't have…"

"No. You have a heart and that is all that matters. Sylvaine, go ahead and prove the path."

Sylvaine cut her finger as well, everyone quite surprised by her resolve. Felix had figured she would be too frail and squeamish about it. It turned out she was quite proficient at cutting herself. The blood again moved in a direction, but not much. Henri stepped back, releasing the wall and the blood moved with a purpose to a small section of the wall.

It fed out from there like capillaries for about a handspan until it had exhausted its blood source.

Ce'Nedra looked at her wall, then at Felix's. "Henri, try it on *your* wall."

The four of them had settled into routines early on, each claiming a wall as their personal property. Henri went to the wall across from Felix and placed his palm upon it. He concentrated, then his eyes widened. "Yes! I do feel it. And yeah, it's *cooler* than the wall."

Ce'Nedra came over and cut his finger. He smeared the blood on the wall as she stepped away again. He focused and everyone brightened as the blood shifted a bit to fill in about three wide veins.

The room's light changed from a soft blue glow to a pale gold one. Sylvaine looked nervous, but Ce'Nedra looked delighted.

"We did it." She looked at the symbols on the walls. "The room is now ours."

"What does that mean?" Felix risked taking his hand off the wall. The glow stayed gold.

Henri and Sylvaine looked at Ce'Nedra.

"It means we can trap him when he comes back."

"Are we now stronger than the amulet?"

Ce'Nedra shook her head. "No. But we will have a few seconds before it gets him out of here. What we've done is make this a first resort instead of a last one. The blood on the walls will make the amulet think we have killed each other and that the room is empty now. Time to start preparing ourselves for when he returns."

# Twenty-Three

"Put your best packer in charge of loading market stalls and your worst one in charge of loading ships."
Kali, The Karmic Hand

Gomez looked at Tanglwyst. "And she really thinks this will work?"

Tanglwyst nodded.

"And you're sure they can't come in here?"

She nodded. "It was something I learned in the Papal City. Let me ask you this: How many people were in here when the freezing spell happened?"

"A half dozen."

"Were they frozen?"

Gomez shook his head. "Not until the stepped outside."

She tapped the floor with her foot. "Holy ground."

Gomez looked around. "Then we need to have our planning meetings in here."

She nodded. "I don't quite know what to do but we need Alexander in here with us. But I saw his Power flare. It won't let him."

"So what do we do?"

"We have to wait. For Dominic, for the army. For Catherine."

"How long will that take?"

She sighed. "That I don't know. But they are coming."

He sighed, sitting, and leaned on his knees. "I'm actually glad you're here. Folks were starting to think maybe we had done something to you."

"I'll try to get my people calmed down. What do you know about that General?"

"Well, I can say that he is an absolute necessity. Some of the Fae customs are strange and if you don't do them right, it's an insult, especially if you have been provided with an emissary from the Fae. He's a military man, so he tries to keep things straight and true. I think Alexander will be alright if he listens to what Johner says and does it. Sometimes it seems odd, but I have watched a man get cut down on the spot for attacking the Queen. They don't take this lightly."

"He'll make it through. He's got to." She exhaled, letting go of her apprehension. Then she turned to him. "Did you threaten my people?"

"Huh?"

"Threaten my people, the ones from the estate?"

"Oh! Well, no, but they seemed to take it that way. I asked to see a missive, and when they refused I might have mentioned how you were a fugitive."

Tanglwyst winced. "How did that work out for you?"

"You pay them really, really well."

"Mhm."

"They were willing to throw me into the barrier if I bothered them again."

"Well, with any luck, Catherine's plan will work and we'll be released from here soon."

"From your lips to Heaven's messenger, my Lady."

Dominic changed his shirt and pants, smiling at his beautiful new shoes. He had them made by a Parduian shoemaker of exceptional reputation. That designer was likewise one that Cipriano kept records on. By now, his name should be on several registers and Cipriano will be contacting him with offers of opportunity and wealth. Dominic could almost count the money now. He checked his hair and teeth in the grand mirror in the King's bedroom, closing the drawer where he had kept his clothes. He had packed them into a bag to take with him. He was not so far gone in his delusions to believe there would not be questions to answer if Alexander returned and found Dominic's clothes in Charles' furnishings.

He took the bag and set it outside with the others his valet had assembled. A couple trunks held everything he owned. It made it easier to gather all of his things if it appeared he was taking everything with him to the siege. After all, he had no idea how long it would last nor what he would need. He was grateful that Tanglwyst was in all likelihood dead so she could not say otherwise. The servants started taking the bags down to the courtyard and he walked slowly to give them time to get everything ready. It was dusk now and he had things to do before dark. He wanted to get the corpse of Elizabeth so he could collect that money too. He heard the rustle of the Letter of Credit from Catherine in his inner pocket. It was all going to be his.

He could barely keep the black swirls from his eyes when he thought of using the amulet. Any thought of amassing more wealth made the darkness within him shriek in delight. It was like having a hairless cat that delighted in the pain of others. He refused to hurt anyone he considered a peer or better, despite the monsters' urgings that no one would be his better for much longer. He had not let it take him so completely that he would do that. In the light of dawn, he was glad Gwen was not around. He had not sought her out since Charles' death. At first, he had just been busy. Then the amulet had showed up and he had avoided her on purpose, despite the amulet begging to see her. He couldn't stop shuddering when he thought of that meeting.

He opened the doors to the courtyard and saw the Castellan still loading the cart. This was good because Dominic still had to get to the body. He expected it to be relatively easy: go to the top of the wall, touch the skull, and take the body through the shadows to the cart. Then he would have someone else bundle the thing into proper cloths for transport. He looked at his hands and thought better of the endeavor. The idea of touching a body in his finery was out of the question. His clothes would be ruined and his hopes for marrying the Princess Gilian or Laura along with them. He turned to one of the servants.

"You. The King wants the body of the former Queen brought here immediately. It leaves with me."

The young man stopped, frozen. "You... you want me to fetch the body?"

"Don't you worry about that, Carl. Finish your duties." Nina Richelieu stepped up and the servant ran off.

"How dare you interfere with my orders!"

"I did it because it wasn't necessary. The body is already here." She gestured to a wrapped body nearby. The linen around it was tied with silk cord and looked to be done well, but not sewn and finished. "Apparently, you were planning to take it with you and His Majesty's letter to the guard requested it. So I had it acquired."

Dominic decided not to mention the money. When he left, he would take the body with him, and there would be no one there to get a share.

It took another hour before the cart looked ready and by that time, he was starting to get impatient. Finally, when the Castellan closed the back of the wagon, he stepped up. He pointed to the body.

"Get that on the wagon immediately. I don't have all night."

The Castellan started to protest but Dominic held up his hand. The Castellan stepped back, shaking his head. "At your service, Sir."

He stood next to Nina and also crossed his arms. He said something to her and she snorted a laugh. Dominic tried not to care but it annoyed him. He did not consider Nina or the nameless Castellan as his peers and he got a perverse joy in thinking of ways to torture them. Another set of servants carried the body gently between them, supportive hands all along the linen. Dominic pointed to the front of the cart.

"Put it there."

They glanced at Nina, who nodded, and they carefully placed the body on the front boards where the driver would put his feet. The cart was yet to be hooked up to horses but that didn't matter to Dominic. He planned to take the whole mess through the shadows as soon as Nina and the Castellan turned their backs.

Let them figure that out.

He dismissed them both with a wave, then motioned his nervous valet over to him. The other servants looked to the Castellan who nodded and motioned for them to come with him. They stepped back from the cart and Dominic grinned, one hand on the body and one hand on the boy. He put his foot on the cart and jumped up, using the boy as leverage. He started to command the amulet when the load buckled under his weight and the whole cart shifted forward. He fell, hand on the corpse but lost his hold on the boy and the rest. He went through the shadows and fell on his back at the feet of the King.

The body fell on top of him with a splat. Black scum oozed out of the linen like he had escorted twelve full chamber pots disguised as a corpse, and he threw the body off in disgust. He turned over onto his hands and knees. Alexander turned to face him and beside him stood a magnificent knight in head to toe silver mail.

"Dominic?"

The knight looked down upon the man, then his eyes fell upon the corpse. Rage filled the man. He drew his sword and when Dominic looked up at them, Alexander frowned. The stench of lemons filled the tent and the steel cut through it coming for Dominic's neck. His mind went blank and the amulet seized control.

It took him to the safe room.

Dominic felt giant barbs tear through him, vicious teeth shredding him from the soul to the skin. His face and eyes bled from the cuts while his body and spirit liquefied from the poison. By the time he made it through the spell surrounding the Papal City, the man who planned to rule Mande was reduced to a bag of bones and sludge.

# Twenty-Four

"Justice is rarely delivered by the hands of the victims."
Shiva, The Karmic Hand

Alexander knelt beside the linen. The smell hit him and he knew instantly what had happened. If this was Elizabeth's body, she had clearly been part Fae. The shadows had devoured her, even though she was two months dead. The ooze stained the linen and the General took Alexander's shoulder in his hand.

"Step back, Your Majesty. That fluid is toxic. If it touches you, the Queen will never speak to you."

Alexander stood. "Why?"

"It is poison to any Fae kind. Those touched by the Shadow are damned in our world. She would be required to burn you from this place to save her soul and yours."

Alexander stepped back and tried to stay calm. He remembered holding Gwen's body and being soaked in the foul fluid. "How long does the taint last?"

"Forever. That will slay Fae upon contact. Even possessing it will be grounds for War."

He blinked, trying to figure out what to do. He couldn't tell Johner about Gwen and if his touch truly was toxic, why was Johner not melting like Gwen had. He looked at Johner's hand and realized he was touching through mail and Alexander's clothing. He doubted direct skin to skin contact would be so benign. Now he was nervous and needed to make sure he did not poison the General. This man was important. He had too much information to lose. Alexander stepped away from Johner and turned to face him.

"Johner, I need to get away from it then. I can't risk it tainting me. I believe that was the body of Elizabeth. I take it she was part Fae?"

He looked at the goo and nodded. "Apparently."

"How much Fae does your blood have to contain for this to be the fate of whomever is touched by the shadows?"

"No less than a quarter."

*Damn. That means Emmy can die if Dominic takes her through the shadows.* He closed his eyes and felt for Dominic. He was ready to Summon Dominic if he was still a danger.

He cast around for almost a minute but Dominic was nowhere to be found. He kept looking until Johner tapped him on the shoulder with a finger.

"Sire?"

"I was looking for the person who did this but I can't find him now."

"You can look again later. Now, we must go. Have you another place to stay?"

Alexander thought about mentioning the cabin but decided to try something else first. "I know a place in town. Can you get me in there?"

"I cannot without bringing down the barrier."

"Then bring down the barrier. I'm here after all. She has what she wants."

"That is not my decision to make."

Alexander sighed. "Then yes, I have a place. This way. But I will need you to disguise it."

Johner nodded like this request was as casual as requesting salt at a meal.

He took the General to the cabin on the cliffs. The General stopped at the doorway. "This place is Land."

Alexander looked at the small home. "Yes. It is."

"This is unacceptable. The Champion of Heaven cannot headquarter in a temple of the Land."

"I'm kind of running out of options here, General. I have a place to headquarter in St. Giles but you can't get me through there."

"You cannot stay here." Johner gave a slight bow and an apologetic smile. "I will cut you where you stand if you try."

The threat was the most simple, direct, unflustered comment, again, as if just politely refusing the roast beef at a dinner. *Would you like the roast beef, Johner? Oh, I couldn't. It gives me gas that would murder everyone in this valley. So sorry. Oh, then please, try the veal.* Alexander was completely out of his depth here.

He looked towards town and the road. Johner's reveal regarding the goo of Elizabeth's body was unsettling, but it gave him an idea. "The substance that Elizabeth's body became: Why is it so bad? Why is it toxic?"

Johner stayed straight as a soldier, no change. "It was designed to destroy us. Centuries ago, your Church chose this weapon against our kind. It was uniquely suited for destroying Fae."

"And anyone who came in contact with the shadows was destructive?"

"No, Sire. Simply the ones who came in contact with the dead from it."

"Why?"

Johner hesitated and Alexander knew he was on the right track. "Because our magic cannot affect it."

Alexander set his mouth. *I knew it.* "So it is an advantage to my people to be in contact with it."

"Sire, I advise against any course of action for spreading the substance."

"Then get me through the barrier."

Johner sighed and glanced at the ground. He looked back up at the King. "I have told you the truth, Sire. It is not within my power to do so."

"But you can pass between the town and the barrier?"

"Of course. It is Fae magic."

There it was. Alexander bowed. "Johner, how long must you serve as advisor and emissary to me?"

"Until a more suited emissary comes along."

"How much do I need you?"

"Apparently, quite a bit, Sire."

"And what would break that?"

"I must serve you until a more suitable emissary comes along."

"And then what?"

Johner didn't even hesitate. "Then I join the forces of war that stand against you."

Alexander's demeanor reflected the unwillingness to tread this path he had in his mind. "General, I do not want to insult you, and I don't want to be on the side of a conflict you do not support. I can't let you continue to advise me against your will. I am potentially going to be fighting every member of this army. I can't ask you to stand by my side."

The General cocked his head. "You're... releasing me, Sire?"

Alexander stood taller. "I am. Stupid and dangerous as that is, I fear I must. I can't, in all conscience, let you be with me when I will have to employ strategies that might put you in contact with weapons that will destroy you."

"All wars are peopled with weapons that will destroy you, Sire. That's why they are wars."

"Then let me put it this way: If you had a weapon that would destroy, or at least impair, you opposition, would you reveal it to the emissary of your enemy?"

"No, Sire. But I cannot let you be unadvised."

Alexander narrowed his eyes. "Why not?"

"I am the Voice of Command. I am the right hand of the Midsummer King Corrigan Starshadow, the Warlord of Sovereignlumin. He sent me here to oversee the battle and give the greatest aid. This is where I can be the greatest aid."

"Until another Emissary can be found."

"Yes."

"What does it take to be an Emissary?"

"Knowledge of the ways of the Fae."

"Who would you recommend as a better emissary than yourself in this situation?"

"Someone who knows Fae, knows their magic, their taboos, their ways, and understands war?"

"Yes. But also understands humans."

Johner's eyes flicked away in thought, then nodded. "I know exactly the person to get."

"How long before you can get them here?"

Johner held up his finger, then looked at the ground. He reached down, through the soil like it was the surface of a lake. He grabbed something, then pulled it from the ground like a turnip. Before them stood a man about in his thirties, with bright green hair. The man shook the dirt from himself, dusting chunks from his hair.

Raven Grasshair looked at Johner. "Bart! How are you?" Raven hugged Johner, very much against the General's will, the stepped back. "How's Father?"

"Not here." Johner gestured to Alexander. "You are now the Emissary to the Mervol contingent for this conflict. Handle this so that your Father does not feel the need to arrive."

Raven frowned and nodded, pursing his lips. "Okaaay…" He turned to Alexander. "Hi. I'm your Emissary."

Alexander held up a hand. "Don't hug me."

"Oh, alright. Johner, what's going on here?"

Alexander turned to Johner. "Please, let's walk while you fill him in. It would be dishonorable for you to drop him into this conflict and not explain what has gone on before. Could result in bad advice."

"Indeed." Raven looked at the cabin behind them. "Ooh! Nice temple."

Johner nodded, but seemed to know what Alexander was doing. They walked to the place where Elizabeth's body lie as Johner explained everything that had gone on. Raven listened with growing seriousness and ire, but he did not interrupt. He shook his head in sorrow when the report of the freezing spell came. When it was explained that the environment of the area was not frozen as well, this made Raven very upset, but again, he did not interrupt. By the time they got to the pile of Elizabeth's body, Alexander had expected the goo to be soaked into the ground but it sat upon it like a bead of water on glass.

Raven stopped short of the goo. He put his hand up in revulsion, covering his nose and mouth. "By the Stones, is that…"

Alexander nodded. "A man possessing an amulet brought it here through the shadows."

Raven looked about to vomit and apparently decided not to hold it back. He ran over to a bush by the side of the road to expel his stomach. Alexander didn't look at him. Instead, he shook his head.

"I don't know what to do about this."

"I do." Johner held up his hand and flames began to encompass it.

"I thought you said it was immune to Fae magic?"

"It is." He cast the spell at the grass nearby. "But Fire is its bane."

The grass caught and Alexander looked at the area. The valley was completely unprotected on this side. The barrier may stop people from getting out but it would spread to the forest with ease. All of Mervolingia would be at risk.

"Johner no!" Alexander grabbed the man's wrist, pulling him off balance. Johner fell, cartwheeling his arms to try and recover his balance. Alexander noticed his Power flaring to protect him from the Fae armor and the contact seemed to be the cause of the unbalancing. Johner hit the ground upon the linen wrappings and the goo splashed upon him. Raven stumbled to the scene. Alexander grabbed Johner's hand and pulled him to his feet but the goo was eating through the armor.

"Raven! Do you have any gloves?"

Raven looked confused. Alexander grabbed the coat around his waist and wiped the goo from Johner's armor, trying to save him. Johner panicked, his eyes wide with fear. He tried to unbuckle the straps but the goo was creeping towards the buckles.

*Dammit.*

Alexander dropped the coat and grabbed for the buckles. "Can you help me get this off him?"

Raven nodded. He closed his eyes and suddenly, the buckles popped free. Johner shrugged off the armor and backed away kicking. He saw some goo getting on the cuisses covering his upper thighs and he unbuckled the belt to drop the legs. Alexander pulled them off, tossing them aside. Johner got to his feet and started taking off the smoking pieces of his gambeson. Alexander stepped back, now seeing exposed skin on the man. He didn't dare do more. He took Tanglwyst's coat and tried to beat out the fire instead, trying to kick dirt onto it but it was too late. It was starting to spread and he couldn't get ahead of it.

Suddenly, dirt thrust up from the ground in the midst of the fire, raining down upon the fire and stopping it from taking off. Within seconds, the fire was smothered out. Alexander looked at Johner and found he was, strangely, just a man. He had an ethereal beauty to him, and Alexander didn't know what he expected, but he truly wasn't expecting just a man. "You... You're not a Fae?"

Johner shook his head. "I was a musician and weaver from Glarren. I created this woven fabric of many colors and made a coat from it. The fabric became known as plaid and was worn by a group of warriors who went into a conflict to protect the Fae forests from invaders. I played the battle song and my friend banged the war drum. We ended up using our instruments to repel a flanking force. Our group was almost slain, but Corrigan Starshadow saw us. He turned the tide of battle and we defeated our foes. I offered myself in service to him for the deed and he took me in. He said he would accept my service for a year and a day. That was eight hundred and one years ago."

Alexander was shocked. "Has he just never released you?"

Raven stepped in. "No. He's actually never collected it."

Johner nodded.

Alexander looked at the goo. "Then this wouldn't have killed you anyway."

"No, but it would have stopped me from being able to fulfill my duties to the Midsummer King. Not being able to have contact with any Fae would be a violation of my contract with him. The result would have been the same. I am, after all, over eight hundred years old." He stepped up and bowed. "You have a new Emissary. I need to go to the Queen and tell her."

Alexander bowed in return. "Thank you."

Johner nodded and moved off, his armor now back on him, despite it smoking upon the ground. Alexander looked at Raven for explanation.

"Fae magic is mostly illusion, but the Fae Lords can grant certain things to their Seconds, like the ability to create armor for themselves or hide at will. One Second can disguise herself as anyone at all. She spent a couple years as a cook in a palace kitchen somewhere, I heard." Raven frowned, stepping back. "Hey, I know you."

Alexander nodded. "You do?"

"Yes! You shot my sister!"

Alexander blinked, looking around. Raven's excited tone confused him for such a horrible accusation. "I… I'm sorry?" Then he remembered the cat. "Wait. Were you a cat?"

"Yes!"

"You buried me up to my head!"

"Yes! That's right!" Raven pointed to himself. "That was me!"

Alexander thought Raven might dance a little jig. "Is she okay?"

Raven waved his hand. "Oh yeah. She and Octavius are trees now. Everything's fine."

"Octavius? Catriona's Octavius?"

"No, Estelle's Octavius. Catriona was just a friend."

"He's a tree?"

Raven nodded. "They both are. Don't worry. They're happy trees." He turned to the goo. "Tell me about this."

"A young man named Dominic D'Medici got hold of an amulet that could teleport him through a shadow place. It does this to Fae."

"Mhm. And how did you get tainted?" Raven waved at the bundle. "Cuz this didn't do it."

Alexander swallowed. "I have been given a gift by Saint Brigit, the Patron of healers. On holy ground, I can heal wounds, even ones that will kill someone. My…" His voice choked off.

Raven frowned. "You took a Fae person through the shadows to a church to heal them and this happened."

Alexander didn't try to speak. He just nodded.

Raven folded his arms. "I see. And now you don't know what to do here. Because this is a powerful weapon against that mess over there," he nodded to the fires of the encampments, "and that's a village you need to protect." He jerked his thumb at the lights of St. Giles.

Alexander nodded again. "And there's a barrier spell on it, trapping the townspeople. Including someone very special to me." His voice wavered a moment, then steadied. Now that he was thinking about her, he could feel Tanglwyst's presence. She was worried about the panic and had been hammering upon him since the arrival of the fire. He reassured her and felt her calm.

"I'm gonna tell you something now: I won't touch that. I'm half Fae. That will kill me outright. But I can get rid of it because I'm also a mage. I don't rely on Fae magic. I tap into the Arcane. And I can do stuff with fire."

Alexander stared at the goo. He had an entire kingdom to protect, and putting this on his soldiers would mean they could fight the Fae army if necessary. They could tip the arrows with it and kill the sharp-eyed monsters. Their hands could destroy them. He knew other humans would not be effected by it, because he had come in contact with several people since Gwen's death. No Fae illusions would cover a soldier touched with this so they would not be able to infiltrate.

He looked at Raven. "You're supposed to be my advisor. Do you know anything about war?"

Raven blinked, shaking his head. "I fear I know far too much about war." He looked at the pile of goo, then at Alexander.

Alexander swallowed. "I don't need this. And I don't want it."

"Good." Raven wiggled his fingers and the linen caught on fire. He put a barrier of earth around it as close as it would get, stopping the fire from spreading.

Alexander watched until it was consumed, which took surprisingly little time. Within a couple minutes, the entire pile was less than ash. After that, Raven turned the earth over it and the ash was taken into the ground. He looked at Raven.

"I take it that means it's been purified?"

Raven nodded. "Fire does that." He looked to the city. "Now we need to deal with that."

Alexander glanced at him, tying Tanglwyst's coat back around his waist while a wry smile claimed his face. "This I can handle."

They strode to the barrier and Alexander held up his bare hand. The Power flared when he came in contact with it, but then he willed that away from him. He needed to touch the barrier. When he did, the energy crackled from it, spreading like a fire across paper, leaving a yellow line across the air. He lowered his hand, ready to put it back if the barrier came down again, but it didn't. He and Raven watched the spell disintegrate and Raven nodded his approval. They stepped across the red line on the ground.

A shout went up from a man lighting a street lamp that had gone out. Townspeople turned to see what Alexander was doing and several started walking towards him. As the barrier was destroyed, a man came up to it and poked the air with a stick. When nothing happened, he stepped across the red line to freedom. Others saw this act of bravery and did likewise. Soon, about twenty people stood behind Alexander and he felt the fealty oaths of all of them. Shouts alerting the world that the barrier was down filled the air. As more people left the town, some to run to farmsteads outside the barrier, he got patted on the shoulder and back. With every touch, he saw fealty oaths behind his eyes. They were real, and he was glad because he was finally getting them for the right reason.

Raven patted him on the back and Alexander panicked. He spun to look at Raven but nothing was happening. Raven raised his eyebrows in question.

"You're not disintegrating."

"Oh." He held up his hand. "I may be Fae but I'm also arcane. I kinda have a layer of dust on me at all times. It's protecting me."

"Alex!"

Tanglwyst ran down the street to the pair and Alexander ran to her, grabbing her in an embrace and spinning her in joy. Her arms hugged him tight as well and he kissed her like he had been underwater and she was precious air. He set her down and put his forehead to hers.

"I'm sorry. I should have told you."

"Yes. You should have." She kissed him. "Don't do it again."

Raven stepped up. "Hi. I'm Raven." He embraced her and spun her around as well.

She was startled and stepped back when he set her down. He went to kiss her and Alexander intervened.

"That's not a common greeting here."

"Oh. Well, you never can tell with foreign places."

Gomez ran up and Alexander hugged him as well. Raven arched an eyebrow at Alexander.

"Honest. It isn't a common greeting here."

A woman ran up to Tanglwyst and hugged her as did several others behind her. They seemed to be coming from the docks. Tanglwyst returned the gestures and squeals of joy, even planting a few grateful kisses as well. Alexander sighed.

"Ok, maybe it is."

Raven smiled and joined in the merriment, hugging Gomez and the folks hugging Tanglwyst. She took Alexander's hand and pulled him to her.

"Family, this is my friend, Alexander. He has helped me get here to you and he's going to help us get our home back."

They slapped Alexander on the back. A woman with long greying blonde hair clasped his hand. "Thank you for helping us."

Alexander bowed to her. "It is my honor, my lady." He looked to Gomez. "We need to talk. Is there anywhere we can go?"

Gomez nodded his shaggy ginger head. "It turns out there is."

Dominic's body fell to the floor, scaring everyone in the room. His blood pooled on the floor and they all heard the hissing coming from the walls. Everyone looked at the walls, watching for the shadows, but none came out. Ce'Nedra gestured to the protection symbols the inhabitants had drawn in their blood.

"Those seem to be doing the job."

Henri went to Dominic and turned his face. "He's dead." He looked at the others. "He's been ripped to shreds."

Sylvaine stepped towards him. "His coat survived. Who is it? How did he get here?"

Felix brightened. "The amulet!"

Henri looked around Dominic's neck and found the thing. "It's here."

"Let's get out of there then." Sylvaine grabbed for it but Henri moved it away.

"Not until we know what killed him."

Ce'Nedra examined the wounds. "These are Fae inflicted. I'm sure of it."

"How can you tell?" Felix held Sylvaine to keep her from touching the amulet.

Ce'Nedra pulled something out of Dominic's chest. "This." She dropped a thorn the size of a small dog onto the floor. "This is a Fae spell. I read about this from a fairy tale as a child." She looked at the ceiling. "Somewhere out there is a wall of thorns."

Felix crept towards the body. "What's that?"

He reached into the well-made coat Dominic as wearing and pulled out a letter. He looked it over. "This is the Royal Seal of Catherine." He blinked, then raised the paper to his nose. He looked at his friends, excited. "There's a secret message here."

Everyone's excitement level jumped.

"How do we read it?" Henri looked at the letter, seeing no identifying marks.

"I need some fire."

They pulled together and put Ce'Nedra's flint and steel with scraps torn from Dominic's linen shirt. Felix struck the sparks to get the small flame going. Once he had a little more than a candle flame, he brought over the paper. He carefully waved the paper over the flame until brown writing formed out of nothing.

"What's it say?"

Felix looked over the lines. "It's to us."

"Felix,

I know you are in the company of Ce'Nedra and Henri, as well as Sylvaine. This is important. DO NOT USE THE AMULET TO RETURN TO PATRAS. There is a spell around the Papal City WHERE YOU ARE, and it will kill anyone who tries to pass through it."

Henri looked at Dominic. "That explains what happened to him."

Felix nodded. "The spell extends around the entire city, but it doesn't look like you are within its range. What's more, you are in a cellar in the Papal Palace. There is space around you. Concentrate on the area fifteen feet away from you in any direction and you will be out. Be careful."

Everyone looked at the walls. Henri sighed. "Well, who wants to try it?"

Felix held out his hand. "I'll do it. I'll scout and come back."

"No!" Sylvaine gripped Felix's hand. "What if you are killed?"

Henri shook his head. "We got into this together. We'll get out together." He nodded to the wall where Ce'Nedra's rune was. "That wall. Fifteen feet on the other side of that wall." He held the amulet out.

Ce'Nedra reached out, then stopped. "That's not right." She looked at her wall. "That one was the first rune I did. The energy was strongest there. That means there's solid earth beyond that wall." She felt the walls, then tapped on the one Felix had chosen. "This one. This has lower Land energy."

They touched the amulet and looked at Henri. "On three…"

# Twenty-Five

## "What is this strange creature?"
## Kali, The Karmic Hand

Alistair saw Johner pull Raven from the chamber holding Catriona and stepped back from the Pillar. He wasn't sure what just happened but he also thought that was a really bad thing. Without Raven to sustain her, she would die for sure. This was unacceptable. He needed to get down there. If he went into the chamber, maybe it would take him. After all, he was Karma. He turned and Lucifer was standing there, his arms folded across his chest.

"It won't work."

"What do you mean it won't work?"

Lucifer nodded to the scene in the Pillar. "You going there. It won't work." Lucifer uncrossed his arms and walked over to it. "You think if you go there, it will take you instead of her. You're wrong."

"She's just the First Dûcesa. She's a servant of the Land. I'm the embodiment of Karma. How can she be more powerful than me?"

Lucifer smiled. "I'll let you puzzle that one out yourself."

Alistair shook his head. This was the proprietor of Hell. He wasn't known for his honesty. "You're lying."

Lucifer turned to Alistair. "You want to try it? Go ahead. I'll give you a staircase into the room itself. But when she gets rescued, promise me you'll leave the chamber empty. That means you can't be in there when she is released. You understand?"

"You can get me down there?"

"Yes. But only if you leave that place empty."

"Why?"

"It traps souls. Why would you want anyone left in it to be drained to death?"

Alistair blinked. "That's a really good point." He pointed at Lucifer. "But why do you care?"

Lucifer looked at Alistair. "Because my stock and trade is souls. I can't utilize them for my own insidious purposes if they are trapped in a magical chamber."

"What does one soul matter over another?"

Lucifer looked at the chamber again. "One soul may be the thing that tips the scales. All souls have weight, you know."

Alistair studied the Archangel. "So you know how to get her out?"

"Nope. Not my purview."

"What do you mean?"

Lucifer stepped back from the Pillar, his warm gaze going to Alistair. "That ain't my work. I have no power over it."

"Who does?"

"Well, that sounds like an adventure for someone else, my friend. But I meant what I said. I can get you there. You just can't be there when she's rescued."

"How do you know she'll be rescued?"

Lucifer leaned against the Pillar. "Call it a lucky guess." When Alistair didn't seem to accept that, Lucifer sighed. "Because I'm doing my best to facilitate it."

"Why?"

"I have a use for it. I'd tell you all about it but two people can keep a secret if one of them is dead. For me, it's just smarter not to reveal my evil plot just yet."

Alistair looked at the Pillar, then at Lucifer. "Alright. Take me there."

"Not a problem." He looked Alistair over. "You're not going to wear that, are you?"

"What?" Alistair looked at his clothing. It was the white with black embroidery that he was wearing when he met Lucifer. The hat was sitting on the bed. The feathers had started to annoy him when he was here alone. "What do my clothes have to do with it?"

"Well, ya see, you're a big entity of the afterlife now. If you just show up being all afterlife-y, you'll draw attention to yourself. Then you'll be accosted by all sorts of well-wishers and do-gooders and people who want to have their lives improved or their ultimate questions answered. Trust me. You spend a few days speaking at scholarly gatherings and you'll get what I mean."

Alistair pointed to the Pillar. "It's the deserted wasteland of York. No one is going to be there."

Lucifer shrugged. "Suit yourself."

He waved his hand and a door appeared in the blank whiteness of the realm. It was purple with a crystal knob. Alistair pointed to it. "Is that it?"

Lucifer nodded.

Alistair opened the door and looked out onto a lush green pasture. He turned to Lucifer but the Archangel was gone. He stepped through the door and closed it behind him.

The King, Gomez, and Raven slipped away from the crowd to a spot next to a couple buildings by the red line. Gomez looked around, keeping his voice low. "The Church here can't be affected by the Fae spells. It even protected the people inside from the freezing spell until they left it."

Alexander sighed, keeping an eye on the street and the crowd. "That's good. Holy Ground is good." He looked at Raven's hair. "Any way you can tone that down a bit? This place was just held hostage by a bunch of Fae. I don't want you grabbed and hung for you hair color."

Raven looked up at his hair and brushed his fingers through it. It changed to a dark brown of similar shade to the green.

"Perfect. Since this happened in the dark, I can hope people didn't notice. Now, where is the Church?"

"Other end of town. This way." Gomez started to head down the road. Raven stepped out as well but Alexander lingered.

Raven looked to see him watching the lady he had kissed. "Do you want me to get her?"

"I.."

"Alright then." Raven walked over to the crowd. He bowed to the Lady. "His Majesty needs you."

A large woman with bright eyes and long red hair furrowed her eyebrows. "His Majesty?"

"We're just friends."

A shorter man with a paunch and balding head snorted. "That's not what I saw."

Tanglwyst shook her head. She came to Raven's outstretched hand and took his arm. "Where are we going?"

"I think we're going to a secret meeting."

Alexander came over to her and took over escorting her. "I'm sorry to pull you away from your family."

"What's going on?"

"We need to talk about what's going on."

"What's going on?"

"Strategies."

She sighed, and turned to her family. "I'll come visit tomorrow. Get some rest, everyone."

Many of them waved and some stepped outside the red line to test the validity of the rumors. The King's group walked up to the Church and everyone entered but Raven. The divine threshold there would strip him of all but the barest of his magics. It made him nervous. He remembered the things the Church did to "cleanse the world of vile magics." Those atrocities still haunted him. None of his companions had yet noticed his hesitation but they would before long. Maybe they didn't need his advice.

He felt a gentle tug from inside. He looked but no one was touching him. Then he saw the shimmer. He took an instinctive step, crossing the threshold, and the shimmer solidified. She smiled, her short, dark hair still bound in a simple kerchief of white linen. She wore a red, short-sleeved woolen dress with a black underdress and long detached red sleeves that kept her outfit clean when she did weeding or milking. Her soft, brown eyes smiled to see him. She reached out her hands to him.

"Raven. My friend."

"Clara!"

Tanglwyst looked at him. "Did you say Clara?"

"Yes. Clara of… Where were you from?"

Clara smiled. "Weltonshire was where you found me, but I came from Glarren."

"Would they call you Clara of Weltonshire or Clara of Glarren, then? I hope it's the former. The latter sounds silly."

Tanglwyst came over to him and he saw he had everyone's attention. "Clara who? Do you know about the fountain and the Pillar of Saints?"

"Well, yes, I do, but how do you know about it?"

Alexander came over. "We saw it. In the basement of the Papal Palace."

"So, it's still there. Well, at least they didn't destroy it."

Clara took Raven's hand. "They can't. We made it. They can't unmake it here."

Raven looked between Tanglwyst and Alexander. "Did it say her last name or anything?"

She shook her head and he sighed in relief. "Good. Then it's Clara of Weltonshire. Way better than the other one. Clara, this is Alexander, his friend, and a lady he likes to kiss who is just a friend."

"Just a friend?" Tanglwyst looked at Alexander.

"It was something I told them because I didn't want to talk about it."

"Um, my name is Gomez, actually."

They all looked around the Church. As one they asked, "Who are you talking to?"

Clara smiled. "They can't see me, actually."

Raven put his fists on his hips. "Well, that's incredibly inconvenient. Now I'll look like a crazy person."

Alexander raised and dropped his hands. "Oh, now you'll look like a crazy person."

Tanglwyst seemed to be a bit more receptive to the idea. "Can she see or hear us?"

She nodded.

Raven nodded as well. "Apparently both."

Clara put her hands on Raven's shoulders and he felt calm and… organized. He pulled back. He'd never felt organized. It was almost like he could think.

"What did you do?"

"Nothing."

"I could think and I don't do that."

Gomez looked at Alexander. "This is your new advisor?"

Alexander shrugged. "He seemed alright in a pinch."

Clara put her hands on Raven's shoulders again. "Communicate with me in your mind. Don't speak out loud anymore for a few minutes. You need to be able to talk coherently to these people. What they are doing is important."

*He did as requested. What are you doing to me?*

*I'm helping you organize. I'm helping you teach.*

*Oh. I've never been able to do that.*

She smiled. *I know. Now go sit down.*

Raven looked at the others. "She's still here. She's just making it easier to explain things."

Alexander sat in a pew. "Can she talk to the other Saints?"

She nodded and Raven interpreted.

"Can she talk to Saint Brigit?" His tone was grave.

She nodded. "Does he need that right now?"

Alexander shook his head. "No, but if you could let her know." He looked to Gomez. "Tell me what you have seen and done."

Gomez explained the happenings of the invasion, the spell, the horrible aftermath. Unfortunately, the environment had not frozen too and the horrors were abundant. When Johner had arrived, Sovereigna had released the spell on everyone, like that's what she was waiting for. The barrier was discovered to be in place then. They found out people could pass in but lost about a dozen people as they decided that if people could enter, they could leave too. After proving that wasn't the case, the monsters patrolling the streets thinned out to join the main army. The *Sulocco* had pulled into port and Tanglwyst's estate had arrived the next day. The goods the ship offloaded helped the town with food supplies. Things could come in, and people started showing up with food at the roads to the north and south, sliding baskets of eggs or fruit across the barrier.

They painted the red line on day three, when a child playing had thrown a stick to see where the barrier was so she could stay away from it. They thought that was brilliant so they did likewise everywhere they could. The woods to the west were unmarked on the ground but the trees had marks on the trunks. They had tried to send out birds in the beginning but they died on impact. They tried from everywhere, including throwing them directly up from the tallest building. They all died. That was the last of the messenger birds. Attempts were tried to toss letters through but they, too, were destroyed. About day ten, the messenger arrived. He had been warned about the barrier. He ended up being held there for hours as people asked questions. He finally left amidst protests when it was starting to get dark.

"Johner stayed with me the whole time, observing but not interfering. He helped a few folks with packages and caught a kid that fell off a roof when the birds were being released. He was strangely unobtrusive, for being such a blatant sign of the occupation. He advised me on dealings with the monsters when they were in town, but when they left, he had nothing to do. He said he was waiting for you." Gomez nodded to Alexander. "What about you. What happened?"

Alexander sighed. "More than I can possibly say. The lady I pursued to marry refused me. She was right to. I discovered a lot of things about myself and this responsibility along the way. I learned a lot about things I never would have guessed existed. Mostly, I learned that there is still magic in the world, and not a small bit of it. I'll mention the appropriate lessons as they apply but for now, I think we need to focus upon what affects us here and now. Saint Clara, why are you here?"

"My main purpose is to help Raven. He has a condition (I do not) that stops him from being easily understood. It has to do with being alive so long, I think. Regardless, he was never a good teacher and that is vital right now. I can't help outside these walls but know that within them, Heaven is not only aware of you, but watching and listening. We'll offer guidance where we can."

"Thank you Clara, and thank you Raven for being her interpreter. Tangl, did you have something to tell?"

"I do, but I don't know what, if any, will be useful. None of it is helpful except that these symbols," she gestured to the ones in the walls, "were put here after the Soulless War. All the Augustinian Churches in the world were redesigned to include them. It was done to boost the strength of the divine in an area. It is part of why St. Giles is so safe despite being on the edge of the Black Forest."

"What is the Black Forest?" Gomez looked at Tanglwyst. "Everyone refers to it as so dangerous but I looked in the records and there are no incidents in the Black Forest at all."

Raven raised his hand. "I know this one. Raven, not Clara. That is a Fae prison. Our most irredeemable monsters go there. Once a Fae enters, it can't leave."

"Like griffins and dragons?" Gomez asked but Alexander's eyes lit up a bit at the mention of them.

"Those are beasts. They are hidden elsewhere. These are Fae, like goblins and ogres and trolls. Basically the full versions of what you said was out there." Raven gestured to the valley.

"Wait, griffins are real?" Alexander leaned forward.

"Well, yeah. They're air creatures so they live if Yokotama. I have a friend there."

"Hunh." Alexander crossed his arms and leaned back. "What about the stuff regarding Clara?"

Tanglwyst shrugged. "Well, I know that there is a pillar under the library in the Papal Palace. It is in the center of a fountain that heals. On it are written the names of all the Saints. Raymond was not on it, but you were, Clara. That's especially odd because of the words written upon it, that these were the words of Heaven."

Gomez cocked his head. "If Raymond is not there, does that make Clara the Patron of Barren Women?"

Raven nodded. "Clara says that Raymond was cast out for causing the Soulless War. Wait. For causing the Soulless War? That took a lot of effort from a lot of people."

Clara nodded. "Yes, but he was the contributor from Heaven. They needed a scapegoat and when I came up, they got rid of him. He still walks the earth."

Raven frowned. "According to Clara, he was cast out and still walks the earth."

"I read up on the Soulless War in the Papal City. There was a lot of horrible decisions made after that. One was these amulets that are created with dark magic. They corrupt the souls of those who touch them." Tanglwyst looked at Gomez. "Dominic has one."

Gomez rolled his eyes. "Like that ass needs more corruption."

Alexander pointed to her. "That reminds me. He popped in at my feet when I was out in the south area with Johner." He related all that happened with Elizabeth's body and the fact that he couldn't find Dominic now.

Tanglwyst smiled. "Is that so? Really scared him?"

"Yes."

"Then I think he accidentally went to the Papal City. And if he's not showing up anymore, then that means he's probably dead. From Henri and Ce'Nedra or from going through the thorns, it doesn't much matter. Can you see those two?"

Alexander closed his eyes and saw four people wandering around away from the place he had seen them before. "Yes. They are safe. Felix from the messenger's office and Sylvaine from St. Andrew are with them." He opened his eyes. "I wonder what they did to gain his ire."

"As much as he was traveling, I can't imagine he had much sanity left. It could have been as simple as delivering the mail. If I didn't know better, I might say he fell prey to whatever was affecting Charles."

"Luckily, we do know better."

Gomez looked confused.

Alexander glanced over. "He was being poisoned by Elizabeth."

Gomez nodded.

Raven pointed to the road behind them. "That Elizabeth?"

Everyone nodded.

"Was Charles the king before you?"

"Two months ago."

"So she was executed for righteous purposes." Raven sat back. "That changes everything."

"How?"

"With a righteous kill, the Krakten Queen has no grounds. She cannot command a price, she can't invade, she can't do anything by the Fae Concurrence. She's not allowed to be here, not according to those laws."

"So this really was an invasion." Alexander ran his hands through his hair. "What do I do?"

Raven shook his head. "I have no idea. It means you probably don't need a Fae advisor though. This isn't Fae business. It's human business. You don't need a Fae lawyer. Your human laws are all that needs to be invoked here." He stood. "I should be getting back. I'll tell Johner when I go."

"Wait." Alexander stood as well. "Don't I need you to talk to Clara and Brigit?"

Raven looked around the church. "Not in here. Good night." He walked out of the building and into the night.

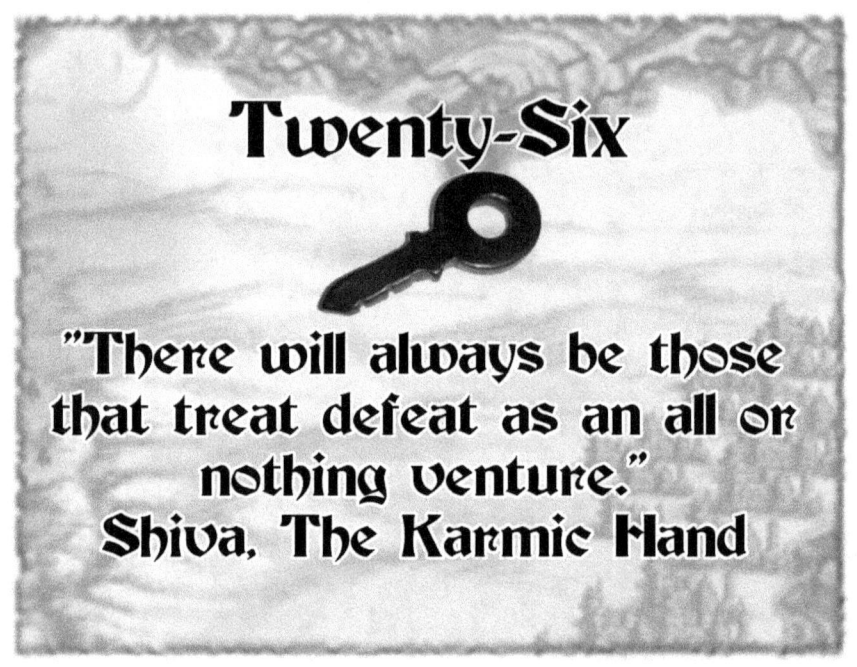

# Twenty-Six

"There will always be those that treat defeat as an all or nothing venture."
Shiva, The Karmic Hand

Alistair stepped out onto the green pasture and looked around. A black horse grazed nearby, looking content. Water flowed from a new spring and had already started cutting its way towards the sea. The ground was alive and lush far as the horizon and he was not certain it didn't go beyond his view. He tried to figure out where he was. This obviously wasn't York.

He saw a figure riding a horse about a mile away. The horse was at a walk and there was a dog running alongside the animal. He decided this person was as good as any to find out where he was. He hailed the rider and moved to intercept him or her. The rider saw him and kicked the horse to a run. The dog accelerated in the springy joy of youth and ran to meet Alistair. As they got within greeting range, Alistair nodded.

"Hail, friend. What place is this?"

"Alistair?" Myrgen's voice was surprised.

"Myrgen?"

The man stopped his horse and dismounted, coming to Alistair to greet him with a hug. "Where have you been?" Myrgen looked him up and down. "And where did you come from?" The dog jumped on the pair, putting dusty paw prints on Alistair's clothes. "Drake, down."

"That's a long story. Where are we?"

"York. Near Persephone according to my map."

Alistair looked around. He looked at the horse and gestured. "May I?"

Myrgen nodded and stepped aside. He went to the wolfhound puppy who was barking at the newcomer and calmed him. From the higher perspective, Alistair could see the old village. The towers were not there, which was why he had not recognized it. He dismounted.

"What happened?" He motioned to the grass. "This place is a wasteland."

"Apparently not. I have been sent by the Land to fetch a weapon that will 'aid in the upcoming war.' It really wasn't any clearer than that, outside of the fact that it's underground."

"Underground?"

Myrgen pointed to the ruins of the covenant. "Over there."

"Hey there."

The two men turned to see Raven walking up. Lauriel walked beside him. The two dogs sniffed each other in greeting and Alistair hugged Raven.

"Old friend. How are you?"

Raven looked at Alistair, his eyes suspicious. "You look different…"

Alistair swallowed. "I do?"

Raven looked him up and down. "You cut your hair?"

"No."

"Hm. Taller? Shorter?"

Alistair pursed his lips. "Nope."

"Oh!" Raven snapped his fingers. He grabbed the lapels of the white coat. "New clothes!"

Alistair tapped his nose. "Nothing gets by you." He looked at the green ground again. "How far does this extend?"

Raven pointed behind him. "All the way to the Mervol border. I was surprised too." He looked at Myrgen. "Hey! I know you too."

Myrgen exchanged a quick hug with Raven as well. "I thought this place was supposed to be barren."

"It was." Alistair pointed to Persephone. "That was the only place that still had anything green near it, last time I was here."

"Same here."

Myrgen looked at Alistair. "When was the last time you were here?"

Alistair thought. "Maybe a few years ago." He looked at Raven. "What about you?"

"About twelve hours, give or take."

Myrgen frowned. "This happened in twelve hours?"

"Oh, I doubt it. The Dûcesa has been underground for almost a tenday."

Myrgen blinked. "The Dûcesa?"

"Yeah."

Alistair put his hand on Myrgen's shoulder. "There's a lot to talk about. Do we want to do it before or after we save her?"

Raven shrugged. "Depends on how many times you want to tell the tale."

Alistair nodded. "Good point. Catriona is going to want to know about all this."

Myrgen walked over to the horse. "Won't she just be able to look and see what's happened?"

Alistair pursed his lips. "If she reads this, she *is* a supernatural creature." He looked at Raven. "Is there enough life here now for you to earth ride?"

Raven nodded. "Plenty. That's how I got here so quickly. Try and keep up, Myrgen."

Raven raised a sled of soil and Alistair stood beside him. He made a crest for a handhold and the whole thing started moving fast towards the ruins of Persephone. Lauriel jumped onto the sled and barked to Myrgen's dog. The other dog looked at Myrgen who was getting on the back of his horse.

"C'mon Drake. Let's run!"

The horse was spurred forward and the dog ran after the sled. Persephone was not far but far enough that the other dog ended up slowing down before they got there. Myrgen rode hard to keep up but when the wolfhound slowed, he did likewise. As a result, Raven, Lauriel, and Alistair arrived a few minutes ahead of Myrgen. The place was simultaneously worse off and better off than Alistair expected. Better off because it had been two-hundred fifty years since the towers had been brought down by the armies of the Church and most of the homes still seemed intact. Worse off because the overgrowth that was reclaiming things really made it look ancient.

"Hunh. That's odd."

Alistair looked at Raven. "What is?"

Raven let the land sled sink back into the ground without a trace. He looked for Myrgen and nodded to him, waiting for him to join them. As Myrgen dismounted, Raven nodded to the grass-covered area inside the perimeter of Persephone.

"When I came here a couple days ago, all this was barren. Not even weeds could grow here. Now look at it."

Ivy covered every house and fallen tower, almost hiding them completely. Trees about twenty-five years old were growing from the cracks where Raven and Wilge's room had been. They were even bearing fruit.

"So, you said you wanted to wait for Catriona. She's gone off to Glarren. Were we going to meet up with her afterwards?"

Raven looked at Alistair, but Alistair decided to ask the question. "Myrgen, what's this weapon you were supposed to grab?"

"Dunno. All I know is it's under there." He pointed to the base of the towers.

Raven leaned in to Alistair. "That's where the *čaro* vault is. It might be something in there."

Myrgen shrugged. "What's *čaro*?"

"It's the stuff of pure magic. It gives your spells a boost. Personally though, I think it's probably the Dûcesa."

Myrgen shook his head. "Who is this Dûcesa? Do you mean Anika?"

Raven shrugged. "I don't think that's her name. I might have been told but, in the end, it won't matter soon. She's going to die and be reborn and then, she won't remember anything."

Myrgen paled, leaning against his horse. "By the Stones. Catriona."

Alistair nodded. He put his hand on Myrgen's shoulder. "Yes. And we have to hurry. Raven's right. She's on the verge of death now. If she dies, she'll change."

Myrgen ran to the edge of the wall and jumped, trying to get over it. The barrier repelled him, knocking him to the ground. Raven and Alistair ran over to him, kneeling to see if he was injured. Myrgen waved them off.

"What was that?"

Raven remembered something. "The Gold Wife. She said it would only admit those who had been here before."

Alistair shook his head. "It admitted Catriona. If it's going to let her in, it should let him in too."

Raven disagreed. "When the Dûcesa entered, she was still the Dûcesa, just in her resurrected form." He pointed to Myrgen. "That's a reincarnated form. Very different."

"What are we going to do?" Myrgen looked back and forth to the two men.

"Raven and I can go in. We've been here before. But we'll need you here when we come out with her. She's... she's gonna need you."

Myrgen looked confused but Alistair and Raven nodded to each other. They went up to the barrier above the low wall and jumped over it into the courtyard. They looked at Myrgen. Alistair held up his hand. "Raven, what is this spell?"

"Marica did it."

Alistair turned to him. "The Gold Wife? How?"

"Remember the spell we put up against the Church's army? It's that one."

"That's still up?" Alistair turned to face Raven. "Then bring it down."

"Can't. I need something from the Land from before her."

"Like what?"

"Like..."

Myrgen held up his hand. "Like one of these?"

In his hand was a cloudy black stone with gold flecks.

Raven stepped over to the wall. "Yes!" He put his hand through the barrier and Myrgen put the stone in his hand. He pulled it through. He opened his hand to look at it.

"This has a lot of flecks in it. I need an earlier one. Very few flecks."

He tossed that one back to Myrgen who then pulled a dozen of the stones from a pouch on his hip. He looked them over and tossed another one through. "This one work?"

Raven caught it and looked. "Yes."

"Why is this working?" Myrgen looked at the barrier. "Why can I toss these through? Does it work for anything inanimate?"

Alistair shook his head. "No. Only with something significantly touched by the Land."

Myrgen nodded to the fallen tower. "Then how did that happen?"

"Cannonballs. Significantly blessed by Heaven."

"Heaven... blessed cannonballs?"

"Sort of. The Church cast them, then cooled them in holy water from a Saint."

Raven closed his eyes. He held the stone in his hands and Alistair watched the barrier, waiting for it to fall. He saw it flicker, and smiled. Then Myrgen shouted.

"Behind you!"

Alistair managed to turn in time to see the golden fist slam into Raven's back. He fell forward across the wall, dropping the memory stone.

"Marica!" Alistair tried to push her away from Raven but she set her mass to immovable, a trick she proved she could do when she was protecting the covenant from the Church Army.

She made a horrid noise, like a fork scraping on a metal plate. He covered his ears against the sound, as did Myrgen. Raven dangled unconscious over the wall. Alistair looked at the gold golem. "Marica! Stop! What are you doing?"

She turned to Alistair. Suddenly, her voice was dulcet, like the gentle tinkling of bells. "Protecting the covenant."

She pulled Raven from the wall and put him across her shoulder. Alistair grabbed her ankle, trying to trip her but she just dragged him along.

"Don't you see, Antoine? The country is being restored. This is all due to me."

Alistair flinched at being referred to by his birth name. It was so very long ago that he changed it to be that of the prince of York. "Marica, this isn't right. This isn't..."

Then he remembered what Lucifer said.

"You've been corrupted." He looked at the Gold Wife. "You serve Hell now."

The Gold Wife dropped Raven on the ground and swung at Alistair. Her hits were lethal. He had seen that in the Inquisition War. She punched a cannonball out of the air and sent it flying back to the unit from whence it came. She was a Servant of the Land, probably the earliest one. She knew countless things.

But Alistair realized something himself. He was already dead. She couldn't kill him.

He put his hand up and caught her fist. She punched his hand right into his face. Alistair went flying back and slammed into a small house that, coincidentally, used to belong to him. The familiar wall broke in and he saw some ceramic shingles spill from the roof onto the street, shattering. He got to his feet, shaking off the blow, literally. His nose was bleeding.

*Well, that worked not at all.* He looked at Raven and caught a glimpse of him muttering something. *By the Balance. He's still working on the spell.*

"When did you fall, Marica? When did you start working for the Infernal?"

The Gold Wife had been about to bend down and pick up the now still Raven, but she turned to face Alistair. Her eyes glowed red.

"I have not fallen. I was sent a dream. It told me about Persephone's power and how to get to it. It said if I released the power source, a stronger one would arrive, one that could heal all this," she gestured to the lush area, "and it was right."

"It did so at the cost of another's freedom, Marica! How could you let that happen to a Servant of the Land?"

"She's only got a small amount of time before she awakens as the First Dûcesa. Once she does, she'll be more powerful than ever. If she awakens more than once, think of what she might become!"

Alistair watched Raven unraveling the spell, and needed to keep her talking. As long as she was paying attention to Alistair, Raven could work.

"At what cost? What could she possibly become that would be a good idea?"

The Gold Wife's eyes were wild with excitement. She stepped closer to Alistair in her zeal. "What cost?" She waved her hands at the countryside again. "How is this a cost? Look! The plants are coming back! This is rebirth, regrowth. Restoration. For over three hundred years, this country has suffered from the scarring of the Soulless War. But now it's being fixed!" She pointed to Raven without looking at him.

"He showed us all that she renews. Now, she's renewing this place. And if she dies again, she'll die in this magical trap, and be reborn *from that.* She takes on the properties of the place she returns, remember?"

Alistair backed away, acting slightly frightened. *If Catriona renewed here, what would she become?* He scrambled back towards the entrance to the village. Behind her, Raven managed a small flash of light and the barrier came down. Alistair wasn't sure what to do next but he needn't have worried. Raven seemed to have a plan.

Raven groaned, drawing the Gold Wife's attention. Alistair got up and ran for her back but she caught him as he was about to strike her and she threw him hard against the broken onyx tower near the center of the courtyard. Raven opened his eyes and looked at her.

"Marica? What did Alistair mean?"

Marica knelt beside Raven. Her voice returned to the screeching sound. Alistair remembered that she could make her voice beautiful and understandable, but only to one person at a time. She seemed to be sympathetic to Raven, almost remorseful and apologetic.

Raven hissed as he tried to move. His legs were unresponsive. Marica looked at them, her expression becoming concerned. "You broke me. You broke my back. I can't feel my legs."

Her fist went to her mouth and she looked to have tears in her eyes. She started to look around and Raven shot a look to Alistair. He wiggled his fingers just behind his back in a very distinct gesture, part of the combat language they had learned during the wars.

*Play dead?*

Marica started to look his way but he did as told when her gaze swept over him and she didn't come over. She picked up Raven's body and took him into the basement of the tower Alistair lay upon. Raven hissed in pain, either real or pretend, and she seemed to respond. Once they were out of sight, Alistair raised his head, then nodded to Myrgen and motioned him over. Myrgen joined him, staying quiet when Alistair motioned to be so. He got up, staying crouched. He pointed to the green house windows near them and Myrgen nodded when he saw Marica enter with Raven's body.

Myrgen leaned close to Alistair. "What do we do?"

"We need to get you to that chamber to get Catriona. She might be able to stop the Gold Wife. She's sacrificing her life to restore this place."

"How do we do that?"

"We have to go there and sneak past Marica."

"You mean she took Raven right where we need to go?"

Alistair waggled his hand in a wishy-washy gesture. "Technically, yes, but there's a small amount of space to work with."

"What if she sees us?"

"Then we fight her."

Myrgen helped Alistair to his feet and then followed Alistair to the under-tower access. The room used to be a great bath house with elaborate water ways and steam rooms. One could walk through here, even with half the covenant's occupants in here, and still have privacy. Now, it was just a large open room and they tread carefully to make sure their footsteps didn't echo. The doorway at the end was open and Alistair motioned to Myrgen to get to the far left side. He took the right and looked to see if she was watching the door. Her back was to them and gave the signal to Myrgen to get in the room.

He followed Myrgen into the shadowy area inside and pulled him into a corner. The door to the *čaro* vault was in the middle of the wall on the right, directly across from Raven's door. Luckily, she had put him on the bed and that was just out of sight from the door once you were across from it. That was the good news. The bad news was that, to get to that spot, they had to cross a wide stretch of light coming in from the broken tower above. Alistair kept an eye on Marica while he waved Myrgen across the sunlit room.

Myrgen stayed close to the wall and trusted Alistair, looking at where he was walking rather than watching the Gold Wife. He made it across without a sound and that was impressive given the terrain. Onyx debris in every size from dog to dust coated this floor. Walking across this was like trying to sneak across a carpet of corn husks filled with beetle carcasses. But Alistair was a thief before he was a Prince. He had broken into that *čaro* vault a couple times, much to the anger and contempt of Wilge, the covenant seneschal. He could do this.

His first step echoed throughout the chamber like a cannon shot.

Marica stepped into the doorway of the bedroom and Alistair froze. Then she disappeared for a moment. Alistair ran to the vault door and tried the knob. Of course, it was locked. Myrgen tapped his shoulder and pointed. He looked over his shoulder and stopped his actions immediately. Marica had grabbed Raven and had him by the throat, dangling above the floor by a good twelve inches. Raven tugged at her grasp but she was, in fact, made of metal.

She snapped Raven's neck and twisted his head completely around, then tossed the dead body into the room.

# Twenty-Seven

## "Sometimes, the strongest is not the one we think."
## Shiva, The Karmic Hand

Myrgen's scream filled the room. "No!"

He slammed his fist into the ground and the onyx chunks in the room all flew at the woman made of gold. The onyx ripped through her thin outer shell like vellum. One of the dog-sized chunks hit her in the face and knocked her to the ground. She rolled over, damaged, and got to her hands and knees.

"So, you are the new Stâpân."

Myrgen's heart blazed with strength granted by the Land to protect his companion. He no longer saw the woman as an ally led astray. This was a monster now, and the Land had control over the monsters.

"No. I am the new Hunter."

He hit the ground again and this time, she countered it. She had the same magics he did and merely neutralized his. He looked at Alistair. "Can you get that door open?"

"Yeah."

Alistair scrambled to the door and Myrgen kept his eyes on the Gold Wife. She picked up the chunk that hit her now-ragged face, and raised it above her head like it was a pillow. She hurled it with a frightening amount of force and Myrgen hit it with his fist as it came at Alistair's back. It pulverized to dust, spraying the men with a cloud of black. Myrgen was hit by a second stone, this one the size of a cat and then another the size of a bird. They caught him off guard and he started bleeding.

A wind picked up and the Gold Wife screamed in frustration and surprise. The dust spun around the room, then lifted in a cyclone moving towards the broken tower ceiling. Myrgen and Alistair shielded their eyes from the flying debris to see Raven in the bedroom, casting the spell.

"Raven!" Myrgen and Alistair's voices joined in surprise and joy

"Get to the Dûcesa. I've got her."

Myrgen looked at the body that was on the ground, then at the door. *Fae magic. Illusion.* Alistair was looking around for something to break the lock. Myrgen put his hand on the wall beside the door. "A citizen of Caratia is held prisoner behind this door. Please, grant me acc…"

The door swung open and Myrgen stepped back. "Oh. Right. It wants us to hurry, I think."

Alistair stepped in. "I'm beginning to wonder why I came on this adventure." He wiped the blood from his nose. "I'm proving to be quite useless."

There was a long room with shelves set up like a library and Myrgen ran down it. He got to the back wall and a secret door slid open before he even asked. Ancient runes glowed along these walls and Alistair was pulled to a halt. He looked at the walls.

"Well, whaddaya know? He wasn't lying."

"It's down here. Hurry." Myrgen ran to the end, where a chamber opened. There, suspended above the ground, was Catriona. Her body was limp and she looked dead. "By the stones... Alistair! Down here!"

Alistair looked in from the opening of the cave.

"Help me get her down."

Alistair nodded. "I can, but not from here. This is a Karma trap."

Myrgen went to her, trying to tug at the spiritual manacles draining her life essence. "What does that mean?"

"It means Karma made it." He smiled, striding back down the hallway. "I get to contribute after all."

Myrgen went to the opening and Alistair walked to the place where the runes began.

"When I release her, you get her out. Understand?"

Myrgen nodded and went back to Catriona. Light flared throughout the room and suddenly, Catriona dropped to his arms. She was barely breathing and felt like she was little more than bones and flesh. She weighed less than a hundred pounds. He could feel every bone in her body and he felt a few ribs crack when he caught her. He carried her out of the chamber and past Alistair. He looked around in the vault. There were several herbs and grasses but he didn't know what any of them were. He lay her down between the wall and a series of shelves built out of the onyx.

He stepped out to the corridor. "I need help here."

Alistair nodded, still holding the runes. "Gimme a second. Raven! Can you bring her in here?"

"No! There's no air in there!"

"Damn."

Myrgen looked up. "I've got this."

He put his hand on the opposite wall and opened the rift in the onyx from the other room, continuing down the hallway. He saw no runes on the ceiling of the vault so he continued to tear it apart. However, once it got to the area with the runes, his power to control the stone ended.

"That's all I can do!"

The howling of the cyclone grew and her screeching was beyond tolerable. Raven brought her into the vault, carefully holding her in the open air very much against her will. He looked at Alistair. He nodded to the cavern. "Is that your plan?"

Alistair nodded.

"Get ready to move."

Alistair stepped aside and Raven sent a huge gust of wind at her, throwing her down the corridor. Once she got about halfway down, she dropped hard to the ground, heavy. Myrgen looked at Raven. They nodded and both men hit the ground. It rippled but Marica took a knee and rode out the earth tide. It parted around her, only shifting her back a few feet.

Raven frowned. "Two feet down, another twenty to go."

"How did you counter her before?"

"Air magic, earth's natural counter. But there's no air down there."

Myrgen kept the ground rippling so she didn't get her balance but he made no progress. Then she dug her hands into the ground and she became immobile. He couldn't even make the small nudges back that made her have to recover the same few feet. She braced herself, then started clawing her way back to them.

"Figure it out, fellas." Alistair didn't move but his voice showed his resolve. "Catriona's running out of time."

Myrgen got an idea. "Raven, make the ground tilt toward the cavern."

Raven made the ground tilt as asked, and Myrgen turned the top layers of the corridor to pea gravel. Her grip on the surface disappeared. She slid backwards into the chamber almost immediately and Alistair flared the lights again. Tendrils grabbed her, dragging her to the spot where Catriona was just hanging. Her screeches cut the air like knives thrown in their direction, and Alistair let go of the runes.

Alistair shook out his hands. "Well, it isn't empty, but I doubt she'll be a problem for him."

Myrgen looked at his companions. "There are a million stories I need to hear but I have a priority first." He took Raven to Catriona. "Is there anything in this room that can help her?"

Raven looked around the room. "Nearly everything was taken after the assault." He rubbed his head. "And I'm not good with body magic." He looked at Alistair. "But we know someone who is."

Alistair frowned. "Merrick? Do we even know where he is?"

Raven nodded, looking at Catriona. "Yeah, we do. But we need to stabilize her or she's gonna die."

"How do we do that?"

Myrgen shrugged. "Simple. We encase her in earth."

# Twenty-Eight

"There is no peace in living for the dying, and no peace in death for the living."
Kali, The Karmic Hand

Raven lifted the earth sled with Catriona on it, the cradle he made keeping her immobile. There was a little room for her to breathe, but everything else was like a cast: self-supporting and firm to prevent jarring or movement. He looked at Myrgen, who nodded, his hand upon Catriona to maintain her connection to the world. He whispered to her, calling her name to make sure she stayed with them. On occasion, she moaned, but those were faint, and far between.

Alistair took a deep breath. "What if this doesn't work?"

Myrgen looked up. "Which part?"

Alistair acknowledged the fragility of the mission with a nod.

Raven started moving toward the entrance. "In truth, the best thing you can do is let her die. The Land will return her. It always does."

"But she'll look different."

Raven looked at Myrgen. "Do you love her, or only how she looks?"

"She'll be a different person entirely."

"That will happen once she gets those stones in your pouch."

"Maybe."

Raven and Alistair turned to face Myrgen. Alistair took the lead. "No. In truth. Because who she was before she met you is very different from who she was after. When she remembers everyone she was, do you want to change the woman you recognize into someone you don't but wearing the same face, or do you want to be able to let that go because it isn't a familiar one?"

"She's already dying, Myrgen." Raven put his hand on Myrgen's shoulder. "Chances are very good she will pass away before we even get to Merrick."

"It is a long journey?"

Raven shook his head. He pointed to another section of the vault. "No. It's right over there."

Myrgen frowned. "Then what in the Hell are we waiting for? Get moving!"

They hurried to the entrance to the Fae realm and Sovereignlumin. The earth sled was very stable and Myrgen was quite surprised but glad. The run wasn't smooth so the fact that Catriona wasn't jostled at all was amazing. He didn't want to, but he made himself think about what Raven and Alistair were saying. Did he only love her because of how she looked? He shook his head. It wasn't that. It was that they had not even gotten time to be a couple in this incarnation. He wasn't ready to try for a fresh start with another one. Yes, she would change. He knew that. But if he recognized some part of her, at least he could use that to ground her. He had been with enough strangers. He wanted someone familiar.

He heard the dog barking outside. "Drake! Raven, the dog, can he come?"

"Sure. Lauriel!"

The Fae wolf sprung to Raven's side.

"We're going to Sovereignlumin. Bring the others."

Lauriel bounded away.

They punctured the Fae realm and Myrgen felt the change in everything. It still felt connected to the Land but everything else was new. It felt and looked like the cabin on the Enigma, when he visited Estelle. There was a huge tower that pierced the sky and they made straight for it. The adrenaline in his body kept him running and they got to the tower in a couple minutes. When they arrived, Raven pulled the sled to a halt.

"We need to go in the right door." He had them enter on the side facing them. Inside, there were several other doors, three from the outside at the secondary compass points, four interior doors at the compass points. Around the entire inside was a staircase that was one part impossible, fifty parts beautiful. Raven pointed to the door with the cornucopia and water.

He picked up an apple. "Here, give her this. It will help."

Myrgen looked at the mage. "How am I going to give her this? She can't eat."

Raven looked at her, then at the apple. "You'll figure something out." He went in the door and turned immediately like he was going up a set of stairs.

Myrgen looked around and saw a bowl for the water. He got it and filled the bowl. He wasn't sure she could even swallow. He took his sleeve, soaked it in the water, then put it to her lips. She didn't even open her mouth. Tears started to roll down his cheeks.

Alistair put a hand on his back. "What do you want to do?"

Myrgen shook his head. "I don't know. I don't want to have her die here. She doesn't know this place."

"Where do you want to be?"

He stroked her hair and a clump of it came out in his hand. That was the final blow.

"Ashstone." He looked at Alistair. "I need to get her to Ashstone."

Alistair nodded and closed his eyes. "Let's hope he was right about this too."

Myrgen felt the world shift and for a brief moment, he saw a white place that he knew he couldn't enter. Then he felt the world solidify beneath his feet and the meditation chamber formed around him. The pile of stones covering Tib was before him. The earth sled was no longer with them. He laid her now clean form upon the ground beside her son.

She opened her eyes and looked around. "Where...?"

He didn't bother trying not to cry. "I brought you home."

"...Tib...?"

He nodded to the stones. He couldn't speak. The room seemed to be helping her and a faint spark of hope caught in his chest. If he could keep her here long enough, she would recover.

She turned to the stones and he saw her throat catch. Her eyes squeezed shut and her body began to shake in silent sobs. She tried to turn and he helped her to embrace the bier. Her body wracked and her cries filled the chamber. Her sorrow broke more bones but she clearly didn't care. He lifted her to lay across Tib's burial stones. Several of them tumbled, exposing the blanket beneath. Every movement caused more damage and he tried to support her weight while she mourned. She started to sag and her crying ebbed.

That was when he noticed his hands were wet.

He turned her over and bone shards were poking through her skin. He pressed her to his chest, rocking back and forth as he felt her slip away. Her final breath rattled in his ear and then she was gone.

Myrgen screamed his anguish to the chamber and felt it go throughout the castle. All the veins in the rock pulsed once, then went dark. He held her body for a long time in the near-dark until he felt her legs fall into the ground. He opened his eyes and saw the blanket wrapping Tib. He reached over and tugged at the blanket until he exposed a sleeve. He pulled the arm, freeing it. He put his hand in hers.

*Take him. Remember him. Please…*

He let her body go and it pulled Tib down as well. The rocks shifted as the body beneath disappeared. He sighed, smiling. She had done it. Even if she changed, she was with her son.

He sat back, covered in her blood, and cried until he had no more water in his body.

# Book Two

"Death is part of life. We
cannot live if we do not die."
Kali, The Karmic Hand

# Twenty-Nine

## "Our connection is beyond time."
## Shiva, The Karmic Hand

Alexander, Tanglwyst, and Gomez sat in the quiet of the church, trying to sort out what they had just learned. Alexander finally sighed, shaking his head. "I think he has the right idea. It's the middle of the night and I haven't rested at all. We should all go to bed."

Gomez nodded. "I'll show you to the place I'm staying. It's the city's guard bunkhouse. There's an empty bunk you can use. They aren't very comfortable, but they will work for a night or two."

Alexander looked at Tanglwyst. "Well, I…"

Tanglwyst came to his rescue. "I have an apartment here in town. It has a bath you can use."

Gomez frowned. "Where will you stay then?"

"I have a ship in port."

Alexander bowed. "I have a place I can stay."

Tanglwyst looked away. "That's true. And it, too, has a bath area. Well then. I'll turn in." She walked out the door and Alexander cursed his brain.

*What in the hell is wrong with me?* He looked at Gomez. "Escort her, please?"

Gomez stepped out the door and called out to her, then offered his arm. Alexander shook his head and sat back down in the pew. He wasn't trying to offend her, but he also didn't want her to feel pressured or shamed. He could tell she had a positive reputation here but she had also recently been a fugitive and punished publicly for her crimes. He could help her be seen as regal, but not if he let her be seen as compromised. He watched her say good night to Gomez who then walked back to the Church.

"You wanna tell me what just happened there? Because you handing off that lady when you greeted her like you did was…"

"Confusing?"

"Inconsistent." Gomez sat down. "I mean, I made the suggestion as absolutely unappealing as I could so you might get a better offer. You got one. You turned it down. So what's going on? Is she truly just a friend?"

"She is a very dear friend at this point. She has been for a while now." He looked at Gomez. "So you made that unappealing offer in order to get me to join her?"

"At least to get you the escort to her home."

Alexander stood. "I am such an idiot."

He strode to the door and down the street. He got to the Tanglwyst Trading Company office and knocked on the door. He glanced at the church and saw Gomez lean in the doorway, arms folded, watching. A window opened above Alexander a few moments later and he stepped back. Tanglwyst leaned out of it.

"Alexander?"

"I misinterpreted Gomez's comment. I thought he was being judgmental."

"What was he actually being?"

"Accommodating."

She smiled, and looked down the street to him. Gomez looked away, and walked, whistling, to the guard's office. He opened the door, glanced back at the couple, then stepped inside. She looked down at Alexander.

"So, you were just being gallant?"

"I never want anyone to think ill of you, my Lady."

She looked away.

"What is it?"

"I wish I could say I don't care what others think of me but that isn't true. Harsh words cut me like I'm made of spider webs. When someone judges me, I feel their weight, more so if I don't know them or don't know them well. I eventually get to the point of not caring, but for a very long time, I won't be able to stop thinking about how to mend things with them."

"We all want people to like us."

"I don't want people to just like me. I want them to like me instantly. It's ridiculous but I do. And, well, I know how much Gomez' opinion means to you."

He bit his lower lip, not sure how to respond. He felt with his heart for her emotions, to see what she needed but she was already showing him. He didn't know what to do. He sighed.

"My Lady, you have wrought me speechless. I haven't a single idea of what to say to help you right now." He stepped closer. "Perhaps now is not a time for words."

She looked at him, smiling and shaking her head. She wagged a finger at him. "Oh. That was... that was it..." She nodded. "Come on in." She closed the window.

He tried the knob and it opened. He looked around the dark office and saw a faint light coming from the back. Stairs were illuminated and he walked through to them, then ascended to the second floor. The sight of her office was impressive and he admired the design. There were chairs along the front of a desk that was as large as Charles'. Bookshelves lined the northern wall and paintings and sculptures decorated the southern one. A door was open in the southern wall and he went to it. Here was the room with the window she had spoken to him from. The bed was next to it with a chair beside that. The window was large enough to lean on the window sill and read a book. A floor harp sat in a corner nearby. A wardrobe and dresser set along the far wall and a vanity was across from the foot of the bed next to a hearth with a fire going in it. An alcove held a half keg standing tub and a hand pump had its spout over the lip of it. Towels hung on hooks and a robe of silk was draped nearby.

She gestured to the bath area. "The water is cold, but I can heat some up if you like."

He bowed. "I would like that but I will deal with the cold. I can't say how long I will be on my feet after this day." He took her hand and kissed it. "Thank you for your support."

She blushed. "Get in there. I'll not let you near me until you get cleaned… Is that my coat?"

He looked down at the garment tied around his waist. "Yes. It has been my armor all day."

She took it from him. "Yes, it certainly has." She held it up and shooed him towards the bath area.

"Be careful where you touch that. It should probably be burned."

She looked at him as he was taking off his shirt. "Why?"

He took it from her. "Because it has some of Elizabeth on it."

"What?" She stepped back from the garment.

He folded the coat carefully so as to have the slime inside. He set it by the corner of the bath and started explaining what happened after Dominic showed up. He washed as he talked and she asked questions from around the corner. He saw a pair of loose pants with a drawstring get pushed into view with her bare foot and he smiled at her decorum in light of the circumstances. When he was done, he dried off with the towel and used the teeth cleaner and clove oil to take care of his breath. He saw a brush on the counter and used it to de-snarl his golden tresses. He saw several greying hairs in the brush and realized the past two months had indeed taken a toll. He slipped into the pants and robe and stepped into view. She was sitting in a chair by the fireplace, also in a robe and night clothes. The fire was bright and she had set out some wine and a couple glasses.

"Would you like some wine before bed?" The question was not suggestive at all and he waved it off.

"I just used your clove oil. That would be…"

"Ugh." She shuddered. "I stoked up the fire to help warm you after that."

"Thank you." He sat and took advantage of the heat. He had not realized how cold the water was until he was sitting before the fire. Then everything felt like it had been submerged in ice. It took a few minutes to get completely warm again. He stood and turned his backside to the fire, being mindful to not get the silk too close.

"Anyway, then Raven wiggled his fingers and burned the body. And it was gone."

She reached out and took his hand, standing. "That was the right decision."

She hugged him and he held her, enjoying the contact with her. She looked up at him. "Bed."

He nodded, weary and sore, and they went to the bed. She took off the robe and set it on the foot of the bed. She got in on the harp side and he took off his robe and joined her on the opposite. He propped his head on his hand, facing her.

"I'm going to be unable to sleep without you, you know."

She smiled, propping up herself. "That hasn't happened yet. You've slept through quite a lot so far."

He snorted a little laugh, pursing his lips. "Yeah, I'm sure that will change."

She got serious. "The truth is I can feel your absence. When I came up here before, this place was so empty. Even though I knew you were right over there, it felt like you were miles away. It bothered me. I think, had you returned to the cabin, I would have been hard pressed not to go to you by now."

"Had I returned to the cabin, I would have looked around, felt lost with you not there, and come back here anyway. Though at that point, I would have woken you and half your neighbors. There might have been singing."

She laughed, her head falling back to really let it out and he joined her. He was so grateful to be here. There was nothing except her in this room. He was surrounded by her and he felt at home. She kissed him and stroked his hair.

"I'm gonna miss you when you get married."

"You know," he lay on his back, "I was offered to several nobles before I got this job. One was the Queen of York. Lovely woman, very understanding. Wicked smart. Not into men. I was quite grateful. Before I knew those things about her though, I tried to do the dutiful thing. She sat me down, in private and in secret, and asked if I wanted to be there or if I was simply doing my duty as a prince. She was thirty, forty years old. I was sixteen. I told her I was doing it out of love and she looked at me like she knew better. So I broke and admitted that I was actually in love with someone else entirely and completely."

He turned to look at Tanglwyst. "You know what she did?"

Tanglwyst shook her head, smiling.

"She gave me a gown that mother had sent with me as a gift. Probably by that Fucc... Whoever."

"Fuccochio."

"Yeah, that fellow. Anyway, she gave me the dress and said to put it on in my room with some folks she would send to help me. She said, 'Be sure to wear it when I come to see you.'"

Tanglwyst's eyes widened. "I had heard that you wore her gown. I had no idea she encouraged it!"

"No one knows, not even my mother. The Queen understood what it meant to do something for duty and what it meant to love someone for life." He took her hand and kissed it. "I went for a decade avoiding all the intrigues my mother could throw at me, based entirely off the lesson that great lady taught me. If you truly think I will settle for anything other than the person I want to have beside me, then you might need to visit York yourself. I don't need to wed because I already have an heir. I don't need to look for someone to love because I already know what that one looks like. I don't need to try and make an alliance because I already have a full stack of allies and enemies that I inherited and created.

"You, my Lady, are my choice. I will not push for something you don't want, but I don't really feel the need to shop around. I'll be fine going to my grave unwed and unbedded."

She smiled. "Well, hardly unbedded."

"I have had only one lover. And I have been with her only a few times. In truth, I have no idea what I'm doing there."

"You looking for instruction?"

"No. Not without commitment. I said I wouldn't be able to separate my feelings from my body because, in the end, I found sex to be incredibly bonding. I exchanged more than just fluids. And with you, with the connection we have without that, I doubt I could be so detached as to not want to spend every moment with you. It is out of respect for your choice, not a fear on my part, that I do not accept your offer." He ran his fingers down her arm and let himself look blatantly at her body. "But please don't think I would not love to discover myself and you in that intimacy."

She watched his eyes, her breathing shallow and quick. He could see and feel her heart thumping hard in her chest. Then she took his hand from her arm and kissed it. "I can't say I'll ever accept your proposal. But I will say this: I believe you're right on the intimacy. If we ever do go to that place, I doubt I'll come back."

"I waited for years before. I have no problem waiting again."

"Sleep." She closed her eyes and put his hand upon his own chest. "We need sleep."

He nodded and closed his eyes, but it still took a long time before he drifted off.

# Thirty

"Strange things happen all the
time. Revel in them, for they
are always amazing."
Kali, The Karmic Hand

Raven took the stairs two at a time. The woman downstairs was in a
bad way and he hoped he could get Merrick down the stairs fast enough
to save her. He didn't have *high* hopes, but he did have hope. He opened
the door at the top of the stairs and looked around.

It had been a while since he had been here. The last time he visited,
he then spent several years as a cat in St. Andrew. Not a Fae cat, just a
cat. The Fae cat was a different cat. Still, the place looked the same, as
he suspected it would.

Well lit like late afternoon, regardless of the time of day outside.
This was the way of things in Sovereignlumin. The seasons were the
perpetual time of day representing the person. Autumn was the late
afternoon of the seasons, with dusk being the purvue of Winter, noon of
Summer, and dawn of Spring. None of the seasons of the Fae chose night,
for that was the purvue of the Black Forest.

Full bookshelves coated every wall, twenty feet up. Raven was sure
a few walls had been added to accommodate them. There seemed to be
an unnatural number of the things. A full alchemy lab held a place of
honor near one of the corners, a scribal area held another. There was a

bed in another, and a bathing area, a reading nook, a full window, and on and on, filling corners. The bathing area was the only place with fewer books but Raven recognized them as water magic spells and rituals, so they were safe from mold.

A bier was the focal point of the room, with a woman lying upon it. The bier was dressed in velvets and silks in golds, reds, and oranges. The lady herself was in a shimmering gown of brown with the colors of fall wandering through it in a gentle fog of changing color. Occasionally, different motifs would show up, like falling leaves or squashes and apples. Her hair was long and red, streaked with gold. She lay on her side, her knee propped upon a pillow and her hand under the pillow at her head. Her mouth was open like she was asleep and about to snore.

Raven walked over to the bed and shook Merrick's shoulder. The old mage snorted out of his sleep and rolled over with a start.

"Purn?"

"Nope. Just me. I need your help. There's a woman downstairs that is hurt badly. If you don't heal her, she'll die."

"That sounds urgent. Bring her up." Merrick got out of bed and smoothed the blankets to accommodate the patient.

Raven took off back down the stairs, trying not to act as worried as he felt. He didn't know Catriona outside of what he had been told by Myrgen, but he didn't want to be the reason she left this world.

Raven opened the door to the bottom floor of Sovereignlumin. "Ok, bring her up."

Alistair was leaning against the wall. He pushed away from it and stepped in behind Raven, heading up.

Raven looked around at the empty room. "Where did they go?"

"Home. She didn't make it."

"You sure?"

Alistair nodded. "I just felt her go."

Raven leaned against the wall. "Damn."

"Yeah. I loved her."

"You did?"

Alistair nodded, and realized his cheeks were wet. He wiped away the tears but they didn't stop. He drooped to the floor and began sobbing. It didn't matter that she would be reborn. This version was gone, and everything she knew, everything she was. She wouldn't be the woman he protected from bandits in Yantap, or be the woman he made love with on a ship for the first time. She wouldn't be the one who reminded him that other lives were as important, if not more so, than his and his petty ego. She wouldn't be the woman who was tricked by Gwen into drinking Passion Sap in order to stop her from giving herself to him instead of to her true love.

And she wouldn't be the woman who loved Myrgen.

She would become someone who remembered all these things, but she would never be the one who did them. He realized that every incarnation of the Dûcesa was like that. Every one had someone who loved them and who lost them when they died. He wondered how her son was going to handle it, or how her family would. He almost wondered how Gwen would take it, then remembered she was also gone and the tears beat their way out of him.

It didn't take long for pain to turn to anger. He wanted to know why she had died. Why had the Gold Wife turned her back on her life's work to kill Catriona? Why had the trap claimed her and let go of the entity of all magic? Even as the potential First Dûcesa, Catriona had been a servant just like the Gold Wife. Less even because the Gold Wife was ancient. And what could have happened to Magic? Where did it go once it was released?

"By the Balance, I thought I was done with crying now."

Raven had crouched beside him, crying out of sympathy more than knowing the woman, but now, he got to his feet. "What do you want to do now?"

"I don't know." Alistair looked up at Raven. "Should we go to Myrgen? This is probably killing him too."

"You know where he is?"

Alistair nodded. "Ashstone. I took him there. But I want to know a bunch of stuff too. Like what the hell happened to the Gold Wife? Literally."

Raven bobbed his head from side to side. "She just went crazy from loneliness."

"She wasn't alone. She could have left there anytime and returned any time. She knows how to make herself look like a normal person. And there's a guy in the desert nearby named Raymond. He's been near Persephone. Why didn't she go there?"

Raven twitched. "Raymond? Where?"

"At the Standing Stones. A few days from Persephone. Remember that ring of tall stones?"

"Yes. I do. That's the problem. I left something there so I'm a little concerned that someone is living there."

"What did you leave there?"

"Hello?"

Both men leaned out the doorway and looked up to the top of the tower. A woman was leaning over a railing up there, looking down at them. She was so far away, he could barely see her. Raven stepped out into the main area while Alistair got to his feet. Raven waved.

"Hi there! What are you doing here?"

She looked behind her. "Visiting family. What are you doing here?"

"The same thing." Raven looked back at Alistair. "Care for a walk?"

Alistair narrowed his eyes. "Lemme try something first." He put his hand on Raven's arm and willed himself to the top of the tower. Nothing happened. He knew he could travel from here. He took Catriona and Myrgen home. He looked at Raven.

"I think this place is older than Karma."

"That doesn't sound correct. But I don't see anything wrong with your logic."

Raven started for the stairs and Alistair realized that Raven systematically accepted anything that was even remotely unusual. Alistair had closed his eyes to try and travel up to the top of the tower, then realized he couldn't and not explained any of that to his friend. Raven didn't even eye a bat at the strange occurrence. Not even a "What did you try to do?"

Alistair looked at the thousand stairs going around the tower wall. "Hey, I am going to Myrgen instead. You head up and I'll meet you there later."

Raven nodded. "Okay."

Alistair watched his friend get to the stairs where the railing started, then closed his eyes and willed himself to Caratia.

# Thirty-One

## "Captivity harms both the captive and the warden."
## Shiva, The Karmic Hand

Raven looked up the rather impressive set of stairs. They went up at least a hundred stories and had several resting places that looked like accomodations for sleeping. There was food and water the whole way after a certain point on the walk. This was a pilgrimage and Raven realized it had been a while since he made it. At the top was his grandfather, Sovereignus himself. He wasn't holding court or anything, just dead. But that's where he lay, preserved.

The fact that someone *had* made the pilgrimage was startling. He didn't know that many people who could find this place. He looked up at the top.

"Are you okay up there? I might be a while getting to you."

The woman nodded. "I'll be fine. You could just fly or something."

"Well, the stairs don't work that way, but I might be able to speed things up a bit."

He put his hand upon the plants and communed with them. He felt the living wood flow all the way up the stairs, rushing towards the top. When he opened his eyes, he was at the landing where the living wood fed into the sanctuary. A woman was there that was at once foreign and familiar.

"Are you Persephone?"

She frowned. She had faded blue and purple hair that draped in ragged, filthy waves down her chest. Her gown that might once have been respelndent spider silk was hanging on her too thin form like a rag. For the apparent age of the garment, there was no wear except at the shoulders, where her bones rubbed. There were permanent wrinkles in her sleeves and the cuffs were black, defying the observer to find the original color.

Her eyes were pale in their sockets. Not from age, though there was some of that, but from lack of use and lack of light. Even now, she kept her face turned to the shadows, away from the light that fell upon Raven's grandfather.

The frown drew hard, deep chasms in the lines of her face, etched in pain, sorrow, and neglect.

"I remember something saying that a lot. I think… I might have been that person."

"How did you get here?"

She looked at the ground, like it might know this answer. "I… ran…" She nodded. "Yes. That was it." She looked at Raven. "I ran. I didn't know I still could." She looked at her bony fingers with their curling fingernail claws. "I don't remember looking like this."

Raven lifted his hand, palm up, and glanced at her hand, then at his. She looked at his hand and then put hers in it like she was putting her fingernails in a bowl. *She has no idea how to interact with someone. How long was she alone?*

He touched her fingernails and tried to do a restorative spell, but it just absorbed into her, leaving no sign it touched her at all. He frowned. This was beyond his skill.

"Would you come with me? I have a friend I want you to meet."

She looked at her hand in his, then at his eyes. "Do I have to go back?"

Raven shook his head. "N…no." He glanced down at the Autumn door. "No. It's right there." He pointed with his other hand in an awkward gesture over the top of their hands. "We'll just go there. To that door and up some stairs."

"*More* stairs?" Can we get there from here?"

Raven looked around. "I don't think so."

She sighed and went towards the stairs. "How long did it take you?"

"I, well, I know a few shortcuts."

"Oh. Can we use them?"

Raven smiled. "Probably."

He synced his magic to match the plants and roots and again entered the flora to travel down the stairs. He felt the floral railing join and part around the woman, like it wanted to touch her but dared not do so. It was strangely reverent.

Raven and the woman stepped out of the flowers near the bottom of the stairs. She looked at Raven.

"That was much better."

Raven nodded. "Unfortunately, there isn't the ability to do that on the other side."

She shrugged. "I was a bit… younger when I went up the stairs here. I feel a lot older now."

"How long were you there?" He walked her towards the door to Merrick and Calpurnia's chambers.

"Oh, I've never been good with time. That's wasn't my gift."

"What *was* your gift?"

"Magic." Her voice was decorated in memory.

"You were a mage? So am I." He smiled at the sudden common ground. "The person we are going to see is also one."

"Oh. That will be nice. I didn't like being in that place. As long as Sovereignus is dead though, he can't put me back there."

Raven stopped. "Who?"

"Sovereignus." She jerked a finger up at the ceiling.

Raven looked at the room above, a sinking feeling forming in the hollows of his bones. "I was told that Sovereignus loved you."

She looked at him. "I thought so too." She sighed at the painful memory, then went to the door. "Oh, is that water?"

Raven shook out of the thoughts he had and got the woman some water. She drank, resting, then they turned the knob and looked at the stairs going to Calpurnia's room. He looked at her.

"Would you like me to carry you?"

She smiled. "Oh thank you."

He scooped her up and found her to be too light to exist. He shifted her and walked up the stairs.

The lion no longer chased him. It just sat there, consuming the horizon, watching him. Michael felt terror every time he looked at it and that had not faded, despite the amount of time that had passed. It was immense, like he was a mouse before it. He still ran in every dream eventually, and after a few swipes at him, the woman would appear.

This time, he was fixed upon talking to her. He ran from the lion, but not because it was going to catch and eat him. He ran because he knew she was there, ahead of him. This time, he paid attention to his surroundings. There was the Wall of York to his right, and he ran north along it. He heard the wall crumble behind him as the lion's claws ripped it open. He didn't care, he just ran. His legs started to hurt and his breathing got ragged but he forced himself to keep going.

Then the claws raked his back and he fell forward into the ground. The claws slammed down on either side, the air igniting in sparks from the impact. The lion started to drag him back and he cried out, "Help me!"

Then there was a hand on his and the woman was there, her feet dug into the ground to brace herself. She pulled him from between the claws and helped him scramble to his feet.

"What's your name? Please!"

She smiled. "Trimelda. Trimelda Daniels."

The paw knocked him to the ground and he woke up.

Michael opened his eyes to James shaking him. James' eyes were sharp and determined, and he had his hand raised to strike Michael. Michael's cheek was sore already and he raised a hand to block the swing.

"Hey!"

James blinked and let go of Michael, sitting back on his heels. He closed his eyes and ran his hands through his hair. "You scared the life out of me."

Michael sat up. "What happened?"

"You were breathing heavy and sweating. Your legs were kicking out, you were screaming. If we had been anywhere *near* civilization, the guards would have been banging down our door."

"You hit me?"

"Twice. If the third one hadn't worked, I was getting the water. Anything to try and get you to wake up."

Michael leaned his wrists on his knees. "I'm sorry, James."

"It's fine, but this has been plaguing you for days now. What's going on?"

Michael told him about the lion and the dream ever since. When he finished, James glanced over at the Wall, almost visible in the distance. "So, Trimelda's place is near the Wall?"

"Yeah."

"Then, let's head that way."

Michael held up his hand in protest. "James, your family…"

"Will still manage to be there if I take a couple more days. Remember, they don't even know I'm coming so it's not like they're holding dinner."

Michael thought about further protesting, then stopped. "Thank you."

James seemed surprised that this was all the fight he got. "Sure. No problem. We'll head that way at dawn and then go north from there."

Michael nodded and they returned to their bedrolls to sleep.

# Thirty-Two

## "The world turns everything into flowers."
## Shiva, The Karmic Hand

Alistair stepped into the meditation chamber and immediately felt himself being judged. This place was the heart of the Land and it seemed to notice that he was an Incarna. He looked around, sending waves of reassurance. "I'm just here for my friends. This isn't an assault."

Alistair knelt beside Myrgen, who started awake when he was touched. He looked around.

"Alistair. H… how did you get here?"

"The same way I brought you and Catriona here. Where is she?"

Myrgen bit his lip. "She went into the ground there. I know she'll return but…"

"It won't be her." Alistair nodded. "I know. I was thinking the same thing."

Myrgen looked around on the ground for something and frowned. "That's odd."

"What?"

"There's supposed to be a stone here, a memory stone. I saw them. When she dies, they show up."

They both looked around the bier for the stone but nothing was there. Myrgen looked at Alistair, his eyes lighting up. "The forest."

They ran from the room and went outside to the Ashstone wall where Myrgen stopped. He looked out over the huge forest that stretched westward for days.

Alistair looked to Myrgen. "Where is she? Can you sense her?"

Myrgen closed his eyes. After a few minutes, his shoulders sagged. "No. She isn't here. She isn't back yet."

Alistair looked at his friend. Myrgen's hair was matted against his head in dirty snarls and his clothes were filthy. His teeth looked slimy while his skin looked thin and pale. "Have you been in there since I left?"

"Yeah."

Alistair looked around. "How long was I gone?"

"It... may have been a couple days..."

*"Days?"* Alistair remembered that the Fae realm could do strange things to a person's sense of time passing. He thought it had only been minutes.

"I kept waiting, thinking it might just be a few hours."

"Myrgen..."

"I didn't want her to find Tib on her own."

Alistair leaned on the wall. "That's all fine and good, but here's the thing: If the Land wants her to find him first, then it will lead her to him. She serves the Land, and it gets the final say here."

"I know, but..."

"You want to protect her."

Myrgen looked at Alistair. "It's kinda my job. Says so in the title."

Alistair clapped Myrgen on the shoulder. "We need to get you cleaned up."

He led Myrgen to the doors and out into the hallway that connected to the meditation chamber. There was a man by the door, short of stature but very solidly built. He looked concerned, and Alistair realized they had just ran right past him. "Stâpân?"

Myrgen stumbled, sagging from grief. Alistair supported his friend as they walked.

"Thomas... Hello. This is Alistair."

Thomas nodded to the taller man. "What happened?" He glanced past them to the wall outside, then stepped over to give Myrgen his other shoulder.

"He's facing a trial from the Land. He needs to be cleaned up. Where can we take him?"

"I'll tell the others. We'll get things ready." Thomas gestured to a chair he had been sitting in. "Wait here."

Myrgen lowered himself into the chair. "Maybe I'm wrong. It might not have been a couple days."

Alistair looked at him. "Then being in that chamber has aged you."

Myrgen pointed an unsteady finger at Alistair. *"That* may be true. It shows me things…"

Thomas came back with a couple of other men. They took Myrgen and led him and Alistair to a room. Alistair figured it was Myrgen's and looked around for some bathing items. They helped Myrgen out of his clothes and then put a robe around him. Alistair waited downstairs while they got Myrgen cleaned up. He expected it to take a little while so he went outside to the courtyard.

The flowers were uplifting in both color and fragrance. He walked around the garden area until he came to an open area with a single autumn-colored stone tile in the ground, the colors shifting between orange, brown, gold, and light green in the light. He went over to it and saw there was writing on it. He knelt down and saw a name carved there.

Gweneviere Douglas of the House of Kelley
You were well loved and will be missed.
Until Summerland reunites us…

Alistair touched the face of the stone and felt his heart break. This was it. This was where she died. He let his tears fall on his daughter's marker stone.

He was sitting there when Myrgen came out a while later. He was clean and looked healthier. Alistair stood, dusting off his breeches and smiling. He gestured to the stone.

"This was very nice."

Myrgen nodded. "It appeared after the attack by Cipriano. There are others too." Myrgen gestured to a few other stones. They were subtle, one by the rose bushes in a dark red, one by the stables in a chestnut dun. "There isn't one for Tib yet. I think it's waiting for Catriona to return. Same with Drake and Anika. They show up when family visits."

"Do they go away afterwards?"

"I don't think so, but they come on stronger when someone who loved them is nearby." Myrgen looked at the stone. "What was she to you?"

Alistair stumbled, falling back on the cover story he created long ago. "Niece. Sister's daughter."

Myrgen nodded. "These are the memorials. People with no family to visit become the trees and flowers here. It's interesting. I'm told during the Naming Ceremonies that the whole courtyard becomes a colorful field. When I was here, there were too many people to see the ground and I was a bit distracted. I plan to look closer at the next one."

"I hope I get to see it sometime."

Myrgen smiled. "I plan to paint it. Tib's Naming Ceremony."

"You paint?"

"Yeah. You hungry?"

"Yes, but I don't want to go back inside. I want us to walk a bit."

Myrgen looked around and nodded. "Yeah, I probably need that."

They walked down the main street towards the town square. The silence was gentle and the men nodded to people passing by. They got to the grassy square and Alistair looked around.

"What was this attack?"

"Oh. The King of Mande used a Caratian artifact to bypass the protections of the Sea of Blood. Then he used those amulets to get all of his soldiers onto shore."

"And the Land *allowed* this?"

Myrgen shrugged. "It needed him here. In fact, it had to wait until every amulet holder was on the shore before it could destroy them. It couldn't risk a single amulet getting away. As a result, several people died."

"How has the town been taking the losses?"

"These people know what the afterlife holds for them. They are so... *well-balanced.* It's half comforting, half unsettling. It's as if every one of them have seen Summerland with their own eyes and know what's coming."

Alistair gestured to the street and buildings. "There are no signs of the attack. No houses destroyed, no bloodstains." He pointed to the grass. "There aren't even clumps of grass misplaced."

"They appeared on shore. No cannons, nothing. That's because they could get here as soon as they had line of sight. That was before the ships were within cannon range, even for long guns. The battle was over before the ships got close enough to fire a shot, with the land sending the bodies of the soldiers back through the air as flaming arrows. They sank the ships on impact. I suspect there was lava or something involved since I don't think a human body alone could have done that kind of damage."

He looked toward the harbor, then his eyes settled on something. His breathing hitched. "Stones... I don't think I'm ready for this yet."

Alistair followed his gaze and saw four men coming towards him. They carried rolls and bacon-wrapped chicken, a specialty of one of the inns near the docks. They chatted happily amongst themselves, and shouted out a greeting when they saw Myrgen. Myrgen waved back. Thessius, Dreathen, William the Navigator, and Lawrence the Bo 'sun made their way to the grass.

"Hail, Myrgen! Whatcha doin' with this lot?" William gestured to Alistair.

"Just showing him around. Giving the Ashstone kitchen a break from my ugly mug." Myrgen nodded to Alistair. "Figured I'd take him to that inn that makes those chicken breasts." He pointed to the food they were all carrying.

"Better hurry then. They're fresh out of the oven right now."

Myrgen took the opportunity and he and Alistair escaped further discussion. They stepped inside the teeming inn. The smell of bacon and roast fowl was mouth-watering from a block away. They managed to get an order apiece and looked around for a spot to eat it but there were no empty tables. They got tea in bottles to go with it, and Myrgen paid for it.

"My first and probably only pay from my time as Chancellor for Catriona's business."

"You're being quite frivolous with it." Alistair stepped outside. "Where did they get the bread?"

"Grethe. This way."

He took him next door, to a baker and fisher. There was a small box on the porch. Myrgen pointed to that. "Don't touch that. Don't look at that. Don't think about that."

"What's in it?"

"Lutefisk."

Alistair cringed, stopping. "Why are we here? What are you doing?"

"Lefsa."

"Oh!" He resumed his ascent of the stairs and they went inside.

The special bread was made from a root and was the product of several options for the diner. They grabbed the fried slices of bread and found a table here with ease. Each table had butter with it and the bread was still warm enough to melt it a little.

"These two places should open a business together!"

"No need. Best bread here, best chicken there. Everyone has their specialty. The tea at the chicken house is good with the chicken but the tavern best for just drinking is a little ways down. For beer, you head to the tavern near the forest road. The hunters like that place. Wine is done at the wine place and is very hearty. There's only one vineyard in Caratia."

"Why only one?"

"It requires too much space. Did you ever go to Tanglwyst's vineyards in Bordeaux?"

"Oh. No, but I have seen them."

"There's a vineyard about three miles from town towards the mountains. That's where the bulk of the farmland is. The forest takes up much of the country." Myrgen took a bite of his chicken. He chewed with pleasure. After swallowing, he sighed. "Apparently, I really *was* hungry. I may owe you a life debt over this."

Alistair nodded, unwilling to stop eating to converse. He pointed back and forth to Myrgen. When he got a breath, he said, "Next time, I'll buy. And we'll have Catriona there too."

"From your lips to the Land's ears." Myrgen paused, swallowing, his eyes getting weary again. "How long will it take?"

"Just a few days. Never more than seven, according to Raven." Alistair glanced at the pouch on Myrgen's hip. "You should know."

Myrgen frowned. He looked at the pouch, then back at Alistair. "What do you mean?"

"They'll tell you. You are her *Kapus.* Her Memory Keeper. Raven told me about it a long time ago, after he left her service." He took another bite of the bread.

"Oh."

"You'll be able to call them forth."

"But, I didn't find hers." Myrgen leaned forward. "When do they show up?"

Alistair shook his head. "That I don't know. But you need to make sure you don't give them to her all at once. You can kill her."

"Oh." Myrgen frowned, then closed his eyes. "Hey. Why don't you have the rest of mine? I don't feel like eating right now."

Alistair didn't have time to swallow before Myrgen had risen and left the building.

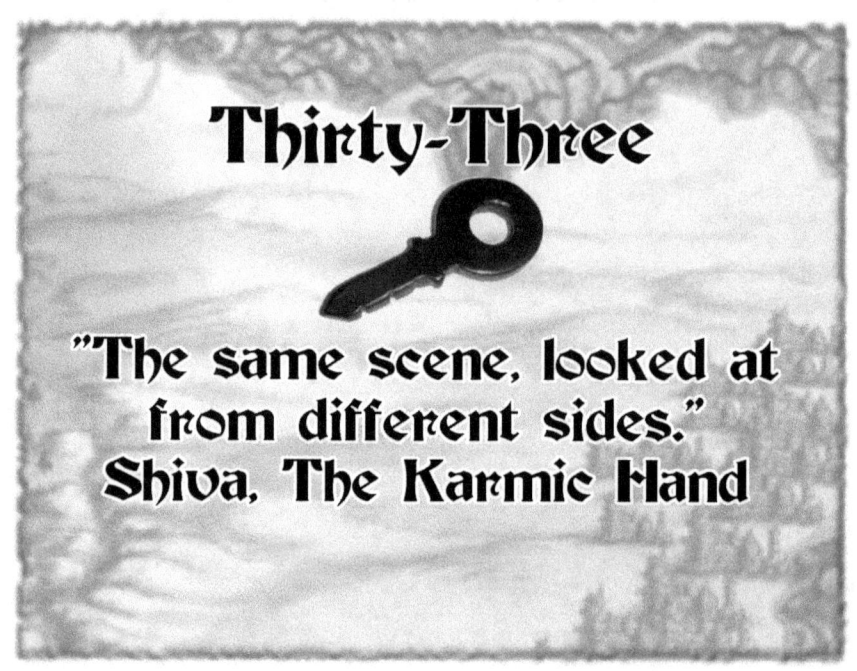

# Thirty-Three

## "The same scene, looked at from different sides." Shiva, The Karmic Hand

"What kept you?" Merrick ran over to Raven.

Raven looked at the old woman. "She was farther away than I thought." He handed her over to Merrick. "And a different person entirely, it seems."

Merrick walked her past Calpurnia towards the bed, but she reached out and touched the sleeping Fae Lord. Calpurnia stirred.

"...Moth...er..."

Merrick stopped, staring at the woman, her body settling back to slumber.

Raven and Merrick both looked at Persephone.

"I need to talk to you, Merrick."

He nodded and put Persephone on the bed. "What happened here?"

"She's been drained of her essence for a couple thousand years, maybe more." Raven nodded to the old woman. "That's Persephone."

"The *čaro* source from under the covenant?"

"Yeah."

Merrick looked as the skeletal woman lay back on the bed. He stepped a few feet away from both women, talking Raven into his confidence. "We were told it was a mage who got too powerful and chose to interfere in human politics."

"Yeah, about that. What was the *source* for that information?"

"Well, Aidan. Our covenant head."

"But where did *he* get it?"

Merrick looked at his books, then wandered around the hall for a few minutes. He stepped onto a ladder and pulled a thick book from the second-highest shelf. The spine said *The Covenant at Persephone.* He took it to a table and the two mages looked it over. Merrick opened the book and started skimming the beginning.

*"A great force remade the world.*

*The people tried to live but it was not possible.*

*The monsters that would end it all could not be killed but they could be stopped.*

*Such a source of magic would be needed to feed the spell.*

*The Land provided it, at great sacrifice.*

*The covenant was struck and all the mage houses echo the pact.*

*For Magic will feed the spell forever."*

Raven looked at Merrick. "I don't think that means what we were told."

Merrick frowned. "Why would they interpret that to mean interfering with human politics?"

"Well, people *can be* pretty destructive. We've seen that." Raven looked at the next passage. A note in the margin claimed it was written in ancient Fae. "Hm… This is not good."

Merrick looked at the writing, then at Raven. "What does it say?"

"No idea. That's the point. The Fae don't write like this. Fae are illiterate. Words in written form make no sense to them. That's why they are so attracted to humans. Humans *write.* Any symbols or writing that is attributed to Fae are actually creations of their human companions. It's also why I have such a difficult time teaching. Only half my mind understands these studies."

Merrick looked at Calpurnia. "That's why she had me transcribe her work. She couldn't do it herself."

Raven nodded. "It's also why the Fae Lords have human lieutenents, in case they have to write something down."

"Who was Calpurnia's?"

Raven shrugged. "Hers was the Elegant Solution."

"What is that?"

"I honestly have no idea."

Merrick rolled his eyes. "Oh, that's right. I had forgotten how infuriating you were."

Raven smiled and slapped Merrick on the shoulder. "It's all coming back now though, huh?" He looked at Persephone. "Do you want to keep her here?"

Merrick nodded. "I haven't seen Calpurnia rouse since Slade walked the earth. If she can do that just passing by…"

Raven understood. "I have some things to look into. Want to see what you can figure out with that book?"

"Yeah, I can do that."

"Thanks." Raven went to the tower door.

"Wait. Where will you be if they ask?"

"Talking to my uncle."

Raven stepped outside of Soveriegnlumin and nodded to the two dogs. Then he frowned, trying to remember why there were two dogs.

"Lauriel, did they leave him here?"

Lauriel nodded.

"Well, you should take them back. I remember a horse or two as well. Get them and take them home, will you?"

Lauriel cocked his head.

"I'm going to find Embertwist. I have a few questions that he might be able to answer. Any idea where he is?"

Lauriel shook his head.

Raven took a deep breath. This was going to be a bit tricky. He looked around as Laruiel left the realm with the other dog. He needed to find some sign of Embertwist. He remembered an inn that his uncle frequented during the beginning of Spring and decided to check that out. Maybe they had seen him.

He started walking towards the forest near Sovereignlumin and felt the air shift when he entered the human world. The Fae realm connected to the human world via several points, but you had to know how to cross that barrier. Raven had no trouble, being equally attuned to both places. He saw the lights through the trees to the west and went that direction.

He came upon the Benevolent Friar and stepped in, noting a presence of guards wearing Mervol livery. He remembered his hair just before stepping into the light of the porch. He shifted it to light brown, then stopped as he saw hundreds of fires in the valley below. He went to the railing and looked out.

"Can I help you, sir?"

Raven scanned the fires. "The army is still there."

"Yes. Do... you know something about it?"

"I passed through there a few days ago. I was hoping the problem would have been solved by now."

"Passed through?"

Raven heard a threat in the voice and remembered the spell that had been on the town, preventing people from leaving or entering. "Well, *near*. Couldn't go *in,* exactly. I wasn't sure if they were going to attack the country or just keep the town."

The guard relaxed, which caused Raven to do likewise.

"My partner says the Fae army and the problem with the Papal City are linked."

"Papal City?"

"Yeah. A dome of poisonus thorns is covering the city so not even light is escaping."

Raven looked around. "It *is* pretty warm for this time of year..."

The guard frowned at the nonsequitor, but Raven had already made a decision. He pointed to the north. "The Papal City is that way?"

The guard shook his head, pointing behind them and to the north. "Follow the road heading northeast. Take you right to it."

Raven nodded. "Thank you."

Myrgen walked past Catriona's room at Ashstone and looked around the courtyard. No stone came to life with color when he did, and that gave him solace. At least maybe she wasn't lost at all. If she *did* remember while she was dead, maybe, just maybe, she would not change. But he knew the stories. He knew the way this worked. She would be a different person, like the statues in the study. She wouldn't even be recognizable to him outside of her eyes.

He turned back to the great doors and went up the stairs. He followed the corridor to the end, passing his room. He had not been in it since he left Alistair at the bakery. He went every night to the chamber to sleep beside Tib's body. Every day, he went to the courtyard to look for her stone or Tib's. Then he went to the tower. He opened the door, and looked at the painting.

Beside the canvas was a bowl with the memory stones in it. The first day, after talking with Alistair, he came up here to paint. He put the stones, still in their bag, on the table next to the easel. He didn't want any other memories but Catriona's and he didn't want to accidentally touch them in his sleep. He picked up the brush and went to work on her portrait. He painted until he cried, then stopped, and sat until he could paint again. When it got too dark to see and he felt he would sleep, he went to the meditation chamber. When he woke, the cycle kicked in again.

Because oil paint took time to dry, he worked in layers and from top to bottom. The sea air was humid and there was no way to remove that. In truth, the best place to paint might be the meditation chamber, but he wanted to use the gift from Drake and Anika. It was something very personal from them to him. Good lighting and good ventilation helped significantly, so he would leave the door open and the window when he fell asleep, letting the small windows in the tower's stairway move the air. Drying agents worked too but were often dangerous to deal with. Painters would go mad or just get too sick to continue. He had avoided them when he did the portraits of Elizabeth and Emmy but with Catriona's death, he found he didn't care. If the Land claimed him, it claimed him. He blew the ground cobalt onto the painting when he was done with a section. The next day, the paint was always dry enough to continue.

He occasionally took the food left by his bedroom door, usually the breakfast, but occasionally the dinner. They stopped making things that could get cold and be inedible. Only bread, cheese, sausage, and water. Every morning had at least one apple with it. He took the plates with him and left them by the door to his room. He had no idea how long it had been but he needed to get this on the canvas while he still remembered everything. Her hair, her eyes. The smile and the excited look before she realized their proximity. That still showed traces in her cheeks, but there was more there. He had to capture that very specific moment when they fell in love.

As it poured out onto the canvas, it left his heart. It didn't go away, but the pain faded. He knew it needed to be done now, because if he saw her again, she would be someone else and he wanted *this* version. *This* was the woman he loved. He may love the one who returned, but he would never be able to love her like this. He knew now why Slade had protected his Dûcesa with his life. He would never change, so his life was expendable. He would just keep coming back, knowing everything they ever experienced, every touch, every tear. This time, he pushed through the crying part and didn't stop.

The tears were mixed with the paint and when that happened, an effect occurred. It was subtle at first, but then it became prominent. The eyes came to life. Not like the started watching him or moving, but they took on that realistic quality he had been hoping for. He added the effect to the luminous part of the moon, and the light foam on the waves. He added it to her lips, and he almost kissed them as a result. He stepped back to see if it held from a distance, and it did. The paint needed time to dry so he moved on to another part of the painting.

He decided this time to work through the night. The paint flowed, strands of hair, highlights, shadows, skin tone, the way the fabric looked. He kept stopping, pulling a separate canvas from the stack to practice a technique, quickly, like getting her lips right or making sure he had the shape of her eyes correct. This time he did a quick sketch of her hands. The painting practically painted itself, and he let his life essence go into it. He had ground stone in vials and used them on the smaller canvases first before applying them to his masterpiece.

Finally, he felt it was done, and he stepped back. He blew the crystal dust upon it to help it set. Then he blew out the candle, letting the moonlight be the only illumination. He poured the stones into the pouch he took with him down to the chamber, the action so habitual, he could do it without touching them. He sat on the bed, and let the vision flow to him. He put the pouch on his belt. He lay down and the soft bed felt strange, but good. He turned on his side and watched the painting until his eyes would no longer stay open, removing something hard on his hip to get more comfortable.

It was the first night since her death he had not slept in the chamber below and when daylight awoke him, he stood and went to the window. He leaned against the window frame and breathed in the fresh sea air. The view here was spectacular, and he took it in, feeling refreshed and awake. Then his eyes settled upon the *Enigma*, still in dry dock. He remembered their talk on the ship after Octavius and Raven left. He remembered when he spoke to Estelle and when he encouraged Catriona to be with Alexander. He remembered his room, and his bed, his desk, his footlocker. He remembered their talks there and his heart threatened to break again.

He took a deep breath and let it out in a rush, then pushed away from the window.

"I miss you, Catriona."

He turned from the window and looked around. Multiple sets of her eyes from different angles looked at him from the scattered practice canvases. A shimmer of light turned his attention back to the bed. On the bed was the dagger with a whale handle. He vaguely remembered removing it last night and it glinted in the sunlight, a perfect complement to the portrait. She had bought it for him because of that moment on the ship, the one he had recreated.

He stepped to the portrait, still drying in places, and touched the face. It was so good, he expected warm flesh, and a curve to the cheek. When he instead encountered flat, rough canvas, his hand dropped to his side. He closed his eyes and shook his head.

"I can't do this anymore. This is madness."

He opened his eyes and went to the door. He would give himself a break, let the room air out for a bit. Get some real food. He chose not to look at the portrait again to give his eyes and mind a chance to see it fresh when he returned. He closed the door and locked it. He would give himself a day to interact with humans and try to restore some sanity and maybe a little body mass. His clothes were loose on him. Get some real rest and then, return to the chamber. He had no idea what day it was but with any luck, he would wake to find her standing beside him this time.

# Thirty-Four

## "Those we love will be with us again."
### Kali, The Karmic Hand

Catherine entered the small keep on the road west through Krakte. She had left the same day as Alexander and Tanglwyst, amid protests from Charles and the guardsmen. She told them it was imperative that they keep up the appearances that both the King and the Queen Mother were still in residence. They needed to do so until the Army arrived in St. Giles. It was a large force and the kingdom pavilions would be visible from the Inn. When that happened, they could take the letters that had arrived and bring them to Alexander. She was going to meet with an ally and try to help another way.

Krakte was a rich and fertile land with several animals native to the region. Many crops were grown here but the main reason it was not an independent nation was the presence of the Black Forest. It took up two-thirds of the land in Krakte and was indestructible. As a result, the country was dependent upon Mervol trade for food, iron, and lumber, and Mervolingia enjoyed the rich skills and engineering of the Kraktens. With little land, they utilized their spaces very efficiently. So much so that they traded all manner of inventions for grains because to the Kraktens, they were common and equivalent.

A zoftig woman with long grey-black hair with purple highlights came down the stairs to greet her. "Can I help you?"

Catherine bowed. "I am a weary traveler. Can you give me a pile of hay for the night?"

The woman bowed at the customary greeting for strangers and gestured to a table by a lit hearth. "Please, we have a spare room for just such visitors. Sit. Get warm by the fire. I shall get you some food and drink."

Catherine sat and removed the cloak and hood she had chosen for this trip. A short, thin man with a balding head and sharp moustache and beard came down as well. They were both adorned in Krakten noble clothing, bright colors of material with contrasting colors of silk spilling from large slashes and holes in the fabric. The legs and sleeves of his outfit didn't match at all, this one in white leather with long strips showing off blood red silk, that one green and burgundy linen with gold silk. The woman was more coordinated, with a purple wool gown slashed to show white. Both of them wore hats that would have doubled as umbrellas, with feathers that matched their outfits making a ring about their brims.

"Where are you from?" The woman spooned stew into an earthenware bowl.

"Patras. More recently, the Papal City. It's surrounded by thorns now. Impassible."

The man brought over the stew and a mug of cider. "We had heard."

Catherine frowned. "There's an army on the valley in Bordeaux."

The woman came over. "We saw that. The Krakten Queen has gone to get her daughter."

Catherine sighed, thinking. "The Queen Mother of Patras is traveling through Krakte as we speak."

The man and woman exchanged a look and smiled. "That's news."

Catherine exhaled and picked up the mug. The cider was excellent and was the stew. "Thank you for your hospitality. I am Catherine."

"I am Albreda Wulftorhüter and this is my husband Reinmar. You know our ways well. Have you traveled to Krakte often?"

Catherine kept her manners about her, not slurping the stew nor the cider. "I used to correspond with a friend here in Krakte. She told me all the things I would need to know if ever I decided to run away from home and visit her. She told me to always offer the host of a house new information before taking so much as a bite or swallow. If you can give them something new within three attempts, they will open their home. If you cannot give them something they don't know, they are allowed to eat you."

Albreda and Reinmar laughed. "Well, we don't exactly eat people, but it is the custom to be able to turn any visitor away. It keeps out those who aren't interesting or who are thieves."

"How does it keep out thieves? They would have the most interesting stories, I would think."

Reinmar pointed to a device on the wall. "That. It tells us if someone is a danger to us. If it rings, then we attack."

On a swivel was a small bell without a clapper. It tipped back and forth in the slightest breeze or shift in air current. It made no sound. She returned to her meal, nodding. "I wish I had one of those for my home. Or at least for traveling."

"There *are* traveling ones. You can set them up in an Inn room or a relative's house or pretty much anywhere."

"Where would I find one?"

Reinmar smiled. "It just so happens I make them."

After food was done and Reinmar had shown her several models of security bell, she had been shown her room for the night. The faint moonlight showering her now was far better than the nights of darkness that she had endured. They kept her hidden but they also made travel slow and treacherous after dark. She had stayed in a barn the first night on an actual pile of hay, and at a school for young women the second. She had not had to result to admitting she was the Queen but she worried about this information getting out and her not having it as a fall back. She didn't know if the secrets were kept from place to place but she didn't want to risk it.

The next morning, she took her new security bell, attached it to her belt, and headed out. She was getting on in years and was concerned that riding this much was going to take a toll, but it was far better than walking. She doubted she could get to the siege before it ended if she had been on foot.

When the setting sun was in her eyes, impairing her ability to see, she turned south towards the Fae army. There were far too many fires and far too many soldiers. She needed to have her counter offer ready for Sovereigna. She only hoped it was still good.

Catriona woke to a beautiful spring day. She could hear birds, laughter, dogs and other animals. A dragonfly entered through the small hut's window, the gentle buzzing of its wings lending a subtle melody to the surroundings. She reveled in the comfort of the bed, a part of her not really wanting to get out to start the day. Of course, she knew she didn't have to, not really. Her decision could be made simply by apathy. If she didn't get up, didn't leave her home, she wouldn't be faced with *choosing* this life. She could just... let it choose her.

"Mom! Can I go to Drake and Anika's?"

Catriona sat up, smiling. Tib's hair was a mess, like he just rolled out of bed too. She heard Rose calling out to Robert to bring her a basket. The sound made her a little sad, knowing where she was. She smiled and nodded. "Comb your hair first. Don't go to them messy."

"Ok."

She heard him canter around the hut on the other side of the stone wall, pause for almost a whole three seconds, then dart out the front door. She knew she would find him later with the messy hair that did not get tamed, eating a roll and petting Drake and Anika's cat, Miguel. She had missed their cat, who had always rubbed up against her and jumped into her lap when she returned home at the end of the season. Catriona always felt it was because she still smelled of the fish-heavy diet, but she never cared why. The cat's purring was always welcome.

She looked around and saw Myrgen's boots by the door to the room. She knew he wasn't here anymore, and it bothered her that he was here long enough to settle in. That meant he wasn't merely hurt and able to see this place. *He was here.* This was *his*... no... *their* home, and his absence made her feel longing and hope at the same time. Three of his shirts were hanging on a rod in the corner and she tried not to cry as she got up and went to them. She pulled one from the cedar wood hanger and smelled it. Xannu's bathhouse filled her senses and she remembered how he had been groaning and sore from falling asleep on the tiles of the bath he used. She had wanted them to have a room with a screen for bathing, but in the end, she had told Xannu to give him his privacy. He had been uncomfortable being around any women at that time, and Catriona determined she was not exempt from that status.

She wept from missing him, her body wracking from the pain. She knelt on the floor, her knees cushioned by the felted wool rug that covered nearly every inch of the room. She missed him, she could not deny that, but a part of her reminded her that he would be here soon enough, and it would be as if no time had passed at all.

Except that wasn't really true. He had been a child of Heaven not two months ago. He could return to that life, now that she was gone, and be lost forever. Yes, she loved him, but when faced with the family and friends around her, was she truly going to leave all of them just for *a man?* She could. She could leave them all here. It wasn't like they were in danger. This was Summerland, where those who died could be at peace. Here, if they died young or too soon, they could resolve those issues, live their lives, fall in love, marry, grow old. They could pursue the hobbies they always wanted to explore, hone talents they wanted to perfect, indulge in their favorite activities with friends and loved ones. If Myrgen had been here, surely he would return. Why would he go to an end he did not know when such happiness could be found here?

But she knew that answer. He had left to be with her.

She stood and stepped to the doorway of the bedroom, still holding his shirt to her body. A woman was in the main room, sitting in a chair and sipping tea. She was blond, which the sculpture in the study at Ashstone had not revealed. Her Yorkish features were pert and pale, her teeth punctuated with a gap in front, also not revealed in the statue. She didn't turn to Catriona, but she didn't have to. The Third Dûcesa knew she was there.

"Good morning! Tib let me in. I made some tea for us."

Catriona looked at the stove. She put on Myrgen's shirt and walked over to the shelf with the hand sculpted mugs on it. She filled one with water and put a small cloth with tea in it, tied with a string, into the hot water. The green-brown substance of the tea started infusing into the water in delicate streams, like the paint from a brush. She leaned against the counter and warmed her hands on the mug.

"Today's the day."

The Dûcesa looked at her, her eyes gentle and curious, but not prying. "Is it?"

Catriona nodded. She had learned much from this lady, and the others before her. She knew that she could choose to stay behind, to be with her friends, her family, her son. She could have this house and watch him grow up, possibly see him start a family of his own. Anika and Drake could tend their garden and play with their grandson a while longer. She could see Rose and Robert actually get married, like they planned for a year. That date would be arriving soon enough. The world would go on without her, like it had for millennia. Her part of the story was simply not important. There would be a new Servant born from where she fell and the legacy would carry on.

But they won't know Myrgen. And he won't know her.

Everything they had done and meant to each other, everything they had learned, all the mysteries they had uncovered would be lost. He might return to her someday, but he might not. *After all, Slade never did.*

She looked at the blond woman before her. She had never been named, not really. When she stepped into Caratia for the first time, all she knew was that she was the new Dûcesa. Her Stapan had been so concerned with not killing her that he never even bothered to ask for her name. Catriona knew that the naming was key to the installation of the soul. Holding names were given as infants, but the Land knew your true name. Until someone asked it, the Land did not give it. So this poor woman had gone through her incarnation with no identity of her own, merely the title of Dûcesa. Her identity was her job, not her soul. It was the reason why Summerland had been her choice. She had come here and someone had asked for her name. And in that second, she became her own person.

"Yes. Michelyne, I was wondering if you could watch Tib for me today. I have an errand to run."

Michelyne frowned. "Is that so?"

"I'm afraid it is."

"Why?"

Catriona took a deep breath. "Because I don't think I'm done yet."

Michelyne looked at her tea. "What is more important than being with your family?"

"Nothing." Catriona set her cup down and went to her predecessor. "Nothing at all is more important than that. But they aren't all here, and everyone who *is* here is safe. I have family left behind and something is wrong out there."

"How do you know that?" Michelyne's eyes searched Catriona's for meaning.

Catriona stood and looked out the window. Tib was talking to Anika while Drake pulled weeds from their garden. Tib was holding their striped orange cat, tilted back like a baby, and telling her some great story. Children played in the fountain nearby alongside dogs, two sheep, and a familiar horse from Gwen's house. Upon a rooftop, almost lost in a shadow, a woman was perched like a cat, looking down upon the scene. She was invisible, but Catriona could still see her. She had silver hair that flowed past her shoulders with eyes that matched in color, and a lithe body accustomed to acrobatics. She was festooned in leather from head to toe and moved soundlessly, no matter the setting. The woman turned to look at her, then lifted her chin towards something on the other side of Catriona's house. Catriona nodded.

"I just do." She walked towards the door to the house.

"Aren't you going to change?" Michelyne looked at the shirt Catriona was wearing.

Catriona looked down at her attire, then back at her friend. "No. I think this time, I won't."

She opened the door and stepped into the light. She stood the street, watching the activities at the fountain. Tib waved at her, and Miguel used the opportunity to jump from his arms. Anika looked at Catriona, smiling as Tib went chasing after the cat.

"You look like a woman who's made a decision."

Catriona did not turn to look at the Sinister Glove. She did not need to. "Yes." She waved to Anika, then turned away from the scene, walking. "What did you want to show me?"

The Glove stepped beside her and pointed. "There."

Catriona looked. A large mansion gleamed in the morning light not far from town. It was elaborate, with ornate arches and shining glass windows. There were still places where she could see through it, but those were the edges only at this stage. "What did you learn?"

"That it isn't here yet. It needs permission to touch this part of the world. But it was made a while ago."

"How can it be touching *this* place?"

The Sinister Glove swallowed. "Because it is painted with this."

The Glove opened a small, white linen cloth that had scrapings in it. A heat rose from it. Catriona touched it and understood. "Lava ash."

"From a righteous fire."

Catriona looked to the mansion and nodded. She had spent enough time here. She needed to get home. She turned to the Glove. "I'll find out what's happened. I'll make sure he's safe."

The Glove glanced at the ash and then folded it and put it away. Her eyes glistened in the sunshine from the tears that were threatening to form. "Can you take me with you?"

Catriona shook her head. "No. Everything with me will burn in the fire as it is. You'll just be right back here."

The Glove nodded, not meeting Catriona's eyes. She swallowed, putting away the linen. She sniffed back the threatening tears and looked at Catriona again. "Then get on it. I know something is amiss there. I don't know if it is just accident or if it's a plan, but either way, it's the beginning of something important." She exchanged a hug with Catriona, then stepped back. "You be careful out there. I don't want to see you back here too soon."

"What's the worst that could happen? If I screw up, you simply toss me back out there."

The Glove nodded and stepped back. Catriona turned towards the fires on the edge of the village and walked into them.

Myrgen took up his accustomed spot before the bier and apologized. If she didn't return tonight, it meant she truly *was* gone, that she had been just a mortal and not some magical fantasy creature. He kind of wanted that, to be honest. If that was the truth, he could die as well. They could be together forever like they were meant to. Be a family.

A noise drew his attention and he turned, drained from waiting and wishing for her. Drained from her never being the one that walked in. This time was no different.

Alistair walked in from the open doors. "You okay? You walked right by me."

"Did I? I'm sorry."

Alistair nodded to the ground by the bier. "Anything?"

Myrgen shook his head. "I was thinking, with today being the last day, that maybe she *isn't* this reincarnation. Raven told me the stones show up after they die and are committed to the ground, but no memory stone has arisen. It's possible she was just a woman."

Alistair glanced at the ground, then back to Myrgen. "And if she *is* just a woman and not a legend?"

A moment of silence passed between them. Myrgen looked about to speak when the ground cracked behind them, light and lava seeping from the crack. The ground opened, revealing a pool of lava. Heat shimmered from it and both Myrgen and Alistair shielded their eyes from the glow. Something rose from the molten rock, a figure dripping liquid fire as if it were oil. The figure looked human and was crouched, holding its hands covering its face. A moment later, the figure turned from brilliant orange and yellow, to black-grey rock. The pool beneath it started to cool as well, solidifying. After about a minute, the humanoid shape remained, cooling in the room. Myrgen and Alistair waited, not sure if this was a message or something else.

The figure shifted and the hands broke away from the face. It lowered its arms, causing the stone to shatter in puffs of ash and smoke. It pushed its hands along its head, clearing away the stone more with each move until she stood, clean and nude, before the two men. Her emerald eyes turned to the pair.

"Myrgen?"

Myrgen stepped forward at her familiar voice but Alistair held him back. "Wait."

Myrgen looked at his friend and shook off the hand. He ran to the woman and stopped before her. He moved her long, wavy hair aside from her face and feasted upon features he knew so well.

"Catriona?"

She smiled, nodding. He took her in his arms and hugged her, laughing. He lifted her in the air, kissing her, and she returned the kiss like they had been too long under water and this was air.

"You're here. You're you."

She nodded. "Yes."

"How? I thought you were going to change."

She nodded. "I decided not to. We'd come too far and…" She looked past him. "Alistair?"

She went to him and he took off his coat for her. She put it on and hugged him. "Thank you."

"Well, I can't have my fiancée roaming the streets undressed."

She smiled and then looked beyond him to the pile of rocks. "What's this? My grave?"

"No. Catriona, wait." Myrgen's voice was strange and horrible. She turned to look at him and he sighed. "That's not… yours. It's Tib's."

# Thirty-Five

"We were never enemies. We were simply opponents."
Kali, The Karmic Hand

Raven looked at the dome of thorns that covered the entire area where the road just stopped. The guard was right; not even light could be seen. He looked closely at the thorns but the sliver of moon was shedding too little light to be helpful. He produced a light in his hand with magic and examined the thorns.

*Yup. That's poison.*

He stepped back. The change in temperature meant that Embertwist had expended his power for the season in one go, and that summer was already in power. With a Fae army camped out in Mervolingia, that meant Corrigan was going to be on the move. Raven wanted to figure all this out before that happened or he would just cut down the army of Krakte.

Or worse, side with them.

The angel was standing right beside him when he stepped back, and Raven tried very hard not to jump or scream. The angel was looking at the dome as well, his arms folded. He wore simple hunter's garb and looked very normal, but Raven could feel the divine aura cutting his connections to magic and Fae down to nothing.

"You came here looking for Embertwist, huh?"

Raven nodded.

"So, you don't know what happened either."

Raven turned, the concern in the angel's voice a bit odd for an enemy of the Fae. "Do you?"

"Not really. I came here because of something I overheard." He gestured to the dome. "I found this."

Raven nodded.

"I knew it was Fae magic." The angel turned, beckoning Raven to follow. "And then there was this."

They walked about twenty yards away and Raven saw a hundred red poppies scattered in an area. There was a hole in the ground where something sizable and pointy had landed. The angel turned and pointed to a spot up on the dome.

"And there was that."

Raven looked but the darkness prevented seeing what the angel was pointing at. Then the giant arrow glowed. It was wrapped in the tendrils of the thorns and was torn up.

The angel looked at Raven. "That is a Fae Slayer. There are siege weapons in the city that fire them." He turned back to the field of poppies. "It's what made that hole."

Raven nodded.

"I think my friend is dead."

Raven frowned. "Friend?"

The angel nodded. "My name is Uriel. Emberwist was my friend."

Tanglwyst arose, her night far too fitful to be restful. Alexander was finally asleep and it had taken all her will to not continue talking to him. Had they continued down that path of discussion, she knew she would have bedded him, even if that meant accepting his proposal. He was right. With everything they were sharing emotionally, making love would be exactly that. As desirable as that might be, she knew she couldn't. She had something else to do.

When she had entered her office after the church meeting, there had been a letter on the floor. She knew the handwriting and had skimmed the letter but Alexander's arrival caused her to panic and hide the letter amongst a stack of papers on her desk. She had barely disguised her feelings as being irritated with Alexander, so he wouldn't suspect anything. She checked him again to ensure he was asleep, then read the letter for the first time.

*"Mistress Tanglwyst,*

*It has come to my attention that my daughter Elizabeth is dead. I understand this is a result of a flawed plan you orchestrated which put my daughter in jeopardy. Since you survived and my daughter did not, I take exception to this. Until this inequity is settled, your holdings and businesses will find Krakten ire. Unlike your own country, I will not be exacting revenge upon the people who had the misfortune of associating with you, only your holdings. Buildings can be rebuilt, but lives cannot be returned once taken.*

*Since this is a thing well known to us, I only require ONE life for that of my daughter. I can invoke the Right of Lineage if necessary but it is not my preference, for I seek justice, not blood. I will leave it to your king to decide whose life comes to me for this purpose: the one who killed her, or the one who let her die.*

*Sovereigna, Queen of Krakte"*

She couldn't show it to Alexander. If she did, he would offer himself, or worse, just go to war. She wouldn't let this escalate to that point. She didn't know if Sovereigna would kill her or simply take her to Krakte. Luckily, the trading company was already being transferred to Kyri. She had seen to her affairs. Now she just needed to let the others know.

She sat at her desk and scratched out a letter to Preston, and another letter she needed to have on record anyway. She told Preston in his letter to give it to the appropriate parties. She trusted him with these. When she finished and sealed them, she put them downstairs on his desk. It was getting light out by then, and she yawned. She wanted to spend just a little more time with Alexander, but she worried that doing so would simply make her course of action harder. Better to not do it than to not be able to let go. She slipped back into the room and got her clothes from the day before. She got dressed in her office and when she had pulled on her boots and still heard no one stir in the other room, she took it as a sign that she was doing the right thing.

She took the final letter and went outside. Gomez had said that the barrier had stopped the Fae army from occupying the town, but with it down, she suspected there would be something guarding the Queen's interests. She was right. She walked up to a half-goblin-looking thing and curtsied.

It looked around like it was not accustomed to being shown respect.

She held out the letter. "I have a message for the Queen. Can you deliver it?"

The goblin looked her over, then took the letter, nodding. She curtsied again and pointed to the Wise Wench Tavern. "I'll be in there waiting. Ok?"

It looked where she pointed, then nodded and ran off.

She took a deep breath and glanced back up to the window of her room. She felt like crying and stopped herself immediately. She couldn't risk waking him right now. If he woke up, he'd ruin everything. Instead, she sent calm, soothing, loving thoughts to ease his mind and heart. She concentrated on those as she walked to the Tavern.

Raven sat across from the angel, the poppies decorating the ground around them.

"I met Embertwist centuries ago. I was invoked against his tricks and we chased each other for a hundred years. He played pranks on me and eventually, I started returning in kind. Then it became a game with us. When the Soulless War came, I stood guard outside the road to Mervolingia, destroying anything that made it through. My brother, Michael, was already inside so that was the best I could do. I needed to be ready if the season changed and released the monsters within.

"After that, we became friends. We would meet in that tavern at the beginning and end of the Spring season to talk and share stories." He gestured to the inn where Raven had gotten the tip about the dome. "But he isn't here now, and this," Uriel looked behind him at the thorns, "this has me very worried."

Raven looked around at the poppies. "Actually, *this* has *me* worried. If Embertwist were hit by that arrow, he wouldn't have had the energy to erect that dome."

Uriel blinked. "Y… you're right. Those arrows were *designed* to slay powerful Fae." Uriel stood, looking at the dome. "This is very powerful. I can't do anything to it."

Raven stood as well. "I'm a mage *and* a Fae. I can't do anything to it. The power that went into this effect would have drained him for the rest of the season, bringing on an early summer. This took *all* his power, not some residual…"

Uriel turned to Raven. "What?"

"I just figured out where he is."

Raven took off running and Uriel ran along with him. Raven went for the forest and turned back for a second when Uriel vanished.

*Of course. Heaven can't go here.*

Raven resumed running and returned to Sovereignlumin. He went to the door with the growing leaves and flowers and entered. He wasted no time getting up the stairs and stopped when he his fear was realized.

On a bier in the center of the room was Embertwist.

Alexander started awake when the knock came on the door. He looked around, confused. Then he remembered where he was and cast about for Tanglwyst. He didn't see her, but the knock came again. He wondered if she did something to lock herself out. He got up and opened the door. Preston was there and he bowed. He looked nervous, maybe even frightened.

"Is the Lady in here?"

Alexander leaned back to look in the bathing room. He shook his head. "Why?"

"I think she might have left."

Alexander looked around the room. The dress she had laid over the chest at the foot of her bed was gone. So were her boots. He brushed past Preston into the office and saw her night gown over the back of her chair. *She changed in here so as not to wake me.*

He looked at Preston, who held out a sealed letter. "For you, You Majesty."

"Preston, what's going on?"

Preston nodded to the letter.

Alexander opened it and read the first words, then dropped it on the floor. He was not ready to read her Will.

Preston stepped in front of Alexander, blocking his exit.

"Move, Preston. I won't let her do this."

"Sire, I am sworn to stop you."

"You would stand against your King?" Alexander didn't want to hurt the man, but he was not about to allow Tanglwyst to die.

"I *am* loyal to you, Sir, but I am loyal to the *kingdom*. And she is doing this to save us all. You included." He handed Alexander his own letter and it included the letter from Sovereigna.

His eyes took in the words on the page. *"She'll be executed!"* He balled his hands into fists, crushing the letters. "I will *not* allow her to be harmed because of *my* actions."

He felt her notice him, felt her heart trying to calm him. He could feel her saying this was *her* choice, *her* decision. And he pressed back with it was not *her* responsibility. It was his. He was sovereign, and unless she had made a decision she had not revealed to him, then it was his responsibility to be sacrificed for the kingdom, if need be.

"Preston, I love her. I am trying to save her life."

"And she's trying to save *yours*."

*"My life is not more valuable than anyone else's in this kingdom."* He closed his eyes, calming himself. "I am not above any of you. I am *your* servant. That is my role. Without that understanding, I become a tyrant." He opened his eyes. "I will not be that kind of king."

"How will you stop the Queen then?"

Alexander thought of the coat in the other room. He knew he could end this conflict if he could just get close to her. But he knew Tanglwyst would never approve of that. He would not use it.

Yet.

"Preston, the Queen is holding my people hostage because *her daughter killed the King.* Elizabeth was put to the sword because she poisoned my brother. Tanglwyst was under a spell that Elizabeth cast, forcing her to help with that task. She blames herself for Charles' death *and* Elizabeth's, and I'll not let our Lady go to that fate because she feels inappropriately *guilty.*" The Power of Sovereignty was glowing around him and Preston's eyes grew large in wonder. "Now, please, step aside so that I may save our friend."

Preston did so and Alexander ran to the stairs. He ran out into the street in the silk pajama bottoms, no shoes on his feet and no shirt on his back. He saw the General and several half-ogre guards walking down the street and ran towards them.

"General!"

The man turned and stopped. He bowed. "Your Majesty."

"You can't take her." Alexander looked between the monsters for the Lady. He caught a glimpse of her dress and hair but the view was cut off between them by the gigantic creatures.

"Sire?"

"I didn't authorize this. Please let me take her home."

The General stepped over to the king, taking him into his confidence. "Are you saying she did this of her own volition?"

"Yes. She doesn't speak for the kingdom. Her sacrifice will do no good."

"Sir, is that wise?"

City guards ran over to the group, standing behind their king. The General glanced at them with an assessing eye.

"What do you mean?"

"The Queen wants the one responsible for the death of her daughter. This lady has sent a letter saying she will offer herself as hostage until the responsible party is brought before the Queen. She offered herself in lieu of the daughter's body that cannot be recovered. The Queen is invoking the Right of Lineage."

"What... What does that mean?" Alexander glanced through the ogres, then back to Johner.

"It means that if the body of the Princess Elizabeth is not returned, then the child of the Princess is to be brought to the Queen in her stead."

*"Emmy?"* Alexander shook his head. "No. No, I won't send a child to someone who could do all this."

"Alexander." Tanglwyst's voice cut through the morning.

Johner looked behind them and he nodded, parting the ogres. Alexander started to go to her, but his guards grabbed him, holding him back.

"Don't, Sire. It could be a trap. It's just a woman."

273

Alexander growled and elbowed the guard in the chest *hard.* The man let go. Alexander turned to him, seething. "Never use that tone about her again. You *came* from a woman, you fool. Show some respect." He shook off the other guards and walked up to Tanglwyst.

"My Lady."

"Alexander, you don't understand."

"I do. You're protecting Emmy."

Her eyes got damp, despite her attempts to stop them. "Not just her. You. The Kingdom. Sovereigna has the right to call for her granddaughter to be sent to her. Charles is dead, as is Elizabeth. It is not unreasonable for her to go to be raised by Sovereigna."

"Except that she is my heir."

"That simply makes her *more* desirable." She raised her hands to hold his and the manacles upon her wrists shifted, showing sear marks like they were hot when they were put on her. She winced and he felt her pain.

"What in... *General!*"

The Fae soldier stepped to the corridor and came up to the couple. "Sire?"

Alexander reached for the cuffs and was instantly scalded by intense heat. Tanglwyst pulled back with a cry of pain. He held his reddened hand and glared at the Fae. *"What is the meaning of this?"*

The General looked at the damage on both parties. "A countermeasure, Your Majesty. You are the Champion of Heaven. The Church has been a very destructive force among my people. The Queen required the Lady's manacles be made of Fae Silver, to protect our people from the scars of Heaven."

"Champion of Heaven, you said that before. What do you mean?"

"There is a mark upon you. Do you not know this?"

Alexander looked around at the others surrounding them. The Fae nodded. The humans did not. "No."

"Then you need to talk to the one you Champion. You need to understand what this means. Nonetheless, the lady is bound against the powers of Heaven."

"She's not the Champion. She has no magic from the Church. Why is it burning her?"

"She is a virgin. The silver says it is so. That makes her blood very valuable. She also follows the Church…"

"Wait, what?" Tanglwyst put her hands on Johner's shoulders. The half-ogre guards pulled her away.

Alexander tried to go to her but another one of the city guards grabbed him. "Sire, don't. We don't want a battle here before the army arrives. She'll be the first casualty."

He looked at Tanglwyst, returning her confused gaze. Then he realized what had happened. "When I healed you."

She shook her head, not understanding.

"I healed you at the Inn at the top of the mountain. I healed... everything, apparently."

"Well, what in the hell did you do that for?" Her eyes were wide with disbelief.

"It was an accident. I didn't tell it to do that. But, it's happened before, in St Andrew. The body loses all signs of... being savaged."

She held up her hands to stop him, then flinched and hissed when the silver scored her again. She set her lips. "That's great. That's just great. Look, your mother should be here soon. Wait for her. She's the one that told me about the Right of Lineage. She has a plan. She knows what to do."

Alexander shook his head. "No. No you can't take her." He started to surge but the ogres stepped between them. Alexander battled his own guards, screaming against the action, but Tanglwyst nodded to Johner and the ogre escort surrounded her again. Several city guards were needed to stop him from pursuing her.

The Fae group peeled away towards the north east just past the church, skirting it with a wide berth. Even in his distress, he noticed the maneuver. He shook off the guards and started walking to the church. He looked at the group and saw her shaking her head and muttering to herself. They turned again towards the north and went out of sight. He looked down, locating the boot prints of the sizable ogres.

"Get me a measuring tape. Quickly, please."

One of the guards went running towards the market area while another came up to see him. "Is there something wrong, Your Majesty?"

Alexander knelt by the print. "Get Gomez please. I need him right away."

The first guard returned after a few minutes and Gomez arrived not long after. Gomez looked at the king, then at the ground. "Sire?"

"Gomez, get a stick or sword or something, quickly. Several."

Gomez gestured to the two guards and they grabbed some wood from a nearby woodpile. They handed the split logs to Alexander and he placed them on the ground. He moved and placed, moved and placed. Then he stood up and stepped back.

"Do you see it?"

Gomez looked at the layout of the wood. The edges of the pieces had been placed to line up with the edge of the footprints. Everything was almost exactly three feet away from the church. "That's pretty precise for just walking down the street."

Alexander looked around, then snapped his fingers for another piece of wood. He laid out another footprint farther down the church from a smaller print. He did this three more times with various sized prints and Gomez nodded, taking out the tape measure. He confirmed they were also three feet from the edge of the church.

Alexander stood. "They can't go near the church. It's not just an unwillingness to. They can't physically go there." He looked at the building, then at his friend. He put his hands on Gomez' shoulders. "I know what to do. I know how to defeat them."

# Thirty-Six

"We do not know our enemies until they move to harm us."
Shiva, The Karmic Hand

Johner brought Tanglwyst to the Queen's encampment. The guards were dispatched back to their duties and Sovereigna glided down from her throne to meet him. He and Tanglwyst bowed.

He gestured to the lady. "Where would you like me to put her for her stay here?"

Sovereigna gestured to a pole erected in the middle of her encampment. There were sticks piled up around it for lighting on fire. Johner frowned but took the lady to the stake and helped her climb the small stairs to the stage for the display. Tanglwyst paled and she looked about to vomit but she swallowed and brought herself under control. He had seen her do this several times and hoped she could keep it up. This was just a trick on Sovereigna's part to frighten the poor woman. It was ridiculous posturing. Unfortunately, the wood and stake were real and not illusion. She must have assembled it after getting the message from the lady offering herself as hostage.

He hung the chain from her manacles to a hook fashioned from a longsword. It had been bent around the stake and Johner could see palm marks from the effort. Then the sword was twisted to form the hook and the whole thing pressed tight around the top of the stake. The effort required to do such a feat was not out of the realm of any of the creatures here, but he suspected a troll or ogre had done the work. Possibly more than one since this effort would have scarred the poor creature forced to do it. Steel was an iron alloy and although it was not as effective as wrought iron, that didn't stop it from being sharp. The Queen's disregard for the Fae in her army was disgusting. This matter was not even Fae related. Part of the reason he had been so willing to pull Raven Grasshair from wherever he was had been because of this fact. Johner doubted he could handle the situation without resorting to Fae logic and that had no place here.

He walked over to Sovereigna's throne and bowed. "Is there anything else you wish, Your Majesty?"

Sovereigna stood from her throne of green velvet and mahogany. Her long, brown hair flowed down her back in an elaborate braid woven with flowers and vines. Some of the vines seemed to be sporting grapes as well. Her doe-like eyes took in the woman on the stake and she sighed. Her gown of emerald velvet was stamped with the cockatrice of Krakte along the bottom edge and she wore a ring made from the eye of one of the beasts. Her crown sat easily upon her head as she glided over to Tanglwyst. She glanced over her shoulder to Johner.

"Bring me the head of Alexander Angloume."

What?" Tanglwyst struggled against the chains and the spike at the top curled around to grip the Fae silver. "No. You have me as hostage. You said that was what you wanted. Me or him. You have me."

"True. But I know you and have questions for you. He is just a murderer."

Tanglwyst set her jaw. "No. No."

"Your Majesty, the girl is a virgin. Clearly she is the greater prize."

Sovereigna scoffed. "She's no virgin. Her virtue was claimed before she even met my daughter. She and her brother were lovers."

Tanglwyst paled.

"Oh, you didn't know Elizabeth told me? How unfortunate."

Johner pointed to the wounds on her wrists. "I think you are mistaken."

Sovereigna stepped forward, looking intently at the scars. Tanglwyst lashed out at the woman and kicked her in the face. Sovereigna fell back, hitting the ground in a lovely, delicate heap. She grabbed her chin and Johner stepped over to the Queen to help her to her feet.

"Kill her!" Sovereigna snarled through the blood on her lip as the ogre guards came to her aid. "Kill her now."

Johner stepped between Tanglwyst and the ogres, drawing his sword. "This woman is a hostage from your opponent, given of her own free will. She chose to come here."

"Then she chose poorly." She stepped back away from the stake, raising her hands. Fire licked from her fingertips.

Johner took a deep breath and glanced at Tanglwyst. "My Lady, perhaps this was not the best choice."

"She was calling for Alexander's head."

"I would not have taken it. I owe him my life."

"Oh."

The ogres moved closer.

Johner took a swipe at one of them and they backed away, cut. "Of course, nothing stops one of these monsters from going after that prize."

She grabbed the manacles and hauled herself up, kicking an ogre in the face. It barely flinched but she distracted it enough to let Johner get his sword on it. The blade bit in and the ogre staggered back. A ring of blue fire sprung up between Johner and the ogres, surrounding him and Tanglwyst.

"Sovereigna, stop this immediately or I will destroy your entire army." Johner's authority was deep and strong.

Sovereigna seethed, but she stepped back and lowered her hands. The ogres glanced back at her for instruction and she nodded. They pulled back.

"Don't think this gets you out of paying for your crime, girl."

Johner put his sword tip to the ground. "While she is here, she is under my protection, Your Majesty. You'll not harm her."

"You will do no such thing." Sovereigna snarled through bloody teeth. "You are here to serve me in this."

"I serve Corrigan Starshadow, not you. If you would prefer he pass judgment on this issue…"

She raised her hand and walked back to her throne. "No, no need for that."

"Then I have your word you'll not try to harm her nor Alexander while the negotiations are ongoing?"

"Yes, of course. So long as we are still talking, they are safe."

He lifted his chin and narrowed his eyes. He turned to look behind him at Tanglwyst. "My lady, no harm will come to you. You're safe now."

"Thank you." She looked at Sovereigna. "So much for hoping to talk to her."

"She may yet wish that. Remember, she is grieving. Would you be any less had she killed your beloved?"

Tanglwyst's eye flickered and her mouth twitched. "No. Especially not when she's tried for a month to get a reply and she got nothing." She looked at the ring of blue flame. "Will this just stay here, then?"

He glanced at the effect, then nodded. "It might be best. I will return." He bowed to her and with a judging eye upon Sovereigna, he left the encampment for town.

Alexander's heart slowed again and he was able to stand. He had been gripped with a crippling fear and had looked in on Tanglwyst to see what was happening. He used the connection between them to force himself to the scene through her. He heard the oath of the Queen not to harm him or Tanglwyst, and saw the protection Johner put around his friend. He also felt a small pang of joy when Johner asked about her beloved and her thoughts had turned to him. A raft in a sea of danger. He looked up at Gomez.

"She's fine now. Johner protected her."

Gomez leaned against the apartment wall. He put his head back and rubbed his hands through his hair. "I really like that man."

"Me too." Alexander finished putting on his boots and picked up the coat he had bundled for safety's sake the night before. He had not wanted to use the body of Elizabeth against these creatures but that display was trouble. He hoped Johner could keep Tanglwyst safe. He didn't want to use this if he didn't have to, but he wasn't blind to the need. He needed to implement his plan even more so now. He pulled the coat on and found it was too tight. The clothes they were wearing were borrowed and they must have sized this one for her. He tied the arms around his waist in his now customary fashion.

"Let's go."

Gomez nodded and they walked to the church. The priest was waiting for them, located by the city guard. He bowed respectfully to the king, who returned the gesture. Alexander motioned to the inside of the church and they all entered.

"How can I help you, Your Majesty?"

Alexander gestured to the overlapping mark on the back wall. "Do you have any carvings or any brandings with that symbol?"

The man looked behind him at the wall. "No, but they might in the Papal City. It's not far. I could make a trip…"

"The Papal City is cut off." He thought for a moment, then looked at a watchman. "Is there a blacksmith in the area? Or a wood carver? Maybe an alchemist?"

"All three sire."

"Would you get them and bring them here?"

"At once, Sire." He and another man left.

The priest gestured for them to sit in the pews. "What do you have in mind, Sire?"

Alexander sat. "The monsters roaming these streets and valley cannot go near holy ground. They cannot touch it nor go any closer than three feet. I want to see if there is a way to duplicate that symbol and place it all around the battlefield. I think, if we can drive them towards the Black Forest…"

Gomez snapped. "They can't get out. Sire, that's genius."

"I have this coat in case I get attacked. I can also get it to our troops. But it is dangerous."

"Why?" The priest looked at the innocuous jacket sleeves around Alexander's waist.

"Because it is covered with a magic solution that kills them."

Both the priest and the city guards behind him took in deep breaths. One of the guards cleared his throat. "How did you get it?"

"Not in any way I can duplicate. At least, I don't think I can. I haven't seen what it can do to a Fae." He looked around. "I know you may be thinking that this weapon is a powerful one, but it will also call every Fae in existence down upon us if it is used. I don't want that to happen. I don't think we can fight that fight."

The priest stood. "It is our duty to fight those monsters. The Church says so."

"Be that as it may, Father, we can't fit every citizen in Bordeaux in this room forever. And I will fight them, but it needs to be in a way that saves people, not risks them."

The guards that left returned with a woman and two men. "Here are the people you asked for, Your Majesty."

Alexander looked at each. "Who's who?"

The older man with the circles of glass upon his face raised his hand. "Alchemist."

The blond man with the long nose and striped shirt nodded. "Woodworker."

The woman, a redhead with burly arms and torso crossed her arms. "Blacksmith."

"Good." Alexander pointed to the symbol on the wall. "I need a lot of those in any form as possible as quick as you can. What do you suggest?"

The blacksmith cocked her head. "I can make a brand." She turned to the woodworker. "If you can slap off several chunks of wood, slices maybe, I can make one and we can brand a bunch in a single day."

"How long will it take?"

"Take me a day to make the brand. It's pretty complicated. It's not like it's just laying down string. It's bending metal."

The alchemist stroked his beard. "String..." He looked to the blacksmith. "Do you have a piece of metal you can pound flat in about an hour?"

She thought about it a second. "Yeah, I think I can. Why?"

"I have acids that I can soak on string. We make the symbol in this string, then add the acids. When it gets put on the metal, it will eat away the metal where the string is." He looked at Alexander. "It will make a negative image, where the light is the symbol, but I think we can do it by midday that way."

Alexander nodded. "Go. Let me know when you have an example. We'll need to test it."

They left, chattering about what was needed and what size to make it.

Alexander turned to the priest. "How much holy water can you make?"

"As much as I can find."

Alexander turned to Gomez. "Can you oversee that?"

"Of course, Sire." They left to begin their task.

Alexander leaned against the pew in front of him and looked for Tanglwyst. She was always active in his mind, but when he looked for her, he could feel everything she was going through. She was calm, but nervous. He sent her comforting feelings, letting her know he was working on this. She seemed to calm a bit and he lifted his head and opened his eyes. A rock skittered to a stop on the floor beside him and he turned to look out the open door. Johner was standing outside.

"General, come in."

"Um, no."

Alexander realized what he was asking. He slipped the coat from his waist and left the building. "Is there a problem?"

"Not yet. You need to begin negotiations with Her Majesty. The life of your friend depends upon it."

"What's happened?" Alexander crossed his arms and listened to the account of the delivery of Tanglwyst. He tried not to grin when Tanglwyst kicked the Queen in the face but he failed. The situation turned grave when Johner explained he left the lady there in the Queen's company.

"You left her there?"

"The Queen assured me she would be not be harmed. Understand, she will undoubtedly also not be comforted either."

"Meaning?"

"She will receive no relief nor dignity while there."

*So, Sovereigna would let her stand there and piss herself than give her the dignity of a chamber pot. How noble.* "What do I need to do?"

"Well, that is up to you. What do you want to do?"

"I wish to take care of my friend."

"Then Sir, do so."

He looked up and down the street and nodded. "Thank you, Johner."

The General bowed and went off towards the encampments.

Alexander stepped back inside the church and sat in the pew. He studied the symbol on the wall. St. Giles and St. Michael overlapping. Protection against monsters, courage and strength to fight. He thought about what could help Tanglwyst, then got an idea. He grabbed her coat and went back to her apartment to look around on her vanity. He opened drawers until he found a jewelry box. He searched but didn't find what he was looking for. He left, tying the coat around his waist again, and went to the Church again. The priest was not yet back so he left and went to the market area.

He found a jeweler and stepped inside. The jeweler, Rowena of Avalon by the sign outside, looked up when he entered. She was a plump, very pretty woman with long brown hair with a large white streak on the right front. She smiled as he entered.

"You're new. What can I do for you?"

"There's a symbol in the church. Would you happen to have something with that symbol on it? It's St. Michael and St. Giles overlapping."

She looked at her stock. "You know, I don't. People don't generally wear religious symbols around here."

"Why not? The Papal City is right over there."

"Probably because the Papal City is right over there. They undoubtedly have every form of Augustinian do-dad known to Heaven. No reason to try and duplicate it from scratch."

"Well, unfortunately, I need one as quick as you can. Are you available?"

"What's your rush, hon?"

He shrugged. "I need to get it on my friend before the Fae Queen kills her."

Rowena blinked. "Silver okay?"

"Hey, is that it?" James pointed to a small house just within sight.

Michael squinted. "Can't tell. But let's see." He kicked his horse and galloped towards the building coming into view.

About a quarter mile before it, Michael and James pulled their horses to a stop. The ground around the house was green with grass and vegetation. A paved road wove from a gate in the wall and made its way to the cottage. It was small, a one family home, and one, maybe two bedrooms. There was a garden on at least two sides and it looked like the garden might extend to the opposite side as well. Flowers, herbs, even food grew there like it was upon the sole reservoir of growth energy in the entire kingdom.

James and Michael looked into the city down the road, then back at the cottage.

James swallowed. "Why do I suddenly feel like there's a witch inside that roasts children?"

"There's got to be an explanation but we certainly won't find it here." Michael spurred his horse to a walk again and they approached it. There were several gifts along the road. Food, pottery, bottles of things in dark sacks to protect the contents, toys, trinkets of every shape and size lined both sides of the road. They came across two comfortable-looking chairs as well as a painted table. The furniture was not together, but in their own spots along the way.

They got off their horses as they approached the front door, which was open to the public. Michael looked around.

"Hello? Trimelda?"

"In here."

James and Michael looked in the front door as the woman from Michael's dream stepped away from the sink, drying her hands on an ornate towel. She stopped when she saw him.

"Michael?" She set down her towel and went to him like he was an old friend. "Michael. I'm so glad you made it." She put her arms around him in a hug.

Michael glanced at James, then hugged her back.

James stepped forward and extended his hand. "I'm James. I've heard a lot about you."

Trimelda waved her hand. "Psh. I ain't nobody. I just take care of this house, grow a few things, offer advice."

James gestured to the paved road lined with items. "What's all this?"

"Oh, those are things people leave as thank yous and offerings. They are here in case someone needs them. If someone out there needs one of these things, they just come and get it. If they don't need something anymore, they bring that by."

"Why?"

Trimelda looked at James. "Because that was Clara's way."

"Clara?" Michael didn't know that name.

"Yes. Saint Clara. This was her home."

James looked like he just met a hero. "Clara? *The* Clara? The one whose footsteps saved the world?"

Trimelda was taken aback. "Well, yes, young James. That's the Clara. You know her story?"

"Yes, my uncle wrote about her. She walked the earth here in a spiral so Raven could collect it. Then he sprinkled it around the battlefield and contained the Soulless so they could be destroyed."

"That's very impressive, James. I would love to read that writing of your uncle's. Now, what brings you boys to my home?"

"You know me from my dream, right?" Michael felt nervous asking about this. It sounded insane.

"Yes. You were running from something." She thought for a second, then snapped her fingers. "Your spirit guide."

"Wait, my what?"

"The animal guide you acquired during your rite of passage. You were to kill the first beast you came across in your rite. This becomes your spirit guide."

"Oh. I'm sorry, I was never told that. I was captured by slavers as soon as the lion was dead."

"Then you never had the ritual sealed. Come, let's work on this now."

James started to follow them but Trimelda turned to look at him. "I'm afraid this ritual is highly personal. It can't be attended by anyone not part of the process."

"Oh."

Michael looked at James, then Trimelda. "My tribe used to attend these all the time."

"They were your tribe. They believed as you believed." She turned to James. "Tell me, do you follow the Fang and Claw?"

James shook his head, his cheeks a little red from embarrassment. "Uh… no. I don't even know what that is."

"Well, I'll have to hold off then." Michael looked at James. "We're actually on our way to deliver some bad news and I should be there."

James held up his hand in protest. "I disagree. C'mere." He motioned to them to step away from the cottage. He pointed to some buildings about two miles away. "See that? That's Kilgorran. Across the bay is Kilmory. They're sister cities. I'm already home. This is where we used to go to sell our wool. I'll go, tell my family and return for you."

Michael shook his head. "Not a chance. I'm here to help and I'll help. Both Myrgen and Catriona would be intolerant if I abandoned you."

286

"You're not *abandoning* me, Michael. You're tending to a very personal task, just as I am. Think about it. I'm telling my mother that my sister, and her brother are both dead. It might not be the best time to also have company."

"You mean, they might spend energy on making sure I feel comfortable, rather than tending to their own grief."

James nodded. "That is exactly what I mean." He gestured to Trimelda. "This is incredibly lucky for me. How long will this ritual take?"

Trimelda smiled. "A couple days. First, we must re-acquaint Michael with the spirits of the beasts that surround him."

"That's perfect then. You haven't been able to sleep and if you had another a dream fit like this morning at my house, my mother might die herself. You wouldn't want to cause my mother's death, would you?"

Michael smiled. "No, that would be bad."

"Precisely. So, I'll scamper off, do my thing, and let my family know about Gwen and Alistair. Then I'll swing by here and we'll..." James shrugged, "we'll sort out our next move from there. I need to get back to Mande to get to the *Raven's Watch* so I might be catching a ship from here to sail south. We can drop you off in Zara on the way."

Michael nodded. "That sounds good. Thank you James." He held out his hand.

James grasped it in friendship and nodded to Trimelda. "My lady, you take good care of him now."

"Oh, I aim to."

The friends smiled and parted company.

# Thirty-Seven

## "When we return, our souls will not be less intertwined."
## Shiva, The Karmic Hand

Myrgen told Catriona everything, from being captured by Boots, to the loss of the White Granite Sword. He told of the amulets Cipriano had, that the Land drew them to it. He told of Cipriano's bragging and how the Land waited until every amulet was on hard ground before it took them and destroyed them with fire. He told the tale of Drake and Anika's passing, how they directed him to the Succession Stones and all three of them had been taken. He told of the assailant that got inside the keep, and how everyone told him that Tib had taken up a sword and attacked. How he had died protecting his people.

Her tears waited until the talk of Tib and his bravery, then they fell. She stayed standing, but she felt her knees trying to give up.

"Leave me. Please."

Myrgen sighed. She knew he wanted to stay but she needed him to go. Had she asked kindly, he would have protested. The only way to get him to understand the seriousness of her request was to be commanding. He bowed and left.

When he had closed the doors behind him, she went to the bier and the blanket that stuck out from beneath it. She pulled it and the stones fell away from it. Something rolled from within and rested at her feet. It was Tib's severed head. Horror coated her body, then anger. Myrgen had not told her that he had been beheaded, only that he was killed. When he said she took the body with her when she went into the ground, he must have assumed the whole thing went. But the separate pieces would have required separate efforts to commit them to the Land.

She knelt down and touched her son's face. "Make him whole."

The head sunk into the ground, and a bluebell grew for a second in the dark lava stone. She sent it to the garden outside where it would prosper and multiply.

"Now, bring me the one who did this to him."

The stones of the bier clacked together to form a towering creature made of red, pulsing rock. It took a knee before her, bowing its head.

"I do not possess that soul. It is not within my purview."

"Who has it?"

"All I know is that it is in the hands of Heaven."

She spat. Her eyes blazed dark, and vicious, and deep jade. "Then I guess I need to make a visit there to seize it."

She looked away, and the stones sank into the molten rock and disappeared. The blanket flared in a fiery glut and disappeared.

Catriona emerged from the doors, her expression unreadable. Myrgen watched her, letting her set the tone now. She walked to him and hugged him, and he and Alistair both relaxed. He held her until she was done.

She looked at them. "We should probably talk."

Myrgen nodded. "Let's get you dressed first, then we'll go talk, alright?"

Alistair glanced at her. "Do you two need to be alone?"

Myrgen looked at her. "Your call."

She looked Alistair over. "I don't think so. Stay with us. I have the feeling you know a few things and I have questions. Do you need to be anywhere?"

"No, not really."

"Good."

They walked down the hallway to the stairs. Myrgen gestured to a set of doors in a wall. "That's the study. We'll be right back."

Catriona put her hand on Myrgen's arm. "I know my way here. I'll be fine."

"Are you sure?"

She smiled a brilliant smile. Now that she was in full light, Myrgen could see the differences clearly. Her hair, her body, her voice, all were pretty much the same. But her eyes were... different. First of all, they were cloudier, like jade instead of emeralds. They were also shaped a little differently. Still, they were very *familiar*. He *knew* these eyes.

She kissed him. "Yes, I'm sure. I'll be right back." She looked at Alistair. "Alistair, see to it he has a drink in him by the time I show up."

"Aye, my lady."

She went down the stairs, a few shocked and excited gasps in the courtyard. Myrgen watched her until she was out of sight, then succumbed to Alistair's sleeve tugging.

They entered the study at Ashstone and Myrgen went to the decanter of brandy near the fireplace. The room was huge, with book shelves, stuffed sofas and matching chairs, a large desk, statues, paintings, and a fireplace you could roast a pig in. Myrgen poured three brandies, setting one aside for her. He handed Alistair one and took the last for himself. He downed half of it in a gulp to start on fulfilling her request.

Alistair took a sip of his. "You alright?"

Myrgen looked up at the portrait of the First Dûcesa. "I don't know yet. This was a turning point here." He turned to Alistair. "Did you see the difference?"

"Nope. It was all familiar. Facial structure, hair," he sighed, "alluring figure."

Myrgen raised a finger from his glass to point at Alistair. "Hey. Manners." He smiled.

Alistair put his hands up in surrender. "Couldn't help it. But no, there was no difference."

Myrgen walked over to the smaller portrait of the Third Dûcesa. "It was subtle, but with her, I kind of expect it. Her eyes were just barely *not* her own, but they were *someone's*. I know those eyes. I just can't place them." He walked over to the statue of the Second Dûcesa. "Hunh. The sword is missing. I wonder what happened to it." He looked around for a moment, then looked back at the statue. "I wonder why they stopped after three." He turned, nodding to the portrait over the fireplace. "And why they started with her. I mean, I remember Raven telling me about her being the first ruler over this area. But there's *no* record of any other..." He groped for an appropriate word.

"Incarnations?"

Myrgen sighed. "Yeah. I guess you do know something about all this."

"Can I tell you something? I'm looking forward to talking it all out with someone. I might be able to get things straight on my head."

"I know the feeling. I have pieces to put together, but I worry other people have them too and I can't get the right picture without everyone's contribution."

"Do you want to wait for Raven?"

Myrgen looked at Alistair. "Let's see how far we get on our own. He's... not always the easiest to understand."

The doors closed and Catriona stood there, leaning against them. "What are we talking about?"

Myrgen got her glass of brandy and she looked appreciatively at the level in his glass. Her eyes were back to being emerald and her own. "Comparing notes."

She nodded, then sipped her brandy. "I think that's a really good idea." She took a deep breath. "So, I think I know the starting point to this talk, the common ground. Do we want to go with before or after we all died?"

Myrgen almost dropped his drink. He looked at Alistair. "You *died?*"

Alistair nodded.

Myrgen sat on the sofa facing the two chairs. "This just became a much more interesting story than I expected."

Alistair took a chair across from him. "Yeah. Well, it came as a bit of a shock to me. I didn't think I *could* die."

"Why not?"

"Because I'm over three hundred years old."

Catriona brought the brandy decanter to the sofa and set it on the table between them. "I've always wondered about that. You were able to get my innermost secret from me, but you never divulged yours. It's part of why I didn't marry you. You never trusted me."

Alistair nodded. "I'm afraid that's true. I was never the right one for you and I knew it. When we were together, I kept getting this feeling that there was more to you than I understood. It was enough for me to speak to a friend of mine named Raven. He assured me you were not Fae, which was my first suspicion. Your ability to read people could be explained by you being half Fae. I was, and maybe *still am,* indebted to the Fae Queen of Winter, Gloriana Talnig.

"We fell in love during the Soulless War, or rather, *she* did. I was not expecting to live through the war. When the Prince of York died saving my life, no one knew it except Raven. Raven was the one who suggested I become him, at least for a little while. He had a really good reason for it. He said it would be too dangerous for the kingdom to lose all their royals in this. They needed something to rally around during this crisis. So he shaped my face and body to resemble Alistair Hapsburg. I returned to Persephone literally a new man, but the plan was for me to find a real heir to the throne after the war was over. Then I'd turn it over to them.

"Well, it turned out Alistair and Gloriana had fallen in love. He left before they even had their first kiss. Exchanged gifts and everything. I just went with it." He shrugged. "She was incredibly beautiful and I didn't see a way this could go awry. She took me to her bed and I thought myself the height of lucky. The next day, Raven came into my room and said we should get Merrick to permanently change my face. That's when he saw I wasn't alone. Gloriana was furious. So she decided to take care of that herself and said that since I had stolen his face and her affection, she would make sure I never forgot it. So, it was made permanent and she bound me to her service. She said, 'Since I will no longer be able to speak to the man I love, I can at least see his face.'"

He looked at the brandy in his glass, swirled it, and swallowed the rest. "Raven didn't even try to stop her. He was pretty angry that I had done this. He told me it was rape, and that I should have told her I couldn't sleep with her. I didn't have to tell her why. I could have just kept putting her off. I tried to con my way out of it but he was right. She refused to see me after that and I didn't know what to do. I talked to Wilgefortis and she kinda of knew what I was going through because she had been forced to marry the Baron of Canterbury in order to keep Persephone's land. Wilgefortis and Raven were in love but she did it out of duty.

"She told me to go to the Fae Queen and ask her what she needed for it to be right. She told me to accept whatever the terms were. I went to Glarren, fought my way to her castle, set myself before her, apologizing. She made me her servant. Usually, these only last for a year and a day, but they don't start until the Fae says they start. Until that time, you stay in pretty much the peak of your life and health so they aren't getting an old, frail person when they need a young, spry one. I was to remain in that limbo until I repaid the debt owed to her."

He pointed to Catriona. "You did that."

She tilted her head. "When you saved me from those attackers my first night in Yantap."

Alistair nodded. "That's also why I took it so hard when you told me what I did to those sailors in my pursuit of Tanglwyst as the Black Sparrow." He looked down at his empty glass. "I realized I was doing the same thing all over again. Anyway, turns out the gestation times of the Fae are somewhat fluid. She had chosen to put the pregnancy on hold until such time as I repaid the debt. When I saved you, that's how she knew. She... gestated."

Myrgen shook his head. "Wow."

"Well, save your judgment. It gets worse. I found out when she sent the child to me shortly after you and I met, Catriona."

Her eyes grew wide. "The baby."

He nodded. He looked at Myrgen. "Catriona wanted to raise him as our own but then she got attacked by Giovanni's forces and he almost got killed. So, I took him to a relative of mine in Glarren. She and her husband had never been able to conceive and I knew they would love him. After you left me," he nodded to Catriona, "I returned to Glarren and found out he was growing up really fast but when I was around, that growth slowed to normal. That's why he hadn't changed until after I dropped him off with my sister and her husband."

"Sister? You're three hundred years old."

"She didn't know that. It happened during one of my bouts of self-loathing. I went on a twenty year binge of celibacy. During that time, I was a monk in a place near Glarren. She was a nun. We left the church about the same time, and helped each other find a place in the world. She always called me brother, I always called her sister. People assumed, as intended, that we were relatives. She called me Sparrow, because I kept flitting in and out of people's lives. I never married because I couldn't

293

figure out how to explain to a woman that I would never age until the Queen of Winter released me. Then I would die instantly. I also couldn't have another child. Gloriana took that as well.

"So James was my only son."

"James." Catriona looked at Myrgen. "You mean *Gwen's* James?"

Alistair nodded. "I said it got worse."

She shook her head. "He's a man. A full grown man. That baby came to us seven years ago."

"Well, remember how I said Fae gestation times were strange? The same with aging times. Before adolescence, they are in flux. According to Orabilia, my sister, one day he was an infant, the next he was a toddler. Then he would return to infancy, then a month later, he was five years old. Luckily, they were sheep herders so they weren't around other people much. The folks in town just thought they had a whole passel of children, all boys. After the first year, the aging became more consistent. It changed every season. So, an infant for a season, then a toddler, then a three year old, then a five. Then it started all over again."

Myrgen frowned. "How did they take that?"

Alistair smiled. "With the strangest delight. I'm pretty sure she was blessed at birth by some great being because the changes were new and exciting to them. They took the entire thing in stride."

"But, if they couldn't have children, how did Gwen happen?" Catriona leaned forward, delighted. "Was the proximity of a Fae child enough to correct the issue?"

"Um… not exactly. When you and I parted ways, I stayed with Orabilia and Gavan for a bit. Having me around stabilized his growth. When the season change came, he didn't change with it. But I was depressed. I loved you and I didn't want to live without you. So, I left Billi and Gavan and sought out Gloriana. I begged for her to let me fulfill her service and die. She refused. She said she would not only forbid me from ever leaving the earth, but that the only thing she had that would ever allow her to forgive me was dead and I had his face. She stormed out and when she went into a room, I thought I heard a baby cry.

"Well, I'm first and foremost a thief. So, I stole into the room to see what was going on. It turned out, the pregnancy resulted in twins. She went from warm to the child to cold fury around her. Every time she was angry, the child cried, and coughed. She was getting sick from the endless mood swings. I couldn't let her stay there. I figured I would do both of us a favor, something that would save the child and possibly make Gloriana so angry, she'd kill me outright.

"I kidnapped her daughter."

Catriona almost dropped her glass. She looked at it, like it was a traitor, and put it on the table to avoid any other incidents.

Myrgen sipped his brandy. "Yeah, that tactic, it doesn't really work."

Alistair gestured to Catriona. "It worked for you."

Myrgen shook his head. "*Catriona* didn't kill me."

"Well, we can't *all* be right, can we? Anyway, I took the little girl to my sister and handed her over. They named her Gwen. I thought, maybe with his twin around, James would stabilize."

"Did it work?"

"Did I mention Fae aging is weird?"

Catriona rubbed her face. "Gwen is barely twenty years old. James is a few years beyond that, maybe four?"

"That's what it evened out to be. Having the extra relative around *did* make their growth consistent. Baby to toddler to young child and so on. He was in that three to four year old range when I showed up with Gwen. But having the extra *Fae* part accelerated the growth. I came back around a year later and they were both adolescents. Gavan said that maybe it was time to take James away for a while, that maybe it was the proximity to Gloriana that kept them accelerating. So, I took James with me, much to Gwen's anger and disappointment.

"We left and his aging slowed. We grew quite close. I ended up teaching him to be a ship captain and he showed an aptitude for strategy. After you and I had our encounter outside Tanglwyst's house and you judged me, I returned to Glarren. Gwen was aging as fast as James had. I knew she needed to be away from the Midwinter Realm, so I..."

"You put her in my way."

He studied his glass, nodding, then poured another brandy. "I thought she would be a good companion for you. We made up a story that she was to be married to some noble against her will and let that story be sown through the town. They all believed she had a dozen brothers and sisters by then so the additional seed that the Kilmory lord was marrying another sister took just as well."

They were silent for a minute, then she nodded. "Thank you. I could not have gotten through this winter without her. Though I must say, she never once let on that she had no other relatives except James. I don't know how that was kept from me." She looked at Alistair. "I'm going to blame you."

Alistair nodded. "And well you should." He raised his glass. "For our fallen."

Myrgen and Catriona raised theirs as well, agreeing. They all drank.

Myrgen set his glass down. "So, is that what happened? Gloriana tracked you down and killed you?"

"Uh, no. That was Duncan McVryce. Killed me with a dart in St. Andrew about a month ago. Right after we met, Myrgen."

Catriona blinked. Myrgen stayed bent forward, his hand still on his glass. They both stared at him. They slowly turned to look at each other and then back to him. Myrgen's mouth did a few acrobatics in an attempt to remark and Catriona's eyebrows did the same. She recovered before he did.

"So…"

Myrgen nodded. "Yeah." He pointed to her. "What she said."

Alistair looked back and forth between the two of them. "What?"

Catriona frowned. "Why did he kill you?"

"Oh. He doesn't like me."

Myrgen twitched. "He…?"

"Mhm. He didn't like that I broke Tangl's heart. So, he killed me." Alistair frowned, rubbing the spot on his neck where the dart hit. "It was *fast* too. I didn't even know I was dead until Karma told me."

"You need to stop hanging around with Raven." Myrgen nodded to him. "You're not connecting things."

Catriona stood up. "I need a break. Anybody else hungry?"

Both men nodded. Myrgen stood. "Let me go. If you show yourself in the kitchens, we'll never see you until we come looking for you."

"Why don't we all go then? In truth, I think we've spent enough time apart."

Alistair nodded and the three friends left the room.

# Thirty-Eight

"To unscramble an egg, feed it
to a chicken."
Kali, The Karmic Hand

The reception in the dining hall at Ashstone was exactly as predicted. People greeted Catriona, and Myrgen saw her eyes return to their customary emerald with gold flecks when she saw them. It truly *was* her again, and he took her hand and celebrated her return alongside everyone else. Alistair was likewise buoyed by the festivities and the trio stayed talking until well past midnight. Finally, Alistair stretched and yawned.

"I wasn't expecting a party."

Catriona, wrapped in Myrgen's embrace, smiled at him. "Stay. We'll carry on with our talk in the morning. We need some joy to counter the grief."

Alistair nodded. "It is, in fact, my job to balance things." A lovely, mature lady came over to them and Alistair smiled to his friends. "I believe my date is here anyway."

He stood and excused himself, and was led away.

Myrgen looked at his beloved. "Are you okay?"

Her face relaxed from the joyful smile she was wearing. "Not quite." She looked around the room at the well-wishers and mourners. "But I know where he is now." She tapped his chest. "So do you."

He nodded. "I do. What impresses me more than anything is that these people accept that on faith. You and I have seen it. We know it to be true."

She grinned. "That is the Land, my love." She took his hand and pulled him towards the door. "Come. Take me to bed. Remind me I'm alive."

They went to her room, the opportunity to be alone feeling rare and desperately needed. He didn't think, didn't allow thought to disrupt things. He almost felt reality try to intrude and he put it down like a Mandian royal. This was *their* time. No one else's. Clothes became laundry, flesh became a canvas they made beautiful with their passion. When they screamed their pleasure, it was with all the release of a full on earthquake. The collapse in the aftermath brought such a complete stillness, they didn't dare break it with talk. Myrgen's heart felt settled and Catriona rested easy beside him.

He thought about what she had been through, and wondered if he could have weathered such an ordeal with as much grace. He doubted it. His journey to find the "weapon" had been for naught, a ruse by the Land to locate his beloved. It had supplied all the information he needed to save her, to keep her *her*, through his dreams after he left Caratia. He was glad he knew what to do when the time came. The Land had provided the guidance. It was no wonder the people of this place trusted it so wholeheartedly. He wondered if everyone here had a story like this to tell.

Judging from the tales he'd heard of others who had suffered losses, yes. The whole time they were downstairs celebrating with the people of Zara, he had heard story after story of great deeds, or terrible pains, and the sending of those to Summerland. When Catriona was told of the battle in the town square, of Drake and Anika's deaths and how the Land took them and Myrgen when the Stones of Intent rose, each person spoke warmly of the Dûce and Dûcesa as if they were happy where they were. Myrgen could attest they had seemed so and Catriona assured him that was her experience too.

"Death is not a thing to fear, Myrgen," he was told over and over. "Even the young, like Tib, will have their whole lives to live out in

Summerland. The Land takes them from this world and still nurtures them in the next." He wondered if it was a kindness that he let the dog live instead of…

He sat up. *Drake.*

Catriona sat up, startled. "What is it?"

"Drake, Tib's dog. He was with me in York."

She frowned at him. "You brought his dog to a wasteland?"

"He insisted."

"He's a dog."

"He insisted!"

"By the bloody Stones." She got out of bed and looked around for her clothes. He did likewise. "Where did you leave him?"

"We were at Persephone." Then he stopped. He turned to her. "No, wait. We were somewhere else. Someplace with a tall tower."

She stopped. "In *York?*"

"I think so. But maybe not…It was lush there. Verdant. Raven took us there." He snapped his fingers. "Alistair would know. He took me from there to here."

"Lush? There's no place lush in York."

He pulled on his pants. "Well, that's not quite true nowadays."

"Huh?" She frowned at him.

He went over to her and put his hands upon her shoulders. "You were drained almost to death in that chamber. The Gold Wife dispersed your life force into the grounds above."

She stared at him. "Get some horses."

They finished dressing and ran to the stables. Within the hour, they were heading towards the mountain and the inn at the top. They heard barking when they got to the inn and a growl as they approached. They reined in and waited, looking.

A great spiked beast snarled from the shadows, eyes glowing green in the moonlight. Catriona got off the horse against Myrgen's hissed warnings. He dismounted as well and moved before her. He drew the White Granite Sword from the ground, the handle slipping easily into his hand. He squinted, trying to see the beast.

He blinked.

"Lauriel?"

The beast came forward into the light, ears forward. It stopped crouching and wagged its tail. Myrgen dropped the sword and it fell back into the ground, disappearing. He went to his knees and the Fae wolf licked his face.

"Where's Drake?"

The wolfhound bounded from the inn, a small girl rubbing her eyes behind him. Drake bowled Myrgen down, and licked his face until Myrgen cried to Catriona for help.

"Is he hurt?" Catriona knelt by the trio and checked Drake over. She found no wounds.

"It doesn't…" Myrgen tried to talk but got a mouthful of dog tongue. "Blah!"

He rolled over and tried to get up but the Fae wolf jumped on his back and held him down while Drake licked Myrgen's entire face. He reached out for Catriona and when she took his hand, he pulled her to him. They rolled around on the ground together, getting filthy and doggy, until their laughter had the whole inn on the porch. Catriona noticed the audience and got to her feet, dragging Myrgen with her.

"How long have they been here?"

The little girl, Erica, yawned before answering. "A few days. They caught a rabbit and ate it. We knew you would be back to get him."

Myrgen checked them both over. "Where there any signs of wear, dehydration, damage?"

"No. Drake had grass stains on his fur in fact. And they smelled weird."

"Weird?"

"Like pumpkins and honey."

Myrgen looked at Catriona. "That's where Raven took us." He lowered his voice. "In the Fae realm."

Catriona looked at both dogs. "Well, they seem fine now. What do you want to do?"

Cecelia opened the door. "Well, I'm gonna get these young ones back to bed. Are you comin' in?"

"Actually, was there a horse with them?"

Cecelia nodded, gesturing to the side of the inn. "Back there. Two of 'em."

"Thank you!"

Catriona arched an eyebrow. "I would have made boots out of your hide had you lost that horse."

"That was… incredibly graphic and unsettling. Nice to know where I stand in the hierarchy of pets." Myrgen looked at Lauriel. "Are you coming with us, or going back to Raven?"

Lauriel looked at York.

"Thank you then. Thanks for bringing them back to us."

Lauriel snuffled, and licked Drake. Drake barked, and turned back to Myrgen.

Catriona got the other horses as Myrgen left some money inside for Cecelia. The pair got on their horses, Drake and the other horses trailing behind them, and went back down the mountain.

Alistair rolled over in his lover's bed and reached for her, but the bed was empty. He could smell bacon cooking and opened his eyes. He was surprised to see the snow white environment of the Hand of Karma. He sat up and looked around. There was a hole in the ground and he went to it and descended the spiral staircase to the area below. He was scratching his shoulder blades, chasing an itch, as Lucifer looked up. The archangel in charge of Hell was frying bacon in a very stylish kitchen. There were eggs in a pan as well as some cinnamon-sugar turnips and fresh bread. He was wearing a red shirt and matching pants, with a kerchief covering his head and a leather apron. His arms had sleeves covering his shirt sleeves, snug to the arm but not impairing.

"Hi honey. How did you sleep?"

"How did I get here?"

Lucifer pointed with a spatula. "Stairs. Too much brandy last night?"

"No, but I was with a lovely lady and now I am not with a lovely lady. I find this to be inequitable."

"Pah!" Lucifer waved his spatula at Alistair and went back to stirring the bacon. "You can head back there anytime. I just can't go there to see you."

"Why not?"

Lucifer looked at him. "Are you insane? Me, a representative of Heaven, in the heart of the Land? That would be an act of war."

"You said you *want* war."

"I don't want to die in it." He nodded to the bread. "There's fresh butter and honey. Get a plate and get started."

Alistair walked over to the bread and smelled it. It was divine. He spread the butter on a chunk and added some honey. "So, what did you need, Luci?"

"Well, Allie, I was wondering what your plan is now that the young lady has been returned to the Land?" He winked at Alistair. "Nice work with that Gold Wife, by the way. Good solution."

"Well, it isn't empty like we discussed but she shouldn't be any trouble."

"I think it will be an interesting match when I drop my guy in there, if all goes well. But tell me your plan."

Alistair frowned. "Why should I? I mean, you're the bad guy."

"Oh, undoubtedly. I probably just want to make sure you aren't going to interfere with my insidious plans."

"Well, we're going to compare notes. See what's going on."

Lucifer nodded his approval. "Sounds good. Then what?"

"Then we put a stop to it."

Lucifer smiled. "I like the sound of that."

Alistair didn't understand. "But we're gonna be stopping *your* insidious plans."

"Mhm. I want you to think of my actions as indicative of what you'll get with any archangel."

"So, I can expect fresh butter and honey in all my Heavenly encounters?"

Lucifer fought a laugh and settled for a chuckle. "I would love to see that exchange."

He finished cooking the bacon and poured the grease into an earthenware jar. Then he laid the individual chunks onto a cheesecloth and nudged the plate towards Alistair. The entity of Karma took the bacon and added eggs to his plate. The turnips were especially buttery but he added a little more and some honey to that mix as well.

Alistair found a fork and took a bite. The flavors were beyond what he had encountered in the world. He moaned in pleasure, his eyes rolling back in joy. "Oh, this is excellent. Why does this taste so good?"

"Eh, probably because it's seasoned with all the stuff that isn't good for you."

"I don't care, I'm already dead."

"Exactly. So, are you going to invite your little friends over?"

"Um, not sure. Can they get here?"

Lucifer nodded. "If they're dead. This *is* the afterlife, after all."

"Well, that wouldn't be a problem for two of them, technically, but what about the ones that can't reincarnate?"

"Oh, they'd stay dead. Probably best not to bring them."

Alistair nodded. "Riiight. Well, now that we've cleared that up, why should I bring them around?"

Lucifer looked at Alistair, leaning on the table. He nodded to sealed missive on the counter that Alistair had completely failed to see before that second. "Because there's a war coming between Heaven and Earth and you need to be prepared."

Alistair walked in the bedroom door of the lady whose bed he had shared, bearing a loaded plate of food. She groaned pleasantly and smiled.

"Did you cook?"

"A friend of mine did so I grabbed a plate and left for better company."

She scooted up to sit in bed and took a chunk of bacon from the offerings. "Cooked exactly how I like it. I must meet your friend."

Alistair smiled. "That would be both sad and hilarious."

They spent the morning relaxing and talking. When finally she sighed, making those noises that said she was ready to be about her business, Alistair kissed her. They parted company and Alistair looked at the castle in the mountain. He smiled and walked up there, then, at the gates, he felt something pull him away from it. He furrowed his brow in confusion.

*A Fae ring? When did that happen?*

He almost went that way, but realized that the Fae ring had not been there when he and Myrgen had gone to lunch the other day. He had always been sensitive to them, ever since his service to Gloriana was imposed. But one was definitely here now. It occurred to him they might have a different purpose than he originally thought. Now the visit with his friends was more important than ever.

He steeled himself and went to the dining hall. He looked around and didn't find his quarry. He stopped a young boy carrying plates from another part of the castle.

"Excuse me, have you seen Myrgen and Catriona?"

"Not this morning. Have you checked their room?"

"That would be the height of indiscretion, my good friend. Can someone knock for me?"

A girl came up beside him. "Did you ask about the Stâpân? They are in the bath downstairs."

"Ah. Not sure that's better. Is anyone else with them?"

"No. But they have said it is alright for people to join them." She handed him a towel. "Here. Go ahead."

She gave him directions and he went to the room with the steaming scent of clean. He heard laughter inside and a lot of splashing. He opened the door and was instantly consumed by steamy fog. He closed the door behind him to keep the warmth in.

"Hello?"

"Alistair?" Her voice was as sultry as he remembered it. He followed it through the steam to a tiled rectangular tub that could fit eight people. There were several others nearby in different shapes.

"Good morning."

"Good morning to you! Join us!"

"I feel I would be imposing upon your privacy."

She smiled, leaning upon the edge, her long hair flowing behind her and obscuring the view. "Then use that one. We can still talk." She pointed to a nearby smaller round tub, only fit for six.

"I really can't. But Myrgen, I owe you dinner, for the other night. I'd like to make good on that."

Myrgen nodded, smiling. "Sure. Before or after the bath?"

He smiled. "Best make it after." His tone grew serious. "There's still much to say."

Myrgen looked at his hands. "Well, I'm getting wrinkled. How about you, my love?"

She looked at her own fingers. "I guess we have been here a while." She looked at Alistair. "Where do you want to meet?"

"There's that tavern you mentioned. Specializes in beer?"

Myrgen nodded. "The Stoic Stag. A block from here down the other street. Towards the woods to the west. Turn right at the gates of Ashstone and it's on the left."

"Thank you. An hour?"

"Sure." Catriona exchanged a glance with Myrgen. "Do you need us to hurry?"

"To be honest, I'd like you wearing your best. I have someone you need to meet."

They both frowned, but nodded.

He turned and left the room.

Alistair went to the gates and turned right, then walked past the tavern to the woods. He felt around for the Fae circle, knowing he had felt one when he looked that direction. He knew that was probably where Catriona had come from. He wanted to see if her stone was there. He suspected that Fae circles were far from related to Fae activities, but had instead been appropriated by them once the Bringer no longer needed them. The one in the woods here was new, which meant in the last day. He looked to the forest.

He stepped into the Fae ring and reached out spiritually to Raven.

The mage looked up from the bench he was on, still in Sovereignlumin. "Yeah?"

"I have a meeting I need you to attend. You busy?"

Raven looked at the stairs going up to the upper floor and the bier of his grandfather. "No. I seriously got nothing better to do."

"Great. Meet me here."

Raven nodded.

Alistair stepped out of the ring and walked over to stand under a tree. A few moments later, Raven did as well.

"What's going on?"

Alistair leaned against his tree, folding his arms. "I've got a meeting to go to. What did you discover in Sovereignlumin?"

"More than I ever wanted to know."

"I think we're about to get a lot of that." He pulled an invitation from his coat. "We have a meeting and I think you need to be there."

He handed Raven the invitation and he opened it. He glanced up at Alistair. "Is this real?"

"Yup."

"Why?"

"Because I've talked with the man a lot lately and he has some insights. There's something bigger going on and we need to come to grips with that."

Raven sighed, closed the invitation and handed it back. He nodded to it. "How many is that for?"

"As many as needs be."

"How many is that?"

"Right now, four."

"Open ended?"

"I think so."

Raven nodded. "Okay then. I'll talk about my discoveries when we're all together. Do we want to reveal all there, or away from there?"

"I was gonna wait until we were all together before making that decision." Alistair cocked his head, narrowing his eyes at Raven. "Are you alright?"

Raven shook his head. "No. Definitely not."

"You up to this?"

"I kinda have the feeling I don't get to choose."

Laughter caught their attention and they saw Myrgen and Catriona step away from the Ashstone gate. They turned towards the tavern Alistair mentioned.

"She's not dead?"

"Not anymore." Alistair pushed off the tree and stepped out into the sunlight, waving. They waved back.

"Is that the same woman?"

"There are occasional changes. When her eyes turn jade, they change shape a bit too. Other than that, I guess this is close to her truest form."

"How often has that happened?" Raven stepped into the sun as well.

"No idea, but I expect this is the end product. She was confronted with the rather horrible death of her son yesterday. There was nothing she could do about it. Myrgen and the Land already killed the murderer."

The couple paused at the tavern but Alistair waved them over. They looked at each other confused but joined the friends.

"What's going on?" Myrgen looked back and forth at Alistair and Raven.

Alistair handed Catriona the invitation. "This is where I wanted us to go for lunch."

Catriona opened the missive and read it along with Myrgen. They both looked at Alistair.

"Is this real?" Catriona looked at the signature again.

*Please join me for lunch at your earliest convenience.*
*I have an apocalypse to discuss.*
*This invitation will be your key to get to our meeting place.*

*~Lucifer*

"Lucifer? Like the archangel?"

"Stricken from the Annals of the Saintly Record but still in place in Heaven." Raven glanced at the back of the letter. "I've seen it."

"What does this mean?" Myrgen frowned, anger starting to spark in his eyes and voice. "Is this some sort of betrayal?"

"No. But we have a lot to discuss and I really don't want to do any of it in public. This is a meeting that has to occur and frankly, it's better to do it on neutral ground than anywhere else."

"What's neutral ground?"

"Well, believe it or not, this invitation is to neutral ground."

Raven shook his head. "This is the monster in charge of the infernal aura."

"Yeah, I know. And I know why he did it too."

"What is neutral ground to a divine entity?"

Alistair swallowed. "Karma."

# Thirty-Nine

"Never bargain with a Fae or a high-ranking church official."
Shiva, The Karmic Hand

"Where are we?" Myrgen looked at the mansion before them.

"It's an area of Karma's Hand that is literally neutral ground. Everyone has all their powers here and they are all equal. It's pointless to fight here because no one can win. It took a lot of effort to make it touch every border so no one was excluded and anyone could be here without dying."

Catriona recognized the building. "I saw this, in Summerland." She looked at Alistair. "It was not quite materialized though."

"That's because I had not yet gotten permission to let it be there."

"How did you plan to do that?"

"Find someone who lived there and get their okay." A handsome man in a beautiful long, black coat of velvet leaves stood at the door. He bowed, golden eyes shimmering in the morning light. Alistair gestured to him as they approached.

"Catriona, Myrgen, this is Lucifer."

Lucifer bowed. "A genuine pleasure to meet you finally. I've heard a lot about you."

Catriona nodded acknowledgment. "Personally or professionally?"

Lucifer laughed. "A bit of both. I tend to watch and listen a lot. Please, come in."

He took them to a study of impressive proportions. What appeared to be every book ever written lined the shelves, and maps and scrolls were stacked in cubbyholes along one wall. Overstuffed furniture appointed the room in clusters for conversation, and there was a warming fireplace that was not too hot and not too low. Windows brought in the morning light on two sides and from above in skylights. There was enough space in here to fly a kite.

Alistair held up a bottle. "Brandy?"

Myrgen looked at Catriona. *Do we trust it?* She nodded and he held up two fingers.

"Where's Raven?"

"He…" Myrgen looked around, "was right behind us."

"Oh," Alistair glanced at the door, "he didn't step into the Fae circle with you?"

"It really wasn't large enough for more than two."

Alistair looked at Lucifer. "He'll be fine. I know he's coming. He'll be here within the next minute. Please, relax." When they hesitated, he added, "Look, there is literally nowhere else to go when he arrives. The invitation can only bring you here."

Catriona sat on the velvet couch facing the fireplace, taking her glass from Myrgen when he brought it over and joined her. "This room is beautiful."

Lucifer bowed. "Thank you. I decorated it for this occasion. All the pieces were designed and built just for this."

Myrgen looked around. "This is a significant enough event to build furniture for it?"

"Well, understand that this was inevitable, so I started work on it a while back."

"How long ago?"

Lucifer sipped his brandy. "About a hundred years." He held out a fancy tray with miniature cakes on them. "Oh! Petit four?"

"Ooh!" Both Catriona and Myrgen set upon the cakes and ate them, relishing the flavors.

Myrgen rolled his eyes in pleasure. "Tangl had the best pastry chef in Mervolingia. Her petit fours were divine."

"It's one of the things I miss about working with her." Catriona tried not to moan while chewing but failed.

Lucifer picked up an orange one with a little carrot in frosting on the top. "This is one my favorite things about being me: Supporting creativity to the point where I can eat it."

Myrgen and Catriona looked at their half-eaten cakes, now suspicious. Alistair came over and grabbed a blue one, devouring it in one bite. He clinked glasses with Lucifer in a show of solidarity. Catriona and Myrgen shrugged and finished eating. A knock came on the door and a servant opened it.

"Master Raven Grasshair, sir."

Lucifer started and looked at Alistair. "A Fae?"

"Not really. A mage with Fae ties. I thought having as much insight as possible for this couldn't hurt."

Lucifer nodded and stood. "Would you like a brandy, Master Raven?"

Raven looked around the room. "Looks like I'll be the odd man out if I say no bytheFaearethosepetitfours?" He skirted the couch in his excitement about the tiny cakes. He grabbed a pink one and a green one as Lucifer poured the brandy. He bought it over after Raven managed to eat each one with equal abandon. Raven took a swig of brandy to help wash them down.

"We will have lunch brought in about an hour. I have some pheasant being prepared."

Alistair smiled. "This is the best council meeting I think I've ever been to."

Raven raised his hand. "I nominate this fellow for hosting all future council meetings."

Alistair gestured to Lucifer. "Lucifer."

"Lucifer. Excellent name. Sounds familiar. Have we met?"

"No."

"Hunh. You're still my pick."

Lucifer nodded and raised his glass. "I graciously accept."

"Good. Now that we've settled that," Catriona put her glass on the table between them, "what is this meeting about?"

Alistair took a deep breath. "There's a war coming between Heaven and earth. Heaven has been choosing its champion for a while and they seem to have settled on someone."

Catriona's blood froze. *I know this.*

Alistair looked at Myrgen. "It's Alexander."

Myrgen took Catriona's hand. "I probably don't need to ask but who is the champion of the earth?"

"No, you probably don't." Alistair looked at Catriona. "It's you, of course."

She closed her eyes.

Myrgen looked around. "Are we waiting for another person then? Alexander?"

"Well…" Alistair gestured to Lucifer.

He nodded. "I can represent Heaven in this matter. In fact, it's best to only deal with me. Your reception from the others will not be positive."

Raven shook his head and took another petit four. "I have friends in Heaven. We should have a representative from them here."

"You mean the Saints?"

Raven nodded, taking a bite.

"Then I agree. Who would you like to be here?"

Raven swallowed. "I get to choose?" He searched all the faces in the room, then slapped his knee. "That's fantastic. I choose Clara."

Myrgen frowned. "Who's Clara?"

Alistair looked at Lucifer, who nodded. "It's a saint that was never acknowledged by the Church. She was a hero of the Soulless War. She enabled the living forces to defeat the monsters."

"The ensuing Inquisition was in part because of our trek to the Papal City to get her recognized." Raven took a sip of the brandy and then looked at the glass. He turned to Lucifer. "Is there any chance I could get some tea? This doesn't feel right with the adorable cakes."

Lucifer tugged on a bell pull and the doors opened a few moments later. "Tea for everyone, please? And check on lunch, if you don't mind."

The servant bowed and left.

Lucifer continued. "When she was brought in, her name was engraved upon the registry in the Papal City. But since she was from York, and determined to be the reason the entire war happened in the first place, she was denied."

Raven nodded. "That's actually not allowed. But I spoke to her recently, at the Fae army invasion. She's around."

Alistair looked at Lucifer. "Can you contact her?"

Lucifer looked at Raven. "Why don't you do it?"

"Um…Well," he looked around, "is this place holy ground?"

"Of a sort. It's neutral territory. That's why your magic still works in here."

Raven looked at his host, then at his fingers. He wiggled them and ran them through his hair. The hair turned from brown to green. "Oh!"

Catriona shifted her gaze to Lucifer. "Isn't that dangerous? Leaving your enemies with their powers?"

"Who said I invited any enemies to this function?"

"Well, you said a war between Heaven and Earth."

"Oh. That's because I plan to start one. I won't be bringing any of them in here."

Catriona and Myrgen looked at Alistair, who nodded.

Alistair went to the brandy decanter. "Karma told me when I became its successor that there was a war coming over the Well of Souls. I was to be the judge to see who the actual winner was."

Catriona shook her head. "The Well of Souls?" She looked at Myrgen, who was just as confused as her. "What is that?'

"Apparently, there is a well in Heaven that is the fountain of all the souls that get dispersed into the world. It's running dry. So Heaven wants a war to refill it."

"How does that help?"

Lucifer motioned to refill his brandy as well. "When people die, their souls have a chance to return to the Well."

"Only a chance?"

"Oh yes. People change beliefs all the time." He motioned to Myrgen. "Like you. A year ago, you would have gone to the Well, but now, as you know, you won't. People experience things that change their minds about the afterlife. Alistair here has been a follower of several faiths in his lifetime. It was that experience that made him uniquely qualified to be Karma's successor."

"So, if they die and they don't have a faith they follow," Catriona looked at Myrgen and Alistair, then back to Lucifer, "who gets them?"

"Well, it returns to the Well, sort of. It goes to the Great Table and is measured. If it measures that it did more good than evil in its life, it goes back to the Well. If it falls the other way, I get it."

Myrgen's mouth shifted in distaste. "So, you really *are* in charge of the Infernal realm."

"Yes. It beat the alternative."

"Which was what?"

"Staying in Heaven." Lucifer sipped his refilled drink, then pointed at Myrgen. "You know how the Church says the path to Hell is paved with good intentions? That's a lie. *Intent matters.* If you try to help someone and things turn out badly, that's not *your* fault. You just get blamed. If you did nothing but set out to help people, *truly help people,* and never had a single thing go right, you would still weigh towards Heaven and not me. What matters is that when you get *blamed* for something, you end up *accepting that blame.* In so doing, you accept the responsibility of that action that you didn't intend and *that* will stain your soul. That's what guilt is really all about: Getting you to take on sin whether you deserve it or not. If someone *tells* you it's your fault because *they* feel guilty, you end up carrying their guilt and I can assure you, they are unloading themselves of it so you get the stain."

Myrgen reached over and squeezed Catriona's hand. He looked at her and she didn't have to read him to know what he was thinking. Her guilt over Nicolai's death, real *and* imagined, her guilt over Alexander, everything was being examined now through this new lens. She sat back, sighing.

Lucifer smiled. "Looks like you spent a lot of time carrying other people's burdens."

She and Myrgen both nodded.

"You know, even people who make mistakes are allowed to let go of that guilt and make things right. They are allowed to be happy. Suffering when you aren't at fault turns your soul black, because you eventually start believing you deserve it."

Raven's eyes narrowed. "You're supposed to be the enemy of all life. Why should any of us believe you?"

"Have I lied yet?"

Alistair looked to Catriona, surprised.

She shook her head. "No. But I might not be able to read you."

"I've never saved your life. Of course you can. You've been subtly doing it since you walked in."

"That's why I suspect I can't read you. You can't possibly be speaking the truth about all of this."

Lucifer leaned forward. "It's true. I lied about nearly everything since you came in here."

Catriona frowned. "That's a lie."

"Okay, maybe only *half* the things I've said."

"That's a lie too."

"One quarter?"

Catriona shook her head.

"The quality of the petit fours?"

She sighed. "Hm."

"Would you feel better if I lied more?"

"It would balance with what we…"

Lucifer tilted his ear towards her. "Yes?"

"With what we…"

He nodded, coaxing her to speak more to the ear presented.

She looked at the floor. "With what we have been told all along."

"And by whom?"

She didn't speak.

Myrgen did. "The Church."

Lucifer leaned back, pointing at Myrgen and smiling. "Exactly."

She looked at him, her gaze intense again. "So, what mistake did you make and what are we here to do to correct it?"

"Well, my lady, *that* is a horrendously long story that I shall try to get out before lunch."

## Forty

## "The most important contacts a business owner can have are a good eatery, a clean brothel, and a discreet poisoner." Kali, The Karmic Hand

"The whole story would take a day to relate, so I'll simply give you the basics. I used to be human."

Everyone looked surprised, including Alistair.

"We all were. All five of us. We lived in a village with our families during the early times. Earthquakes were common and we had monsters back then. Great beasts roamed the ground, sea, and skies. You never knew how long you had to live. As such, people clung to anything consistent or stable. Now, back then, two things you could count on was the Giver of Life, and the Bringer of Death."

Catriona frowned at the titles, like there was some memory trying to step from the foggy depths. Myrgen kept an eye on her as Lucifer continued.

"These entities were the epitome of truth in advertising. When the Giver visited, plants germinated, animals were bred, people got pregnant. When the Bringer came, she took the dying from the world, brought in the harvests, turned the soil to fallow. You didn't give birth until the Giver arrived and you couldn't die until the Bringer claimed you. It was all part of the cycle.

"That wasn't to say births and deaths didn't occur. Your baby comes to term and is going to be an easy birth, well, that just happened. You get hurt badly, you die. I had a wife and she was pregnant with our daughter. She was attacked by wolves near the end of her term and she managed to cut our daughter out of herself before she passed away. They were found and my little girl was almost dead. We saved her, but she was attached to her dead mother for who knows how long. That caused her to have problems.

"My brother and his wife were barren, so my daughter was all our family had. We didn't want her to die. So, we called out for the Giver to help us. She came to deliver another baby in the village and my daughter, barely two years old, was suffering. We asked her to heal my daughter."

*"I cannot do this thing you ask."*
*Lucifer's tears flowed unhindered. "Why?"*
*"She is not within my grasp. She has been touched by death at her birth. It is a sickness within her that will burst forth and hurt others. You must call the Bringer to take her. She needs to be put into the earth so she may be reborn. I am sorry for your loss."*
*Raphael held his brother as he cried, and the Giver bowed and walked away. When she was out of sight, he looked at Lucifer's face. "We'll try to find a solution. I'll not let her die. There are great beasts and great magics in the world. Something has to be able to save her. We'll go tomorrow to seek a cure."*
*"What if the Death Bringer comes while we're gone?"*
*Raphael stared at his brother, trying to find an answer. "I don't know."*

"I decided the Giver was right and I called out to the Bringer to take my daughter and end her suffering. But she didn't come and didn't come. After a year of watching my daughter in pain, I finally said to Raphael that I was willing to do this quest to save her. We went to another village, for none of our women were pregnant. It took several stops, during which Raphael would speak in private with the elders, seeking rumors and stories of fantastic beasts that might heal Persis. At the fourth village, we found a couple of pregnant women and we waited for the Giver.

"Raph said we would follow her to her home, for she often seemed dormant around that time of the year. Such a fountain of life *had* to have herbs or creatures around her. We would steal a few and take them back. She came and went, and we followed her back to a waterfall and pond. She entered the pond, weary and wrinkled from the year's travel, and when she emerged, she was young and whole again. We had found what we needed.

"She left the water and went to sleep on the far side of the pond. We looked about for something to carry this water in, like a gourd or something. Then Raph saw an earthenware jar at the bottom of the pond. I quietly went to the bottom to get it and when I returned with it, I… Well, I looked like this."

His coat turned into light and he unfolded wings from his shoulder blades. They were glorious, feathered as if with a crossbreed between mother of pearl and a sunbeam. His hair turned to fluid opal and he was the kind of beautiful that could not be described without weeping. He hovered a moment above the group, then he touched down and resumed his human form. Everyone in the room was speechless but he sat down, retrieving his brandy.

"As you can see, it was not common. Raphael was stunned to silence and I didn't realize I was different until he finally could speak. The water was still rippling from my emergence and we didn't dare stay there, so we left with the jar. We skirted the other villages along the way and did our best to make straight for home, but that was not easy. We didn't have food with us, expecting to visit villages along the way or eat from trees, roots, and berries. With my transformation, Raph worried we would be killed. At the time, I didn't know how to hide it."

Alistair shook his head. "That form is awe inspiring. How could you have thought you would be attacked?"

Lucifer's lips formed a small sneer. "Oh, well, that was Raphael's fault. It turned out he had been attacking the Death Bringer for a year."

Catriona flinched. Myrgen took her hand. "What is it?"

"I don't…know."

Raven watched Catriona for a moment, then turned to Lucifer. "Attacked?"

"Yes. He decided to prevent Persis from dying by basically killing the Death Bringer. It *kinda* worked too. It turned out that the private meetings he was having with the elders along the way was to warn them about the Death Bringer. He wanted them to fight against her too. He figured the more people who fought her control, the longer we would have to find a cure for Persis."

Catriona squeezed Myrgen's hand, like she might be in pain. Myrgen turned her face to him. "Are you sure you're alright?"

Catriona closed her eyes, like she was fighting a headache. "I know this. I have seen this over and over in... a dream." She looked at Lucifer. "They shot her, from a tower, stopping her before she even left the woods. They would take her body and throw it into a pit in a mountain."

Lucifer nodded. "A dream, you say? Sounds more like a nightmare."

"They kept doing it too. And, she had a companion. They... tortured him..."

Myrgen swallowed, looking at Raven. Raven returned the look, then glanced over Catriona.

Lucifer shrugged. "I don't know anything about that, but I wouldn't be surprised. Anyway, our trip home was fraught with problems because of this. He didn't dare go to the villages, in case they were fighting the Bringer. And with me looking different, he couldn't risk them deciding I was something worth slaying. I no longer needed to eat, but Raph wasn't so lucky. We hurried home before he collapsed from hunger.

"We arrived home to a pit of cooling lava. The entire village had been destroyed. Uriel and Gabriel were still in the tower, but they were burned. We could hear Michael screaming from a crack in the cliffs that surrounded the area. The lava went up to a large earthen wall, preventing it from going to the forest or anywhere outside the edges of the village. I flew over to help my friends, but the heat was such I could not breathe. My wings started catching fire. I grabbed Uriel, but could not grab Gabriel. Then Raphael was suddenly beside me. He had touched the pot's water and become an angel as well.

"We rescued all three but they were all poisoned, burnt, and in so much pain. It was impossible. We tried to find out what happened but they either couldn't speak or couldn't stop screaming when they did. All we figured out was that the Death Bringer got fed up with being killed and decided to destroy the village. Raphael told me we needed to put them out of their misery and I agreed. I took my dagger and tried to cut Uriel's throat. The cut stopped his screams, but he was still very much alive. I tried to cut deeper, but it did not matter. He stayed alive.

"The Bringer had refused to let them die, no matter what happened to them."

Catriona stood, her breathing ragged. "Excuse me. I need some air."

Myrgen stood with her and Lucifer nodded to the door they came in. "This is a long tale. Let's take a few minutes. I'll check on lunch. To the right is a solarium, to the left is a garden. Feel free to go where you feel comfortable."

Myrgen bowed. "Thank you."

He escorted her out and they went to the left.

Raven watched them go and he nodded to Alistair. "Walk with me, would you?"

Alistair nodded and they, too, excused themselves from Lucifer's company. They went right to the solarium. The room was warm and fragrant, a stunning view of Sovereignlumin commanding the skyline.

"Well, *that's* interesting." Raven frowned.

Alistair nodded. "Karma's Hand touches every aspect. It has to, to maintain balance." He crossed his arms. "What's up?"

"Remember the lady at the top of the stairs?"

"Yeah."

"Turns out she's not just *any* stair-climber. She's Magic."

"Magic? What, like, a mage?"

Raven shook his head, his eyes wide and earnest. "No. I mean she's the source of Magic. She was held prisoner under Persephone for millennia. I thought she was just some *čaro* source put there by the Order because she interfered in human politics. But no. She's the actual reason there is magical stuff in the world."

"How did she get there? Did the Order trap her?"

"No." Raven glanced at the tower. "My grandfather did."

*"What?"* Alistair looked at the tower too. "Why?"

"I don't know. I talked to Persephone and she didn't know either. Merrick is hoping to speak with her at length, but when she lay down, she fell into a deep slumber. Alistair, she's the *third creature* to do this. Calpurnia is in her tower, but there is a dome of thorns over the Papal City right now and Embertwist is in *his* tower, laid out just like Cal. He spent his energy for the entire season to cast that spell.

"And, I think the Sinister Glove is dead."

Alistair dropped to a bench in the solarium. "Any idea what happened?"

"Uriel said it looked like the city fired upon them and the Glove was shot with a Faeslayer bolt."

"Lucifer's Uriel?"

"No, Embertwist's Uriel, though they are probably the same person." Raven held up three fingers and counted them off. "Calpurnia, Embertwist, and now Magic. And a trap made by Karma released the source of *all magic in the world…*"

"To grab Catriona." Alistair looked to the garden area. Myrgen and Catriona were talking. Myrgen was showing her the stones in his pouch and tapping his head, then he pointed at her. She nodded, then glanced at the stones, putting her hands behind her back.

"She's more than just the Dûcesa reborn. I think she's the Death Bringer. It's the only thing that makes any sense."

"Except why would the Death Bringer return life to the wasteland that was York?"

Raven stumbled at that, frowning. He stroked his chin. "Yeah, that's true. It would make more sense for her to be the Life Giver. Either way, she would be the only thing worth more to that trap than Magic itself."

"What do you want to do?"

Raven shook his head. "I don't know. If she were the Death Bringer, she could maybe talk to my grandfather and find out why he imprisoned my grandmother in that trap."

Alistair held up a finger. "And if she's the Life Giver, she can reanimate him to the same end. So, how do we find out which she is?"

"I don't know yet. But as soon as I do, I'll let you know."

James rode to Kilgorran and made it there by sundown. He knew the ferry rode all through the night in the summer but this was early spring. He needed to check on it. He rode directly to the docks, surprised at the growth since he had been here last. It was near this bay that Catriona defeated his strategy to take down Tanglwyst's company. That had been only a couple years ago but so much about this place had changed. New buildings were everywhere. He got to the docks without getting lost and found a building marked Office of the Ferrymen.

*An office, huh? That has grown too then.*

James dismounted and entered the office, its windows still lit up and people still visible inside. The man behind the desk surprised him.

"Hamish?"

The man looked up and his weathered, bronze face and blond beard broke apart in a smile. "James Douglas! As I live and breathe!" He came around the counter and the men embraced.

James gestured to the room. "*Office* of the Ferrymen? Not bad, Hamish. Not bad at all."

"Well, York made a deal with Glarren to get wood from the forests. It made the villages and town expand as sawmills started springing up all along the coast. Come, have a look."

They stepped outside and Hamish pointed to the opposite coast. There were at least four sawmills on the shore that James could see, with several torches around them to give off light.

"After that trade agreement, people started coming from all over to work there. Glarrens are very selective about what they cut from the forests to keep them healthy and strong, and Yorks are very skilled in the running of mills. It was a perfect match. It will be years before they need to move to the other side of the land bridge to cut."

"So, that's kept you pretty busy, I guess."

"You'd guess right. We have four ferries running dawn to dusk to get the workers here and back."

"Do they work all night too?"

"Nah. They do have security crews to keep the Fae and local wildlife from setting up shop in the workings. Hence the continued lighting, even after the crews have left. Lost a couple folks to a thrown blade the first month before they started that practice."

James glanced over his shoulder to the west. "Am I too late to get across, then?"

"We have the last ones over there already, getting the final shift's workers. Why?"

James frowned. "Bad news. Gotta get home."

"Oh no." The cheerful fell right out of Hamish's features. "What's happened?"

"Gwen was killed. And we suspect Alistair is dead too."

"By Gloriana's Cloak. I'm so sorry, James." He stared a moment at the floor, then got a determined look on his face. "I'll take you over myself. I have a small boat for runs to York and back."

"You sure?"

"Completely. No one should have to do something like this and I'll not make it harder on you."

James sighed. "Thank you, Hamish."

# Forty-One

## "When practicing tolerance, your enemy is the best teacher."
## Shiva, The Karmic Hand

The four friends returned to the study and Lucifer nodded to them all. "Is everything settled?"

Myrgen nodded and Catriona smiled. "I am still recovering from a recent death."

Lucifer nodded. "I had heard. Do you want to continue?"

"I'm afraid so. The things you say are striking memories in me, from dreams and nightmares, as you called them. I found it interesting that the garden overlooks Summerland."

Alistair nodded. "Yes."

"It was… difficult to look upon it, but I was able to see my son again. He waved to us." She squeezed Myrgen's hand and he lifted it to his lips.

"Do you regret leaving it?"

She shook her head. "No. Had I not left it like I did, I would not remember it. That's why the Dûcesas change when they die. The one they used to be decides to stay behind."

Raven cocked his head. "Are they all there?"

Catriona nodded. "Do you realize you never asked the Third Dûcesa her name?"

Raven waved a hand at her. "Pshaw, of course I did. It's…" He frowned. "Uh…" He put his hands on his hips. "Well, *that* was incredibly insensitive of me."

"It's Michelyne, by the way."

"I can't wait to apologize." Raven turned to Lucifer. "Is there more story?"

Lucifer nodded. "A bit more."

"Does it actually get to why there is a war coming?"

Lucifer nodded. "I can skip to the end."

"That sounds good."

"Okay." Lucifer grasped his hands together and took a deep breath. "End of the story is that I know the location of the Giver of Life. My brother angels are holding her captive in Heaven. She is in a cage that was made about the same time as that trap you were in, my Lady, and probably by the same entity. I made a deal with the Death Bringer long ago and I have a bunch of souls for her. They have not been anywhere near Heaven nor Hell. I believe they will be the thing that tips the balance in our favor, if I can get them to her. I cannot free the Giver and she cannot free herself. I need Alistair to do it."

Alistair folded his arms. "All you need to do is ask. I owe you a favor."

"You can't enter Heaven. The only reason you can enter Hell is because the Bringer granted me the lava bed that used to be my village. It has a Land component to it and therefore has a sense of balance. But Heaven has no such thing. If you tried to go there, you'd be powerless and I need you the opposite of that. I need to drain the Well of Souls so the essence of Heaven weakens enough to save her."

Myrgen frowned. "How does a war drain the Well?"

Lucifer gestured to the room. "Look around you. Do you see these works of art? The craftsmanship of the furniture, the food and drink, the sculptures and paintings in the room. All of these exist because the Well has been harvesting souls that are not quite pure. In fact, when people suffer, their souls darken, and when they darken, they access a deeper connection to the essence of the world. The darker the soul, the less like Heaven it becomes. Heaven was actually crafted from the original contents of the Well. But the darker soul has access to imagination, creativity. The *fantastic,* the *unsusual.*" He pointed to Myrgen. "The reason you can paint so well is due to all the souls that went before you never returning to the Well purified.

"For the last three hundred years, I have been actively turning the Heaven-worshipping populace into darker and darker creatures until their souls are dark enough that Heaven automatically rejects them, sending them to me. This plan is almost complete. Anyone who was born in the last twenty years will fall to me unless they turn to Land worship like you have. Those converted souls will go to the ground, which is *still* not back to the Well. Within the next fifty years, the Well will be dry. The protection Heaven has will go away and Karma will be able to walk into Heaven to free the Giver."

Lucifer looked in his goblet at the brandy he had poured. "Except I don't have fifty years. Raphael and Gabriel have decided to refill the Well with her blood."

Lucifer threw the goblet into the fireplace, his anger finally exploding. The liquid flared and everyone stepped back from the angel. He turned to the assembled entities. "So, you see, I have run out of time. Michael was imprisoned during the Soulless War and hidden away. Uriel isn't strong enough to stand against both Raph and Gabe alone because of the injuries he suffered at *my* hands. And in Heaven, they are all powerful, so long as there are souls in the Well. I can't fight them *and* sneak Alistair in. I won't sacrifice Uriel because the Giver would never allow it. And if they kill her, they will kill *any* chance of another birth in the world. If the Giver of Life dies, everything dies. The world ends in a single stroke.

"A war on earth is what they want because they think it will return souls to it. They will pay attention to it. It is the last resort, outside of finding a way to return the Bringer and get her to wage war against them. I have souls for her, should she need them, that I have collected for a thousand years."

Alistair stepped forward, holding up his hand. "Wait. You have the untouched souls of Land Worshipers? How?"

"If a person converted but died before their naming ceremony, they would come to me."

"Is the Prince of York amongst them?"

Raven nodded. "He was in love with Gloriana. He wouldn't have been devoted to the Church, not with that in play. He's probably with the Land's souls."

Alistair nodded, his face turning pensive. Raven knew he was thinking of exchanging his life for that of the real Prince of York.

"Possibly. He died in the Soulless War, right?"

Alistair nodded.

"I was collecting for her during that time. The Land has accepted souls through attrition, but in circumstances like that one, where they were worshiping Heaven or nothing right before, and turned to the Land, those were more of a judgement call. Fae supporters weren't Fae *worshipers*, per se. They didn't automatically go anywhere. If it was a soul that might be in contention, I tucked them away. At the very least, they should have the chance to choose where they wanted to go."

Raven thought about what he found out in Sovereignlumin. The Father of all Fae had put the woman he loved into a trap that would drain her existence to feed a spell. But that spell *wasn't* just the covenant at Persephone. Magic (the spell stuff, not the person) hadn't *left* the world with her capture. It had simply been used in a different way. It took away her *choice* of how it was distributed, like the trap took away Catriona's choice to disperse her renewing life energies into the area. Magic was why York was a wasteland. Replacing Magic with life changed the dynamic.

*Why did the spell need an eternal force? What was it feeding?*

Raven understood magic, even if he couldn't explain it. He knew that a spell fueled by a mage was strong, but that a spell fueled by a čaro source didn't need to be monitored. It just had to be cast and the feed left open, and it would run perpetually until the source was exhausted and went away. That's why the spell repelling anyone who had never been in the covenant was still up after all those centuries. The source was Marica.

This made him think. *Marica was the source of the protection spell, but now she's the source of the spell feeding... whatever that other spell was. If a mage changes the čaro source of a spell, that changes the nature of the spell. She was a protector, so chances are that the spell has taken on a protective nature instead of the original, um, magical(?) nature. If they use a weaker source, the spell will end when the source is used up.*

But the trap spit out Magic in favor of this woman. What was she that would be more important than Magic? If Catriona was the Death Bringer Lucifer had met, why did she *replenish* York instead of killing everything further? If she was destruction and endings, why did she bring renewal? Was it just that she couldn't die? Or was she…

They were in the afterlife now. He could find out.

Raven looked at Myrgen. "Can I see those stones?"

Myrgen nodded. He took the pouch from his belt and handed to Raven, confused.

"There is information from the time of the Bringer in these."

Raven poured them out into his palm and when they threatened to spill, he caught them with earth magic, holding them all together. The firelight danced across the gold flecks within and they stirred in the air. He rearranged them into what looked almost like a cohesive piece of stone, a pyramid that had the top stone as the one with the least flakes. The pyramid was a nubbly jumble, but he knew it would work. He looked at Catriona.

"Remember."

He hit her in the chest with all the stones at once.

James stepped out onto the front stoop of his mother's house. He could still hear her crying, though it had been an hour since he broke the news. The loss of Gwen and Alistair was overwhelming. His father had recommended he step outside while he tried to comfort her. James had obliged.

He looked at the saddle on the rail in the stable. He had not yet unpacked his saddlebags for his time home. He expected his mother was going to make him stay in his old room. He walked over and untied the bags. He heard the box shift and pulled it out to make sure the contents were safe. The box had not been fully closed since Gwen and he had opened it since he needed the contents available. He saw that the locket had tried to escape and he picked it up.

"Where do you think you're going?"

The trinket twisted, glittering in the moonlight. The inscription twinkled at him.

*Gloriana,*
*That you will know the faces of our children.*

He looked to the mountains beyond the forest. He had another mother to tell.

# Forty-Two

## "When seeking the truth, don't be afraid to break a few rocks."
## Kali, The Karmic Hand

As evening started to settle, Alexander showed up at the Queen's encampment, carrying a set of saddlebags. Tanglwyst looked at him and smiled, then winced as the silver manacles burned her skin when she shifted. He didn't even bow to Her Majesty, but walked straight to the Lady. Johner bowed and Alexander returned the gesture. He looked at the hardware on the lady and frowned.

"I see what you mean, General. That is a nasty piece of work up there. However," Alexander turned to the saddlebag, "I think I can help with this."

He reached in and pulled out a small vial. He walked up to her and dumped the vial on her wrists, his hand on her shoulder. He fed some healing into the holy water in the vial and her wounds went away. Then he touched the bent steel and it shimmered and revealed it was simply bent up in a slight spiral but definitely not gripping it tight. He eased the manacles up over the hook, allowing the lady to put her arms down for the first time in hours. She practically collapsed on him.

Sovereigna came over to the scene and frowned. "Who are you? What are you doing with my prisoner?"

"I was sent to see to her needs, Ma'am. I was told she would be given no comforts here but would suffer no harm either. She came here of her own free will, so I'm obliged to remove these manacles."

He pulled out some cold iron shears from the blacksmith. It took some work to get them under the wrist pieces, which were already burning again, but he was able to cut them off. Sovereigna watched carefully, not commenting but not going away either. Tanglwyst dropped her wrists to her lap and sighed in relief. Alexander reached into the bag and pulled out a chamber pot. He offered it to her and she smiled a pale replica of her usual mirth. He set that aside near her pile of sticks.

Then, from around his waist, he pulled off the coat she had worn, that had been his armor. He looked in her eyes to see if she understood what this meant. She looked at him, and nodded. He put it on her shoulders.

"It's just in case someone decides they don't have to abide by the accords of negotiations."

She nodded. "I understand."

"It's permanent, so don't let it touch you."

"I know."

He took off her boots and socks, and pulled out a water skin and some of her soap. She looked at him. "Are you planning on...?"

"It seemed like the saintly thing to do."

He washed her feet and then rubbed them with scented oil also from her apartment. The oil helped him rub the knots from her calves and she squeezed his hands.

"What do you plan to do now?"

He glanced at the Queen. "Well, I can't take you from here, because you chose to be here, but I can do my best not to leave you alone." He stood and faced the Queen. He bowed and took a knee.

"I am a weary traveler. Can you give me a pile of hay for the night?"

Sovereigna looked at him, her eyes great with shock. She glanced to the guards around her, then she bowed to him as well.

"Come and join me at my table," she looked at Tanglwyst, "you and your companion. I will have food and drink brought. There is a place for you to stay."

Alexander rose and helped Tanglwyst to her feet. She looked at him but he didn't return the look. Instead, he followed the Queen to the large dining chamber in the heart of the great pavilion. All manner of food and drink were laid before the couple and Sovereigna gestured for them to join her. He offered a chair at the far end for Tanglwyst, to the left of the chair at the end. He took off the coat around her shoulders and draped it over the back of the chair, easily accessible. Tanglwyst looked at it and realized what he had done. Her heart thumped and he had his match it. He sat in his seat at the other end of the table, placing himself as the adversary.

Sovereigna looked at him, waiting.

"I am truly sorry for the loss of your daughter. She loved your granddaughter very much. I fear she had the *Einberufung der Strähnen* from being away from the Forest for so long. It seems the Fae blood within her was too strong to be among humans without the help of a Fae around."

"I surmised this from her letters. She was very unhappy where she was."

*One down.* "Her daughter shares the best features of her parents. She has golden hair like her father and deep green eyes like her mother."

"I know this as well, for I have a miniature of her that was painted for the change of seasons to spring."

*Two.*

Sovereigna smiled, her lips beautiful and wicked. "You only have one chance left, boy. If you don't give me something I don't know, I am allowed to eat you." She looked at Tanglwyst. "And your friend. And it will be a fitting end for the monster who killed my child."

Tanglwyst took his hand but he smiled and squeezed hers.

"My mother is right behind you."

Sovereigna sat up, her eyes disbelieving and she turned.

Catherine stepped from behind a tent flap and bowed to the Queen. Sovereigna got up and flowed over to the Queen Mother. "Catherine?"

"Sovereigna. I got your last letter. I'm sorry my son was out of town when it arrived. As it stands, he still has not been home, but he is at least now informed."

"And what about my request?"

"You are right, you deserve to have vengeance. We have sent for the body of your daughter. It should be here any day."

Alexander's adrenaline spiked and he tried to settle his heart by breathing.

Sovereigna took Catherine's hands in hers. "Really?"

"Yes. Now as to the other part, where you take the life of the person responsible or the person who let her die, I offer that person to you now."

Alexander stood, knocking his chair over. "Mother, don't." He wasn't about to let her turn over Tanglwyst just to keep control of him.

"I offer myself."

"What?" Tanglwyst got to her feet as well.

Catherine put up her hand to her son's protests. "You want the responsible party for Elizabeth's death. I chose her. I did so for selfish reasons. I wanted to know about the Fae and the tales of Krakte. Seeking this knowledge is forbidden by my religion but I hoped I could learn it in secret."

"And did she teach you?" Sovereigna's eyes had softened, hearing about her daughter.

"Of course not. You taught her better than that. She converted to Augustinianism the day she wed Charles and never spoke a word of her homeland." Catherine looked down at their hands. "I fear it is what killed her."

"The *Einberufung der Strähnen* your son spoke of, the *Summons of the Wisp*, claims many from my Land who move to other places. That's why so many of them open inns and taverns. They keep the ways of the Fae and help travelers as well."

Tanglwyst tugged on Alexander and they took their seats again. Clearly, Catherine was not in danger from this woman, but he did not yet understand *why*.

Catherine sighed. "It was something I thought of repeatedly, but there is no place in Patras where the Fae can walk. I tried to encourage her to visit you, knowing she would be able to encounter Fae on the road, but she refused. It appears she had fallen in love with my son." Catherine looked at Alexander.

Sovereigna turned to him and he stood again, sliding his hand from Tanglwyst's. "I did not know until she was already poisoning my brother."

"So, the one she loved was the one who slayed her?" The Fae Queen's eyes started to get that edge again, but Catherine turned her gaze back to her.

"She sent for a love potion. You knew what she was doing."

Sovereigna wilted, and reached for her chair like she was beyond weary. Catherine guided her there and sat to her left, still holding her hand.

"I thought she was trying to get her husband to leave his mistress. For the sake of their family."

Catherine shook her head. "Charles already had a true love. He's with her now."

Alexander swallowed at this secret being revealed, but it appeared Sovereigna took it differently.

"When one love dies, the ones left behind are often faced with that choice. I am glad she chose to be with him. Many lovers choose suicide to be with the ones they love."

Catherine patted Sovereigna's hand. "I'm glad that was not your choice."

Sovereigna turned to look at Alexander, who had folded his hands in front of his mouth to stop himself from interrupting. *Tangl is right, she has a plan. I need to not mess it up.*

"Is that why you killed her? Because she tried to give your brother the potion?"

"Your Majesty, she meant the potion for Alexander." Tanglwyst stood to speak. "I found her workshop and her notes. She was poisoning Charles so she would be free to be with his brother."

Catherine looked at her son. "The potion would not have worked on him either, for he, too, had a true love. You know the penalties of tampering with such power." Catherine stood and knelt next to her friend. She lifted Sovereigna's hand to her lips, and kissed it. "We learned that lesson together."

Catherine and Sovereigna let the tears flow without concern and as they did, the tension in the bodies of the half-Fae bled out. The guards did not relax per se, but the rest of them did. Sovereigna touched Catherine's hair and cheek, then took her face in both hands and kissed her. The kiss was warm, like it was far too long in coming. They hugged, a long embrace of sharing, then Sovereigna nodded. "I will accept your offer. I have long wanted to show you the beauty of my Forest."

"I have long wanted to see it."

Alexander leaned over to Tanglwyst. "I did *not* see that coming."

"I knew your mother had a plan. I didn't know what it was outside of she knew the Queen's weakness. I never expected it to be *her*."

The Queen opened her arms to the table. "Please. Stay and eat, drink. You are welcome in my home."

They did. Sovereigna wanted to know what had happened and Tanglwyst provided those details without letting Alexander speak. He worried that the truth would only hurt the Queen more, but in the end, the tale was such that Sovereigna raised a glass to her daughter and to those who thwarted her. "The tales of the Forest are fraught with these sorts of endings. She will become a story that will be known throughout the world. It is the way of our people."

"How did you find out about the power of true love?" Alexander took Tanglwyst's hand and kissed it, then turned his attention back to the other couple.

Sovereigna beckoned them down to sit closer. Alexander stood and escorted Tanglwyst to the other end. He sat beside his love and let her sit beside his mother. He did not want to have her out of his sight, at least for the next little while.

Catherine looked at Sovereigna. "We met when we were young and we felt things for each other, but we were not free to pursue them. Your father discovered our letters after Francois was born and he said he would ignore them if I stopped pursuing his mistress, Diane. I did. But after you were born, he decided in a rage that he would expose me to the court. The connection to the Fae would have been enough to have me killed by the Church. He had decided he wanted Diane as his queen. Sovereigna was visiting and..."

Alexander searched her face. "Did you kill him?"

She nodded, her tears unimpaired. "I did. She gave me a recipe for a potion that would stop him from telling the truth. It ended up making Diane kill him in a jealous rage, then herself. He never got the chance to say a word to a Church official."

He looked at the Krakten queen and then closed his eyes. "I see." He nodded. "That's what you meant. He had true love."

"No. Diane did. Henri loved only himself. He had numerous affairs on both of us, with impunity. The Saints only know how many bastards there are ready to take the throne."

He looked at her again. "That explains it. I was told before, by..." he glanced with guilt at Tanglwyst, "by Catriona..."

Tanglwyst glanced away, settling the beast that was between them so recently. He felt it in her heart. She let her eyes join his again, and nodded.

"She told me that you had the best interest of the kingdom as the basis of everything you did. That was where your loyalty lay, and that I should not judge you so harshly."

"I am sorry I never met her then."

He looked at his hands. "Me too, though at the end, it's probably best you didn't. I didn't really handle things well with her." Tanglwyst took a deep breath and he saw this and moved on. "But you taught me a lot of things of great import and one of them is that a woman is just as competent as a man when it comes to ruling a kingdom. That's why I made Emmy my heir."

Sovereigna sat back, her tears drying. "You did?"

"Even if I someday have children of my own, she was in line before me. She was passed over because she was a girl, but that was foolish. In my life, I have known more women who have the potential to rule well than I think most kings are allowed. I think she will make a fine queen."

"So," Catherine's smile was reserved, "you would deny your own children their birthright?"

He laughed. "Are you honestly trying to tell me that I should put my own children in the path of the throne? With any luck, they will never have to worry about such a thing and can live their lives as they see fit." He nodded to Sovereigna. "To love whom they want to love. Without reservation."

Catherine looked at the Krakten queen as well, but Alexander's gaze slipped to Tanglwyst. She smiled, wiping away a few tears of her own.

"Do you mind?"

"That a woman will be on the throne next? No. That is really all I ever wanted in life." She looked at Sovereigna. "It's what Elizabeth wanted as well, clear to the end."

An owl hooted nearby and Sovereigna looked to the roof of the tent. "The hour is late and there are matters to attend to on the morrow. First," she turned to Tanglwyst, "there is the rebuilding of your home here."

"That will take months, Your Majesty."

"Yes, but I have an army and they are…"

"Fae?"

"*Krakten.* We will have your home rebuilt within the summer, should you wish it."

Tanglwyst ran to Sovereigna and hugged her. "Thank you. Thank you so much."

Sovereigna seemed confused, but delighted she had earned such affection. She returned the embrace, patting Tanglwyst on the shoulder.

Alexander rose as well, bowing to Sovereigna. "May we take our leave of you?"

"Of course, though you are indeed a guest in my home."

"I would ask that you give my room to my mother then, if you have the extra hay."

She glanced at the glorious pavilion around them. "I will bring some up from the stables myself."

He bowed, and offered his arm to Tanglwyst and they left the Queens to their own.

When they were out of earshot, Tanglwyst bumped his shoulder with hers. "You didn't want to stay?"

"I didn't want to risk it! Things had worked out. I was not about to jeopardize it by hanging about and saying the wrong thing."

"Like you can say the wrong thing."

"It is rare, but when I do, it brings down castles." He grew solemn. "And towns. And ships."

"Alexander?"

"I'm afraid I can't stay here after all to oversee the rebuilding. I have to go make amends in St. Marguerite."

They stopped by the church and she stroked his arm. "What happened there?"

He shook his head. "Far too much to tell right now. I won't ask you to come with me."

"Try and stop me."

"My Lady…"

"If this is so important it would pull you away from me at a time like this, it is soul stopping important. I'm going with you. Besides," she tucked her arm into his again and tugged him towards her apartment, "you're going to need a ship to get there in any kind of time and it just so happens I have one."

He smiled, allowing himself to be tugged towards the office. He stopped outside and held her in the faint moonlight.

"I don't deserve you. I don't deserve what you offer. And because of that, I need to take my leave of you tonight. And probably for a while longer than that."

"You're leaving me?"

"For the nights, yes." He kissed her hand. "It was only knowing you were opposed to the idea of marrying me that I did not take you up on your offer last night. I can assure you, I will not have that willpower again. For the sake of our friendship, I cannot spend another night beside you."

"Are you trying to change my mind?"

"I'm trying to make sure you *have* your mind. No tricks."

He kissed her, sharing that love with her and she still held back. He could feel it and he knew this was the right choice.

She lay her head against his chest and sighed. "Marry me."

He smiled at her vain attempt to convince him. "No."

"Augh… You are heartless."

"I am." He looked at her. "It's because you have it." He stepped back from her. "Now go. Sleep. I will see you on the morrow for breakfast."

They parted reluctantly, but he knew it was the right thing to do. He knew there was a horribly uncomfortable bunk available in the guard house so he set his feet on that course and only looked back twice.

"St. Michael, St Giles, I have a weapon to use against Heaven's enemies. A coat that will slay any Fae that touches it. Help me decide what to do. Help me please."

Gabriel heard the call, like he heard so many of the humans begging, but this one caught his attention. *A coat that destroys Fae? What kind of a weapon was a coat?*

The Pillar showed a man before a modest altar. Gabriel didn't know the place but the saints seemed to. The priest in the small church had interrupted the whispered conversations in the room. Clara and Brigit turned to Giles. The Archangel Michael had been drawn away in the Soulless War and could not respond to the prayer, but this was specifically to Giles so he could.

Brigit looked at the image in the Pillar. "Isn't that the priest in St. Giles, the one where the king is?"

Clara nodded. "I thought this was solved. The Queen giving herself up to be a hostage should have brought peace."

Peace? Gabriel was outraged. So, apparently these exalted humans have been working to stop the war, not forward it. Clearly, they have plans for the Well that they are trying to hide from me.

They were leaning on the table around the Pillar, their backs to the door.

Clara looked to Giles. "What do you want to do?"

Giles shook his head, but Gabriel had heard enough. "We start the war."

They turned to see Gabriel in the doorway, his hands clenched in fists. All of them paled as they realized he had heard them.

Giles held up his hands to the angel. "Saint Gabriel, let me explain…"

Gabriel grabbed Giles by the throat and threw him into the women. Giles hit them both with enough force to send all three sprawling. They crashed into the wall, cries of pain from them.

"I'm really not interested in any explanations. You knew we wanted a war. You have been working against that."

Clara got a knee under her. "What you want is *wrong*. A war won't do what you think."

"That is up to me to determine."

Brigit checked Giles, who tried to get up. He glared at Gabriel. "We won't let you slaughter thousands just to allow your reign here to go on a few more years."

"Luckily, that's no longer your problem."

Gabriel waved his hand and the floor opened beneath the trio, dropping them from Heaven. Their screams of terror lasted moments before the floor closed again.

He walked to the Pillar of Prayers and put his hand upon it. A glow filled the church below and the priest shielded his eyes.

"Where is the weapon?"

The priest stuttered. "Th… the k…King went to the Fae encampment. He was wearing it. It was a coat that had something on it that destroyed Fae on contact. He wasn't wearing it when he returned just now."

"I see." Gabriel looked around the area and found the object draped over the back of a chair in an illusionary tent. He saw a few half-Fae monsters around and smiled. He blew on the image of the coat and a small sound same from it, like a trumpet call. A Fae with large ears turned to the sound and beckoned its patrol to join it. They listened, hopping to the pavilion. The sound continued to come from the coat and the Fae reached over and leaned on the thing to hear it.

Johner saw the movement and saw what the Fae were touching. He shouted to them to get away, but one brushed against the back and the body of Elizabeth of Krakte came in contact with that Fae. The others were too close and the sludging was instantaneous. Three Fae were killed in the space of a second.

Johner stopped short of the puddles and looked at the table. The food and wine were eaten and drank. He pulled his sword and put the tip in the ground.

"Now, this is a Fae matter."

# Appendices

# Appendix A: Characters of the Saintlands

Aggie- Innkeeper of the Fair Winds Inn and Tavern in St Margeurite. Husband of Flora, brother-in-law of Martin.

Aislyn Cortright- Nubian woman in St. Giles.

Alan Moriarity: Catriona's son. After his Naming Ceremony, Victor Tiberius Morstadora.

Albreda Wulftorhüter- Noblewoman of Krakte. Her and her husband Reinmar are inventors.

Alexander Angloume (ANG-loo-may): King of Mervolingia, Alexander succeeded the Throne after Charles. Alexander is also the Duke of Anjou, the family lands of the Angloume house.

Alistair MacGlarren: In service to Gloriana, the Midwinter Queen, Alistair is also the bloodline heir to the throne of York. The original Black Sparrow, he retired from this position after succeeding in learning about Tanglwyst's pirate operations. He stopped when Catriona, his former lover, found out. Alistair is also the father of James and Gwen. Since his death at the hands of Duncan McVryce, he has been serving Karma in the afterlife.

Allen Hobbs- Royal Patrolman for the Bordeaux Highway between St. Giles and Cliffbase.

Anika Zapolya- Dûcesa of Caratia. Holder of the Hearstone.

Antoinette: Cook in the mornings at the Patras Royal Palace.

Archbishop Alonzo de Patrone: Archbishop of Patras.

Artemisia: Mythical name of the Moon and mother of the Sea Goddess Calista.

Bartolemous Johner- The Voice of Command (Lieutenant to Corrigan Starshadow).

Black Sparrow: Notorious pirate who attacked the Tanglwyst Trading Company. Taken out by Catriona Moriarity.

Brigit- Patron Saint of Healers. Alexander's personal patron saint.

Bringer- Short for Death Bringer. An entity of Power that has been missing for centuries. Counterpart to Giver.

Calpurnia Allegheri (cal-PUR-nee-uh AL-uh-GAIR-ee) the Autumnal Sovereign - Fae Lord of Autumn. Currently asleep in the tower of Sovereignlumin.

Catriona Moriarity (CAT-tree-OH-nah MORE-ee-AR-it-tee): Stâpâna of Caratia. The Stâpâna is the Protector of the Land's People in the country of Caratia, the second highest rank in the country. The Stâpâna is chosen through a secret ritual known only to those in Caratia. Lover of Myrgen.

Cecelia A-Kandalló/ de Firenze- Simultaneously the proprietor of the Brew Ha House in guardianship of the Caratian Pass to York, and the head of the kitchens at the Royal Palace of Patras, respectively.

Ce'Nedra van Oppal- Innkeeper of the Black Cat and Anchor Inn in St. Andrew.

Cipriano- Annibal Cipriano Malatesta, King of Mande.

Charles Maximillian IX: Former King of Mervolingia, ruler and instigator of the St. Michael's Day Massacre.

Clara of Weltonshire- Patron Saint of Barren Women. Hero of the Soulless War, her holy footsteps blessed the soil where she walked. This soil was gathered by Raven Grasshair to corral the Last Child so that he could be captured and banished by Calpurnia. Although Heaven accepted her as the new Patron Saint of Barren Women (displacing Raymond non Nonattus after his ejection from Heaven), the Papal Council never acknowledged her.

Corrigan Starshadow the Midsummer King- Fae Lord of Summer.

Diane de Poitiers- Mistress to King Henry II. Murdered Henry in a jealous rage and then commited suicide due to being fed Cyprian Herb by him.

Dominic D'Medici (DOM-uh-nik dee MED-ee-chee): Fiancé of Gwen. As Acting Chancellor of Mervolingia, he is in charge of all funding and expenses for the entire kingdom.

Don- A general title of noble station. In Augustinian countries, it means Lord.

Drake Zapolya: Dûce of Caratia. The ruler of Caratia can be either male or female and is chosen directly by the Land through a ritual involving several trials and finally culminating in a ceremony in the town square of Zara.

Duncan McVryce: A notable member of the Back Streets of Patras, Duncan has played a role in several events involving members of the Royal family, the Augustinian church and Tanglwyst's interests.

Ealusaid (EL-uh-SASH)- Proprietress of the Benevolent Friar on the road to the Papal City.

The *Enigma*- Catriona's ship, it houses a Fae spirit named Estelle, that is the daughter of Corrigan, the Midsummer King. Estelle is wife to Octavius.

Entivia "Boots" Malatesta- Horse in the Stable of Assassins owned by Giovanni Sangiardo.

Embertwist Apocraphix the Vernal Monarch- Fae Lord of Spring.

Estelle Starshadow- Daughter of Corrigan and wife of Octavius.

Father Benjamin: A priest in service to Marco Giovanni, he was killed helping Catriona escape her captivity in the breeding pens of the Giovanni estate.

Felix Benivieni - Official messenger for the Royal Palace in Patras. Childhood sweetheart of Sylvaine Rochefort.

Flora- Innkeeper of the Fair Winds Inn and Tavern in St. Marguierite. Wife of Aggie and sister of Martin.

Fuccochio, Benivito (foo-KAH-chee-o)- Clothing designer in Florintine, Mande. Known for his fairness and incredible designs, his patrons are catalogued by the royalty and nobility of Mande.

Gabriel- Archangel. Patron Saint of Autumn.

Gilian Malatesta- Princess of Mande and daughter of Cipriano.

Giver- An entity of power being held captive in Heaven. Counterpart to Bringer.

Gloriana Talnig the Midwinter Queen- Fae Lord of Winter.

Gomez de Santander: Head of Alexander's personal guard, Gomez began as a guard at the Giovanni estate.

Gweneviere "Gwen" Douglas (GWEN-eh-veer DUG-lus): Handmaiden of Catriona, Gwen has the distinction of being her most trusted companion. Daughter of Alistair and Gloriana, twin of James.

Hamish Ó Caoindealbháin (HAY-mish oh CAY-lin)- Chief Ferryman for the Office of the Ferrymen in Kilgarren, York.

Helen Brightwater- Chatelaine for the Sanctuary Vineyards, held by the Tanglwyst Trading Company. Wife of Matthew Brightwater.

Henri de Porthos (OHN-ree dee POR-thos)- Chief Bookkeeper for St. Andrew. Beloved of Ce'Nedra.

Isabella D'Medici- Lawyer for the Tanglwyst Trading Company and cousin to Dominic D'Medici. Wife of Othon of Burwick.

James Douglas- Captain of the *Crimson Veil.* Brother of Gwen.

Jess Beck- Goatherd in Caratia. Husband of Rae.

Johannes- Bo'sun on the *Enigma.*

Karma- Entity of Balance. Worshipped by default in Yndia.

King Henry II: Father of Francois I, Charles, Alexander and Margaret, husband of Catherine, Deceased.

Kyri de Holloway- Daughter of Tanglwyst. Lives in Pardua, Mande, in the Storm Catch. Proprietress of the Storm's Catch Inn and Tavern.

Last Child- The last child left from the original children resurrected before the Soulless War. These children were returned by the Land to walk the earth, but their souls were already returned to Heaven with their deaths. As a result, they searched the world, draining life and destroying souls in their attempts to get one of their own. The Last Child hid away in Clara's basement and escaped because he convinced Mephistopholes to turn against Lucifer and serve him instead. Mephistopholes took him through the ground, thereby destroying all the farmland in York.

Lauriel- Fae wolf. Caretaker and responsible party for Raven Grasshair.

Lawrence of Cleves- Keeper of the Watch on the *Enigma.*

Lucifer- Archangel. Caretaker of Hell.

Marco Giovanni: Mandian Count and head of the Apolodorus family, Giovanni almost married his cousin to secure a large financial conglomerate but murdered his son and then committed suicide the tenday before his wedding, leaving the Apolodorus fortune to his oldest child. Father of Dominic.

Marica the Gold Wife- First creation of a mage entirely by magic, the blacksmith Hephas used a life spell to animate a metal statue he forged. The Land granted this and infused the Gold Wife with the ability to work earth magic. Unfortunately, Hephas only wanted her to speak to him, but he worded the spell poorly for the sake of rhyming. As a result, only one person at a time can understand her.

Martin- Proprietor of the Fair Winds Inn and Tavern in St. Marguerite, along with Flora and Aggie.

Matthias Lovas (muh-THI-us LO-vahs)- Stable Keeper of Ashstone in Zara, Caratia. Killed in the Second Mandian Invasion protecting Victor Tiberias Morstadora.

Merrick Blackburn- Mage at Persephone and hero of Soulless War. Beloved of Calpurnia, he watches over her as she recovers from the spell she cast to capture the Last Child.

Michael- Archangel. Patron Saint of Summer. Lost in the Soulless War.

Michael - Myrgen's Nubian Slave. A very large man who is fiercely loyal to Myrgen.

Michelyne- The Third Ducesa, her name was only discovered after she died and was asked what her name was by the inhabitants of Summerland.

Miguel (MIH-gel)- Anika's cat from before she became Ducesa.

Monique Delorme- Proprietress of the Wise Wench Tavern in St. Giles, and author of the Wise Wench Tavern Book.

Morgan Wolf - Vicar in St. Marguerite, and Myrgen and Tanglwyst's brother.

Myrgen "the Grey" de Sablonierres (MUR-gun dee SAB-yon-air): Former Chancellor to Mervolingia, he was accused of the regicide of King Charles. Wandering the world in search of his path, he is Catriona's lover.

Nicolai Moriarity - Husband of Catriona Moriarity and father of Tib. A guard in the Patras Palace. Dead by poison.

Nigel - King Charles's Castellan before Myrgen.

Nina Richelieu – Guard in of the Royal Palace at Patras, she is Gomez' second in command.

Octavius - First mate of the *Enigma* under Captain Catriona Moriarity, husband to Estelle.

Osondrea- Scribe for the Sanctuary Vineyards belonging to the Tanglwyst Trading Company.

Othon of Burwick- Former personal bodyguard of Tanglwyst. Husband to Iabella D'Medici.

Persephone- Covenant tower of Mages in York that was the war effort agains the Last Child in the Soulless War. Also seen as the name of the entity that was the source of magic under the Covenant.

Pope Gregory - Head of the Augustinian Church.

Preston Cowley- Manager of the St. Giles Home Office for the Tanglwyst Trading Company. Married to Steve.

Princess Isabelle - A Mandian Princess of marrying age

Princess Marie-Elizabeth - The daughter of Elizabeth and Charles.

Queen Elizabeth of Krakte - Queen of Mervolingia, married to Charles Maximillian IX. Mother of Marie-Elizabeth. A school friend of Tanglwyst's along with Adriana Capaletti.

Queen Elizabeth of York- Queen of York, and friend of Alexander.

Queen-Mother Catherine D'Medici - Mother of Charles and Alexander. Married to Henry II.

Rae Beck- Goatherd in Zara, Caratia.

Raphael- Archangel. Patron Saint of Winter.

Raven Grasshair- Mage from the Covenant at Persephone, son of Corrigan, in sworn service for Calpurnia. Ward of Lauriel.

Raymond non Nonnatus- Patron Saint of Barren Women, expunged. Cast from Heaven after granting babies to a dozen Glarren women after they converted to the Augustinian faith. The women rejected the faith and returned to worshiping Fae once their children were born.

Reinmar Wulftorhüter- Krakten inventor and husband of Albreda.

Richard of Kent, Sir- Noble knight in service to the Covenant at Persephone. He and Raven went on a quest to get Clara's name in the Saintly Record. This quest failed, but exposed the corruption in the Papacy. His death at the hand of Inquisitors sparked the Emilianite movement.

Rowena of Avalon- Jeweler in St. Giles.

Sinister Glove of Embertwist- Lieutenant to Embertwist.

Slade Stormchest- Stapan to the First Ducesa. Died protecting her from the Last Child right before it was banished into the void by Calpurnia's spell. The Last Child touched him instead of her and was then taken by the spell as he turned into a soulless.

Sovereigna Shwartzwald- Queen of Krakte, Elizabeth's mother, Marie Elizabeth's maternal grandmother.

Sovereignus the Eternal- Father of all Fae and beloved of Magic.

Svein (Sven)- Proprietor of the Benevolent Friar and husband to Ealusaid.

Sylvaine Rochefort- Widow of the Lord Rochefort who terrorized the families of St. Andrew. Childhood sweetheart of Felix.

Symonne- Proprietriss of the Drum and Nightingale Inn and Messenger Service, guardian of the Caratian Pass to Mervolingia. Wife to Tomas.

Tanglwyst de Holloway (TANG-gul-wist dee HALL-oh-way): Owner of the Tanglwyst Trading Company and Catriona's secret partner. Sister of Myrgen and Morgan Wolf.

Thessius- Glarren member of Catriona's crew on the *Enigma*. Former First Mate to Ramirez on the *Crimson Veil*. Quartermaster on the *Enigma*.

Thomas the Diminutive- former Stapan of Caratia, only one of two members of this order to resign the post without dying.

Tomas- Proprietor of the Drum and Nightingale Inn and Messenger Service, guardian of the Caratian Pass to Mervolingia. Husband to Symonne.

Trimelda Daniels- Dreamwalker for the Fang and Claw. Caretaker for Clara's Way and Clara's Bed. Clara's Bed is the monument to the Soulless War that is held in trust by the Crown of York. Couples who are seeking to get pregnant went here to conceive. As such, this became a royal honeymoon spot for post-coronation copulation.

Tristram Wulfschlager - Captain of the *Righteous*, one of Catriona's ships.

Tulio d'Or- Bandit king that holds the Contested Forest.

Uriel- Archangel. Parton Saint of Spring.

Urien Atreides - Husband of Tanglwyst de Holloway, a Latian Merchant who owns The Atredes Trading Company, which along with the Tanglwyst Trading Company controls 73% of the Mervol - Mandian trade.

Ûr- Caratian form of noble address

Wilgefortis- The wife of Raven Grasshair, she was also the Baroness of Conterbury in York and the Seneschale of Persephone during the Soulless War.

William- Navigator on the *Enigma*

Xannu (ZAN-noo)- Proprietess of the Open Lotus Incense and Bath House in Rouen.

Zachary Crow- Stable hand for the Benevolent Friar and adopted son of Svein and Ealusaid.

# Appendix B: The Augustinian Calendar

The world of the Saintlands has four seasons, and those are the purview of the Fae Lords. Embertwist Apocraphix, the Vernal Monarch, rules over spring, Corrigan Starshadow, the Midsummer King, rules summer, Calpurnia Allegheri, the Autumnal Sovereign, reigns over fall and Gloriana Talnig, the Midwinter Queen, rules winter.

The combat these lords, the Church originally invoked the Archangels against them. These were sufficient but as Heaven gave the Church the Saints, these former humans were invoked in addition, adding to the strength of the protections against Fae trickery. The saints were originally celebrated upon the day of their ascension and delivery by Heaven into the Rolls.

However, 300 years ago, the Church, in the aftermath of a great war, decided to write down a formal calendar, honoring saints for their purviews instead of their date of ascension. This was to battle non-church beliefs, unify the masses and establish lines of Church control.

Pope Richard I told the cardinals to which he assigned this task to begin the year prior to the apex of Gloriana's control, so as to get ahead of the rise of her power. The Cardinals discussed it and Cardinal Cosimo of Pardua offered up Genevieve, invoked against disasters, to start the year. Richard approved and the calendar was begun.

Genevary became the first month and the months were divided into 31 day sets with 10 day tenday. In the center of the month, the 16th, is the Devotional Day, where all work stops for a day to pray and invoke the saints of the month. This strengthened the divinity in the realm, repelling anything not Heaven related. Although the new calendar reorganized the role of Saints during the year, many days are still known by the saint who ascended upon that day, though the Archangel's days were established during the Augustinian Calendar.

# Months

1$^{st}$: Named after Saint Genevieve, **Genevary** 16 honors Sebald, Martin of Tours, and Raphael the Archangel. Genevieve is invoked against disasters, which abound in the Saintlands during the winter. Sebald once burned icicles in a poor woman's home to proDûce heat. Martin of Tours cut his cloak in half to give to a naked beggar. Raphael brings the heat of the sun and dawn to battle freezing cold.

2$^{nd}$: Named after Saint Vitus, **Vitusary** 16 honors Medard, Catald, and Barbara. Vitus is invoked against storms, but is also the Patron saint of dancers so balls abound in Vitusary. Medard is invoked against bad weather because he sheltered the beautiful queen Angelica, granddaughter of Saint Marie Angelica, when she fled the intrigues of the Mervol court during a storm. Medard gave his own tent so she would be safe and dry. An eagle sheltered him from the weather, creating an umbrella for him as he rested. Catald cured the ill and is invoked against plagues, which often abound from bad weather. Barbara was saved when lightning struck her attackers during a siege.

3$^{rd}$: Named after Saint Florien, **Florias** 16 honors Vincent, Jude, & John of Nepomuk (bridges & flooding). Florien is invoked against floods, a common problem in the Saintlands the third month. Saint Vincent Ferrer is the patron saint of builders, often put to work during this time. Jude helps the hopeless. John of Nepomuk strengthens bridges during floods to save the towns.

4$^{th}$: Named after Saint Elmo, **Elmos** 16 invokes Fiacre (gardeners), Phocas (market gardeners), and Uriel the Archangel. Elmos starts the sailing season, so Saint Elmo, patron saint of sailors marks this month. Fiacre and Phocas bring the first harvests from winter, began indoors or in warmer climes to feed the masses while Uriel protects the people from the lies and trickery of thieves.

5$^{th}$: Named after Saint Walburga, **Walpurgisnacht** 16 invokes Valentine, Rose of Lima, & Theodore of Sykon (reconciling the unhappily married). Walpurgisnacht 1 allows the young and amorous to pursue each other unhindered and as such, this month marks the beginnings of many marriages. Valentine honors true love. Rose of Lima honors florists and flower growers. Theodore, known for his counseling skills, reconciles the unhappily married, reminding them of the way they felt their first month of marriage.

6th: Named after Saint Wilgefortis, **Vilgfort** 16 honors Felicity (women wanting sons), Monica (wives), & Marie Angelica (nun who married). Felicity is invoked by women wanting sons, usually royals, due to her miracle of delivering sons whenever she was a woman's midwife. Monica honors wives as she was Heaven's example of a perfect wife and Marie Angelica was a nun who married for the sake of the world. A čaroion held that Marie Angelica would have a daughter who would alter the church and though she was a nun, she was persuaded to leave her vows to fulfill this čaroion. Her daughter, Tanglwyst Angelica, inherited a powerful shipping company which was destined for the hands of a corrupt Church. Her sacrifice honors all women who must abandon their own dreams for the sake of a greater good.

7th: Named after Saint Maurice, **Maur** 16 honors Elizabeth (war), Clara (savior in the Soulless War) and Michael the Archangel. This is the season of war, and thus, the people invoke Saint Maurice to keep their soldiers safe while away from home while Elizabeth is invoked to find peaceful resolutions to wars. Clara was a woman whose role in the Soulless War enabled the plague to be destroyed through the spreading of soil she had walked upon, preventing the plague from crossing it. Michael fought the creatures of Hell to preserve the faithful during the great wars.

8th: Named after Saint Francis, **Franco** 16 honors Hubert (hunters), Andrew, and Sebastian. Saint Francis honors all animals and those who tend them. Hubert honors the hunters. Andrew the fishermen and Sebastian protects archers.

9th: Named after Saint Thomas Aquinas, **Aquin** 16 honors Ivo, Augustine, and Albert. The season of scholarly pursuits, Aquin honors those who devote themselves to study. Ivo honors lawyers. Augustine honors theologians and his ideals of Heaven are the basis for the Augustinian Church. Albert honors scientists and herbalists.

10th: Named after Saint Benedict, **Benedine** 16 honors Gabriel the Archangel, Giles, & Margaret. As this is a time of darkness descending upon the land and things turning cold, people were often creating tales of ghosts and fear. Those who had died in the wars of the summer or in the professions of the year were often "seen" wandering the desolate places during this month. To counter these tales of fancy, the church brought in their strongest saints against fear and superstition. Saint Benedict fought his greatest fear, being homeless, and opened his home as a shelter. As such, he is their patron saint. Giles protects against night terrors. Margaret defends against those being attacked by devils, enabling their escape. Gabriel the Archangel heralds Heaven's will, driving away doubt and fear.

11th: Named after Saint Ferdinand, **Ferdin** 16 honors All Saints (Fer 1), Eloi, and Anne. To celebrate the survival of the month of fear, All Saints Day was noted as the first Church holiday. It also honors those responsible for the greatest achievements of humanity: Ferdinand for Engineers, Eloi for jewelry and metal smithing and Anne for pregnancy.

12th: Named after Saint Brigit, **Brig** 16 honors Cosmas & Damian, Raymond, and Roch. A most notable saint, Brigit was one of the first saints ascended to Heaven after giving her life to heal others. Her blood created a fountain by which those who were ill or damaged could be restored. This fountain is in the center of the Papal Palace in the Papal City. Cosmos and Damian are conjoined twins who became doctors. Raymond honors midwives. Roch is invoked against epidemics.

# Weekdays

Day 1: Honorasday: named from Honoratus, for bakers.

Day 2: Bernaday: Named after Saint Bernadette, shepherds.

Day 3: Rufinasday: Named after Saint Rufina, potters.

Day 4: Simproniday: Named after Four Crowned Martyrs, stonemasons.

Day 5: Julianusday: Named after Saint Julian, boatmen.

Day 6: Vincentsday: Named after Saint Vincent Ferrer, builders.

Day 7: Wencesday: Named after Saint Wenceslas, brewers.

Day 8: Genesday: Named after Saint Genesius, Actors & Comedians.

Day 9: Columbasday: Named after Saint Columba, poets.

Day 10: Dismasday: Named after Saint Dismas, undertakers.

# Appendix C: Religions

### Augustinian (AHG-us-TIN-ee-uhn)

The Augustinians believe God made the world and made Heaven. God set up the ability for Man to ascend to Heaven body and soul by doing good works. If a human is good enough and helps enough people, they can become a Saint. Each Saint in the Augustinian Rolls was once a human and their name appears in the Heavenly Roster when they ascend. The Heavenly Roster is a book kept in the Papal City on the Official Altar in the center of the Cathedral under constant guard.

In the 1300s, the Church stopped acknowledging new names in the Roster after The War of the Soulless which they blamed upon the heathen religions. The reason cited for this denial was the War made it difficult to believe all the reports of ascended Saints. At the time, it was unknown by the populace about the Heavenly Roster but after the declaration and an investigation by nobles outside the church, this information was revealed to the public. Regardless, once the Pope responsible passed away and the scandal was uncovered, the new Pope acknowledged the updated Rolls and the new Saints were canonized.

The main Tenant of Faith in the Augustinian religion is the Saints are the world's connection to Heaven. It is only by praying to the Saints that one can communicate with Heaven. It is against the Laws of the Church to pray directly to God, bypassing his appointed representatives, to make requests, though one can offer praise unto Heaven without invoking a particular Saint. However, if one prays to a particular saint for guidance or assistance and they receive it, it is against the laws of the Church to not acknowledge the Saint who answered the prayer.

### Emilianite (uh-MEEL-ee-uhn-ITE)

After the War of the Soulless and the Scandal of the Unacknowledged Saints, a group of followers broke away from the Church. Citing corruption in the dictations of the papacy, it was determined that apparently the Church could communicate directly to

Heaven without the help of the Saints since they refused to acknowledge the Saints received in the Rolls. They called these Saints "the Abandoned Children" and called themselves Emilianites, after Emilio, the patron Saint of abandoned children.

The Emilianites believe that man cannot be trusted with the will or intent of Heaven through a conduit, for that can be hidden or destroyed. Instead, they believe man can be more assured of correct information if he prays directly to Heaven. If Heaven wants the Emilianites to pray to a Saint, they will communicate that Saint's name to all the Faithful. Until that happens, the Emilianites will pray directly to Heaven. Since the Scandal of the Unacknowledged, no Emilianite has ever noted a Saint's name being given to them. As such, they continue to offer prayers only to Heaven.

### Land Worship

The Maker split in two, creating the Heavens and the Land. Both are sentient and great entities unto themselves. Heaven holds the Well of Souls and deals with all things ethereal such as dreams and thoughts, ideas and concepts. The Land deals with all things physical, be it body, plant or liquid. If it can be held, it is the purview of the Land.

When the body dies, the Land takes it into itself and dissolves the flesh, leaving the soul. The soul is filtered and cleansed of the sins of its life and when all the sin is gone, the soul that is left is returned to the Well of Souls. The Land interacts with the people on a daily basis, feeding them, clothing them, healing them. They trust the Land and count on its gifts for life.

### Calista's Call

Oceanus, Father of Waters, was alone and lonely. He wandered across the world without drive or direction. Sometimes, to relieve his boredom, he would slice through a mountain or sink an island he made but in the end, he was aimless and alone. Then, one night, he heard a stirring song. It beckoned him from across the Land and he fell upon a beach, kneeling before the singer. A beautiful maiden of silver hair and glowing pale skin sat naked on the beach, her voice filling the night. He crept up behind her and she saw him and screamed, then grabbed her clothes and fled to the sky.

Every night, he went to the beach to fall upon the shore, begging her to return. He brought her gifts from the sea and faraway lands, creatures and stones, wood and plants. Eventually she peeked from behind the curtain of night and slowly emerged, a little more each night, until she fell in love with Oceanus and they made love upon the beach. They created a daughter of rich blue skin like her father and glowing white hair like her mother. They called her Calista and the salt from their tears of joy at the sight of her soaked her, making her touch turn water into salt water.

Calista watches the sea and keeps her secrets and those of her followers. She is a fickle goddess though, and prone to fits of fury that can seem unprovoked. When she is happy or dealing with honorable people, her hair is the white of sea foam. Mermaids gather the honored dead and if a sailor is a good follower, Calista recognizes them and grants them the ability to live underwater as merfolk in her cities. Her dolphins and sea mammals guide ships through treacherous areas and are always signs of her pleasure.

But she has her primal side as well and when dealing with the dishonorable, she sends her teeth to rend them. Her hair turns bloody red and her sharks and sirens call the evildoers to their destruction. If there is an argument in ship at sea and sharks arrive on the scene, it means someone in the fight is lying. If a criminal is sentenced to death at seas, the sharks will take him, but if the criminal is remorseful, they take him to the depths where he becomes a Marked One and serves Calista for as long as they breathed air. Sirens call the unjust to the sharks' maws so if one hears a siren's call, the heavier the sins on their soul, the harder it is to resist them.

If a body is rendered with fire at death, Calista will know them not and shall cast their spirit out of her mouth to walk the earth forever.

**The Ancient Ones**

Sovereignus was a good king. He loved Magic so much, that he mated with her, and fathered the Fae. The Fae were everywhere. They were the merfolk in the sea and the harpies in the air. They were the pixies and dryads in the trees and the white-furred talking animals in the snows. All the magical creatures, great and small, frolicked in the love of their mother and father. The Fae loved humans and played with them, guiding them to good places and punishing the lazy or wicked with their games and tricks.

But then a sickness came, one that threatened all the magical creatures. Dark men captured the Fae, torturing them to find the sources of Elemental magic. Sovereignus roared and rode to war against these dark men and felled them. In the battle, he was mortally wounded and returned home to die. He gave to his four eldest his power, divided as to their gifts.

To his youngest son Embertwist Apocraphix, he gave the powers of Spring. The Vernal Monarch is the quintessential thief and like a thief, it comes in the night, stealing the cold of winter and revealing the living things beneath her skirt. To his oldest son, Corrigan Starshadow, he gave the powers of Summer. As the Midsummer King, his paladin nature marches forthright towards the good and just.

To his oldest daughter, Calpurnia Allegheri, he gave the powers of Autumn. Calpurnia so resembled his beloved Magic, she channels the gifts of change and harvest during her reign as the Autumnal Sovereign. To his youngest daughter, Corrigan's twin, he gave the power of Winter. Gloriana Talnig, the Midwinter Queen, uses the cold to stop disease and preserve and heal, but also to punish the wicked and delay the unjust. The children split and went to different parts of the world to preserve their realms from the followers of the Dark Men, but each season, they return to Sovereignlumin, the great Tower That Watches All to transfer the power of the seasons.

### Karma

Karma is all about balance. For each act, there is an equal and opposite reaction in a person's life. As they get closer to the end of their life thread, they can find themselves bound by the threads they have thrown. Negative acts cause sticky threads, positive acts throw stabilizing threads. If a soul has cast more sticky threads than stabilizing, they can be caught up in the negative and it will strangle them. Thus are many of the symbolic gods of Karma multi-limbed creatures.

### The Primordial Egg

The Primordial Egg twitched and cracked and from the shell, four Dragons emerged. They opened their mouths and breathed forth the world. The Earth Dragon formed land and grass, ore and metal, wood and dale. The Water Dragon formed oceans and rivers, lakes and streams, snow and ice. The Fire Dragon breathed the sun and stars to warm the world. And the Air Dragon gave life and the moon. As all things came from magic, all creatures upon the world were magical, and all things communicated with one another in the combined tongue of the elements.

But then, a threat loomed on the face of all and it tried to conquer the magic in the world. It's flashing sword and violent means crushed all but its own belief, slaying the dragons in the world. The Elemental Dragons Rose against it, but to destroy the threat meant to destroy all they loved as well. Instead, they seized their followers and sealed them away in special places. The Earth Dragon hid the giants and Dwarves in the mountains. The Fire Dragon hid her faithful in the ash and lava. The Water Dragon took her children and gave them the ability to breathe water. And the Air Dragon took his children to the sky, to the place between life and death.

At first they spoke aloud to one another, but monsters found their hiding places, so the Dragons broke the world and spoke only in secret languages so none could find their whereabouts. The Earth Dragon spoke through entrails and omens, the Water Dragon through storms. Fire claimed its own hypnotic power and Air spoke through the dead. Together, they all keep the legends and the magic safe, making certain that only those who wish to keep magic in the world can find them.

### Fang and Claw

The practice of having an animal choose to join with a person's soul to guide them is standard practice in the followers of Fang and Claw. They also believe in the consuming a part of the animal allows for that animal's superior quality to enter the consumer.

As a rite of passage, warriors of the tribes will hunt a dangerous animal with which to partner. Shaman may not be led by a dangerous animal, but by a wise one such as Snake or Owl. And those who become the Seers find themselves in the company of spiders.

# Appendix D: Countries

**Caratia (CUH-ray-SHEE-uh)**
Capital City: Zara
Native tongue: Caratian (CUH-ray-SHEE-uhn)
Dominant Religion: Land Worship

**Glarren (GLARE-uhn)**
Capital City: Kilmory (kill-MORE-ee)
Native tongue: Glarren
Dominant Religion: The Ancient Ones

**Krakte (KRAHK-tuh)**
Capital City: Austra
Native tongue: Krakten
Dominant Religion: Augustinian, Emilianite, the Ancient Ones

**Latia (LAH-tee-uh)**
Capital City: Cheryb (SHARE-eeb)
Native tongue: Latian (LAH-tee-uhn)
Dominant Religion: Calista's Call

**Mande (MAHND)**
Capital City: Vincenzia
Other Cities: Pardua, Florentine, Calais, Aquila, Balona, Trieste, Naplles, Genoa
Native tongue: Mandian (MAHN-dee-uhn)
Dominant Religion: Augustinian

**Mervolingia (MER-vole-LIN-jee-uh)**
Capital City: Patras
Other Cities: Rouen (ROO-en), St. Giles, St. Andrew, St. Marguerite
Native tongue: Mervol (MER-vol)
Dominant Religion: Augustinian, Emilianite

**Nubia (NOO-bee-uh)**
Capital City: Leeus Brul (lee-OOS bruul)
Native Tongue: Fangspek
Dominant Religion: Fang and Cḷaw

**The Papal City (PAY-puhl)**
Capital City: None
Native tongue: Mervol
Dominant Religion: Augustinian Church Seat

**Toledo (toe-LEED-dough)**
Capital City: Tuscan
Native tongue: Toledan
Dominant Religion: Land Worship

**York (YORK)**
Capital City: Landen
Other cities: Canterbury, Kent, Oxford, Cambridge
Native Tongue: Yorkish
Dominant Religion: Emilianite

**Yndia (YIN-dee-uh)**
Capital City: Yantap (YAN-tap)
Native tongue: Yndian
Dominant Religion: Karma

**Yokotama (YO-ko-TAH-mah)**
Capital City: Kūki doragon
Native Tongue: Yokotaman
Dominant Religion: Dance of the Air Dragons

# About the Author

Tonya Adolfson has been a member of the Society for Creative Anachronism since 1988 and has met thousands of people with very interesting personas. Many of these people have made it into these books and she is grateful to them for enriching her life.

Tonya lives in Boise, Idaho with her husband, two children, two housemates, four cats and three dogs and yet, strangely, the house is actually pretty clean.